Louise Voss has been in the m[...]
working for Virgin Records and [...]
manager for an independent label in New York. More
recently she has been Director of Sandie Shaw's company in
London. She lives in south west London, and has one
daughter.

Louise Voss is the author of three previous novels, *To Be
Someone*, *Are You My Mother?* and *Lifesaver*, all published
by Black Swan.

Acclaim for
LIFESAVER

'Compelling suff' *Heat*

'Painful and poignant, *Lifesaver* is a very touching account
of the effect that having children – and not being able to
have them – has on relationships' *Candis*

'Poignant and funny . . . A compelling, honest, moving and
powerful story of self discovery' *The Last Word*

'A thought-provoking, all embracing novel of the role of
mother, lover, wife and above all, life-saver'
Western Mail Series

Also by Louise Voss

TO BE SOMEONE
ARE YOU MY MOTHER?
LIFESAVER

and published by Black Swan

GAMES PEOPLE PLAY

Louise Voss

BLACK SWAN

GAMES PEOPLE PLAY
A BLACK SWAN BOOK: 0 552 77170 8

First publication in Great Britain

PRINTING HISTORY
Black Swan edition published 2005

1 3 5 7 9 10 8 6 4 2

Copyright © Louise Voss 2005

The right of Louise Voss to be identified as the author
of this work has been asserted in accordance with sections 77
and 78 of the Copyright Designs and Patents Act 1988.

Set in 11/12pt Melior by
Falcon Oast Graphic Art Ltd.

Black Swan Books are published by Transworld Publishers,
61–63 Uxbridge Road, London W5 5SA,
a division of The Random House Group Ltd,
in Australia by Random House Australia (Pty) Ltd,
20 Alfred Street, Milsons Point, Sydney, NSW 2061, Australia,
in New Zealand by Random House New Zealand Ltd,
18 Poland Road, Glenfield, Auckland 10, New Zealand
and in South Africa by Random House (Pty) Ltd,
Endulini, 5a Jubilee Road, Parktown 2193, South Africa.

Printed and bound in Great Britain by
Cox & Wyman Ltd, Reading, Berkshire.

Papers used by Transworld Publishers are natural, recyclable
products made from wood grown in sustainable forests. The
manufacturing processes conform to the environmental
regulations of the country of origin.

In memory of Betty Reeves.
She was a matriarch in the truest and
best sense of the word.

1

Susie

It was a very unsettling feeling, knowing that your life was going to change so completely, whether you wanted it to or not. You realized your old life wasn't perfect, but it worked, in its own way. You thought you knew where you were going, you thought you'd learned from your past mistakes – you weren't *asking* for perfection or bliss or enormous wealth, just enough happiness and security to carry you over the hot ashes of the discontentment that were inevitably left once the initial flame died down. You'd learned that the first thrill of sex eventually palled; that friendship was what was important, and trust, and enough money not to have to lie awake and worry about paying bills. You accepted this as a truism vital for the survival of your relationship and your own mental health.

That was where I was, anyway, settled in the sugar-pink clapboard house that Billy and I bought together in Lawrence, Kansas. It was a good place to be, literally and emotionally. The house was much humbler than the six-bedroom mansion Ivan and I had owned at the height of his career success, but it didn't bother me at all. Billy and I fitted this house. I always thought that Ivan, Rachel and I used to rattle around in the mansion. I remember Rachel cycling her tiny turquoise tricycle along the shiny parquet hallways. You couldn't ride around on anything in *this* house – the rooms all open out of one another, like multiplying cells, and there's too much comfortable clutter on the floors.

So I was happy back in Kansas, under the vast skies, entertained from our verandah by the extreme weather and the innumerable stars at night. I felt smug almost, like I'd finally, at the age of nearly forty-five, got it cracked. After the peripatetic existence of my marriage to Ivan, trailing around in the shadow of his success and his ego, I had this deep urge to root myself in the earth, like the marijuana plants Billy grew in the back yard and whose leaves he smoked too often.

I missed my daughter and, oddly, I missed my ex-mother-in-law almost as much: Gordana had been such a solid presence; the consolation prize for being married to her emotionally stunted son.

Nonetheless, I thought I was rooted in Kansas. I'd escaped from Ivan, and met a good, solid man who treated me with respect and whose only real fault was staying up too late and falling asleep in front of the TV with a burned-out joint in his hand. I didn't like it particularly, but I couldn't complain. No one was perfect, and his pot habit was as much a part of him as his dimples. In fact, the first words he ever said to me were: 'I'm so stoned I could hunt ducks with a hand-rake.' It made absolutely no sense, and yet perfect sense at the same time; and it made me laugh. Billy always made me laugh, which meant I forgave him a lot. Including his strange selection of stoner friends who turned up at the house, night or day, spouting rubbish and wanting to be fed.

Then out of nowhere, everything changed. Maybe it was my own fault for being complacent. Sometimes I thought that I was just destined to be different (not special, just different). But it turned out that the man I'd been with for nine years, and whom I thought I'd be with for ever, didn't love me any more. Even though we'd been engaged for most of that time. I was kind of surprised that he even had the energy to get off the couch and find himself another woman, but he had; leaving the faint outline of ash around him on the sofa cushions.

It was a fatal mistake to assume that just because you didn't get particularly turned on by the sight of a tubbyish middle-aged man in a too-tight faded Grateful Dead T-shirt, nobody else would either. I guess I took him for granted – ironically, in the same way that I used to grumble that Ivan took me for granted.

On the day after Billy left me, I stood for a long time in the front room and stared at a photograph of us with our arms around each other, taken on the gravelly shore of Clinton Lake. We'd gone there during the hottest week of last summer for a swim with some friends who had a trailer there, but it was so hot that even the murky waters of the lake didn't provide any respite, not unless you dived (*dove*, as they said over here) off the jetty right down to the cloudy grey lake bed and lay there half buried in the silt, like a plaice or some other bottom-feeding fish. Only the deepest two feet of water was cool and quiet. I wished I could be back there.

We looked happy in that photograph. I studied it, realizing two things about us: that I had finally lost the slightly harried expression I'd worn throughout my marriage to Ivan; and that Billy was far more attractive than I'd given him credit for. I looked at him through another woman's eyes – Eva's, the woman who'd stolen him from me – and saw the delighted smile, the warm sleepy brown eyes, the dimples. Billy was a lovely, cuddly man, and I hadn't appreciated it.

In fact – and how much Ivan would hate to hear this – he had actually ended up being far more attractive than Ivan: Ivan, the erstwhile sports pin-up, who'd had women falling over him when he was the star tennis player, eighth best in the UK, hundredth best in the world, voted Most Gorgeous Man in some British tabloid survey of 1984, 'Ivan the Terribl(y) Sexy', that sort of thing. Who'd have thought that a shortish, pudgyish midwesterner, who not only possessed but actually wore a pair of denim bib and braces, would outshine Ivan in the sex-appeal department? I mean, I knew these things were subjective and perhaps I was exaggerating Billy's charms because I'd lost him, but Billy had mellowed into his looks, whereas Ivan had just gone to seed.

I saw him in December a couple of years ago, for the first time since the divorce. I'd gone back to England to spend Christmas with Rachel, to watch her play in some tournament or other, and to catch up with Gordana. I would have preferred not to cross paths with Ivan at all, but it was fairly unavoidable under the circumstances. So it was gratifying to see that Ivan's once washboard stomach had developed a little paunch; it was smaller than Billy's, but somehow more noticeable because he was so self-conscious about it. And where Billy's chubby face had matured into warmth, Ivan's face looked as if someone had taken a pencil sharpener to his nose and chin and an eraser to the crown of his head. His broad shoulders had begun to droop and his skin had developed a grey tinge. I remember thinking it was funny that he seemed to have taken on the stressed look that I used to have. Probably because his awful girlfriend nagged him so much. That was karma for you.

I decided to phone Rachel, having remembered that it was her birthday next week. If I called her now, I might catch her before she went training, and I could ask her what she wanted. She was so hard to buy for: she just wasn't into clothes or make-up or music or books. She only liked sports: pool, darts, table football; and tennis, of course. She was a tomboy. I'd thought she'd grow out of it, but she didn't seem to have.

I missed my daughter. I knew she didn't miss me, but she was still the only good thing which had come out of my marriage.

I wished that Billy and I could have had children. We did try, but not that hard, if I was honest. At first we thought we'd wait until we got married. Then, as time went on and I realized that I still felt too superstitious about taking the plunge for a second time, and Billy was too indolent to chivvy me into it, we thought we might just have a baby anyway. But when it didn't happen, neither of us could face the tests: the legs-in-stirrups indignity of it, the nail-biting risk of disappointment. I couldn't shift an unpleasant image of Billy's testicles like dried-out seed pods, full of ganga seeds. That was the trouble with Kansas men, they were nearly all potheads.

I dialled Rachel's number, hoping that neither Ivan nor the awful Anthea would answer, and thankfully neither did. Rachel and I had a little chat, but she sounded tense and miserable, not at all like a girl rocketing towards the peak of her career. I tried to worm it out of her, wondering if maybe it was boyfriend trouble, but she said she and Mark were still together.

'So what's up, honey?'

'It's just *Dad*,' she spat out, as if he were a cherry stone she was in danger of swallowing. The vitriol sounded odd from her; she was usually so placid. 'Would you believe, he's actually trying to ban me from seeing Mark? I mean, does he think I'm still a kid?'

I tutted sympathetically. 'Well, you know your father's always been ... single-minded. Is he telling you that a boyfriend is too much of a distraction?'

'Yeah. He's got it into his head that my game's

slipped since I started going out with Mark. Which isn't true. I'm just tired, that's all.'

'I bet you are. You need a vacation. Why don't you bring Mark over here for a holiday soon?' I said, moving four feet across the polished floorboards of the front room to deflect a serious buzzing sound which had infiltrated my cordless phone. 'Show him the sights. You know – Dodge City; The Eisenhower Museum in Abilene; the World's Largest Ball of String in Cawker City. Hey, if you came next August, you'd be here for Annual Twine-Winding time – winding on Friday, picnic and parade on Saturday. Don't say there's nothing to do out here.'

'That would be great, Mum, if either of us ever got time for a holiday,' she said, not even laughing at my snide remarks regarding the dubious attractions of the Sunflower State. I'd have been offended if *she* had made jokes about my adopted home, but I was allowed to. But she obviously hadn't been listening. She had inherited her father's irritating habit of not acknowledging parts of a conversation.

I hoped that this Mark was worth all the aggravation. I supposed he must be – I'd never even known Rachel to have a boyfriend before, at least not a serious one.

'Hang in there, Rach. Ivan will just have to get used to the idea. You have to have a life outside of tennis.'

'Thanks, Mum,' she said, and I felt happier. I hated to admit it, but it was nice to be united with my daughter against my ex. I'd never tried to poison her against him, but I wouldn't put it past him to do that to me at any opportunity.

'We should go on holiday together some time,' I suggested, knowing that in all probability it would never happen.

'Sure, Mum. Anyway, I've got to go. I've got squad practice in a minute, and José hates it when we're late.'

I debated whether to tell her that Billy had left me,

but decided against it. Not when she sounded so down already.

'OK, Rach. Take care. I'll call you again next week. Bye.'

It was only after we'd hung up that I realized I'd forgotten to ask her what she wanted for her birthday.

2

Gordana

I watch her face, when she doesn't know I'm watching. She is mad about that arrogant boy of hers, I see it in every one of her expressions. Her eyes dart around searching for him, sliding towards the main gate of the tennis club, looking to see if it's his car which has just come in, and then comes that moment of disappointment, a teeny pull down of the skin around her mouth when she realizes it's not. She's outside on court now, dancing to the ball the way she does, but even though she doesn't break her swing, she still watches the gate.

I love my granddaughter. I don't want her to be hurt by men, but of course she will be. We all are. I told Ivan, though, that it is ridiculous to forbid her to see this Mark. Ivan usually listens to his mother, but for some reason this time he wouldn't budge.

'She's not a child any more,' I told him. 'You can't ban her, it'll only make them want each other more. Let him break her heart – which he will, in no time at all – then you won't be the villain, and Rachel will have got him out of her system.'

Poor little Rachel, I think to myself. Ivan wanted her *purged* of Mark, he wanted to give her some kind of laxative to make all her feelings shoot out and be gone.

Rachel has been on court for ten minutes, having a warm-up hit with her coach José. Hitting and looking for Mark; hitting and looking. I do understand why she looks. He is very a handsome boy, with black hair and many muscles. Almost too many for a pro player; sometimes I think surely they must slow him down. But he seems to be able to run fast. I think that if Ivan carries on making a fuss about him and Rachel, he will soon run – in the opposite direction to where she is. Then, like I tell Ivan, Rachel will hate him. She will look and look for Mark, and he will be off smiling at some other pretty girl. It's funny: he is a lot like Ivan was at that age. Same colouring, similar build. Almost as arrogant too.

I go to make me and Ivan a cup of tea in the club kitchen. It gets me cross, the way the Intermediate section shamelessly steal teabags out of the Midweek members tupperware box. I know for a fact that it was half full only two days ago. Then the Intermediates played, and look! Now all that is left is five bags and a lot of brown powder at the bottom of the box. Of course they never leave any money in the tin provided. Someone (not me, too boring) will have to bring it up at the next committee meeting. Maybe Elsie. Elsie always likes to have something to make a fuss about.

I carry a mug of tea out to Ivan, who is restringing a racket for Rachel. I put the mug down on the table next to him – his favourite mug, it says 'STRESSED' on it in wavy brown letters – and watch him threading the catgut so fast in and out of the holes around the edge of the racket head, spinning it back and forth in its clamp so he can weave it back through again, pulling it taut each time.

He has always been good with his hands. When he was a little boy, he would sit for hours building Airfix models and then taking pains to decorate them with a particular shade of paint, the one he always used, what was it called? It came in tiny round tins whose lids I had to prise off for him with the edge of a screwdriver. Once the lid was off the paint, he never needed any further help. His tongue would stick out the

17

corner of his mouth, and his frown lines started when he was nine.

'Olive drab!' I remember, out loud. Ivan looks at me as if he thinks I have lost my marbles. 'Sorry,' I say. 'Seeing you do that reminds me of those models you used to make when you were seven or eight. You got through a lot of olive drab. Do you remember, we made a pyramid from the empty tins? It was big.'

He permits himself a small smile. I reach out to ruffle his hair, but he jerks his head away. He doesn't like his hair being touched nowadays, I think since it got all thin in the middle.

'You should smile more often, Sonny Jim. You are much better when you smile. At the moment you look like a black cloud. But it's nice to see you down here. Helping you buy this place was the only way I get to see you these days!'

I am joking, of course, but he frowns and looks even more like a black cloud. I think it is because he didn't like to be reminded that he'd had to borrow money from me and Ted to turn this place from the small-town tennis club I've been a member of for years, and where Rachel started playing, into what it is now: this big smart 'academy', with six new courts, a new bar and changing rooms with wooden mats on the floor, and Ivan's name above the door in big letters. But perhaps I am wrong, for all he says is: 'Don't let anyone hear you call me that, Mama, it's embarrassing.'

I laugh, but he doesn't. Sonny Jim is a nickname I've used sometimes for him since he was a little boy. The shopkeeper at the end of the road used to call him that, and even though I had been in England for years, I'd never heard that expression before. I thought it was a term of endearment mixed up with the wrong name. I thought it was *Sunny* Jim, and I remember saying to this shopkeeper, 'No, his name is not Jim. It is Ivan.' But she kept on calling him Sonny Jim. Enormous bosoms, she had, that shopkeeper. They went from her neck to her waist. *She* could never have played tennis.

'Do you think Rachel and Mark are still seeing each other?'

'No, I don't. Rachel's a sensible girl. Zurich's a huge tournament for her, and she knows she needs to get focused. There's too much at stake.'

'She needs to have fun too, Ivan. She is starting to look as serious as you do. All she does is play tennis and work out all the time. At least I managed to persuade her to come to the party tomorrow. Are you coming too?'

Ivan ignores me, just threading the catgut back through another hole. Sometimes he pretends I'm not there when I talk to him. It drives me mad. But I know he will come to the party. He moans about the Midweek and Intermediate sections, all us oldies. If he'd had his own way, he'd have got rid of the whole lot of us when he took over, but I wouldn't let him. It was our club first, and so I made it a condition of the loan that he wouldn't change when we could play. It's a funny mixture here now of young foreign girls bouncing around learning to be pros and the likes of me and my friends who just want a sedate set or two of doubles, and then a nice cup of tea.

He'll come to the party, though, I'm sure he will. He loves the attention. It takes his mind off whatever has bothered him for some time now. Years, I think, this particular thing has bothered him. I keep asking him what it is, if I can help, but he just ignores me. I think it is more than just his disappearing hair, or his unsatisfactory career, or the money he owes me and Ted.

I must confess, I was terribly disappointed when Ivan didn't succeed as a professional tennis player. He looks so dashing on court, so tall and handsome, and I was so proud of him. I really thought he could be the British Number One. I used to dream of him holding up the Wimbledon trophy and blowing me a kiss from where he'd be standing, next to the Duchess of Kent.

I'd think of my cousins back in Korčula, in their ill-fitting nylon dresses, drinking their bitter coffees and watching my gorgeous son win Wimbledon on a wall-mounted television in an austere café on the square.

I had even planned out in my head the letter I'd write to them, alerting them to the fact that the very same Ivan Anderson who was through to the quarter-finals was my own boy: Ivanovic Korolija's grandson. I wouldn't want to tempt fate, so I wouldn't post the letter until he got to the quarter-finals, and then I'd have to send it Next Day Delivery, to make sure they didn't miss the semi or the final. I'd address it to Sabrina Franulovic; from what I heard she was still the town gossip. I'd pretend that I was merely being solicitous, enquiring about the wellbeing of her and her family, then I'd drop in the part about Ivan being through to the quarter-finals, hotly tipped as the winner. I would have to get somebody to check my Croatian though, it's got very rusty since Mama died.

I imagine us going back to visit, with Ivan, walking triumphantly into their dreary cafés and their dreary lives, probably unchanged since we were last there, when Ivan was just five years old.

Mama used to tell me how shocked they all were when she and Papa brought me over to England, and how they sucked their teeth and told each other we'd never survive in this big noisy country with no family around us, but they were wrong. We did. If those cousins could see the house Ted and I live in now, they'd think it was Buckingham Palace.

I don't believe this is just because I married a rich man, either. Ted wouldn't be as rich as he's become if it weren't for me. I taught him to make more out of his money. I would never let one penny go to waste. It's our money. Our house.

3

Rachel

Tennis, tennis, bloody tennis. Even my social life revolves around it. Sometimes I feel so bored by it that I can hardly bear to pick up a racket, and the sight of those damn endless balls makes my heart sink.

Not always, though. It's great when I'm winning, of course, and I love the challenge of it. Most of the time I feel grateful that at least there's something I'm really good at – and I am really good.

Too good to give up . . . but not yet good enough to give up, either.

It's just that I sometimes wonder if perhaps everyone could talk about something else for a change? Not much chance of that in my family, though: Dad – ex-British hopeful, coach, my business manager, Mr flaming Ambitious; my grandmother, Gordana – even more ambitious than Dad, if such a thing were possible. Only my mother doesn't seem afflicted by this particular sporting obsession; she escaped nine years ago to live in the back-end of nowhere in mid-America.

So, because trying to imagine my family not talking about tennis is too much of a stretch, I try and imagine a different family altogether. A mum and dad in safe white-collar jobs, home at six every night for dinner; siblings; regular family outings to Areas of Out-standing Natural Beauty; queues for the bathroom;

bickering; hugging; laughing conspiratorially . . . I hate being an only child.

It's really hot in here. When Dad took over and revamped this place, a bit of air-conditioning wouldn't have gone amiss. I wish I was out in the cold night air, participating in the men's training session, under the sickly yellow glow of the floodlights. Instead I'm squashed up at one of five trestle tables occupied by forty club members, mostly female and of a certain age. They're all chatting loudly about house prices and school fees, their burgundy cheeks and shiny foreheads signalling that they're as hot as I am. The lady opposite me, Margery, delves into her handbag and rather ostentatiously pulls out a silver compact. As she powders her nose, I see the compact is engraved with the words 'Runner Up, the Winnie Wainthrop Midweek Trophy 2004'.

I'm sandwiched between my grandmother, Gordana, and another of the old club stalwarts, Elsie, and I wish I was pretty much anywhere else at all. I only agreed to come because Mark is training outside, but with Dad bound to turn up at any moment, I think it's unlikely I'll even get the chance to talk to Mark after his practice finishes.

'Can't we get some fresh air in here?' I say, forgetting my alternative family daydream (we'd all be sitting down to shepherd's pie and carrots about now, perhaps planning a holiday for next year, even though we should by rights all have grown out of the desire to go on holiday with our parents. They'd tease us, and make jokes, 'When are we ever going to get rid of you all?' but we'd know they were delighted we want to be included . . .)

I fan myself with a copy of the fixtures list. Through the stubbornly closed window, I watch Mark execute a perfect slice backhand on Court One, spreading both his arms wide after the shot as if he could take flight. The sight of him out there, his face ruddy with exertion, makes me feel even hotter.

'And let all that warm air go to waste?' Elsie frowns at me. 'Do you have any idea how expensive it is to heat a place like this? No wonder our subscriptions are so high, with people like you going round opening windows willy nilly!'

Elsie is probably the same age as Gordana, early sixties, but behaves as if she is from a completely different generation. Gordana wears a nifty Nike ensemble on court: a tightish skirt and blue and white top which she absolutely still has the figure for, and in which, at a distance, she could pass for a woman in her forties. Elsie, on the other hand, plays in a hideous navy garment circa 1952, with about five million pleats in it to enable it to encompass her enormously wide hips. It rides up at the back to expose buttocks drooping in Billy Jean King frilly tennis knickers, and perfectly accentuates her Delta map of matching blue varicose veins and blancmangey legs.

She hates what's happened to the club since Dad took it over. She hates all these young, fit people around. I wonder why she still comes? Habit I suppose. She doesn't even seem to enjoy her tennis any more. She has so many stipulations to be fulfilled before she'll set foot on a court that it hardly seems worth it: she will only play on one of the two red courts and not on any of the green ones (too slippery), using Wilson balls, not Slazenger (I have no idea why); she refuses to play with men (too aggressive); she won't stand for anybody chewing gum on court (too uncouth); and has a problem playing with anybody under forty (because they soon realize that she's got a gammy leg and therefore can only hit the ball if it lands right at her feet).

When the conditions are acceptable for her to play, she's a nightmare on court. Although she can't run, can't serve, can't volley or lob, she finds it necessary to give 'constructive' criticism to whomever has the misfortune to partner her in doubles: 'Don't swing at your volleys!' 'That should have landed *inside* the baseline!' I sometimes watch her out of the corner of my eye when I'm training on the next court with José, and I can't believe some of the things she comes out with. Plus she's a horrendous gossip, and nobody likes her. She lives in our street, which makes it worse: she's always trying to cadge lifts off Dad, and he can't stand her.

I gulp down half a glass of tepid white wine, and try to stop myself looking at my watch yet again. Only a few minutes till the men's training finishes, and then perhaps there'll be a chance of a furtive kiss with Mark before he goes off to the pub with the rest of his team. Providing Dad doesn't turn up.

'Where is Ivan?' Gordana asks me, reading my mind. There is an empty seat at the head of our table, and an expectant air to the other women around me. They all adore Dad.

'I don't know,' I say. 'I haven't seen him all day. But I went to the gym at six this morning, and I haven't been home since.' My muscles ache as if reminding me of this, and I think longingly of my cool, firm mattress.

Bang on time, somebody switches off the floodlights, and the courts outside are plunged into pitch darkness. A few moments later six sweaty men burst through the door, shouting and laughing, causing a momentary hush in the chat of the women inside as we turn as one, some disapprovingly (Elsie: ugh, men); and some admiringly (Gordana and I).

'Coming to join us, boys?' calls Gordana in her husky voice, waving her wine glass merrily at them. Her English is still slightly imperfect at times, even though she's lived in this country since childhood. I am convinced she cultivates a Croatian accent for added sex appeal.

Mark smiles at me, but manages to make it look as if

he is actually smiling at my grandmother. 'Sorry, Gordana. Tempting, but we've got pints with our names on them waiting for us. Thanks anyway.'

They all jostle into the men's changing room, and the chat in the room resumes, although the wistful looks on some of the ladies' faces suggests that their minds are more on the fit, naked male bodies not ten feet away in the shower, rather than who is responsible for laundering the clubhouse curtains. There are *some* compensations for having their club overrun by youngsters . . .

I'm not at all surprised that Mark and his friends declined Gordana's invitation. The Ivan Anderson Tennis Academy's Autumn Social supper isn't exactly a riveting social occasion if you're under fifty. I am the youngest person here by a good fifteen years. Dad and I are the living breathing trophies of the I.A.T.A., the club's crowning glories – well, so Gordana believes, anyway. Ivan got to the last sixteen at Wimbledon once or twice in his heyday, and I'm currently ranked five hundredth in the world; tenth in Britain.

Since we moved back here from Kansas when I was a baby, this clubhouse has been a second home to me. I've grown up here; I learned to play tennis here. Despite the often petty squabbles and small-mindedness inevitably found in any collective, committee-run organization, the place and people give me a level of stability crucial to my nomadic existence. I'm glad that Gordana made Dad keep things the same when he took over – well, as much the same as possible. I'm travelling to tournaments around the world thirty-five weeks a year, so any stable community, however flawed, would feel like a blessing.

Five minutes later, two beeps on my mobile phone alert me to the arrival of a text message, and earns me a frown from Elsie. The text is from Mark: 'MEET ME AT THE BACK OF COURT 4, SEXY BEAST'.

I grin hesitantly, although my body is already

responding to the mental image of him, freshly showered, running his large hands over me. We've not actually gone all the way yet, although we've talked about it, and he keeps teasing me. I do really, really fancy him. It took me quite a long time to pluck up courage to tell him that I'm still a virgin, and he was surprised. I don't know why – I mean, he lives the same life as I do; he knows how hard it is to maintain a relationship when tennis has to be the focus of everything. He hasn't had many serious relationships either, although I guess that, unlike me, he's managed to find opportunities to have sex. But he's never had Dad breathing down his neck, forcing him to 'concentrate on his career' instead of going out to meet potential partners.

Much as I want him, though, I'm not going to be pressured into it. I don't want to get hurt.

But right now, I think how nice some fresh air would be . . .

I stand up. 'Just got to go and make a phone call outside,' I say to Elsie, who disapproves of mobile phones.

The men, including Mark, emerge from the changing room and leave the clubhouse in pungent wafts of aftershave and spray-on deodorant, heading for the pub in the next street.

I'm glad Dad's not here yet. He'd have a fit if he saw me slipping out behind them. Although it's bound to get back to him – I see Elsie's eyes narrowing – what can he do about it? I'm twenty-three tomorrow, for heaven's sake, he can hardly lock me in my bedroom to prevent me from having any contact with Mark.

He and Mark clashed, horribly, a couple of years ago, back before I was with José, when Dad was still coaching me. He took Mark on too, and the relationship lasted about three months until their regular shouting matches and ego clashes proved too much for them both, and Mark fired him. Dad hasn't spoken to

Mark since, but the way that Mark stood up to him served only to intensify my long-standing crush on him. I couldn't believe it when he finally asked me out.

I leave the clubhouse, pretending to dial a number on my phone. The air is cold on my hot cheeks as I walk along the verandah, doubling back on myself once I'm sure I can't be seen from inside. I creep underneath the windows until I get to the end court, silent in my trainers. I have a sudden fear that Mark has gone to the pub after all, having not received a reply to his text, and I'll be standing around on an empty tennis court in the dark, feeling like a prat. The gate is slightly open, and I go inside, holding my breath with anticipation. There's no sign of him, and so I am relieved when I think I can faintly smell his aftershave.

'Pssst,' I hear from a distant corner. 'Over here!'

'Where?' My eyes are still adjusting to the darkness. There is a pause, and then a hand suddenly grabs mine, making me jump.

'Hi, sexy,' Mark says, pulling me towards him. 'Are you a naughty girl?'

I laugh softly and kiss him. He smells of tennis balls and shower gel, and lust courses through my body. It's such a physical sensation, like the feeling of an icy drink travelling down my oesophagus to my belly.

'Me? Not at all. It was your idea.'

'I don't hear you complaining,' he says, dragging me over to the back of the court. I glance uneasily towards the lit-up clubhouse. Through the window I can see Gordana holding forth to her entourage, gesticulating wildly at her own table; the queen of clubs; a big fish in a pond she and Dad both wish was a lot larger.

'By the way . . .' Mark whispers, sliding his hands under my T-shirt.

'What?'

'. . . I love you soooo much,' he says, and his breath

27

is warm on my throat and my ear and in my heart. 'You are just so beautiful. You make my heart jump, you know.'

This is a different Mark to the cocky player on court, the bad loser, the racket-thrower, the stroppy muttered curser. This is *my* Mark: sweet and romantic and passionate. Nobody else has ever made me feel like this, not ever. Mark is in a whole different league. I hug him hard, my chin fitting perfectly into a bespoke notch at the side of his neck. 'I love you too. I *love* you!' We kiss.

'What are you doing after this?' I whisper. It would be so easy to go home with him, to continue what we kept starting but never concluded. Perhaps I am ready. Perhaps it's time.

'Pub with the lads,' he replies, stroking my breasts gently. I wait for him to invite me to come with him, but he doesn't. 'They're waiting for me.'

'Can I come?'

For a moment his hands stop moving, then continue, like a missed frame of film in a movie. 'Oh babe, aren't you wanted in there? Ivan'll throw a fit if he shows up and you've disappeared.'

Not for the first time, I wish he and Dad hadn't fallen out. Then Mark could come with me, sit next to me, and everyone would know without a doubt that we were an item, rather than having to gossip and speculate about it. But then I swallow down a needling worry that it wouldn't make any difference; that Mark would still do exactly what he wanted, even if Dad weren't a problem.

'Let's concentrate on what we're doing right now, shall we, instead of worrying about what we're doing later?' He pushes himself against me, a master of distraction, hard beneath the soft fleecy fabric of his sweatpants.

I look nervously again at the lit-up clubhouse, and pull away from him a little. It scares me when he does that.

'Oh Rach, Rach, you drive me mad. I want you so much,' he moans. He's kissing my neck now, and my skin feels so alive and sensitive it's as if I can feel every tiny cell of his lips brushing against it. Gooseflesh sweeps up and down my back, although I'm not at all cold.

'Sorry. I'm not trying to tease you or anything, it's just . . .'

'What?'

'Soon,' I mutter, 'I know I'll be ready soon.' And I really think I will be, as he pinions me against the fence, and the green wire presses honeycomb patterns into my back. I wrap one leg around his hard thigh, and forget about Dad. After all, twenty-three is ludicrously old to still be a virgin, tennis career or no tennis career. And Mark isn't going to wait for me for ever . . . 'Just not yet, OK?'

He sighs, and kisses me again.

Fifteen minutes later, and rather sheepishly, I creep back underneath the windows to the clubhouse, hoping I don't appear too obviously ravaged. Mark got his own way and I allowed him go off to the pub without a murmur, in an attempt to compensate for not letting him go all the way. Anyway, he was right. Dad would have gone up the wall if I'd absconded from the dinner so early. I plan to slink back to my seat, still clutching my mobile as if the call had just finished; and I am concentrating so hard on looking innocent that for a few moments I fail to register the utter change in atmosphere inside the pavilion.

Whereas before the room had been filled with breathy chat and the tinkle and hoot of laughter, I am greeted with complete silence. At first, I think that somehow they'd all managed to see Mark and me snogging on Court Four, and I instantly blush a deep, panicky scarlet. But they aren't looking at me. All eyes are turned in the direction of Gordana and Elsie, who are standing up, actually eyeballing one another like two cartoon bulldogs. Gordana, usually so composed, looks as if she is going to punch Elsie on the nose.

I run over to the table. 'What's going on?' I hiss at my grandmother, as the entire room follows the exchange with rapt attention. A couple of the kinder souls attempt to rekindle the conversation at their respective tables, but are indiscreetly shushed – this is clearly the most exciting thing to happen at the tennis club since the near-punch-up at the last AGM over allocation of court time for the lowly Intermediate members.

Gordana grasps my hand. 'Elsie has gone too far this time,' she says coldly.

Elsie sniffs. 'I'm only describing what I saw,' she replies.

'Shall we go into the kitchen? Or outside, for a walk?' I ask, trying to drag Gordana away by her sleeve whilst looking at everyone else in the room and hoping that my expression says, For heaven's sake, show a little discretion, *please*.

It seems to work, since a stilted sort of chat breaks out again, enough that I can talk to Gordana without the entire room hearing. She shakes off my hand and continues to glower at Elsie

'What did she see?' I whisper.

'It is slander and vicious gossiping without any truths,' she replies, rather inarticulately. When Gordana is distressed, her standard of English seems to slip dramatically.

'I merely asked,' says Elsie, 'why two men and a woman would come to your house at ten to seven in the morning, stay for two hours, and then take Ivan away with them again, if they aren't police officers conducting a raid?'

She pats her perm, so triumphantly that I want to smack her too. Then, belatedly, I realize that she's talking to me; that it's my house she's referring to.

'Well, Elsie, firstly, I have no idea. But obviously if

they were police officers conducting a raid, we would have been informed by now. Secondly, I don't think Dad, when he turns up, is going to be too happy to hear what you've been implying about him in front of everyone. Lastly, and most importantly, it is absolutely none of your business, and Gordana and I would thank you to keep your nose out of our family affairs.'

My knees are shaking when I finish this little speech, and I can feel the sweat pressing dark under my arms. I have never had a confrontation like this before with anyone, apart from Dad, and it makes me feel sick. But Gordana's stricken face is enough to make me lose my rag. I can tell she feels totally humiliated, in front of all her friends.

'Come on,' I say to Gordana again, 'let's go and get some air.' This time she allows me to steer her towards the door. As we pass, most people's eyes drop towards the dusty floor, although a few smile tight little sympathetic smiles in our direction. Elsie sits down again, but I notice that everyone on our table leans away and studiously ignores her.

Once outside, I drag Gordana into the car park and we hide conspiratorially behind a large and muddy Range Rover belonging to the captain of the Midweek section, Miranda Matheson.

'Where is he?' she hisses at me.

'I don't know. When did you last speak to him?'

'Yesterday, here. He seem OK then. You?'

'Last night. He and Anthea were still up watching TV when I went to bed. I was out early this morning. He hasn't been here all day.'

We stare doubtfully at each other. 'It can't be true,' says Gordana.

'Elsie wouldn't completely make it up, though, would she? And why hasn't he told us?'

Gordana leans against the spare wheel of the Range Rover, which is mounted on the back door of the car like a trophy. She is still clutching her wine glass.

'It does not mean they arrest him. Maybe it is early business meeting.' Then she grabs my arm with her free hand. 'No! It cannot be raid. If it was raid, they take stuff out of house. Elsie didn't say they take anything.'

'That's true,' I said. 'And what would they be raiding the house, for anyway? Illegal money? White slaves? Anthea's diet pills?'

But Gordana didn't smile. 'We must ring Anthea,' she said, balancing her wine glass on top of the Range Rover's spare wheel and pulling out her tiny silver phone. 'Ivan's telephone has been off all day.'

She dials, as expertly as a City trader, and waits a moment. 'Yes, Anthea, it is Gordana. Is Ivan there? . . . No, he is not here either . . . Where has he been today? . . . Out where? . . . You don't know. Was anyone in the house today, this morning, I mean, early? Elsie say she saw some people . . . Right. I see. Please tell him to ring me when you see him. Thank you.'

'Well?'

'She say Jehovah's Witnesses.'

'At seven in the morning? Aren't there usually just two of them? And why would he leave with them?'

'I don't know. She say she went out early too and when she come back he is not there. Something is not right.'

The club's adopted cat, Timothy, trots up to us and rubs himself against my legs. I think briefly of Mark.

'I'm going to go home,' I say, extracting my bike lights from my backpack. 'We can't lurk about in the car park all night. Are you going back inside?'

Gordana draws herself up to her full height, I guess already mentally preparing to face Elsie again.

'She's just a silly, bitter, bored old woman with nothing else in her life,' I say. 'Don't let her get to you. You know that nobody likes her, and they all love you. She hates that. And she's jealous of you.' I hug my beautiful grandmother as if she is my best friend. Which, in many ways, she is.

'Very well,' says Gordana, sniffing delicately, then stooping to stroke Timothy. 'Ted is not coming to collect me until eleven-thirty. Will you ring me when you get home, and let me know . . . what is going on?'

I sigh. 'Of course, if I find out.'

I clip the lights on to my bicycle, unlock the padlock, and cycle home, past the lighted, steamy windows of the pub Mark and his mates are in. I consider going in to tell him what's happened, but decide against it. I'm too anxious to get home and find out for myself.

Entirely selfishly, my heart sinks as I realize that if Dad's really been arrested, he won't be able to fly to Zurich with me tomorrow. It's potentially a really big tournament for me – I haven't had to qualify for it, since my current ranking means I've been automatically seeded. It would be hard to go without Dad. Even though he is no longer my coach, he comes to almost all my tournaments – it's cheaper than paying José to come, and more often than not, Dad has his own players in the same tournaments, so we all travel together.

I cycle on for another ten minutes through the dark quiet back streets, gulping in deep harsh breaths of cold, wet, air, the thrumming rotation of the wheels and the whiz of tyres on tarmac calming me down. It's starting to hail. I hear the little stones rattling on my bike helmet and see them bouncing on the road around me.

I'm sure he hasn't really been arrested, and this whole thing is a ridiculous storm in a teacup.

4

Gordana

What has he done? What has my silly, silly boy *done*?
Oh, I knew there was something going on. He has been
in funny mood for ages now. Elsie is a bitch and a
gossip but she would not invent such a story. Those
people came and took him away.

No, Gordana, wait.

It doesn't mean he has done something bad. Think.
Many explanations. Business meeting? Maybe. No
way can it be Jehovah's Witness, Ivan would shut the
door in their faces, never invite them in for two hours.
Maybe it was secret meeting he didn't want to have at
club. Yes. He will be so angry with Elsie for saying it,
if that's the case.

I go back inside but everybody now is looking at me
like it is me who is a criminal. Rachel has gone away
on her bicycle. I should have rung Ted and told him to
come now. I don't want to be here, although my
friends are trying to cheer me up: they talk too loudly
about the proposed plans for the new court surfaces;
they peek anxiously at me over the rims of their wine
glasses as if suddenly they are worried I will explode,
pffff, and shower them all with my criminal
tendencies – for of course whatever evil is in Ivan has
come from me.

Listen to me. Shame on me, for assuming my Ivan
really has done something bad. It's probably a

complete misunderstanding. Ivan has made mistakes in the past, but that was in the past. I don't even think about those now, unless I have to remind him of something. I think basically he is honest. So honest that he would buy a Permit to Travel on a train platform at night when he *knows* there will be no inspector on board the train. That's how I brought him up. I smacked his bum over and over, that time he stole a water pistol from the toy shop; smacked him right there in front of the shop owner. He never did it again.

It's part of life, to make mistakes. I make big mistake by letting that butcher's boy get me pregnant, when I was young and silly and didn't know any better. Ivan make mistakes too . . . like when he went to live at that university in Kansas and came home with a wife and a baby, so young himself and his scholarship down the drain. But still, that baby was Rachel, and I wouldn't be without Rachel for any of the tea in China. Sometimes mistakes work out for the best. My own mistake turned into Ivan, didn't it?

Yes. If it is not a misunderstanding, it is more likely to be a mistake than a dishonesty.

I tell this to Andrea and Maureen. Then to Liz and Lorraine, and Esther and Helen. They all nod and purse their lips and put their heads to one side with sympathy. I have another glass of wine. Nobody will speak to Elsie, and she sits on her own until a little Indian man comes inside and tells her the taxi is ready, then she goes and no one except Humphrey says goodbye. Humphrey loves Elsie, even though she once told him she has a garden gnome who is the spitting image of him.

I feel better now . . . but still something niggles at me. I don't like to not know everything that is going on with my son.

It is only after Ted has picked me up, at eleven-thirty on the spot, and I am in the car telling him everything about this awful night, and how after all that Rachel rang to say Ivan is in bed with migraine, when I suddenly stop and clap my hands over my mouth.

'What is it, Dana?' says Ted, looking worried.

'I left my wine glass on Miranda Matheson's car,' I tell him, and burst out with something, which I'm not sure is laughing or crying.

Ted shakes his head, and drives on.

5

Susie

The first time I came to live in Lawrence was in 1979. I was nearly twenty, on an exchange programme with my British university, where I was halfway through a degree in American Studies. Myself and another girl, Corinna, were allocated places at the University of Kansas, and, boy, were we ever pissed off. Everybody else on our course got to go to one of the various colleges of the University of California: surfers' paradises, home of the stars, year-round sunshine ... We got *Kansas*. All we knew about Kansas was that it was bitterly cold in winter, boiling hot in summer, and in the middle of nowhere. Wheat, tornadoes, rednecks, Toto, the Wicked Witch of the West.

Corinna was distraught. She had visualized herself spending a year in a bikini, on a beach, surrounded by gleaming bronzed hunks, and with a pop of a pitchfork that bubble burst. She tried to cheer herself up by imagining handsome cowboys and lewd acts in the back of straw-strewn flatbed trucks, but she was devastated at the loss of her very own American dream, and moaned about it all the way through the flight to Kansas City. I was none too happy about it either. We believed our exile to be a punishment for being the worst students, a cruel joke by our lecturers for being the ones who always handed in their essays late and who missed the most tutorials.

I met Ivan the week after Corinna and I moved into our rented house: small, grey, clapboard, as all the houses were (we wondered for ages why nobody ever had firework or bonfire parties, until somebody pointed out that it's not the wisest form of entertainment when the whole town is built of wood). It had a square, scrubby yard, and a noisy air-conditioning unit which hung precariously out of the living room window. Kansas was in the grip of an Indian summer, and we found it hard to stay cool in our new home, especially after the climate-controlled halls of residence we'd stayed in when we first arrived. We ran the air-con day and night, until our ears rang with its constant watery roar.

It was our remarkably inquisitive mail-carrier, Raylene, who occasioned the initial meeting between Ivan and myself. In the process of delivering our letters from back home, she noticed the British postmarks and thereby deemed us interesting enough to invite to Sunday brunch. It was how she'd met Ivan, too.

Corinna and I were a little taken aback to be invited to lunch by our postwoman, but since we were woefully short of any better offers, we decided we'd go along. Corinna got all dolled up in her best gypsy top and glitter socks, and I put on my turquoise satin jacket, although neither of us held very high hopes of the gathering.

Raylene's house was not dissimilar in size and shape to our rented one, but whereas ours contained the bare minimum of rented furniture, every conceivable inch of surface space of Raylene's was full of clutter: newspapers old and new; cassette tapes, LPs, posters. Piles and piles of letters and papers littered the floor, and cut-out articles and cartoons were sellotaped all over the walls. A small table was balanced perilously in the middle of the living room, covered with plates of strange-looking cold meats (which I later discovered included pastrami and salt beef); various salads, and baskets of bread, but none of the several guests present had touched any of it.

'What a lot of magazines you must subscribe to,' said Corinna politely as we came in. There was the inevitable chorus of, 'Oh my gahhd, I LOVE your accent!' but she ignored it – we were already getting used to the reaction.

'Oh no,' said Raylene gaily. 'I don't subscribe to any of them. I'm a mailwoman. I get them free.'

Corinna and I exchanged glances. 'How come?'

'Well, you know how things can get "lost" in the mail,' Raylene said, tapping the side of her nose. 'Let me introduce you to some folks. This here's Calvin, and Patty, Brandon and Sara, and a fellow European – Ivan.' They all raised their plastic cups of beer and nodded or said hi, except Ivan. He barely even bothered to turn around from where he was kneeling (on a messy pile of Calvin and Hobbs cartoons clipped out of the *New York Times*), flipping through a stack of LPs.

Calvin was a tall Rasta with bloodshot eyes and bedraggled dreadlocks, but he had a cute face, and Corinna immediately engaged him in conversation, then led him away into the kitchen. I felt annoyed and abandoned, but at that moment Ivan straightened up, holding out a Velvet Underground album. I took one look at his thick black hair, lanky, muscular body and arrogant eyes, and promptly fell madly in love, instantly forgetting about Corinna's defection. It goes to show, doesn't it? You should never trust love at first sight.

'Cool,' I said, like an over-enthusiastic Labrador puppy, 'I love the Velvet Underground.' I watched him intently as he held the LP between his middle fingers and dropped it delicately over the spike in the centre of the turntable.

'So where are you from?' I cringed as I said it.

Corinna and I were already fed up with being asked that, but I couldn't stop myself bouncing round his feet asking questions.

'England. Like you. But my mother is Croatian, from Yugoslavia.'

'I know where Croatia is,' I said, forcing a high laugh into my voice so he wouldn't think I was criticizing him.

'Yes. Sorry. I'm used to Americans asking me. Most of them have never heard of it. I'm here on a tennis scholarship.'

'Oh.' I might know that Croatia was part of Yugoslavia, but I'd never heard of a tennis scholarship. 'So that means you must be pretty good at it?'

Ivan looked at me through half-closed eyes, as if he thought I must be joking.

'I turned professional two years ago,' he said with an air of finality, implying that was all I needed to know. In fact it didn't enlighten me much further. How good did you have to be, to be professional?

'Do you play?' he asked, sounding bored, as if he already knew the answer.

'No.' I glanced at the table of food, realizing that I was starving, but still nobody else was eating. Odd: I hadn't been hungry when I arrived. I decided that it must be all that lust coursing through my veins.

Raylene and Sara came up to us. I was about to broach the subject of lunch when Sara produced a huge joint, held a match to it and inhaled. She handed it wordlessly to me, and for a moment I considered dropping it. It seemed like such a fierce, un-controllable thing, and I'd never held one before. But I didn't want to appear naïve or square, so I held it tentatively to my lips and puffed. Raylene engaged Ivan in conversation, and I looked away, disappointed. Ivan had turned his back on me with such alacrity that I thought he'd probably been dying for an excuse to escape.

The smoke went straight to my head, but in a pleasant way, so I took another drag. My hunger instantly left my stomach and swam up towards my brain instead, where it circled gently for a while. It was quite a nice feeling, I decided. I looked for Corinna, to offer her the joint too, but she was ensconced in the kitchen, laughing with Calvin. Their heads were almost touching, and the sight of his black dreads was striking against her bleached blonde crop. They looked good together, and I wondered if she was feeling better about not going to California.

The small, cluttered room seemed to be getting a bit stuffy, so I excused myself and went to stand on the porch for a while.

It was so hot, even in mid-September. I hadn't got used to the particular sort of cloying heat that blew in across the wheatfields and prairies, as if an enormous oven door had been opened somewhere. Baking hot, literally. I'd never been in a house with air-conditioning before either, and kept forgetting the thirty-degree hike in the temperature every time I stepped outside.

Raylene's street was a neat block of detached cube houses, but there was nobody about – as usual. I rarely saw people walking. It clearly wasn't the done thing to walk anywhere. Occasionally a huge, low-slung car, usually containing at least five people, would drag itself past, as if the heat affected acceleration; otherwise everything was still, bleached out, exhausted.

I began to feel ill. My mouth dried up, and my legs started to jiggle and weaken, like someone was unfastening nuts at my knees. I sat down, too suddenly, in the stillness, and felt the rough planks of the porch under my thighs. I was embarrassed – two puffs of a joint and I was out of it? Pathetic. I groaned, and felt worse. I wanted my mother, but she had died six years earlier.

Things went from bad to worse. As I sat there

sweating, enormous tears, the size and solidity of hard-boiled eggs, squeezed themselves out of my eyes and rolled slowly down my face, and when they dropped off the edge of my jaw and crashed to the floor, I felt relieved and terrified in equal measures. Moments later I began to confuse my tears with my eyes, as if it were my eyeballs which were coming out. I'd recently heard a story about an old schoolfriend who had a severely over-active thyroid, and as a result her eyes bulged so much that they did actually pop out onto her cheeks (twice, once when she was making love, and once when somebody unexpectedly clapped her on the back). It wasn't a *major* drama, allegedly, since the doctors had taught her how to stuff them back in again; although how that could be anything other than a major drama was beyond me.

I cupped my palms over my eyes and leaned my head forwards so nobody would see my eyes falling out.

'Are you all right?' said a curious voice somewhere miles above me. I peered through my fingers and saw two very long and very hairy legs. They went on and on, up to a pair of brief shorts, and on, up to the face of the man I'd fallen in love with about half an hour earlier. It was a lovely face, but it was looming down at me in a way which made me feel even more nauseous.

'I don't feel very well,' I confessed, as the fence in Raylene's yard undulated and receded. I heard Ivan's knees snapping like gunshots as he sat down beside me on the porch step. His legs were so long that I imagined them having to fold in several places, not just once in the middle.

'Have you smoked Kansas grass before?' he asked conversationally. I shook my head.

'Never smoked any grass before,' I said, proud that I had managed a whole sentence through all the cotton wool that had mysteriously appeared in my mouth. It tasted horrible.

'It's supposed to be very strong. I wouldn't know, myself, since I believe that only morons do drugs.'

'Oh,' I said in a small voice, sensing that I ought to be devastated by this indictment. I wrapped my arms around my knees and rested my forehead on them. 'I want to go home.'

I meant that I wanted to go *home* home, back to England. People there did occasionally smoke pot, but as far as I'd ever been able to make out before, all it did was to make them laugh like hyenas and then eat lots of biscuits. Why did I have to be in this awful place where two puffs of a joint made things move and wobble and stopped time dead in its tracks?

'I've been sitting here for hours,' I announced in a muffled, aggrieved voice, my head still on my knees.

'No you haven't,' Ivan said. 'I saw you come out here just now.'

'Must have been someone else,' I insisted. 'It was lunchtime when I sat down.'

'It's still lunchtime,' he said.

'Where's Corinna?'

'She left with Calvin.'

I started crying again, enough boiled-egg tears for a Boy Scout picnic. I put my hands back over my eyes, just in case.

'Oh dear,' said Ivan. 'You're in a bit of a state, aren't you?' He sighed with what appeared to be deep irritation, and extracted a car key from his shorts pocket. 'I suppose I'd better take you home then. Come on.' He stood up, held out his hand and hauled me to my feet. Not that I could feel them.

The car journey seemed to take several hours, which was odd, considering Corinna and I had walked to Raylene's house in only ten minutes: a few blocks north and halfway up Mount Oread.

'This is not a mountain,' I said, trying to make conversation. 'Why do they call it a mountain? It's a little hill, that's all.'

43

Ivan, behind the wheel of a battered Subaru, looked bored again. 'In Kansas, this counts as a mountain,' he said. 'This is 1044 Connecticut. Is this your house?'

'I think so,' I said doubtfully, squinting at it. It looked identical to all the other houses on the block.

'Let's go and find out, shall we?' he said. Even in my less than compos mentis state, I could tell he was taking the mickey.

'I'll be fine from here,' I said, promptly falling out of the car on to the sidewalk. Ivan didn't even try to disguise his laughter, and I decided that I was rapidly going off him. Nonetheless, I permitted him to escort me up the path and help me with my key in the lock, which suddenly seemed much too large for it. I felt like Alice in Wonderland. 'Drink me,' I muttered, and Ivan gazed at me. We stood there on the threshold, staring at each other for what I was convinced was at least twenty-five minutes, and then he leaned forward and kissed me, so gently that I thought I'd float away.

'Come on. I'll make you a cup of tea and you'll feel better,' he said with authority, opening the door and ushering me inside. 'Go and have a lie down.'

I did as I was told, but two hours later, there was no sign of him. I began to worry. What if he had stolen all our things and run away? Not that we had anything to steal, beyond our passports and clothes. But where was he? Perhaps he'd gone to the grocery store to buy some milk – although something must have happened to him. Maybe he'd been hit by a truck on the way back! Oh no, I thought, struggling to sit up. I'd have to call the police, and I was really in no fit state. Plus I didn't even know Ivan's surname . . . Alarmingly, the bed suddenly took off, with a force which pushed me flat on my back again. It was whizzing through the wide Kansas night sky and stars were rushing past me on either side of the bed. I felt freshly sick. I knew it wasn't real, but I couldn't stop it. At least with a nightmare you could stop it. I cried out.

The bed juddered to a halt, and Ivan appeared in the doorway carrying a mug of something steaming. 'Are you all right?'

I was sobbing now. 'The bed was flying ... I can't stand it. How can I make it stop?'

He sat down, putting the mug on the carpet (since our furniture-rental budget hadn't stretched far enough for bedside tables) and patted my hand awkwardly.

'You can't make it stop. It will stop when it stops. This is a very extreme reaction for a couple of hits – maybe that grass had some PCP, you know, angel dust, sprinkled on it. It makes you hallucinate.'

'Was everyone else having the same thing?' I asked weakly, sniffing. When I'd left, none of the others looked as if they were struggling to focus on wavy fences and popping-out eyeballs. I was glad for Corinna's sake that she hadn't partaken. It was terrifying. And now, to add insult to injury, waterfalls appeared to be gushing from my nose.

Ivan handed me a Kleenex. 'They're used to it. They smoke all the time, morning, noon and night. It probably only gave them a little buzz. Also, it's a very bad idea to smoke in the morning, especially when you never normally smoke at all.'

How do you know so much about it? I thought crossly, Mr 'Drugs Are For Morons'. I became aware of some mellow music, Van Morrison's *Astral Weeks*, which Ivan must have put on the cassette player in my room, although I hadn't noticed him doing it.

'But it's nighttime now. I should be getting over it.'

He laughed and pointed out of the window. 'Wow, you are in a bad way, aren't you? It's two o'clock in the afternoon.'

I closed my eyes and lay back, willing the bed not to move. It did move, but I realized belatedly that this was because Ivan had climbed on to the mattress and lain down next to me. I felt his hand slip under my

45

lacy charity-shop blouse, and gently rub my stomach. The sweat which had burst out all over my skin after sitting outside on the porch had chilled, and appeared to be coating me with jelly, like the sort found around the sausage in a pork pie. 'Why is he singing about oil drains?' I muttered.

'What?' Ivan propped himself up on one elbow and looked at me, amused. I thought I ought to remove his hand, but it was comforting; anchoring. I hoped he didn't mind my clammy jelly texture.

'Van Morrison. He's saying something about viaducts and oil drains.'

Ivan laughed at me – again. 'I think he's saying "your dreams", not oil drains.'

He had this annoying knack of making me feel about two inches tall, even when I was completely out of it, which was quite a feat, considering. I finally managed to lift his hand off my belly. It was as heavy as a lead weight.

'I hardly know you,' I said, as haughtily as I could.

'You will,' he replied confidently.

Within minutes his hand was back again, resting warm and heavy on my bare skin. I peeked at him as his eyelids slid down, black eyelashes feathering his cheeks, wondering if he was right, whether I would know him. In a moment of lucidity, I scrutinized his body: the hard muscles of his legs, the little whorls of dark hair sticking out of the top of his T-shirt, the way that his suntan stopped in an abrupt line across his bicep.

I must have fallen asleep too, because the next thing I knew was a shortness of breath, a sensation of being smothered. Ivan was on top of me, gently kissing my neck, and with his fingers creeping like a spider up my leg, under my skirt.

'Get off!' I shouted in panic, for a moment not even remembering who he was.

At that moment, the screen door slammed and I heard voices in the house.

'Corinna!' I yelled as loudly as I could.

Ivan rolled off me immediately. 'Sorry,' he muttered, sitting up and combing his hair back into place with his fingers.

'Susie? Are you all right? Oh, sorry.' Corinna had stuck her head round my door, but retreated immediately when she saw Ivan.

I sat up too. Thankfully, everything seemed to have stopped whirling. 'Yeah, I'm fine,' I called back. 'Just checking it was you.'

'It's me – and Calvin,' she said, and I could hear the smile in her voice. 'See you in the morning, OK?' We heard giggles, and the sound of her bedroom door shutting.

'I'd better go, hadn't I?' said Ivan, not meeting my eyes.

I touched his face gently. It was such a relief to feel a bit better, although I could tell that I still wasn't back to normal. My voice sounded as if it was coming out of a long tunnel. 'Yeah. I need to sleep more.'

'Can I see you again?'

I pretended to think about it for a minute. 'If you promise never again to try it on with me when I'm sleeping.'

He hung his head in mock contrition. 'Sorry.'

'OK then. Thanks for looking after me today.'

'You're welcome. I'll be in touch.'

Then, with a small heave and creak of the mattress, he was gone. I immediately fell asleep again, grateful for the escape from the torment of the past two hours (masquerading as nine hours), and vowing never to touch pot again as long as I lived.

And I haven't touched it since. It's sort of odd that I ended up living with a total dopehead, but there you go.

6

Rachel

It's three in the morning. My eyes hurt and my head is fuzzy, but I woke up about an hour ago, and I know it's going to be a long time before I get back to sleep tonight. I kind of wish I had gone in to see Mark at the pub on the way home after all. What's the point of a relationship if you can't confide in the one you love? A hug and a kiss from him would have really helped.

Perhaps Mark's and Dad's mutual antipathy made me worried that some small part of Mark would gloat, or make a joke about not having to hide our relationship any more if Dad really had been arrested and was going to jail; and I would lose it with him. I love him deeply and completely, but that not to say I don't sometimes feel just a little bit scared of his unpredictability.

What would Dad be going to jail for? It's preposterous. Bloody Elsie, putting ideas into everyone's heads. I mean, if *I'm* worrying about the possibility that it might be true, what must everyone else at the club be thinking?

It was dark and quiet inside the house when I got home. I couldn't see if Dad's car was there, because he keeps it in the garage at the back, but I knew Anthea must be in, because her car was in the drive, the heating was turned up full, and there was a faint smell of vegetable soup in the air. Anthea lives on a diet of

48

vegetable soup, Ryvita and vodka and slimline tonic. It's probably why she goes to bed so early (no energy to stay up later than nine-thirty) and always has the heating on full (too enfeebled by her lack of calories for her body to generate any heat of its own).

'Anthea?' I called up the dark stairs. After a moment I heard the swish of her bedroom door across the carpet.

'Yes?' She sounded grumpy, as usual.

'Where's Dad?'

There was a brief silence, then she appeared, her ash-blonde hair sticking straight out in an unruly thatch at the back and one thin strap of her lilac lace negligee falling off a brown freckled shoulder.

She glided downstairs, the haughty expression on her face born, I knew, from her intense dislike of anyone seeing her without her make-up on. She was exposing far too much flesh, and I hoped against hope she was wearing something underneath the negligee. I fixed my eyes on her from the knees down to avoid seeing anything I didn't want to see. She had a great body for a woman in her late forties, although the skin on her legs was getting a little baggy. It fell in creases just above her kneecap. I bet she'd have a knee-lift, if such a thing existed. (Needless to say, she seemed utterly paralysed by envy at my mother's relative youth and beauty, and wouldn't even have her name mentioned in her presence, referring to her only as 'Her'. When Mum came over, Christmas before last, it threatened to turn ugly. Gordana forced us all to have a Boxing Day lunch together, and Mum kept looking at Anthea with such obvious pity that Anthea was nearly beside herself with anxiety. She thought Mum pitied her for being too old or too baggy-kneed, or whatever; whereas in fact Mum just felt sorry for her that she'd got lumped with Ivan.)

'Have you seen him?' I demanded. 'He was expected at the club tonight, for the Autumn Social.'

She raised her eyebrows, and a faint expression of shock flashed over her face. 'I thought tonight was the committee meeting.'

'Um . . . well, maybe there was a committee meeting earlier, but I was there for the dinner thingy.' Damn Dad and his big fat fibs. Trust him to pretend to Anthea that he'd be going for a meeting, not a party.

Anthea clearly didn't believe me – well, I never have been a very convincing liar. She looked so totally different to her daytime self, standing there on the stairs with her tanned, wrinkly skin; vulnerable and much older. I felt sorry for her. Despite living with Dad, she has such a fragile, tenuous hold on him. I think it must be just sex which keeps them together. They don't appear to have anything else in common.

A muscle twitched in her cheek, but I knew she'd never let on to me how hurt she was about not being invited. Dad is terrible about including her in his work life. He recently told one of his squad members that he had a live-in girlfriend and they laughed, assuming he was joking. He hasn't once brought Anthea down to the club (although she sometimes comes in on her own, to try and sell the dreadful tennis gear she designs. He avoids her whenever she does).

Still, I had more important things to worry about than Anthea's pride.

'So where is he?'

'He's upstairs. In bed. He had a migraine. He got home about five and went straight to bed. You know what he's like when he gets one of his heads. He said he wanted to sleep it off so he'd be fit for Zurich tomorrow.'

'Oh. So . . . did he say what he was doing today?' I asked, but already I felt relief draining through me. He couldn't have been arrested if he was going to fly to Switzerland with me tomorrow. They didn't let you leave the country when you were on bail, did they?

'No, he didn't,' she said shortly – fair enough, since

she never knew anything about Dad's movements. I decided not to ask her outright if he'd been arrested. It seemed faintly ludicrous now that I was home, and Dad was simply upstairs asleep. And anyway, if the Jehovah's Witness story was a cover-up, she wouldn't admit the truth to me. She was ridiculously loyal to Dad.

'Well, never mind. I'm just going to ring Gordana – we were worried when he didn't show up – and then I'm going to bed too. I've been up since half five this morning.'

Later, after I'd placated Gordana, had a shower, and climbed gratefully into my single bed, I heard Anthea whirring away on the exercise bike in the spare room. She was at it for hours. I thought I could hear a faint moaning sound too, although that could have been the bike's mechanism. It was like being haunted by a manicured ghost. She's going to collapse with exhaustion if she carries on like this, I thought; or else exercise herself into oblivion. I had a vision of breaking down the door to find nothing left of her except a pair of false eyelashes floating in a puddle of sweat, next to an empty crumpled Chanel tracksuit.

Clearly all was not well with her and Dad. I felt a surge of anger as the whirring kept me from sleep: Dad ought to get his nose out of *my* love life and concentrate on his own for a change. But I still wondered if it had anything to do with Dad's early visitors. Feeling guilty at my annoyance – poor Anthea, I felt sorry for her really – I got up and made her a cheese sandwich, which I left outside the spare bedroom door with a glass of milk, for when she eventually finished exercising. I called through to tell her it was there, but received no answer.

It took me ages to get to sleep. My room seemed too big and too empty as I sat up in bed in the dark like a child waiting to be tucked in. I wished that I'd accepted

Gordana's offer of company. She was always such a rock – I once overheard Mum saying that the hardest thing about moving back to Kansas was not having Gordana's shoulder to cry on any more. (I was quite put out by that, actually. Surely, bearing in mind I stayed with Dad because of my career, it ought to be *me* she was upset at being apart from?)

All of us in different places, not being there for one another: Mum in Kansas with Billy; Dad in a place somewhere inside his head that nobody has access to; Gordana at the club getting drunk; me here with old Anorexic Annie – although she's about as much support as a custard bra.

I eventually lay down and closed my eyes, willing my overactive imagination to put a sock in it. I tried to sleep by conjuring up my alternative, imaginary family, but somehow they wouldn't come, not tonight. They were as flat and lifeless as paper dolls. Then I tried listing all the former Wimbledon Ladies title winners, chronologically, in my head.

Just as I got back to Billie Jean King, and was finally drifting off to sleep, the elderly Blu-Tack holding up my signed Steffi Graf poster gave up the ghost. One corner drooped down with a disconsolate flapping sound next to my head, which woke me up again with a jerk. I sat up, peeled off the dry grey lump and squeezed it to try and activate some life into it, then pushed the poster back up into position over my bed. For heaven's sake, I'm twenty-three years old today. I ought to be investing in some proper art, not sticking posters on walls like the naïve kid I was when Steffi signed it for me.

It occurs to me that Mark didn't mention my birthday when I saw him earlier. The Swisscom tournament in Zurich is a WTA one, so of course he won't be entered in it; which means that unless he seeks me out at training tomorrow – today – I won't see him until I get back. Great . . . not.

Perhaps I'll skip training, for once. It's my birthday, after all. And I'm flying in the afternoon. I have a deep yearning to slob about at home all morning in nothing but a T-shirt, knickers, and big socks.

Through the dim light cast by the fluorescent numbers on my clock radio I can just make out the outline of Steffi, her arm stretched out in a lethal drive volley, her black-scrawled name written over the net. She looks distinctly shabby now – I've never even had time to put her into a proper frame. But I can't bring myself to take her down.

I think about her career, and how I envy her her numerous Grand Slam titles. That's what Dad and Gordana want me to be. That's who I want to be, and maybe still might. If I keep training, and playing, and keeping positive. I can do it. I *know* I can. The prize money for the winner of the Swisscom tournament is 189,000 dollars. Just imagine. One single win would probably pay back everything anyone's ever invested in my whole career. It would be so wonderful . . .

7

Susie

Ivan was right, of course, as he always liked to be: I did get to know him. After the awful day of Raylene's brunch, we started to see more and more of each other. He would ring me up, very non-committal, at odd times of day and night: midnight, or seven a.m, and invite me out places with him – an early breakfast at Perkins, the big diner on the edge of town, or to see his favourite band at Cogburns, an eye-wateringly terrible cod-reggae act called Penury Wanks. Sometimes we went to Harbor Lites, a bar on Massachusetts Street to drink beers and watch fat bikers in flares playing pool; a couple of times he let me come and watch him play tennis (which greatly impressed me. He was so fast on court, so agile and accurate. He took my breath away). But for the first few months he seemed to do it under sufferance, as though someone was laying a big guilt trip on him for not looking after me properly. I often felt like saying, 'You don't need to do me any favours, you know.' But I liked his company – and I was crazy about him. Besides, my room-mate Corinna was well and truly ensconced with her Rasta, and I didn't have anyone else to hang out with.

Ivan didn't kiss me again, not for weeks, and I began to wonder if he might be gay, but he didn't seem to hang out with anyone else. And the way he looked at me sometimes, so intensely, through narrowed eyes as though he was weighing me up – well, it wasn't the way that any of my other friends, gay or straight, had ever looked at me before.

'I have to focus on my tennis,' he said abruptly one night as we sat in the Jazzhaus at two in the morning, drinking White Russians. There was a candle stuck in an empty wine bottle on the table in front of us, and I was breaking off bits of warm, soft wax and moulding them into little cubes. 'I don't have time for more than one friend.'

'I'm flattered,' I replied sarcastically, lining up my wax cubes, but he just nodded as if to say, 'So you jolly well should be.' I rolled my eyes and shook my head.

'What?' he said, that edge of irritation never far from his voice.

I didn't know what to say. If I told him I wasn't really flattered, he'd be offended. And the truth was, I *was* flattered. I loved being Ivan's only friend. I loved hanging out with him when he wasn't away at tournaments: being nostalgic about England; laughing at the way Kansans described a weekend trip to Kansas City or Wichita as a vacation, or the way they put Ranch dressing on everything, or the way that people always seemed to lock their truck doors but leave the windows rolled down . . . We shared a common amusement for the foibles of our temporary home, and it united us. I thought it was more than that, though. I wanted to believe that the sexual tension between us was intense, that something was brewing that neither of us would be able to control when it finally happened, and that Ivan was as afraid of it as I was.

Either that, or he didn't actually fancy me at all, and that moment when I woke to find him on top of me had merely been part of my drug-induced hallucination.

'Can I come to one of your tournaments some time?'

I asked, emboldened by my fourth White Russian. I'd been dying for him to invite me, but as yet no such invitation had been forthcoming. I knew that he drove for miles to get to some of these tournaments, and thought it would be a good opportunity to really talk to him. 'I don't mind missing a couple of days of classes. And I could keep you company.'

'Maybe,' he said, although he smiled at me as he said it.

I couldn't wait to be stuck in a car with him for hours, chipping secrets like diamonds out of him, so much more valuable for the difficulty of their extraction. If his team didn't win, though, the journey home again might be a bit of a nightmare. Ivan was always so down for a day or so after he lost a match. There was one particularly bitter defeat that the KU tennis team had recently suffered in Kansas City, only up the road – which I think made it worse, it was practically a home match – and he'd been so down in the mouth and grumpy that I told him he had 'the Kansas City blues'. Apt, I'd thought, given the city's musical heritage. It stuck, anyway, and became an epigram to describe Ivan's bad moods.

Although he was gradually getting better at talking, at least late at night, there was still so much more I wanted to know. He hardly talked at all during the day, but after a couple of drinks he would speak a bit about his mother, Gordana, and stepfather, Ted; how Ted had brought him up as his own son, and how he, Ivan, had never met his real father but didn't have any inclination to seek him out. Ted was kind and generous, and rich: Ivan had learned to play tennis on the court in his back garden, and then Ted had paid to send him to a very expensive private school, where he'd further concentrated on his game until, at the age of ten, he was the best Junior player in Europe.

It was funny, though, the way he was so monosyllabic during the day. We'd meet for sandwiches in Wescoe cafeteria, or a walk by the pond, and I was almost afraid of him at those times, he seemed so distant. But gradually I realized it was just the way he was. I stopped worrying about it, and would blatantly ignore him right back again, burying my head in my History of Art textbook, or scribbling notes for a term paper. I used to try and make him smile, or tell him snippets of information he might find interesting, but in daylight hours it was tough.

'Have you heard of Jean Arp?' I asked, and Ivan looked bored. Sorority girls on the next table nudged one another and whispered about how gorgeous he was, and if he happened to glance in their direction they would blush and pretend to pick at their salads.

'Arp was a Dadaist, and he went through a phase of being obsessed by navels. Anything vaguely circular, for about a year, in any context, became a navel to him. Look at these: "Mountain, Table, Anchors, Navel"; "Man, Moustache and Navel". I love that!'

If that had been an evening conversation, Ivan would have laughed too, I swear. But because it was lunchtime, he moodily slurped his juice and pointed at the illustration of 'Frond and Navel'.

'That looks like a wishbone and two dots. Doesn't look anything like a bloody navel. It's crap. Modern art is crap.'

I sighed. But even Ivan grumbling at me was better than Ivan not talking to me at all. I was as riveted by him as the sorority girls; I'd let him get away with any amount of monosyllablism or even downright rudeness, just to be able to look at the way his eyes changed from dark gold to hazel to dark brown and back again as the light fell in them, and the dimple which flickered in and out of his cheek when he talked.

'What are you doing this afternoon?' I asked, almost nervously.

'Team practice,' he said, screwing up his juice

carton and flicking his hair out of his eyes. 'Come and watch if you want.'

He stood up, noisily scraping his chair legs. Every woman in the room gazed at him.

'Well,' I said. 'I was going to go and work on my Gertrude Stein paper . . . but OK, I'll come.'

8

Gordana

I look at myself in the mirror after Yolanda has just set my hair the way I like it: with a curl, but not an old-lady curl like Elsie's perm. Yolanda dyes it to cover up all the grey, and I wonder why any woman would want to keep her hair with grey in it. I look so much younger. So, I look, and I smile good-graciously, and I think: Yes, Gordana, you have done well.

Nobody my age at home look this good, I bet. Last time I went back it seemed that every woman over forty-five had grey hair. They cannot afford to have the dye done every six weeks.

It's nice to have money. I chose well with my Ted; it has turned out so well for the girl with such a humble origin. I want Ivan and Rachel to know how it was for me, so I tell them this story many, many times. Rachel loves it. She always asks me to tell her again.

I came to Dagenham from Croatia with my parents when I was seven, in 1949. When I left school at sixteen, I went straight to work as a punch-card operator at the Ford Motor Company, the same job at the same place – although a few years earlier – that this singer Sandie Shaw had done, before Adam Faith discovered her. Sandie was only there for a short time though, while I must endure seven years of it until Ted rescued me.

I was not happy when Sandie's career was launched;

in fact, I was as sick as a parrot (or is it pigeon? I never can remember). Years, I had been slaving away in that factory, just waiting for the time when *my* singing career could begin for real. Like Sandie, I used occasionally to sing on stage with the local dance-hall bands in Ilford and Dagenham. I even had tickets to the Hammersmith Odeon show where Sandie – when she was still plain old Sandra Goodrich – pushed her way into Adam's dressing room to sing to him, but I was not able to attend. Why? Because I was at home, fetched back there by my mama because little Ivan was throwing up. I think from the Spam sandwich he had eaten earlier. My mother didn't mind looking after Ivan during the day when I was at work, but she drew the line at allowing her daughter to be out gallivanting while Ivan sprayed all the surfaces of the house with his vomit.

'How will I ever find a husband if I can't go out?' I wailed.

'Well,' my mother said, in Croatian, 'it serve you right for getting yourself knocked up by that useless butcher's boy, doesn't it now?'

'That useless butcher's boy' was Paul Tyler, son and heir of Tyler's Butchers in Dagenham, eighteen at the time, spotty and very complaining. He hated working in a butcher's shop but his father insisted that he would only inherit the empire by starting at the bloody sawdust and fake parsley of the shop floor, and working his way up to the filets mignons later. Ivan has never even met his father, and says he never want to. I don't blame him, really. All I remember is the acne and bad moods, those awful Stay-Press slacks and the Adam's apple which look like it belong on a giant.

We met in 1959 when Paul began to chat me up each time I go in for the family mince. Before long he is pressing me up against closed gates in back alleys, sucking lingering raw-meat kisses from my smudged lips. I kept it a secret but the truth was I had never been kissed before. Sweet seventeen, and I thought it was quite nice, but I couldn't help visualizing the big fat ox-tongue in Tyler's window. And besides, Paul's Essex accent was so difficult for me to understand that kissing – the Universal Language of Love – was easier than talking.

We had sex within a month, in the shed on Paul's dad's allotment, squashed in between an upside-down wheelbarrow and a black plastic tray of purple sprouting potatoes. I was left with a spider's web draped on my beehive, blood on my pantygirdle, and an Unwanted Pregnancy: a tumbling ball of cells which was to become Ivan. My relationship with Paul Tyler did not last long – he ran off to join the Navy the day after I told him he was going to be a daddy, and I haven't seen him since.

By the time Ivan started infant school, I was still at the factory, but Sandra Goodrich had changed her name, been photographed barefoot, and released her first single. When it flopped, I was happy. I wanted Sandie to come back to Ford's, shod and sorry, so that I would no longer have to suffer such torments of jealousy. But it was not to be. Sandie shoots to Number One with 'Always Something There to Remind Me', which she follows up with a string of top ten singles, churning them out like they were shiny Cortinas rolling off the assembly line.

'That could have been me!' I wailed when Sandie was voted Best New Singer of 1964. I remember wailing a lot at that time. Ivan was behaving badly at school, and had taken to opening his bowels on the floor at home, and I must spend hours on my knees with a knife and gritted teeth, scraping poo from between the floorboards. It was not how I imagined my life.

When Sandie came back to Ford's the next year for a visit, to see how her old mates were getting on, I locked myself in the Ladies' toilet and cried and swore with my father's handed-down Croatian swear words. That's why I was missing from the group photograph in the local paper, a blurry shot of all the girls in Sandie's department clustered adoringly around their former colleague.

'It should have been *me*,' I cried when I read in the papers that Sandie got to go to a party at Princess Margaret's place, when I was yet again stuck at home. That time, Ivan had mumps — not that it would have made any difference if he'd been healthy — it was still Sandie, not me, hobnobbing with royalty.

In the long evening hours after I'd scraped poo and tucked Ivan up in bed, I would sit silently in the living room dreaming and plotting possible means of escape. But even this I couldn't do in peace, as I no longer had a room of my own: Ivan slept on a fold-out bed in the corner of my childhood bedroom, in the place formerly occupied by my precious gramophone. I had to sell that years before, to buy a cot and a pram.

Frequently, I wished that my mama and papa had made me do what many other parents in those days did: insist that I give the baby up for adoption. I could have gone away for a couple of months, perhaps pretend I had gone back to Croatia to stay with relatives, and returned with nothing more to show for my silly foolishness than a lot of baggy skin on my tummy and a problematical pelvic floor.

My parents thought I was watching TV with them every night — when I wasn't scraping poo, of course — but had no idea that in my head I was twirling on stage in a sequinned minidress, Number One in the hit parade, Sandie Shaw left behind, an unpopular nobody unable to struggle out from behind the shadow of my talent and glamour . . .

One rare night Mama and Papa (Mr and Mrs K, to their English friends) were out at a neighbour's drinks party (I am *not* invited. People take pity on my poor suffering parents, who work so hard to establish themselves in the community, and then have to put up with the illegitimate grandson – but they have no sympathy for me, the brazen hussy), and I was listening to the wireless as loudly as I could without waking Ivan, who never slept good. I thought of the music filtering through the flimsy walls of our terrace, and it was my own small act of rebellion. I made myself a large Campari and soda, put on my best dress – cherry gingham, with a ribbon under the bust – and lit a cigarette, jiving around the living room to the sounds of Les Swingle Singers, tears of rage and frustration beginning to roll down my cheeks. I was on my third big drink, liking the fact that the red of the Campari nicely matched with my outfit, when there was a knock at the front door.

I wiped my face and went to answer it. It was a man, older than me and balding, but not that old, and quite modish. He was clutching a bottle of something, which he pushed towards me.

'Not too late, am I?' he said, smiling and showing teeth which were crooked, but not unattractively so. If he'd bitten into an apple, it would have left Dracula-style puncture marks. I guessed he was in his early thirties. He stepped inside the hallway and held out his hand. 'We haven't met before, have we? I'm Ted Anderson.'

I was more than a bit tipsy from the three drinks, and I didn't know what to say. At first I thought he must be friend of my parents who had decided to call round unannounced. 'Gordana Korolija,' I said, transferring the bottle into my armpit to shake his hand. 'Do come in.'

I liked him immediately for not saying 'Eh? Come again?' as did most people when I spoke my name. Ted Anderson followed me into the front room, where he stopped, with a slightly confusedness. 'Where is everyone, then?' he said.

'My parents are out, I'm afraid,' I replied in my best

English accent, putting my shoulders up straight and sticking out my breasts in their tight bodice. The broderie anglaise along the low neckline of the dress tickled and itched, and I resisted the temptation to stick my hand down the front of it and scratch. 'What may I get you to drink?'

Ted laughed, and winked at my bosom. 'Oh, like that, is it? Parents go out, you decide to have a party – you're a one, aren't you? I'm not as late as I thought then, if no one else is here yet.'

He wiggled on the spot in time to the music on the radio, elbows bent into his sides, digging the toe of one pointy, expensive-looking shoe into the carpet. I watched, wanting so much to have someone to dance with that I almost cried.

'No one else?' I asked.

He looked a little impatient now. 'Well, you don't normally have a party with only one guest, do you? I'll have a gin and tonic water, love, ta.'

Suddenly I realized what had happened. He was supposed to be at the same party my parents were at, four doors down, but he'd heard the music floating through the window and simply got the wrong address. I opened my mouth to correct his mistake, but I was so longing for company that the thought of him leaving sent me almost into a panic. I noticed that his suit was very well cut, and his watch gold. He might not be very good-looking, but I was pretty sure he was rich. You could just tell. I liked him. Perhaps it was my loneliness and desperation for change, but at that point I decided it was more than likely, were he not already taken, that I would marry him.

'Lemon and ice?' I asked in a high little voice, even though I knew my parents' kitchen contained neither of those things, nor indeed any gin or tonic water.

He nodded, taking a cigarette from a silver case in his inside pocket and lighting it, still twisting his hips on the carpet as he inhaled. Grabbing my handbag on the way, I ran into the kitchen and leaned against the counter, breathing heavily. I quickly took out my compact, checked that my mascara hadn't run, and reapplied my lipstick.

I took one of Papa's bottles of ale from the fridge. 'Sorry,' I said, carrying it back into the front room. 'We have run out of gin. I can offer you this, or a Campari, or some . . .' I spotted the bottle he'd brought '. . . wine?'

'Ale'll do me, thanks,' he said, stretching out his arm for the bottle and neatly taking its cap off, having produced a Swiss army knife from his trouser pocket for the purpose. 'Are you expecting many?'

For one brief moment I thought he was asking if I was expecting many children, or was pregnant with twins or something, and I was angry at the personal nature of the comment. 'No! Just – Oh, I see. No. In fact . . .' I blushed. 'I'm afraid there's been a bit of a misunderstanding.' I would have to be truthful. 'This is not the party, actually. I think you want the Murrays at number twelve, they're having people round tonight. I thought you were friend of my parents . . . Sorry.'

I looked down at the carpet. Ted laughed, in a lovely free sort of way. He took a swig from his bottle, then he tipped my chin up towards him with his spare hand.

'You're a pretty girl, Gordana. How old are you?'

'Twenty-three,' I said, ashamed that I was a spinster. I studied his face; it was sharp, thin-lipped, and he had great black shadows beneath his eyes – but his eyes were brown and soft, like a dog's. He had wrinkles on his forehead, and too much of it was exposed by the thinning hair. When he let go of my chin, I could still feel the press of his warm fingers against my skin.

He looked at my party outfit. 'Are you going to this party, then?'

I shook my head. 'No invitation for me.'

Ted laughed again. He looked quite sexy when he laughed – not like Paul Tyler, who'd laughed with discomfort, like there was something sharp stuck in his throat. I decided I would like the experience an older man could offer. Not to mention the cash. Paul had never given me anything – hadn't even offered to buy me new stockings when he laddered one with his clumsy fingers in his hurry-hurry to pull up my skirt.

'Are you married?' I blurted, brave with alcohol and the easiness of his laugh.

'No. Are you?' he replied, moving closer to me. He didn't smell of entrails either, like Paul did. Which was also a plus.

'No—' I stopped. I couldn't quite bring myself to tell him about Ivan, not yet. Not when Fate had brought him to me like this.

'You've got a strange accent, as well as a funny name. Where are you from?'

'Yugoslavia.'

'So, since you're all dressed up with nowhere to go, how about coming to a dance with me tonight?' He said it with such a natural confidence, no stammering or blowing smoke in my face or staring at a spot on the floor, like Paul would have done.

'I would love to!' I cried, instantly forgetting all about the child asleep upstairs. I couldn't believe that this was the first time in five whole years anybody had asked me out.

Ted looked at his watch, sticking his wrist right out of his sleeve like he was punching an invisible person. 'Right, let's go then. I was thinking of heading down the Roxy anyhow. This drinks party sounded a bit of a bore, to be honest. I only said I'd go because Cliff Murray – I work with him – tells me his daughter's a bit of all right. But now I've met *you* . . .' He tailed off, with one of his eyebrows raised up high.

I blushed again, so very delighted. 'Janice Murray has nothing special,' I said, although I had always been envious of Janice's willowy figure and high-and-mighty expression. Privately I suspected that Ted would have loved her. Tough luck, Janice! I said to myself smugly. I actually gathered up my keys and handbag, fetched my cardigan from the back of one of the dining chairs, and was all ready to go. When I finally remembered, that remembering hit me hard with its sudden, cruel reality. I put my hand over my mouth. 'Oh! I can't. I can't come out with you tonight.'

Ted didn't look disappointed enough, in my opinion. He lit another cigarette. 'Why not, then? Jealous boyfriend? Parents going to call the police if you go out?'

I closed my eyes, the crushing weight of all of this responsibility ripping through my body like a labour pain. I thought perhaps maybe not to tell him and leave the house anyway, but the potential humiliation of being found out later was too great. Ivan was bound to wake up and yell about something or another.

'I have a kid. He's asleep upstairs. Ivan. Five years old.'

Ted just laughed again. 'Had you forgotten?'

'No, of course not!' I said, crossly. 'I just . . . Oh, it does not matter. Here, here is your wine back. Number twelve. Janice Murray is the person with the nose in the air, you won't miss her. Have a good time. It was nice to meet you. I'm sorry for any inconvenience.' I was practically pushing him towards the front door, thrusting his bottle back at him, determined not to let him see the fresh tears which were springing up fast.

Ted turned and put his hands on my shoulders – not in a perverted way, but in a kind way which made it unavoidable that the tears spill down my face. 'Poor kid,' he said. 'You, I mean, not the baby. Where's the father?'

'Gone,' I said, not meeting his eyes, feeling his hands almost burning into my shoulders. 'Didn't want to know.'

'His loss,' Ted said. 'I like you. Do you reckon your mother would babysit one evening, and we can go dancing then?'

'She might, I suppose.' I gave a sob. I was so tempted to bury my face in his jacket that I felt pulled like a magnet towards him. He's a stranger, I tell myself. Don't be so forward. But it felt natural. And he'd told me he liked me! Paul Tyler never said anything with nearly so much affection.

'Well then. Shame about tonight, but how about we go back into your front room and have a little dance there instead? I haven't finished my drink yet.'

Ted never made it to the party that night. When my parents returned, they were too drunk themselves to notice the excessive number of cigarette stubs in the ashtray, the two empty glasses left on the floor next to the settee, or the fact that the settee cushions were flattened in the middle in an unmistakable hollow caused by two people, one on top of the other. But the next morning, they noticed how bright-eyed I looked, how willingly I played with Ivan, whistling 'Tonight' from *West Side Story*, and even offering to go to the shop when we ran out of tea.

Me and Ted had been married for nearly three years when, in 1968, Sandie wed the dashing young dress designer, Jeff Banks, and the pair were the most hip young couple of the Swinging Sixties.

'I could have had him,' I lamented to myself as I looked at Ted and sighed. I loved him, but there was no way he'd ever get in a pair of those groovy tight striped trousers like the ones Jeff Banks wore. Ted thought men with facial hair were all damn Commie hippies. But at least he was rich, and I would never have to work in a factory again.

And I really did love him.

9

Rachel

I wake up, again, on the morning of my twenty-third birthday. This time there is a wintry daylight outside – I've really slept in – and there are tears running down my cheeks.

I dreamed I was on Centre Court at Wimbledon, racket in hand, but I couldn't seem to move. Instead of an opponent, tennis balls were firing at me out of the ball machine, flying straight at my head, bang, bang, bang, right between the eyes, pummelling me into the ground until I began to slowly collapse beneath the barrage. Dad was yelling at me from the stands, something about '*footwork!*', fury etched between his eyebrows; but it was no good, I couldn't get any of those balls back, or stop them from hammering me. The capacity crowd jeered and slow-hand-clapped. Gordana and Mum were sitting in the front row, on the opposite side of the stadium to Ivan. For reasons which I was unable to fathom, they wore matching designer wedding dresses. They looked disappointed in me. Then, to add to the dream's humiliation, I wet myself on court; just like I did in my first ever umpired short tennis match, seventeen years ago, as a red-faced six-year-old too embarrassed to ask for the toilet in case Dad shouted at me.

Even though I was awake most of the night, it still takes me a few seconds to remember what happened at the club with Elsie and Gordana, but as soon as it does, I can't stop the worry settling back on my shoulders again like dandruff.

I climb wearily out of bed and put on a tracksuit, but even though the sleep clears from my eyes and my brain slowly unfogs, I still can't shake off the impression of being under attack from those balls. They smacked into my forehead, but the sound it made was the sound of balls hitting a wire fence.

We had some hail yesterday, but today it's downgraded to rain, which is hurling itself at the window, rattling the glass, and I think sourly how it always seems to rain on my birthday. The trouble with being born in October.

I open my bedroom door, noticing that Anthea hasn't touched the snack I left out for her. The milk has gained a textured patina of dust on its surface, and the edges of the sandwich have curled into a dry sneer.

At that moment, I hear the sound of footsteps in the gravel of the front path and – even in the current crisis – I automatically do some nimble cross-overs sideways along the landing and down the staircase to see if it's the postman. My right hand is holding an imaginary racket high above my head, as if I've just been lobbed from the top of the stairs. (After a recent, particularly galling defeat at a challenge in Miami, Dad and José went into a lengthy confab, the result of which was that they decided it was my on-court movement which was to blame. As a result, they encourage me to execute cross-over steps practically everywhere I go.)

I get to the bottom and wait expectantly by the letterbox, realizing that I'm not old enough to be completely blasé about birthdays just yet. For a moment I wonder if perhaps this was the reason for my sleepless night, rather than pre-tournament nerves, or worrying about Dad, but then I decide surely not. I'd be announcing that I still believed in Father Christmas next. But I could remember it well: that breathless anticipation of gifts and attention, candles and cards.

I wonder what Mark will give me?

A few envelopes thud on to the tiled floor, but right away I can see that they are mostly circulars and bills. I pounce on a plain white envelope, and a square yellow one, and leave the rest of the post on the hall table. Nothing from Mum – she is usually late with my present. The yellow envelope contains a card from my friend Kerry, and the white, one from Gordana and Ted – I recognize Gordana's neat writing. When I rip it open a voucher flutters out: fifty pounds, for the big art shop in the local shopping centre! I am delighted. Gordana knows how much I love to draw, and she's always encouraging me, although I always say that I never have time for it. This is not strictly true: there are endless hours of spare time at tournaments, waiting around for matches, or, if I've been knocked out, for the rest of the squad to finish so we can fly home again. I keep meaning to take a sketchpad and pencils in my hand luggage, so I can use the time constructively, but the truth is I'd feel embarrassed suddenly to whip out a pad and crayons. It would seem . . . pretentious, I suppose.

I realize this is daft, and vow to be braver. Drawing is the thing I enjoy most (after playing tennis), so why not? I hear Gordana's voice in my head: 'Who cares what anyone else thinks?' and I know she's right. Although the thought of my fellow players squinting critically over my shoulder makes me cringe . . .

I put the voucher into my purse just as Dad appears on the landing in his dressing gown; his hair is sticking up, and his big yellow toenails loom down at me over the lip of the top stair. He looks grey and shattered, closer to sixty than his forty-four years. He comes slowly downstairs, ruffling my hair wordlessly as he passes, and I notice that he smells strange: of sickness perhaps, although it feels more like fear and fatigue; anxiety trapped like stale sweat.

'Is your migraine better, Daddy?' I ask, following him into the kitchen. I haven't called him Daddy for years.

'Mmmm,' he says, more like a grunt, and fills the kettle.

'We missed you at the party last night. Gordana was really worried.'

'Mmmm.'

'You know Elsie – well, you know what a nosy old bag she is? She – er – thinks she saw some people turn up here early yesterday morning. I mean, maybe she was mistaken and it was next door, but—'

'Jehovah's Witnesses,' he says, his back to me. His dressing gown is frayed and striped in black and red. He's had it as long as I can remember, although the black stripes have got lighter and the red ones darker, as if they're trying to swap places.

'You let Jehovah's Witnesses in? Elsie said they were here for a couple of hours!' I couldn't keep the incredulity out of my voice. Gordana is quite a staunch Catholic, and it has always been a source of sorrow to her that her son is the biggest atheist this side of Hades. Whenever any Jehovah's Witnesses have had the temerity to mount our doorstep in the past, the whole street has heard the sound of Dad banging the front door in their faces.

'Decided I might as well hear what they had to say,' he says sheepishly, with a weary shrug.

I stare at him, speechless. 'No wonder you had a migraine by the afternoon.'

'Yeah. Tea?' He reaches down three mugs, and throws in teabags.

'Yes please. But Elsie said that you got in their car?'

He tuts furiously. 'That bloody woman needs to get a life.'

'*Did* you get in their car? What, have you been

converted or something? Is that what all this is about?'

He turns to face me, eyes bulging, dressing gown open to the waist to reveal his scrubby black-haired chest. I know he's my dad and everything, so obviously I'm not looking at him in *that* way, but I really can't see why women fall over themselves to get to him. Mum, OK, maybe that's understandable – it was twenty-four years ago, and he was young and successful and had all his hair then. But it's a mystery to me why they still go for him. And right now he's looking as rough as I've ever seen him.

'Rachel! Will you please stop interrogating me! Turns out I went to school with one of them – we used to be quite friendly actually. That's the only reason I let them in. Then when I said I had to go to work, they offered me a lift. I knew I'd be drinking at the party later, so I accepted the lift, rather than taking the car to work and having to leave it there. Then I felt ill in the afternoon, so Anthea came and picked me up again. It's really no big deal. I can't understand why everyone is making such a fuss.'

I wonder who 'everyone' is.

'I didn't see you at the club yesterday,' I say in a small voice.

'*Rachel!*' he snaps again, in the tone he used when I was a kid and kept using an incorrect grip for my backhand volleys. 'I really don't see why I have to explain myself to you, or anyone else. I was there yesterday, I just had a lot of paperwork to catch up on, so I was in the office most of the time, until my head got too bad to continue. Now, if you could just shut up long enough for me to have my breakfast in peace, I'd really be most grateful.'

He hands me a mug of terracotta-coloured tea. He always makes it too strong, and I always have to add more milk.

I add more milk. 'It's my birthday today,' I say, trying to sound just huffy enough.

He has the grace to pause. 'Oh, Rach, sorry, of course. I did remember, just what with the . . . migraine and everything, it slipped my mind. Sorry, darling. Happy birthday.'

He enfolds me in a reluctant hug, and I have to hold my breath as my head gets pressed into his shoulder. 'Thanks, Dad,' I say in a muffled voice. 'Gordana and Pops gave me a voucher for the art shop.'

'That's nice,' he replies, away in his own world again.

We pour and eat cereal.

'Are you well enough to come to Zurich today, or should we cancel your flight?' I venture after a few minutes.

'No, I'll come. As long as Anthea doesn't mind. And I'll have to get some sleep today, I'm shattered.'

This was odd, too. I've never once heard Dad even ask Anthea's opinion on anything, let alone seek her approval for any of his actions. My heart sinks slightly at the thought of him and his black mood travelling with me; but it's a relief, too. If he'd said he wasn't coming, then I'd really know something was wrong.

He doesn't say a word to me for the rest of the morning, remaining closeted with Anthea in their bedroom. Making love, probably, I conclude with a shudder, since the only time they do appear downstairs, he practically has to unpeel her from around his hairy neck.

I look up from the sofa, where I've been alternately dozing and aimlessly gazing at Eurosport, having blown out the training session. I'm too tired after my sleepless night.

'Go on then, love, get the present,' Dad instructs Anthea under his breath. Then he calls out, 'Come into the kitchen, Rachel, we've got something for you.'

About time too, I think, uncurling myself and obediently following him into the kitchen, as Anthea retrieves a Boots carrier bag from the understairs cupboard. She hands it to Dad, before wrapping herself back around him.

'Happy birthday, Rachel; it's from both of us,' Dad says, passing the bag over and pecking me on the cheek. Then he looks at his watch. 'I've just got to pop out for a bit, to see Gordana. Our flight's not till seven, is it, so if you book a cab for four-thirty, I'll be back by then.'

I glance up, but when I see how stricken Anthea's face is, I hastily look away, and peer instead inside the Boots bag. It contains a box with a picture of something resembling a very small hand-held trouser press. On closer inspection, it turns out to be a hair-straightening device. What the hell is the point of that? My hair is so curly that it would take hours to iron – when it's tied up in a ponytail, I can barely stuff it through the gap at the back of my baseball cap. I can't even be bothered to blow dry it, let alone straighten it.

I have to say it's a source of huge annoyance to me, the way Anthea only ever gives me presents intended to alter my appearance in some way, as if publicly acknowledging that she doesn't think I'm good enough the way I am. Last Christmas she gave me a book about how to apply make-up properly; the birthday before was a Swiss ball – the same as the one I use every single day in the gym already. Anthea even put a note on it: '*These things are great for bums!*' as if I didn't know. There is absolutely nothing wrong with my backside, anyway, it's just a bit wider than Anthea's baggy narrow behind. Although I soon realized, however, that Anthea had actually bought that Swiss ball for herself. Less than a fortnight after my birthday, it disappeared into the spare room, where it has resided, next to the exercise bike, ever since.

'Thanks for my present,' I say to Anthea, since Dad has already left the room. Couldn't you even be bothered to wrap it? I feel like adding.

'You're welcome. Those things are a godsend for someone like you. Once you've used them a couple of times you'll never want to go back to that messy look. Make sure you let them heat up for at least twenty minutes first though.'

Whatever. I know that those tongs will never leave their packaging. Life is too short.

'Want some soup?'

Anthea shook her head. 'I couldn't. After the night I've just had, I feel sick even thinking about food.'

Nothing new there then, I think. We sit at the kitchen table in silence, both staring at a vase full of fake flowers which Anthea insists on using as a table decoration: lurid and unrealistic blue fabric blooms which obscure the view of the person opposite. The petals, like most of the surfaces in our house, are covered with dust. The kitchen seems too big and empty without Dad's huge presence in it. In addition to being enormous, he's never still, constantly jiggling from foot to foot or fidgeting like a five-year-old needing the toilet. Mum used to say he made her feel seasick.

I notice that the table in the corner which usually houses our ancient Apple Mac is empty, although the printer is still there.

'Where's the computer?' I ask.

Anthea blushes unexpectedly: a deep, mottled, unattractive flush which sweeps over her neck and face. 'I – er – it was broken. I had to take it in to be repaired.' She must have dropped something on it, the daft bat, I think with annoyance. I was planning to check my emails later to see if there was one from Mark. I wonder what Anthea managed to do to it, but since she is clearly embarrassed about it, I decide to let it go. Surely Mark will call me, anyway.

Anthea stands up. 'Well, I'd better go and sort out some clean clothes for your father to take to Switzerland. I don't think he should go, the way he is

76

at the moment, but you know what he's like . . .'
Anthea never thinks Dad should go anywhere. He'd be
indoors twenty-four/seven if she had her way, just to
keep him out of mischief. It must be awful, I think,
to lack trust in your partner to that extent.

The telephone rings, and Anthea lunges frantically
for it. She is undoubtedly behaving even more oddly
than usual.

'Hello? Oh. Right. Rachel, it's for you,' she says, her
face impassive. She hands over the phone and goes
back upstairs, her narrow shoulders fixed miserably
up around her ears.

Please let it be Mark, I beg silently as I hold the
phone to my ear – although I know it won't be. Mark
never calls me on the home phone in case Dad
answers it. I've had my mobile in my pocket all morning, but there's something wrong with it at the moment
– it keeps switching itself off. Another thing I don't
have time to sort out.

'Hiya, Rach, happy birthday, babes. And happy
anniversary to us, too! Five glorious years of friendship . . . I'll give you your prezzie later, OK?'

'Hi, Kerry, thanks for the card. I know, five years . . .
what would I do without you? What time are you
getting to Zurich?'

'I don't know. Me and José aren't on the same flight
as you, are we?'

'No. Ring me when you get to the hotel; Dad and I'll
be there about eight, their time.'

Kerry is hopelessly vague about her travel arrangements, frequently missing planes or else catching
them by the skin of her teeth. Only José's chivvying
can ever galvanize her into action. I thinks it's funny
how somebody who is so incredibly speedy and agile
on court is so infuriatingly sluggish in every other area
of her life. Kerry's blonde hair is often lank and greasy
because she can't be bothered to wash it more than
once a week, and the only reason she isn't on the same

flight as us is because she left it so late to book the tickets that our flight was full.

Kerry Sutherland and I have been best friends since we were eighteen, bonding fast through dozens of tournaments around the world. We are so close now that she moved to live near me, so that José could coach her at Dad's club too. But it says a lot about our lifestyle that we still hardly ever socialize with one another; and our personalities are very different. It's definitely our careers which hold us together.

We first met at one of the more lucrative Futures tournaments. It was the only highlight of a truly horrible day for me: my eighteenth birthday, and I'd been knocked out in the first round, in a humiliating defeat by a Slovakian girl with dead eyes and a killer forehand. Dad barely spoke to me for the rest of the afternoon, not even when he handed me a small box containing my birthday gift (I'd hoped for a car, or at least some driving lessons, but it was a hideous ruby pendant thing with diamonds round the edges which had belonged to my great-grandmother. I've never worn it. And I still can't drive).

We were about to leave the club, slinking out in disgrace, when a voice with a northern accent behind me said, 'Hey, you're Rachel Anderson, aren't you?'

I swung around, banging my racket bag against the doorframe, and saw a familiar-looking, tiny and compact girl of about my age, with four gold rings in each ear and white-blonde hair scraped into a high ponytail. She grinned at me and stuck out her hand.

'I'm Kerry Sutherland, you beat me two years ago in the Nationals. You aced me five times – I never chuffin' forgot it.'

'Thanks,' I said ungraciously, not wanting to talk to her. My eyes were swollen from crying in the toilets earlier, and I knew I looked a state. Dad tutted and sighed and inspected his watch, and at that moment I felt a flash of rage so pure and intense that I wanted to jab him in the throat with the handle of my racket.

I turned my back on him. 'I know who you are too,' I said. 'Everyone says how well you've done this year. Are you through to the second round?'

'Yeah,' she said nonchalantly. 'Don't suppose you've got time for a coffee, have you?'

I glanced back at Dad, fuming in the doorway. It was tempting, but he'd go ballistic if I made him wait. 'Better not,' I said, rolling my eyes and making a face at her that he couldn't see. I hoisted my racket bag higher on my shoulder. 'Next time?'

'Definitely. When's your next one?

'Italy, in two weeks.'

'Yeah, I'm down for that one too. Top. See you at the hotel. *Arrivederci*, or whatever they say over there.' She raised her voice and gave a cocquettish wave: 'Bye then, Mr Anderson! Take care now!'

Everyone, I reflected glumly, knew who my father was.

'She was nice, wasn't she, Dad?' I asked in the car as we drove back home around the M25.

Dad grunted. 'Dyke, I expect . . . I've told José we've got to work on that backhand volley this afternoon,' he said, cutting in front of a large articulated lorry.

'But it's my birthday!'

'So?'

Happy birthday, Rachel, I thought, as I sank back in the passenger seat.

At least one nice thing came out of that horrible day, I think to myself, and here she is, still on the end of the phone talking to me.

'Let's go out for a couple of drinks tonight in Zurich, shall we?'

'I'm not drinking before a tournament.'

'Oh, come on, Rach, two drinks – non-alcoholic if

you want – won't affect your performance, will it? We don't have to be out late. It's your birthday!'

'Crap birthday it's turned out to be,' I say glumly as the whirring and moaning start up again over my head. It sounds horribly self-pitying, but I can't remember ever having a really great birthday. Even my twenty-first was a sombre affair, falling, as it did, during another tournament.

'Why?'

'Partly because I haven't even heard from Mark. More because – Oh, look, I can't go into it all now. It might be nothing, anyway. But I'll tell you this evening. Please don't make me drink, though.'

10

Susie

In Dillons supermarket yesterday, I put an enormous carton of cranberry juice into my trolley. It was about a month after Billy had gone; the only evidence of him left in our house was a dusty sock I found under the bed, and his Dewars Grain and Feed baseball cap hanging in the coat cupboard. But the thing is, I don't like cranberry juice at all (how can something with so much sugar in it still taste so bitter?), but I had picked it up out of habit, because Billy used to drink gallons of it.

It hit me like a punch in the belly: I no longer needed to buy cranberry juice for my fiancé.

Shaking, I took out the carton again in the next aisle and left it next to the jars of babyfood. Then I gripped the handlebar of the trolley, holding it tight, bending forwards so my head almost touched it.

I was almost forty-five years old, and on my own. I'd somehow gone through one marriage, and a long-term relationship I thought would be for keeps. How had it happened? I never thought Billy would leave me. He *worshipped* me. He told me he loved me, every day; he wrapped his wiry brown arms around my neck and nuzzled into me, and I was so used to his smell: sweat, pot, engine oil and something musky which was all his and which drove me mad with desire . . . Someone else was smelling that scent now. She had taken it away from me, without my permission. I reluctantly relived the moment that I found out, trapped in a looped screening of it inside my head. I hadn't been able to stop thinking about it ever since it happened, only four weeks ago.

I'd gone into work in the morning in a light jacket because although autumnal and breezy, it was still pleasantly mild; but when I came out again at lunchtime to get a sandwich from the deli, the temperature had dropped by twenty degrees. Fall had blown in across the prairies early and bitten me, hard, squeezing the breath from me like a mean hug, beginning to freeze the earrings in my ears and cutting the circulation from my feet even though the deli was only a four-block walk. I'd pushed open its heavy glass door and stepped into the warmth inside, the glasses I wore for work immediately steaming up from the lunchtime rush. Once I'd allowed my lenses to de-mist, I saw that black bean soup was on the specials board. I was just thinking I'd have that instead of my usual ham and provolone cheese, when I saw Billy's back in the line, his narrow shoulders familiar in the too-big overalls he wore to work.

'Hi, baby,' I called, and Billy's head whipped around as if my voice had fired a warning shot – which he probably thought it had. For once, his eyes hadn't crinkled up with pleasure at the sight of me; rather, they'd opened wide in the sort of terror I'd reserve for seeing a seriously unpleasant kind of ghost. His hand kind of jerked by his side, and it was only as a delayed reaction that I realized it was because he'd been holding hands with the woman in the queue next to him. I felt momentarily puzzled: why was he holding hands with a stranger? Was she upset? Was this some sort of new law in the deli to engender sociability amongst the customers? Then the penny dropped, and when it did, I thought: what an unbelievable nerve. Nobody could do *anything* in this town without it being commented on, and yet Billy could openly hold hands with another woman and expect nothing to be said? Perhaps that was because everyone already did know. Perhaps *I* was the only person who didn't?

The speckly lino floor began to rock and slide, and I had to sit down on one of the deli's few spindly white chairs. They were metal, with a seat like a flattened colander. They never seemed to have quite enough legs, those chairs, and I gripped mine with both hands, willing myself not to topple over in it. I heard myself gasping for breath, as if I'd just gone back outside into the cold.

The woman with Billy remained faceless, then. Just a body; hands with which she'd appropriated my man. I couldn't speak, or look up from the floor, or do anything, for some time. Not Billy. Not with another woman – he *wouldn't*. Surely he wouldn't. But when he came and knelt down beside me, like a horrible parody of a proposal, the guilty expression on his face told me that he would, and had.

'I was going to tell you . . .' he said, and his voice tailed away in the lunchtime sandwich-production clatter and hum.

I wanted to feel rage; to smash my fist first into his face and then hers, but annoyingly, I didn't. I just felt a rush of painful love, the sort of love you feel the second after your child is born; that hopeless, unconditional, hurting love. I hadn't even known I possessed unconditional love for Billy before – what a time to find out. I'd thought my love for him was qualifiable, tempered and even, if I'm honest, diluted by the knowledge that he wasn't Ivan. He wasn't a successful, temperamental, beautiful man whom everyone was in awe of; he was just good ol' Billy. He wouldn't treat me the way Ivan treated me. Perhaps that was why I didn't even feel I had to marry him. I didn't need to prove to anybody else that he was mine; he just was. He was my Billy.

Not any more.

'I'll go home and pack,' he added nervously.

'But I love you,' I said, and immediately laughed, nervously and mirthlessly. Billy didn't laugh, although I thought I saw pain flash across his face. It had been a kind of catchphrase of ours, a private joke: *But I love you!* We used it as sign-offs on letters and notes to one another, turning it into an acronym which became almost his name: B.I.L.Y. I'd say it to him at nights before we drifted off to sleep together: 'B.I.L.Y., Billy,' and he'd reply, 'B.I.L.Y., Susie baby.' I hadn't meant to say it then, to tug at his heartstrings intentionally. It just came out, through the jumble of my confusion. 'But I love you,' with the subtext being, 'so how can you possibly do this to me?'

Some time later – I don't know how much later, or if Billy had left with the woman first – I walked back to the office, this time not even feeling the bitter cold. My skin felt like latex, a protective sheath holding me together and stopping anything coming out. An icy wind had blown up, whirling funnels of dry orange and yellow leaves around in mini-tornadoes on the sidewalk. I remember walking through them and thinking that everything in my world was moving now.

Carved pumpkins were already beginning to appear in shop doorways and windows, although Halloween was a few weeks away. By the time it came around they'd be collapsed and moulding, teeth turning black, and I'd be trying to get used to the fact that my lover was gone.

Back in the supermarket, I made my first decision: I had to leave town and do something different. Radically different. Maybe even get a new career. I'd had enough of being a realtor, being polite and wearing a suit and trying to be competitive so that the other realtors in town didn't despise me. It didn't come easy to me, and I'd never quite fitted in. After years of having my British accent admired and commented on, it was no longer a novelty; rather, it was something which marked me out as different and foreign and possibly not to be trusted. Or maybe that was just my paranoia. But I had drifted back to Kansas after Ivan and I split up; drifted, then stayed because of Billy. I'd thought it was my home, I thought I had roots here, but now I wasn't so sure. What I did know was that I didn't want to drift anywhere any more. I wanted to settle down somewhere that I'd really belong.

I picked up a six-pack of mineral water and gazed at the labels, all depicting their own little snow-capped mountain ranges, and something inside me twisted with yearning.

'I could go skiing!' I said out loud, transfixed by the thought of seeing mountains for real. I didn't want to live there, but it might be a good temporary stop, to help me gather my thoughts and make my decision. I could almost taste the freshness of the air, and savour the escape of being high above the clouds, away from the choking, biting cold of Kansas. I couldn't believe that mountains could be any colder than these vast plains.

Perhaps Rachel would come with me – it could be her birthday present, since I'd forgotten to send her anything. It was her birthday today, too. I'd ring her and ask her. It would be perfect; she was a competent skier already. I could learn – I'd always wanted to. I wouldn't mind going to Europe, and we'd never been on holiday together. It would cost a fortune, but who cared?

'Do it, then,' said an elderly woman wheeling her trolley near mine. She smiled at me with large brown teeth and straightened what was clearly a wig. 'You can do whatever you like, you know.'

I couldn't quite smile back at her, but I tried to look appreciative.

'I always wanted to go skiing,' the woman said conspiratorially. 'Never got the chance, and it's too late now. My hips don't work so well.'

She moved away, heading for the herb tea, and I thought: wouldn't it be great if I could help people like that; help them make changes in their lives. Give them encouragement, and confidence. I wished there was a career in that.

'There *is* a career like that,' said Rachel when I called her to wish her a happy birthday and to tell her that I wanted to treat her to a skiing trip. She seemed vaguely interested in the idea of me changing careers, but overall was so distracted that I wondered if she was even listening.

'It's called life coaching. It must be big over there – it is here. You can do a course. Why don't you come over for a bit and study for it, after our holiday, then you could go back and be the only life coach in Kansas? If Billy can spare you, of course.'

'Oh, Billy can spare me,' I said grimly.

It seemed like a good idea at the time. But already, by that night, my enthusiasm was slipping, like the wig worn by the old woman in the supermarket who'd given me the original idea. Maybe, I thought. Maybe not. I didn't even want to go to Europe any more. It didn't feel like my home any more than Kansas did. I wanted to see Rachel, but I couldn't face Ivan or even Gordana, having to tell them that my next relationship had failed too. But I'd promised Rachel a holiday now, and once she'd got used to the idea, she'd sounded pleased. Well. Kind of pleased . . .

'Sounds great, Mum. You sort it out and let me know. I'll email you the dates that I'm not at tournaments – no, I can't, the computer's broken. I'll call you with them later. I'll probably only be able to spare a week at the most, though. Anyway, I've got to go. I'm flying to Zurich in a couple of hours, and the taxi's about to arrive.'

She rang off, and I was left with the silence around me. I was going to have to do something.

11

Gordana

'OK, Mama, please keep it to yourself. I *was* questioned, but it wasn't even the police, it was just two brainless jobsworths from Immigration. One of my girls got herself into some trouble; tried to get into the country on illegal documents. Immigration came round to talk to me because they thought I had something to do with it, seeing as I coached her for a couple of years after she arrived over here. You know they're really clamping down on the Eastern Europeans coming in. Then they jumped to conclusions; thought I was responsible for every silly Czech girl who comes in on forged papers – like I'm some kind of criminal mastermind! It's ridiculous. I soon put them right. That's all it was. In fact, I'm really hacked off with them, coming to the house like that so early. The bit about the migraine was true, which is hardly surprising. The whole thing was really stressful.'

I stare at my boy, my eyes narrowy and my lips pressed into a line. I always used to be able to tell if he was lying, but it seems that once his Adam's apple shrunk and his chest got hairy, he also learned to be so good at it that it was no longer so easy to fool me.

'So why did you lie to Rachel and tell her the story about the Jehovah's Witnesses?' I ask. He is driving me back from tennis in his posh car, the one that makes me feel I am in a hovercraft, it is so smooth and floaty.

'I don't want to worry her. You know what a fusspot she is; and this is a huge tournament for her. It could really move her career on to the next level – about time, too. I don't want any distractions for her. None. So you're not to say a word, Mama, all right? Besides, we have to keep it quiet. Mud sticks, you know, and it could do my reputation no end of harm.'

'Very well,' I say, not happy about having to tell lies as well. But I hope I will not see Rachel until she gets back, and then, if Ivan is telling the truth and it is a mistake, it will all have blown away. 'And what happens now?'

It is the day after the horrible row with Elsie. No wonder my boy looks so tired, but I am pleased that he's asked to see me before he and Rachel go off to Zurich. I wonder if he needs more money.

'Nothing happens,' he says crossly, beeping his horn at a poor old lady who had dared put one foot off the pavement. Even the horn sounds smooth and . . . what is that word? It was in Ted's crossword last week, he taught me it. Melluflious? No, that doesn't sound right. Mellifluous, I think. Melly-flewus. 'Nothing except that, thanks to Elsie, all the Midweek ladies get something other than Rachel and Mark to gossip about for weeks on end.'

'Excuse me, Ivan, but I am a Midweek lady,' I say with dignity, forgetting about that tricky English word.

'You're different,' he replies, turning to me and for the first time managing something which was almost a smile. Or perhaps it is a grimace. I am not sure. With Ivan it is sometimes hard to tell.

'I certainly am. So,' I continue, determined to make the most of it, 'how is the club doing?'

There is a tiny little pause. Someone who doesn't know Ivan so well – Anthea, for example – might think it is because Ivan is fiddling with the button which makes his wing mirrors flap in and out, but I know better.

'It's not going well? Is this why you wanted to see me?'

He clucks with exasperation. 'Did I say that? No, I didn't. Honestly. It's fine, Mama. I just wanted to reassure you. And you said you needed to give me Rachel's birthday present, to give to her.'

'It's OK. I already post it.'

I know I must proceed with much cautiousness. Three years ago, Ivan, with a great fanfare and as much publicity as he could beg for, spent a huge amount of money —quite a lot of it borrowed from Ted and me — to relaunch the tennis club as his own academy. It was supposed to be the first of many. Like David Lloyd, only better, he said. At the time I said that ought to be his slogan, but he didn't think that was so funny. It made me chuckle though. I could see the banner outside the club in my imagination: 'LiKE LLOYDY'S ONLY BETTER.'

The real banner, outside our much improved and extended little club, reads 'I.A.T.A'. The Ivan Anderson Tennis Academy. I was so proud when it opened. Me and the Midweek girls all got our hair done first, and lots of real tennis players were there. Elsie nearly fainted when Pat Cash signed her sun visor – I think this is the closest she ever come to having an orgasm – and Valerie drank too much champagne and vomited into a tub of petunias next to Court Six. Ivan and Pat played an exhibition match, and Ivan won easily. Then Rachel played Anne Keothavong, and also won with no problems – and Anne was the British number one at the time. Apparently she had the flu that day, but I'm sure Rachel would have beaten her anyway. It was a perfect day for this proud mother and grandmother.

Most of the pupils at the academy are Eastern European girls who come over for a couple of years at a time. But people are saying there don't seem to be so many of them around any more. Our club remains the only branch of the academy. Ivan has been managing to pay back the money Ted and I lent him though, so I suppose things must not be too bad.

'New players enrolling all the time?' I ask casually, looking close at my fingernails. They are in very poor state at the moment. I think it's because the last time I had a manicure, the girl painted some clear cement on them. It was supposed to make them strong, but it keeps flaking off and taking bits of my nail along. Very distressing. And my hair is getting thin, and my feet are getting ugly. I don't like growing old. Ted just gets more leathery and creased, and grumbles about his bowels. I feel that I am falling apart from inside out. I wonder when we will have false teeth? Soon, I fear. I wonder if Ted's false teeth will be crooked, in the way that his old ones are? I suppose not. I will miss those Dracula teeth.

'You'll get all your money back,' Ivan snaps at me, taking a corner so carelessly that his car tyre rides up on the kerb. Which is most unlike him. 'I don't miss a payment, do I?'

'Ivan! That is not very nice, to talk to me like that. When have either of us ever told you to hurry up and pay back that loan? Never. I think it's great you're paying us back but there is no need to be so cross about it.'

Now Ivan looks like a sulky boy again. 'I don't like being in debt,' he says.

'And I only asked how your membership is going,' I reply. 'I said nothing about the money, so don't be so touchy-feely otherwise I will think I have something to worry about.'

He sighs. 'Touchy, Mama, not touchy-feely, that's different. Anyway, there's nothing to worry about, at least not yet. I just had a bit of a slow year, that's all. Especially since I launched the clothing range . . .'

Ah, yes, the clothing range. Anthea's little project. She begged Ivan to let her design some tennis dresses and tops and things, and he, foolish boy, agreed. He must not have seen the designs before she made them. And the colours! She is very fond of lime green and orange swirls. 'Like Nike,' she said. More like an explosion in a sorbet factory, I thought. I was in Lillywhites the other week and I didn't spot a single item of I.A. tennis wear. Rachel refuses blankpoint to wear it to any of her tournaments, which makes Anthea very cross. Ivan has given up asking her. I think he is embarrassed that his name is on them. He prefers that she wear Nike too.

The only times Anthea ever comes to the club is when she decides to hold a sale. She brings a wheely rail of these garments, then sits next to them all day, pleading with her eyes for people to buy them. Sometimes some of the older, kinder Midweekers do, or occasionally an impressionable Intermediate member, but I don't know what they do with them when they get them home. I only ever saw one girl wearing any of it on court. It was a turquoise and pink swirly top – quite put me off my strides. In fact I think Rachel *should* wear it in her tournaments. It would give her the advantage straight away.

'You will tell me, darling, won't you, if you have any problems?' I keep my voice light; try to sound like I wasn't giving him a hard time in any shape, form or way.

'Don't hassle me, Mama,' he growls back.

'You are so grumpy sometimes,' I say, raising my voice slightly because we have just got on to the motorway and the car fastens away, an easy ninety miles an hour. 'I don't know how Anthea puts up with you.'

'She doesn't hassle me as much as you do,' he replies, shooting me a sideways look.

'I only do it because I care about you, darling.'

'I know, Mama,' he says. He sounds almost sad. My big, beautiful boy.

92

12

Rachel

By the time the taxi drops us off outside Terminal One at Heathrow, I am jumpy with worry and irritation. Every attempt to initiate conversation with Dad is met with grunts; all the way to the airport he just stared either out of or at the car window, at the raindrops which skated across the glass, lit gold from the reflection of the streetlamps.

'Hope it's not raining like this in Switzerland,' I say as we climb out of the cab, resorting to the desperate measure of discussing the weather. Dad doesn't even pretend to be interested in replying, just wordlessly peels off a twenty-pound note which he hands to the driver, leaving me to heft my racket bag and holdall out of the boot. I grit my teeth, biting back the urge to ask him why the hell he was even bothering to come if he wouldn't talk to me or help me with the bags or anything – he'd be sorry if I pulled a muscle in my back, wouldn't he? What a waste of time and money *that* would be, if I couldn't even play once we got there . . . I hate it when he ignores me.

Worse is to come. The queue inside the terminal is obscene. It looks like a ball of yarn, twisting round on itself so many times that it is impossible to know where it begins or ends; it's just a solid mass of fed-up looking adults and disconsolate children sitting on stationary trolleys and bulky luggage.

'Great,' says Dad, breaking his vow of silence. 'Just . . . great.' He stands next to the revolving doors, looking utterly defeated.

Mum had an expression she used to use for crowds of people. It took me a moment to remember what it was: 'Like a Brueghel depiction of hell'. I never understood what that meant until she showed me a picture of his in an art book. I think of it now: hundreds and hundreds of sour-faced harassed people, crammed together in lines. From the second we squeeze through the revolving doors, it is impossible even to see a single tile of the floor for the great mass of bodies inside.

'Computers are down. They're cancelling flights all over the place,' a glum businessman with halitosis informs me as I look desperately around for the end of a queue – any queue. A small boy, trying to wriggle past, trips over the end of my racket bag, which is protruding from the side of my trolley, bumps his head on a suitcase, wets himself, and bursts into noisy tears. His mother swears volubly at me.

'Sorry,' I say.

'Keep your child under control,' Dad snaps at the woman, staring disgustedly at the yellow puddle spreading out near the wheels of our trolley.

The boy's mother rounds on us. She is rather fat, with an orange sleeveless top on, displaying a smudgy tattoo on her left arm. I stare at it, mesmerized, trying unsuccessfully to work out what it says. '*Kevin*', perhaps. Or maybe '*Heaven*', or even '*Devon*'. The complicated calligraphy has not aged well, somewhat like the canvas on which it is painted.

'Oi, misery guts, you don't bleedin' well talk to me like that, *all right*?' She jabs a finger at him, making the fat on her arm wobble, and I feel like asking her to hold still, please, because she was making it even more difficult for me to decipher the tattoo. 'And what are you staring at?' she snaps in my direction.

'Come on, Dad. Let's try down here.' Ignoring the fat woman, I manoeuvre the trolley and Dad (with difficulty) away from the altercation. Her aggression has shaken me but, in the grand scheme of things, it is the least of our problems.

As we pass the First Class check-in, I permit myself a lingering, envious gaze: no queue there, just one supercilious woman in a fur coat carrying a small dog, being fawned over by the uniformed man behind the desk. Just think how much easier everything would be, if you were only more successful, I tell myself. No queuing. No smelly minicabs or sulky fathers. People jumping to attention when they saw you, being nice all the time. Maybe if your volleys were crisper or your footwork better or your stamina higher or your will to win stronger . . . I wish I knew. If I *knew* why I couldn't quite break through into the big time, maybe I could fix it. But I don't know.

Eventually, by asking several different but equally miserable-looking people, we manage to find what appeared to be the end of the line for the BA flights.

'How long have you been waiting?' I ask the woman in front. She is digging her thumb into the skin of a satsuma, and the fresh sharp smell of its juice cuts through the toxic exhalations of thousands of frustrated travellers, making my mouth water.

'Twenty-five minutes so far,' she replies. 'Haven't moved yet, and my flight leaves in half an hour – although it's probably been delayed. They all have.'

Settling in for a long wait, Dad and I automatically go into our ritual queuing behaviour. After hundreds of trips to tournaments around the world, we've honed to perfection our ways of dealing with the tedium of check-in or flight delays. I always doodle, leaning on the handlebar of the trolley (abstract doodles, not drawing, in case anybody sees) and Dad takes out his book, usually a sportsperson's biography. As the queue inches infinitesimally slowly towards its destination, he nudges his holdall forwards with his foot, without looking up from the pages of the book. We rarely speak to one another, as if talking is banned until we are comfortably seated on the plane; anybody observing us would conclude that we were strangers travelling independently of one another. I don't mind. On this occasion, it doesn't make any difference anyway, Dad being in such a strop already.

I swallow down the bitter disappointment that Mark hasn't contacted me on my birthday, wondering if he has a good excuse, or if he is going to make the sort of husband who always forgets birthdays and anniversaries, like Dad was with Mum. And with me, come to think of it. The sort of husband for whom you have to leave Post-It notes around to remind them, with wish-lists of gifts so that you don't end up with some heinously unattractive vase which even your worst enemy would know you'd hate . . .

But Mark is different from Dad. Even if he started out a bit hopeless, I'm sure I could train him. At least he has taste, also unlike Dad, who is sadly lacking in discernment in the gift department. Poor Mum had to endure years of tacky teddy bears and sickly Hallmark-type posters, which Dad would hand over beaming with pleasure, and which Mum would display for the minimum amount of time possible and then stuff into a cupboard.

Twenty minutes later, the queue has still only moved fifteen feet. Bored of my doodles, I pull my mobile out of the side pocket of my backpack, telling myself I'm only doing it to see if Kerry is here yet and trying to contact me. Since all the flights are delayed, she might even end up being on time for once. But the screen is blank again, even though I'd left it switched on.

'That's the fourth time today. Why does my phone keep turning itself off?' I ask Dad, who totally ignores me. Again. I roll my eyes and turn on the phone again.

'Battery's probably low,' says the satsuma woman, turning her head to address me. 'Or maybe you've spilt some water on it at some point?'

'I don't think so,' I say, keying in my code. 'So, aren't you worried you've missed your flight? Where are you going?'

The woman opens her mouth to reply, but there is a sudden commotion in the crowd; people swear and tut as somebody pushes through unapologetically. 'Rachel Anderson!' the person yells, and I beam with delight and recognition, waving manically back in the direction of the familiar voice. At that point, after all the stress of the past twenty-four hours, I couldn't care less that Dad has put down the book on top of his wallet of travel documents and is glaring at me through narrowed eyes.

'*Mark!* Over here!'

'Happy birthday, babe, didn't you get my message?' Mark appears through the crowd and wraps his arms around me, squeezing the breath out of me and lifting me, all five foot ten of me, off my feet. He puts me down and kisses me effusively and passionately.

'What message?' I ask joyfully, when we surface again.

Mark turns and stares hard at Dad, although he speaks to me: 'I know your mobile's playing up so I left a message with Anthea at your house.'

A chilly sensation worms its way between my shoulderblades as I realize the gravity of the situation, as if the blue touchpaper has been lit but nobody is standing well back. It's bad enough that Mark knows that Anthea – or Dad – hadn't passed on the message (on my birthday, too!). But, on top of his migraine (or whatever), Dad now knows for a fact that Mark and I are still an item. And here are both men, in this gun-powder keg of tension already existing in the terminal, almost pressing noses, growling at each other.

Not good, I think. I unfasten my arms from around

Mark's neck and sheepishly allow them to drop back by my side. The woman with the satsuma has turned round and is staring with unsubtle, almost greedy fascination at the unfolding tableau.

'Dad,' I say nervously. 'Dad, um, please don't jump to conclusions.'

'Shut up, Rachel,' says Dad, not taking his eyes off Mark for a second.

'Ivan . . .' Mark pleads quietly. 'Be reasonable, mate. She's twenty-three years old. It's her *birthday* . . .'

'Oooh, happy birthday!' the satsuma lady whispers, nudging me in the side.

'Are you trying to make a fool of me?' Ivan suddenly turns on me, making me back away and bang my hip on the handle of my trolley. By now, several other people have stopped grumbling about the queue and are gazing, riveted, at the free entertainment.

'No, Dad, of course not. We don't see that much of each other, and it's not serious or anything . . .' I stop, catching the momentary stricken expression which crossed Mark's face. For a second he looked young; vulnerable; not at all like his usual confident self, and it makes me love him even more. I slide my arm round his waist, but he shakes it off. Then, without another word to Ivan, he grabs my elbow and steers me, with difficulty, through the crowd to the doorway of a small Tie Rack concession. I don't dare to look back at my father's face.

'Sorry, er . . . Mark, you know what he's like. Nightmare!' I say, hearing the unnatural shrillness in my voice. I wanted to call him 'babe' the way he called me, but my mouth somehow wouldn't quite form the word, and it came out as if I was struggling even to remember his name. I'm just not good at scenes. It's hot in the terminal and I can feel sweat clutching at my armpits and sticking my T-shirt to my back.

'Why don't you ever stand up to him?' Mark demands. I am shocked to see that he is white with anger. 'You let him walk all over you, you live in fear of what he's going to think or say or do next – frankly, Rachel, it's pathetic! You're a grown woman, you make your own bloody decisions. And that's how you see us, is it: "nothing serious"? Well, thanks a million.'

'No!' I say, distressed. 'Of course not! I was just try-ing not to . . . Dad had a very hard night . . . He's really under pressure at the moment and I didn't want to add to it . . . Of course that's not how I see us. I'm crazy about you! You must know that.'

I reach out to touch Mark's hair, but he ducks violently, knocking into a stand containing pashmina scarves encased in clear plastic near the store entrance. The neat coloured packets fall in a slithery cascade across the floor, spilling out into the main terminus, sending a shop assistant scurrying out after them before they get kicked under trolleys or secreted into handbags. The shop assistant probably knows from past experience that even usually respectable and law-abiding people feel more inclined to steal when under this sort of duress, as if being jostled in a queue for an hour gives them the right not to return an errant accessory straying into their path.

'I'm not so sure I do know that,' Mark says. He sounds formal and far away, and I am scared. We stand for a moment watching the assistant grovelling on the floor for the scarves, but it doesn't occur to either of us to help her. 'In fact, is this why you won't sleep with me? Because you don't like me enough? Is that it?'

'No!' I repeat. 'I really *am* crazy about you.' I curse myself because, although it's true, I know that I sound uncertain. For the first time, I notice that Mark is hold-ing a large red paper bag with raffia handles. He sees me look at it, and hands it to me.

'This is for you,' he says, without smiling. 'Happy birthday.' He kisses my cheek then, in exactly the same distant way Dad did earlier when he gave me the hair-straightening device. I want to clamp Mark's head in my hands, force his mouth on to mine, force the passion for me back into his soul, and not let him go. He can go to the pub whenever he wants, I think frantically. I don't care if he never comes to another of my tournaments; I'll come to as many of his as he likes. Just please don't let me lose him . . .

'*Excuse* me,' says the assistant haughtily, her arms encircling a wobbly pile of packaged scarves, which she begins to reload on to their chrome display stand.

Mark leans against the entrance of the shop, closing his eyes.

'Are you all right?' I ask, and he nods with his eyes still shut. I know what he is going to say before he opens his mouth, and I will him not to. When he does speak, it is so quiet I have to strain over the grumbling travellers and the blurred flight cancellations coming over the tannoy. Straining to catch the last words I want to hear.

'Rachel . . . I can't handle this any more. You're a great girl, but, I mean, your dad . . . It's too much. We had a good time, didn't we? Let's just . . . leave it for now, shall we?'

'Please don't say that,' I manage, clutching his hand and forcing him to look into my eyes. 'Please . . . I'm so sorry I said we weren't serious. I'll go now and tell him we are. I'll make him understand, I don't care what it takes. We can start sleeping together whenever you want. You're . . .' I pause. Mark is so many different things to me, I can't decide what to say first: 'You're the man of my dreams' sounds too corny and fake. 'You're wonderful' is too sycophantic, and 'You're everything to me' too desperate. I curse my lack of experience in these matters, when it seems that everything depends on me saying the right thing. I wish it was like tennis, where I would (more often than not) instinctively and without hesitation pick the right shot to play in any given situation in a match.

Words are so much more tricky. But then I haven't had eighteen years of practising words of love, not the way I've practised my tennis shots, anyway.

'You're – so important to me,' is what I whisper in the end, tasting the inadaquacy of the words as they rise like bile into my mouth.

'Sorry, Rachel,' he replies, meeting my gaze for the first and last time. 'Clearly not important enough.'

He turns and starts to weave his way across the log-jam of people, away from me, and away from my father.

13

Susie

Everyone in Lawrence seemed to have an open-door policy. Sometimes it drove me mad, but, as the years passed, most people did seem to get more respectful of the rhythms of family life, especially the folk with kids and rhythms of their own to adhere to. Billy and I still got the loners and the unattached, but I'd become fairly adept at giving them the right amount of welcome and hospitality. I wasn't afraid to kick anybody out when I'd had enough of their company. The problem was, though, that because of Billy's little sideline as the local pot dealer, I couldn't downright turn people away.

So I liked it best when it was just the two of us in that before-supper-after-work hour. Billy would be swigging a beer, tired but alert, stretching and chatting aimlessly to the cats; the three of them drifting around the place in a slow dance of unwinding. Billy was quite feline himself: little and soft and lithe. The way he moved, slowly but deliberately, made me imagine him with a tail. If he'd been a cat, he would have rubbed his head against the furniture as he passed, that tail in a delicate question mark of enquiry.

Newport and Pavonia, the real cats, didn't know what to do with themselves after he left. They didn't dance any more; they just sat at the kitchen window and waited for me to come home; complaining bitterly about what had kept me once I climbed up the steps and unlocked the door. It made me angry, on their behalf as well as mine.

Billy used to retire to the couch and skin up a joint after dinner, but even then, with him immobile in one place for hours, the rest of the house had seemed more animated than it did when he wasn't there. It was as if he exhaled life into the house along with the marijuana smoke: a sleepy warmth which permeated the walls and leached into every room, while he sat in front of the TV.

Once he'd gone, the place felt empty, even with the cats and me inside. The evenings were the hardest. I could just about get through the days, coasting on my normal routine: caffeine; appointments; viewings; valuations; gossip by the water cooler, little cone-shaped paper snippets about who was seeing whom. All the other women at Harvest Realty were divorced, so they weren't at all surprised when I told them about Billy. I think they were secretly pleased. I was the cone-shaped gossip when I was absent from the office, I was sure of it. It was another reason not to want to work there any more.

I wanted Billy back. I kept waiting for him to come back, to be there when I returned from work, smiling hesitantly at me and telling me that it had all been a big mistake. I wanted our life together back again. Everything had unravelled into a chaos of loose ends and needed untangling: everything, from holiday photos to insurance policies, bottles of wine and pictures on the wall. What could have been so wrong about us, for this to happen?

Perhaps it was me. I knew after Ivan, I'd had a problem with commitment, but it wasn't as if Billy seemed to mind. In fact, we used to laugh about it. Every year, on the date of our engagement, I got a joke anniversary present from him: a child's plastic tiara, or some crotchless knickers, or a CD of songs by an unlistenable Bulgarian folk band. The gifts always came with a label bearing a message like: '*real diamonds when we're married, hon*', or: '*for our wedding night – now remind me, when is that, again?*'; and, with the CD: '*Marry me soon else I'm booking them for your birthday party*'. I'd laugh and slap him affectionately and say, 'Yeah, yeah, don't rush me!' whenever he asked plaintively when I was planning to make an honest man out of him.

One year he gave me a baby's dummy – a pacifier, they call them here – as my gift. The label read: 'We'd better get on with it, else Junior will think I'm his grandpa'. We decided to stop trying for a baby quite soon after that, and the subject wasn't mentioned again, apart from some wistful jesting about parenthood when the cats kept us up at night, skidding along the corridors chasing their tails or other, more detachable objects. One morning when we got up, there was a maze of tangled white thread at ankle height wrapped around all the furniture, a vase broken, and an empty cotton reel on the kitchen floor; and Billy said, 'Oh you kids! I'm grounding you. No TV for two days.' I could have sworn there were tears in his eyes. And he hadn't even liked that vase.

Come to think of it, Billy often did try to get around difficult subjects with a quip or a bad pun. And once or twice I thought how closed-down his face looked when he was giving me my anniversary gift for yet another year; even while he was joking about something or other – but he never made an issue out of it, never. I really thought that if it was all that important to him, he'd tell me. I thought we told each other everything. After all, I'd told him often enough how scared I felt of making that commitment again. That it had nothing to do with how I felt about him; and wasn't it commitment enough for us to be engaged, and settled together?

Had I been missing something? With a cold squeeze

of cognizance, I thought that, in all probability, I had.

I needed to get away. I forced myself to try and be positive. I was looking forward to going skiing. Then maybe I would look into becoming a life coach. I could tell people how to live life to the full; to have adventures; take risks, where appropriate; de-clutter; de-stress; de-cide. I would always tell my clients to put themselves first, the doormats of this life who feel second best. I would think of my experience being married to Ivan and I would say: Whatever you do, don't put *anybody* else first, not even if they're some top notch dishy tennis player who thinks he's going to become the next Björn Borg. If you aren't happy, then you don't have a hope in hell of making your nearest and dearest happy either. Think positive. Imagine the outcome of your dreams, and act like they're already becoming reality. We all know these things already – to be honest, from what I've read up about it, it seems like pretty basic stuff to me. I suppose it comes down to having the conviction to make other people believe what you tell them. Perhaps being a life coach gives you authority. If someone will pay you eighty bucks an hour to tell them on the phone to think positive, then they think it's money well spent.

I actually did quite a lot of research on it, online, and Rachel was right, there were courses you could do, by correspondence. Many of the courses were based in England, and you could have tutorials, so that would be my excuse for moving away from Lawrence for a while. I might move back here afterwards, I might not. There was probably a reason why there were no life coaches in Lawrence (I checked), students and hippies didn't tend to rush to pay eighty dollars an hour to be told how to improve their lives. They just rolled another big fat one and put on a Little Feat CD. But that was OK. I'd rent out the house to some graduate students and keep the income, which would have the dual benefit of pissing off Billy. He'd have moved in like a shot given half a chance, but there was no way that I was going to let him and Eva set up home together in *my* house.

Although Billy had more tact than that. He wouldn't really have moved in. Even as I thought it, I knew it wasn't true.

But all the same, I couldn't prevent myself from imagining Billy and Eva in the sauna in the garden, the one Billy had built himself to a genuine Scandinavian design, with fresh scented pine and an iron fireplace to heat the rocks on. I saw Billy lying naked on the slatted wooden seat, leaning back in Eva's arms the way he used to in mine, letting their skin get red hot, turning over and gently sliding inside her in a slick of sweat and heat, then running out in the garden to cool off afterwards. When it was snowing, would they laugh and squeal and try to lie down long enough to make snow angels, the way we used to? Oh *shit*.

It really hurt. But I couldn't stay in Lawrence for ever, just to spite them. I'd go and stay with Gordana and Ted in Surrey. I was sure they'd have me, after the skiing holiday, for a few weeks, and that way I would get to see more of Rachel. Obviously I couldn't stay with her, since she lived with the Spawn of Satan and his mistress, but maybe I could persuade Rach to come to Gordana's too for a little while.

It wasn't much, but at least it was something to look forward to.

14

Rachel

Mark made me feel good about everything. I could train longer, play harder, *know* that I was the best – because he told me I was. Because he'd stroke my face and sigh with pleasure; because he took me dancing, when nobody had ever taken me dancing before; because he cooked for me – nothing fancy, just a baked potato and some chicken in a packet sauce, but it was the best food I ever tasted.

I've messed it up by being weak and pathetic and not even realizing. It's second nature to me to say the things Dad wants to hear. I just slipped up by saying them when Mark was there. He's never been there before when I've been placating Dad, so I suppose I wasn't used to editing what I say. What an *idiot* I am.

I'd bet any money in the world that if we had started sleeping together, he wouldn't have let me go like that. I was so close to giving myself to him. So sure that he was the One. Who wants a twenty-three-year-old virgin? No one, and certainly not a gorgeous red-blooded male like Mark. I should have let him, ages ago. Perhaps the sighs I thought were sighs of pleasure were actually frustration. Mark isn't used to not getting what he wants.

Now he's going to get it somewhere else, because I've messed everything up.

* * *

Once we are finally on the plane and I have to sit next to Dad, speechless with fury and sorrow and disbelief, he tries to console me. He puts his big fat stupid hand on my forearm and squeezes it, and I can't believe what he says. He says: 'You're best off without him, love. If he really loved you he wouldn't have let me come between the two of you. Look on the bright side, eh?'

I want to punch him, but instead I grit my teeth and concentrate on not crying, knowing that once I start, I won't stop for a long, long time. I force myself not to think about Mark, and the feel of his arms around my waist or his warm sweet breath in my ear. I stare out of the plane window as the plane hauls itself airborne and watch everything on the ground get smaller: cars into dots; houses merging into squares and curves; roads into string. I wish the plane was like the Challenger space shuttle, going higher and higher until it exploded and nothing was left of anyone's troubles except a bright firework of loss in the sky, fading into smoke and then into nothing.

At that moment, I decide that I really hate Dad. But the next moment, I am gripped with a new panic: maybe what he said was right. How could Mark have said all those lovely things to me if he could just give up on us so easily? Oh, I *knew* it was because I wouldn't sleep with him . . .

I do not once peek inside the red paper bag with the raffia handles until we arrive at the hotel in Zurich and I lock myself in my room. I had to lie to the woman at the airport check-in desk, saying no, nobody had given me anything to carry, and although lying usually makes me itchy with discomfort, I hadn't even cared.

When I laid the bag flat on the black rubber conveyor belt to pass through the X-ray machine, I permitted myself a glance at the outlines of its contents as they showed up black and white on the monitor screen. The bare bones of a relationship, which I had managed to break as surely as if I had dropped the bag and heard them fracture. I couldn't work out what anything was, amongst the several mystery objects on the screen, although there was one small box which looked like it might contain an item of jewellery.

On the plane I pushed the bag underneath the seat in front for take-off and landing, but for the duration of the rest of the flight I sat with it between my feet, feeling the scratchy thick paper chafe my ankles, wondering – with no excitement, just a dull curiosity – what Mark had given me. When he had wrapped those presents, he'd still believed he loved me. By the time he handed them over to me, he no longer did.

I unwrap them as soon as I am alone in my room, fingers trembling as I peel the sellotape off the packages and fold the used wrapping paper into neat squares. I was right about the little box containing jewellery: it was a necklace, a little silver star with a tiny chip of diamond in the centre, on a delicate silver chain. The note on the box says, '*For my very own star*'. Also inside the bag is a bottle of my favourite perfume, the one he said made him want to rip my clothes off whenever I wore it; and a book called *Will To Win*, which I flick through and then throw violently at the wall separating my room from Dad's. I feel like I don't have the bloody will to live, let alone to win anything. I've always been so positive about everything – you have to be, to be a pro tennis player. You have to believe in yourself. But right now I feel that all the positivity has leaked out of an unseen part of me, like a puncture in a paddling pool.

The last gift is a bright pink low cut T-shirt with 'Babe' spelled out in sequins across the breasts. It isn't really my sort of thing, but I immediately go across to the mirror and hold it up against my body, even managing a very brief smile at my reflection as I see myself through Mark's eyes.

I pick *Will to Win* off the floor, straighten the cover where it has creased, and lay it carefully on the bed with my other presents in a neat semi-circle. Then loneliness descends, and I slide down the side of the bed until I am sitting on the carpet. I start to cry and don't stop until my eyes are swollen and my chest hurts, and there is someone banging at the door. I ignore it, thinking it is Dad, but the person won't stop knocking. Despite the bleary aftermath of tears impairing my hearing, I can make out a reedy insistent voice calling my name.

I wipe my face on the dusty fringe at the corner of the bedspread, stagger wearily up, and open the door.

'*Rachel!* What's the matter, babe?'

Babe. The name I wanted to call him, but couldn't. I imagine Mark in Top Shop, fingering the racks of T-shirts until he found the one he thought I'd look sexiest in. Or then again, I think, full of bitter self-pity, perhaps he was visualizing the porcine lead character in the film *Babe*. If he could just throw away our relationship so easily, perhaps that was how little he thought of me.

Kerry stands on tiptoe to hug me, gathering me awkwardly up in her arms in the doorway. I feel like a sack of potatoes, unwieldy and lumpy. All cried out, I just lean my head miserably on Kerry's bony shoulder. She is dressed for a night out: boots and a miniskirt, lots of jewellery and pink lipgloss. It is comforting to see her, but I still wish I was at home with Gordana and not hundreds of miles away in yet another nondescript hotel bedroom.

'Mark finished with me,' I say dully, and a maid pushing a trolley down the patterned carpet of the corridor gives me a nervous look. The trolley is piled high with covered plates, and it smells of school dinners.

Kerry squeezes me tighter. '*What?* On your birthday? Bastard, wait till I—'

'He came to the airport to give me my present, and Dad gave him a hard time.'

'He chucked you because Ivan had a go? What's the *matter* with him?'

'No. It was my fault. He ended it because I told Dad, in front of Mark, that I wasn't serious about him.'

'Oh.' Kerry heaves me into the room and closes the door, scrutinizing my doubtless ravaged-looking face. 'What did you do that for, then?'

I don't answer. Depression, heavier than gravity, pulls and tugs at me, making me long to sink back down on to the floor again. The thought of playing a tennis match in the morning fills me with despair and a leaden fatigue. I want to sleep for a month.

'I'm sorry, Rach. I know how much you liked him.'

'Yeah. Well. Thanks for coming over, Kerry, and I suppose I'll see you on the bus tomorrow, but I really think I'm going to write today off and go to bed—'

Kerry puts her hands on her hips and raises her eyebrows. 'No way.'

'What?'

'I said, no way. We're going out.'

'Kerry, I'm not going out.'

'You are.'

'Oh come on, look at the state of me! Anyway, it's Sunday night. Nothing'll be going on.'

'You've got ten minutes to put some make-up on and get changed. I'm not taking no for an answer. Clubs are open on Sundays, you know. What do you think I'm all dolled up for? It's your birthday! Which reminds me . . . Here, before I forget: happy birthday, pet.'

She rummages in her backpack and brings out a flat square, wrapped in silver paper with 'Many happy returns' all over it in glittery writing. The halogen spotlights in the ceiling above us catch the glitter in a

111

sparkly dance as I tear off the giftwrap. It's a CD: Kelis's album. I've never heard of them.

'She's really good,' Kerry says, a little self-consciously. So it's a she, not a they. I hope 'she' isn't a rap act. Kerry is into rap, lots of swearing and posing and swaggering. Not my cup of tea at all.

'Thanks,' I say, my eyes filling with tears again. I pick the cellophane off the CD case so I can examine the booklet inside it, and put off the moment when Kerry was going to make me go out. It doesn't work, but at least the album doesn't look like a rap record.

'So come on then, let's go,' she says bossily. 'And don't give me that early night stuff; you know you wouldn't sleep if you went to bed now . . . *Plus* I want to hear what's going on with Ivan.'

I have to think for a moment even to remember the big drama of Elsie's arrest allegations, and the not-quite-ringing-true story about the migraine and the Jehovah's Witnesses. Mark's desertion is such a shock that everything else has been completely superseded in my mind.

'Oh yeah, that,' I say, sitting down heavily on the bed. I catch sight of myself in the mirror and shudder: my nose and eyes are bright red, cheeks deathly white, and hair like a Brillo pad.

'Kerry, do I have to go out?'

Kerry walks over to my holdall, unzips it, pulls out my jeans and my washbag and holds them out to me. 'Ten minutes,' she said, looking pointedly at her watch and gesturing towards the bathroom. 'No excuses.'

Half an hour later we are walking through Zurich's picturesque old town, which is bustling with people out on a Sunday evening. It is a cold, crisp night. I feel convalescent, wrung-out; but deep down I am grateful to Kerry for forcing me out.

'Where are we going? Couldn't we just have had a drink at our hotel?'

Kerry snorts derisively. 'That hotel bar was like a morgue. Anyway, me and José met this gay guy from Portugal on my flight. He fancied José, and told us about this really buzzing hotel near here; he was really trying to get José to say he'd come down tonight. It's called the, um, Goldenes Schwert, and it's got a nightclub in it.'

I manage a smile. 'Was José horrified?' I ask. José's dark curls and flawless olive skin have made him a bit of a gay icon, and women and gay men alike jostle for his attention, although no one has ever known him to have a partner. Kerry and I long ago decided that he was one of those asexual men, like Action Man. Any hint of sexual innuendo throws him into such a state of confusion that he's been known to walk headfirst into floodlight poles in his haste to escape. This gauche charm is what makes him so appealing. He also has an endearing habit of classic spoonerisms on court, oft-quoted by us and the other members of our squad: 'Take a little breast,' he once said, getting 'rest' and 'breather' mixed up. But our favourite is 'Shit your hot' instead of 'Hit your shot.'

'Well, you know what he's like – he didn't admit it if he was. But he told me that he was just staying in his room tonight, reading. Such a waste.'

'Who for: men or women?'

'Who knows?' says Kerry, linking arms with me. 'Maybe one day we'll find out; or maybe he's got a secret double life that we don't know about.'

'Talking of which,' I say glumly, looking in at the lit-up windows of candlelit restaurants and red-carpeted theatre foyers, 'Elsie the Battleaxe, you know she lives in our road? Well, she swore in front of everyone at the social supper the other night that she saw Dad getting arrested at seven in the morning. Gordana nearly punched her lights out.'

Kerry stops in her tracks, causing a large man leading a small dog to walk into the back of her. '*Entschuldigen*,' she says to him over her shoulder

113

– we all know a smattering of words from most countries we play tournaments in; and of course how to score a match in many different languages – and then, to me: 'Arrested? What the hell for?'

'Well, of course it's not true. But I think something else is going on, because he's being very cagey about it. Claims it was Jehovah's Witnesses, whom he just happened to know from school, so he invited them in for a two-hour chat. I mean, how implausible does that sound?'

'Very,' says Kerry with feeling.

'The worst thing about it was bloody Elsie, slandering Dad like that in front of everyone. Gordana was really upset. Elsie wouldn't have done it if Dad had been there, but he didn't turn up – which of course she took as added proof. He had a migraine, and hadn't bothered to let me or Gordana know he wasn't coming. But everyone in the room stopped to listen. They were like a flock of vultures.'

'I don't think you have flocks of vultures.'

'Well, whatever. They couldn't get enough of it. I was half expecting them all to stand up and start chanting *fight, fight, fight*. It was awful.'

I remember the feel of Mark's bulky torso pressing me against the fence on Court Four, and the warm bare skin of his stomach against mine in the cold night air when our T-shirts had ridden up as we kissed. My voice falters.

'It was awful,' I repeat, banishing the memory. 'And I don't know what's going on with Dad. I think it must be some secret business deal or something, but it's obviously not going well. He's hardly said a word to me since – apart from sticking his oar in with Mark, of course.'

'Blimey,' says Kerry, steering me around a corner. 'Sorry, tell me the rest in a minute – this is Marktgasse, so the place should be down here. Number fourteen, the guy said.'

114

'There's nothing more to tell.'

I point at a typically Swiss-looking square town-house, with shutters and awnings and window boxes bravely trying not to look past their prime. We edge past the hardy souls sitting at tables outside the hotel and make our way through the lobby to the nightclub. It's early, and almost completely empty inside, which suits me. We sit down on tall stools at a table around a pillar, and order two vodka cranberries from a pretty boy with lithe honey-coloured legs in tight white shorts. Coloured lights swoop and bounce across the deserted dance floor, and the Seventies disco music has an echoey quality to it

'Is this a gay club?' I whisper after he takes our order.

'Duh . . . what do you think, Einstein? That Portuguese guy on the plane was as camp as a row of tents, and just look at our waiter. I wonder if *Goldenes Schwert* means Golden Showers?'

Tears threaten to overcome me again. What the hell am I doing in a nightclub after Mark has left me? I should have done the decent thing and climbed into bed and pulled the covers over my head. That's what one does when one's world crumbles, surely. I yearn for that white cotton haven; could feel the cave I'd create for myself: the cold sheets which my breath and body heat would heat up until it was a damp, dark place of safety. Although that's not right though, either, I think. If I'm going to be under covers, I want Mark's big solid body there with me, his skin almost burning me with its warmth and security. My own body heat isn't enough. The thought fills me with panic.

'I don't want to be here,' I say frantically. 'There's no way I can play tomorrow.'

'You can. You'll be fine, Rach. Just keep focused. I'll hit with you first, and José'll be there. And your dad—'

115

'*He'd* better not show his face. I don't know why he even bothered to come.'

'What's he doing tonight?'

I shrug. The waiter sashays over with a tray, places our drinks and the bill on the table with a flourish, then stands with his hand on his narrow hip, gazing pointedly off into the middle distance while Kerry fumbles for money, squinting at the Euros in her purse.

The DJ puts on 'Crazy in Love' by Beyoncé – or so Kerry tells me, otherwise I wouldn't have known – and the waiter absently raises and lowers alternate shoulders and clicks his fingers, as if he is about to suddenly launch himself off across the empty parquet dancefloor like the little welder girl in *Flashdance*. I watch him, wishing fleetingly that I had a job which involved no more pressure than not spilling frosty drinks and giving people the correct change.

'Dad? I don't know. He usually goes to his room straight after dinner, but I didn't have dinner with him. In fact, I haven't seen him since we arrived.'

I wonder if Dad heard me crying earlier. I'd heard the sound from the television in the room to the other side of mine, so the walls were clearly fairly thin; although I had been trying to cry quietly. Part of me wanted him to rush round and comfort me as he used to when I was a little girl (although he never comforted me for anything tennis-related: injury, defeat or humiliation) and part of me couldn't have borne it if he had. But there was no sound at all coming from his room.

After two drinks on an empty stomach, I feel both better and worse. My head is beginning to whirl slightly, like the coloured lights, and to add to my existing emotions of grief, shock and bitterness comes another unwelcome addition: the guilt I always feel if I'm not completely abstemious before a tournament. But, as Kerry pointed out, a couple of drinks the night before my first match in these particular circumstances was probably far less harmful than staying in my room, crying and not sleeping.

The lights in the club become dimmer, the music louder, and a glimmer of something more positive gradually begins to shine back in my head: *I'm going to do well in this tournament.*

I'm not even aware I said this out loud until Kerry laughs. 'Of course you are!' she bellows in my ear, over the top of the thumping bass of the music, making me recoil with pain. 'You're the tenth best woman player in the whole of the country, and you're on the way up. You're going to *rock.*'

'Kerry.' I turn on my stool and lean both my hands on Kerry's lap, which earns me an approving glance from a group of three lesbians at the bar. 'I thought I wouldn't be able to do it without Mark. I was even starting to wonder if that was why I'd stayed on the circuit, but at least I know it's not. Sod him. I don't need him.'

Kerry hugs me. She knows that I don't often express such confidence in my game out loud, and, although I am by nature quite a positive person, I've often wished I had her stubborn persistence: Kerry keeps going, even though she is ranked a few places below me, because she really believes that she is the best, and soon everyone else will realize it too. OK, so it has taken a bit longer than she'd planned, but she's had some bad luck: a nagging back injury, bad draws, opponents on better form in crucial matches ... Whereas with me, although I'm fiercely competitive on court, it's been commented on that I always seem more surprised than anyone else when I win.

Kerry starts to say something else, but suddenly stops, gaping with astonishment, her eyes fixed on the door of the club.

I turn and look too, but can't see what she is looking at, other than the spectacle of lots of extremely attractive and well-groomed men bumping and grinding together on the dance floor.

'I could have sworn . . .' Kerry squints through the sequinned and shady disco light, then shakes her head.

'What?'

Kerry drains the rest of her drink, her straw momentarily sticking to her top lip. 'I thought I just saw Ivan. Or somebody very like him, at least.'

I manage a laugh. There is more likelihood of seeing Osama bin Laden in lederhosen, snogging George Bush on the dance floor, than there is of seeing my father in a nightclub, particularly a gay one. Dad loathes any loud music recorded later than the mid 80s, refuses on principle to pay more than the equivalent of two pounds in any currency for a drink, can't dance to save his life, and not very secretly disapproves of homosexuality. I think idly that becoming a lesbian myself would be the ideal way to really piss him off. I glance over at the three girls at the bar, and, unless I'm imagining things, they all give me sultry looks. But then the memory of the feel of Mark pressing himself up against me makes me realize that I'd never want to make love with a woman. I never want to lose my virginity to anyone if I can't have Mark.

'No chance,' I say. 'You must be drunk. In fact, I am, a bit, and I've got a headache. Can we please go back to the hotel now?'

15

Susie

I was sitting near the top of the stairs, a half-full basket of dirty laundry on my knees, still pondering the logistics of going on a skiing holiday with Rachel in Italy. Did I need to take ski gear with me, or hire it there? Would I need a visa? How many lessons should I have? Thoughts whirled round my head like washing in a tumble-drier, making me dizzy. It suddenly seemed far too great an undertaking. I couldn't handle it. Perhaps I'd just stay where I was, instead. Perhaps I wasn't ready to be that proactive yet . . .

A rattle of the screen door made me jump up, hoping against hope that it might be Billy. I ran down the stairs, spilling laundry all the way, to find a man standing in the kitchen – but it was only Flamingo Dan. Disappointment rose up from my belly to meet my sinking heart, and I retraced my steps, collecting up my dirty tights and work clothes. One advantage of being on my own was at least three times less laundry to do, I mused, not even bothering to greet Dan straight away. Not that he'd noticed. He'd gone straight to the fridge and helped himself to some juice.

'No cranberry, man,' I heard him complain.

Of all Billy's oddball, acid-casualty friends, Dan was the worst. For no apparent reason, he was obsessed with flamingos. He had a selection of representations of them all over the inside of his tiny house and dotting his front yard: plastic ones, ornamental ones, tiny ones on swizzle sticks, huge inflatable ones. Oh, and he was afraid of mushrooms – the edible kind, not the magic variety, naturally – and allegedly puked whenever he touched velvet. Go figure, as Billy used to say.

As I picked up a bra strewn over the banisters, I suddenly decided that I was definitely going to organize this skiing holiday after all, if random visits from Dan were all I had to look forward to for the foreseeable future. Sod it, I'm off, I thought. I want out of here.

Dan even looked like a flamingo: long, skinny legs, beaky nose, and a predilection for pink. Billy and I used to joke about him: 'Where's Dan?' one of us would say, and the reply would be, 'Hmm, I don't know. Wait, isn't that him over there, standing on one leg in the pond?'

'Hi, Dan,' I said, carrying the basket into the kitchen and dumping it at the top of the basement steps, where the washer and drier were housed. I then instantly moved to the far side of the kitchen island, so he didn't try and embrace me as per usual. 'What's up?'

'Hi, Susie,' he droned, his pupils so dilated that his eyes looked black. 'You know, nothin' new. Just lookin' for Billy.'

I put my hands on my hips. I could have done without this.

'Dan, Billy moved out a month ago. He left me. You must know that. I saw you out with him and' – I couldn't bring myself to say Eva's name – '*that woman* last week.' It was true. I'd seen the three of them through the window of the Freestate Brewery, laughing and chatting at a table, a half-full pitcher of beer and a plate of nachos in front of them. I'd gone home and got straight into bed, cold with misery, although there was a small part of me which cheered at the thought that *I* no longer had to endure drinks with Flamingo Dan. I couldn't believe that Eva would enjoy his company either. Rumour had it that she was pretty smart. She was halfway through her first semester as a graduate student doing a PhD, something geological, my friend Audrey said. I hoped that it meant she was so academic that she'd soon get terminally bored with Billy and Dan's riveting conversations about spark plugs or which of the Grateful Dead's albums was the best.

'Oh. Yeah. Right. Sorry, I guess I forgot.'

'How could you forget?' I wasn't sure why I asked that, since it was fairly self-explanatory.

'You know. I just forgot that Billy told you already, that's all.'

I digested the implications of this in silence for a moment.

'So, let me get this straight . . . you'd known for some time about him and – her – and you just didn't know that I knew?'

Dan looked confused. 'I guess so.'

'Oh, that's just great, Dan, really great. So who else knew that my fiancé was sleeping around behind my back?'

Dan's eyes opened up wide with panic. Even his eyelids were avian-looking, bald and a bit scaly.

'I guess I don't know, Susie. Sorry. Er, I'd better be off then. What time will Billy be back?'

I gritted my teeth. 'Dan,' I said, trying my hardest not to whack him around the head with the bread board, 'HE DOESN'T LIVE HERE ANY MORE. Now, if you don't mind, I have things to do. I have a vacation to organize.'

'Cool!' said Dan, his panic forgotten. 'Are you guys going anywhere nice?'

Stronger tactics were required. I suddenly remembered Dan's mushroom phobia.

'Hey, Dan,' I said, in an affectedly cheerful voice, opening the fridge door and removing the pack of four huge meaty flat ones I'd bought on my trip to Dillons that day. 'Want to stay for supper? I'm making stuffed mush—'

He was out of the door and gone before I'd even finished the sentence. I didn't know whether to laugh or cry, so I did neither. I didn't fancy the mushrooms much myself, either, so I put them back in the fridge and made myself two pieces of toast, spread with the chocolate body paint that Billy and I had only got halfway through, laboriously warming it and applying it in sticky sensual lines and patterns on each others' bodies.

The cats wove circles of warm sympathy around my shins as I ate.

'Seems a pity to waste it,' I said, through a mouthful of crumbs.

Later that evening, I rang my friend Audrey to tell her of my plans.

'Skiing?' she said with disgust and fear, as if I'd told her I was going to dance naked on a minefield. I heard her take a deep drag of her Camel Light, and then she laughed throatily. '*Europe?* Why in hell do you wanna do a thing like that?'

'Because it's fun. Because my daughter lives in Europe. Because I'm tired of entertaining Flamingo Dan. Because it's good exercise, and a challenge, and I want to see some nice mountains. We don't see many mountains here, do we?'

'Mount Oread's good enough for me, honey, and I don't see why it ain't for you. Hell, if it snows I'll take you tobogganing down it on a tea tray, that do you? Why would you want to spend a thousand bucks for some fancy ski resort where they don't talk English and you gotta fly for days to get there?'

'It's not days. It's only about ten hours or so, and I want to get away . . .'

I wondered why I was having to defend myself to her. Then I realized that what I was actually doing was telling her about the holiday in the hope that she would mention it to at least three other people (which she undoubtedly would) and that it would get back to Billy within days.

I wasn't going to call him and tell him myself, so I'd have to rely on the Lawrence grapevine. There was Raylene, who was still working as a mail carrier in town, twenty-five years later; and Audrey was on her round, so that was a dead cert. Raylene knew Billy, of course, and anyway, once Raylene knew, it may as well be on the front page of the *Lawrence Journal-World*. Everyone would know.

Audrey was somewhat more positive about the life-coaching idea, though, and agreed to feed the cats while I was gone, for however long it ended up being.

'Don't tell anyone I might be away for more than a couple of weeks, will you?'

I didn't want Billy to know that much. He'd probably be pleased that I was going out of town for a few months, and he wouldn't need to worry about bumping into me in the Bottleneck or the Freestate Brewery. And Eva would be ecstatic.

For a moment I almost ditched the idea. There was something to be said for hanging around being a fly in the ointment – Lawrence was a small town, and I usually managed to glower at her at least three times a week, once I'd seen them together enough times for me to be able to recognize her. It had become quite a hobby. I was getting it down to a fine art: lurking around stop signs when I spotted her car and looming up to the driver's window to stare menacingly at her. She was small like me, but much frailer-looking. I could take her out, any day. Could come back from the skiing holiday tanned and fit, and Billy would realize what he was missing.

No. Stop it, Susie, I told myself after I hung up from Audrey. This wasn't a very constructive behaviour pattern for a potential life coach, was it now? Staying

123

in a place specifically for the purpose of intimidating your fiancé's new girlfriend probably wasn't a particularly positive life goal. Skiing would be much better. Sod 'em. She'd soon get fed up with Billy picking his toenails at the dinner table, and I'd be sailing down a vast white piste while a gorgeous instructor gazed admiringly at my rear view.

I went to write my resignation letter to the boss of the real estate agency, and to pay the balance on the skiing holiday before I could change my mind again.

16

Rachel

Incredibly, I *am* doing really well in this tournament. Kerry got knocked out in the second round by a beefy American girl, but, four days after our arrival in Zurich, I have played my socks off, and found myself in the quarter finals. I am relieved I didn't give in to the temptation to stay in bed and not even get on the plane, because the two-odd hours' duration of each of my matches has been the only time I haven't been pining for Mark. I've found I can turn off the insistent wail of misery inside my head, and focus.

Dad and José are really happy with my performance too, although I still can't talk to Dad. I take all my pre- and post-match advice from José, and roll my eyes like a stroppy teenager whenever he says: 'Ivan told me to tell you . . .'

Via José, Dad has plenty to say about all my matches – insider knowledge of my opponents' games, tips on shots, etc. – but, oddly, when it comes to the day of the quarter-final, he doesn't say a word. Even though I'm refusing to be within a ten-foot radius of him, I can immediately tell that something about this match is spooking him. Perhaps he believes I'll be way out of my depth, and this thought makes me even more determined to win. Unfortunately, I woke up this morning feeling really ropy: exhausted and queasy. I put it down to a nerves.

My opponent is a twenty-five-year-old Hungarian

girl called Natasha Horvath. She is my height, and beautiful in an intense kind of way, with straight blonde hair knotted up as if she'd fantasized about twisting my arm behind my back when she did it. She seems vaguely familiar, although I'm sure I'd have remembered if I'd played her before. Every time I look at her, I get a cold uncomfortable feeling in my back, and my shoulderblades tighten up.

She is really unsettling me. She's been glaring at me from the start, not just with the common-or-garden steely aggression that we all employ to try and psych out an opponent; but with a raw, naked hatred which is coming at me in waves from the far side of the court. It's throwing me off my stride, making the sweat dripping down my face just a little more cloying, and for a while all my volleys go straight into the net.

The warm-up is brutal, like she is trying to score points off me already. When I feed her some smashes, I swear she is trying to put them all straight through me. I'm jumping out of the way, under fire. This does not seem normal. I glance over at Kerry, sitting at the front of the stands, and she makes a face at me, then grimaces in Natasha's direction. José, who is next to her, gives me the thumbs up, but when I look over at Dad, he is gazing at Natasha with a strange but unmistakably lustful expression on his face. As soon as he catches me looking, he jumps and shakes himself slightly, acting insouciant – but the damage is done, and it just makes me even more angry. Bloody Dad, he's like a dog on heat. It's embarrassing. Could he not stop thinking about pulling, even for a second? As if a gorgeous woman like Natasha Horvath would look twice at my dad, with his lived-in face and thinning hair . . . He might have been a catch twenty years ago, but no one thinks that now, except Anthea and a few menopausal and bored housewives at the tennis club.

All in all, I am in an extremely bad mood by the time

the warm-up has finished. But this is good. I want to be angry. I want to be in control, and vicious, and as intimidating as Natasha is being to me. I make myself stop glowering at Dad, and glare right back at Natasha, the ferocity of my gaze trying to disguise the fear that she somehow manages to instil in me. She's like an automaton. The crowd must be able to see, or sense, the tension, because the atmosphere is unusually sober, with people sitting as taut and still as the few remaining empty flip-up chairs of the stands. Huge television cameras gaze at us with blank lenses, waiting.

Natasha had won the toss, and chose to serve. Her first serve lands just wide of my service box. I look up at the umpire, waiting to hear her call, but Natasha assumes – or decides – she's aced me, and has already moved across to the left side of the centre T, ready to serve the second point.

'Wide!' I protest, pointing at a non-existent mark on the hard court and wishing we were playing on clay so I'd have my proof. The umpire shakes her head. I blink with disbelief – the very first point! I put my hands on my hips. 'That was *wide.*' My voice sounds small and squeaky with outrage in the echoey stadium.

'*Funfzehn–zero,*' says the umpire impassively. She is a stocky middle-aged woman who looks like she'll never be able to get out of the umpire's chair without the aid of a crane.

A faint smirk brushes across Natasha's lips. I hate her. I hate the umpire. Three more aces follow – genuine ones – and I've lost the first game without scoring a single point. Natasha's serve is a nightmare: hard, unpredictable, left-handed. I have the strangest feeling that this is more than just competitive; it feels personal. What can I possibly have done to Natasha to make her hate me this much?

I manage to salvage a couple of my service games, but the first set is a write-off: six–two. When I glance

127

across at Kerry, she has her feet on the back of the seat in front, and her head buried in her knees. I feel sick again, and swallow hard. Imagine the humiliation of puking on court! I'd emigrate if that ever happened. Nervously, I glance over to the exit, calculating how fast I could get there in the event of an imminent vomit.

At the set break, Natasha sits on her chair at the side of the court with a towel over her head. Her fists are clenched, and the towel is moving as she appears to be shaking her head under there; giving herself a pep talk, I presume.

An image of Mark springs into my head, the way he'd encourage me in my matches. I miss him, sitting up there mouthing, '*go on*', at me, nodding his support, telling me he loved me with his eyes. He used to say that the urge he got to jump up and down and scream for joy when I hit a good shot was awful; as was the way he felt like punching the umpire when there was a bad call. I know what he means. You have to sit and watch impassively, especially when there are TV cameras present, and it's so hard.

Dad was dreadful like that when I was younger. Impassive was not a word in his vocabulary. He actually did leap up and roar, regularly; and more than once he was asked to calm down or leave. Sometimes he shouted at me, sometimes at the umpire. For years, I lived in terror that he'd become one of those tennis dads who got such a bad reputation on the circuit that most of the press their daughters received talked of nothing else. Analyses of their match play was more about how the dad had behaved than how the off-spring had played. Especially since Dad had been quite good in his heyday. The tennis press – and sometimes the nationals, if I was doing particularly well – never failed to point out that I was more successful than he'd ever been. And unsurprisingly it never failed to go down like a lead balloon in our household.

Second set. I've been shaken, but I tell myself that this is a fresh start. I'll look at the annihilation of the first set as the warm-up. Now I mean business. The umpire calls time, and we walk back to our respective ends of the court. When Natasha turns to face me, waiting for my serve, she looks like a bulldog chewing a wasp. Her expression contorts and darkens her pretty face, but this time I refuse to be intimidated. I serve hard and fast to her forehand because her backhand is stronger, and she slightly mishits the return. It is almost the first weakness she's shown, and I'm on to it immediately. She chip-charges – runs up to the net after the shot – but a fraction of a second too late, and I lob her with ease.

Fifteen-love. This is better. Kerry gives me a discreet thumbs-up. I allow myself a brief, fleeting image of Mark; I pretend he is sitting next to her, waiting till I win to rush down to the changing room to give me a big cuddle outside the door . . .

My next serve is even better. Fast, but with a spin which sends the ball richocheting away from Natasha's racket, and she barely scrapes it back into my court. I am there waiting for it, and slam it past her into the far corner. Why could I not have done that in the first set? Sometimes tennis bemuses me. You know perfectly well what you ought to do, you've practised it a million times, so why are there times when you just can't do it? It's at moments like these when I wish I had a nice, easy, non-challenging job, like a manicurist or a house painter.

But for the rest of that set, I couldn't be happier to be a tennis player. I am all over her, triumph and attitude in every one of my shots. I serve harder, run faster, return better than I ever have before. I feel as if wings have sprouted from the sides of my Nikes, and I'm barely even out of breath. Natasha hates it, but she can't do anything about it. Perhaps she became complacent at winning the first set so easily, but something almost imperceptible floats skywards out of her game: its departing soul. She fights hard, of course, and we have some brilliant rallies, but the points are mine. I feel as if I own them before the words are out of the umpire's mouth.

The crowd sits forwards and puts away their sandwiches, and I feel them urging me on. It is euphoric. I wish Mark could see me now. I wonder if there is any chance this match is being broadcast on Eurosport. I'll do it for him. I have another fleeting fantasy, that he'll have jumped on a plane and is, even as I think it, cheering me on silently, one of the blur of faces before me.

I win the second set six–one. Natasha tries desperately to maintain her expression of undiluted evil, but I can see I've upset her badly. Her brow is a furious furrow of concentration, and I can almost see her marshalling her strength to fight back.

We start the third a little more cautiously, gauging each other's respective fatigue and fury but, despite my queasiness, I still have the edge. I am three–one up, at thirty–all, waiting to receive Natasha's serve. She suddenly kneels down and does up her shoelace – I'm sure it wasn't undone, but it is a stalling tactic – and I make the fatal mistake of glancing into the crowd. Hearing a man's voice calling, 'Go on, Rachel!' clear as a bell and sounding just like Mark. I even think I see him, sitting there, beaming at me: my wish-fulfilment fantasy.

By the time Natasha straightens up again, I've realized with disappointment that of course it isn't Mark at all, just somebody who sounds like him, but it is enough to tip the balance of the match again. She aces me; and what makes me catch my breath isn't the loss of the crucial point, but the acute pain of the loss of Mark. My concentration is shot.

I haven't realized that I am holding my breath until I begin to feel literally vertiginous, but as Natasha moves across to serve, at forty–thirty, and aces me again, it is too late to simply exhale. Suddenly I feel very, very unwell, rather than just the under-the-weather sensation I've had throughout the match. The court beneath my feet begins to rock slightly, and I know I have to sit down immediately, before blackness creeps up over me.

'Three-two to Miss Anderson, third set. One set all,' says the umpire, in German, and I realize with over-whelming relief that I have one minute to sit down and get myself back together. I sip cold water, dry the sweat off my face, put my head between my knees, and breathe as deeply as I can, feeling my ribcage expand and push against the tops of my thighs. It's not over. I'm still winning, just. She held her serve, that's to be expected. I've broken her once in this set. I can do it again. I just have to not let her break me in this game. She is not having this game, no way. I mutter to myself in the damp quiet between my trembling knees. It's as if the crowd has vanished, and I know this is good, because if they aren't there, then Mark can't be there either, and I need him not to be there because his absence – or his imaginary presence – is putting me off.

'*Zeit*,' says the umpire. Time. Time to forget about feeling ill. I've got all evening for that. Time to work. Time to win.

Thankfully, I've stopped feeling dizzy, but despite my pep talk, I lose the next game; and the next. It's my serve, and if she breaks me again, it's all over.

I don't serve well, but she makes a couple of unforced errors, and I'm thirty–love up. Then, after a long rally, she runs up to the net to take my drop shot, skids and slips up, her long legs splaying out on the court in different directions. The ball goes in the net and she bangs her racket head on the ground in frustration. We are both desperate.

She's not hurt, although she takes her time walking

back to the baseline. I serve for the game – right into the net. Gritting my teeth, I put a huge spin on my second serve, sending the ball curving up and away, bouncing so high that she has no chance of returning it.

The game is mine. Four-all. I wipe my face with my wristband, grateful that I've stopped feeling sick. Two more, I think. Two more games, then I can go and lie down and cry for my beautiful Mark.

I feel like a gladiator in an amphitheatre, fighting to the death. Natasha wants to kill me, so I must kill her first. It's weird – it's not as if I'm playing the world number one, or somebody who'd boost my ranking hugely. Beating Natasha would hike it up a bit, but it's not about points or rankings or getting through to the semis, or even winning this tournament. I just want to beat *her*, and I feel almost grateful that she hates me enough to get me this worked up.

Perhaps she did hurt herself when she fell, or perhaps she's just cracking under the pressure, but in the next game I break back again, with relative ease. Five-four. The match is within my grasp at last, and it's my serve. As we change ends, I look up and see José, Kerry and Dad like the three wise monkeys, all leaning forwards in their seats, rigid with pressure; and somehow this reassures me. I'm not on my own. I can do this. As long as I don't think about Mark's face at the airport.

As we walk back to our respective ends, the crowd is cheering loudly, expressing their excitement that this is a match which could go either way, a match which is the equivalent of a page-turning thriller that you can't put down. In my head I hear an imaginary commentator's voice: 'Rachel, serving for the match. Can she hold her nerve?'

I jog from foot to foot. The ballboy feeds me three balls; I put one in the pocket of my tight dress, discard one, and roll the third in the palm of my left hand. The lineswomen stand around like policemen, arms behind their backs, legs splayed in their unflattering beige trousers, waiting for my mistakes. I throw the ball high, lift my racket, drop it behind my head, bend my knees, and launch myself with all my strength into the serve. It goes so fast that I'm as surprised as Natasha. When I look at the read-out of the speed, it says 106 mph: my fastest ever.

She gets it back, though, just about, and I have to run like hell to reach her return. I slam it past her, right into the far corner, and the cheers of the crowd gives me an almost sexual fluttery feeling in my belly.

I serve again, not as fast this time, but another ace. There's been a lot of aces in this match. Natasha's eyes are narrowed and she is muttering to herself, staring at the ground.

The next rally is a long, exhausting one. She has me running from side to side, as if she's toying with me again — until one of her shots goes wide, and her strategy fails. Forty-love; three match points. Could I really be lucky enough to win the match on a love game? The crowd are no longer still, but fidgety and murmuring, slow hand-clapping. The umpire has to shush them as I wait for the serve.

It happens in slow motion, my body falling into the positions it knows as well as walking: the ball-toss, the leg-bend, dropping the racket behind my head, hopping forwards on impact, until the ball finally leaves me, flying away to the exact spot I want it to go to, right at Natasha's big feet like a heat-seeking missile, too close for her to be able to react on one side or another. She scrapes it off the ground — straight into the net. It's all over. I've won.

17

Rachel

I have to go and do a brief post-match press conference as soon as I get off court. I hate doing these all red-faced and sweaty, but at least I'm the victor, so I've got a smile on my face for the TV cameras. I'm used to them now; they no longer frighten me as they used to when I was an up and coming Junior. But as I gabble away about my performance, all I can think about is how I'm longing to get to my phone and see if there's a message from Mark.

As soon as I'm released I almost break into a run towards the locker room, stopping only to scrawl hasty autographs on outsize tennis balls for a group of clamouring Swiss schoolchildren. The locker room is empty. I rush over to my locker, open it and grab my phone out of my bag.

No messages. I feel my shoulders sag. Much more slowly, I strip off my clothes and head for the showers. When I get back I check the phone again, just in case he's rung or texted in the last four minutes. Still nothing. I am standing wrapped only in a towel, dripping on the floor, staring at the little blank screen, not thinking about the biggest win of my career, or the fact that I've got to do it all again tomorrow – only this time against the player ranked third in the world. I'm not thinking about my own ranking, or even the fact that I'm in with a good chance of winning the whole tournament . . . I'm just wishing there could be a text from Mark telling me he loves me after all.

Suddenly the phone rings in my hand, making me jump, and my heart hurdle in tandem. As is often the case when I'm abroad, the caller's number isn't showing up, but I'm sure my prayers have been answered. Breathlessly, I press the green button and hold the phone to my ear.

'Hi, darling, it's Mummy,' says a distant crackly voice. 'Is this a good time?'

I sink down on to the wooden slatted bench and begin to sob with disappointment. But the line is bad, and I don't think she hears my distress.

'Just ringing to tell you that I've booked the holiday! We're going to Italy, in three weeks' time, isn't that exciting?'

'Yeah,' I manage. 'But I've got to go, Mum, I'm about to be—' I drop the phone on to the bench as a tsunami of nausea sweeps up from my knees to my throat, and I make it to the toilet just in time.

If I ever needed a bloody holiday, it was now.

I don't tell anybody I vomited, apart from Mum. Actually, I feel marginally better for it, as if I was puking out some of the stress and disappointment. I ring Mum back again later, after the fuss and excitement and congratulations from Kerry and José and a little coterie of British tennis supporters and journalists in the players' enclosure of the stadium.

Mum is thrilled to hear I'm through to the semifinal, and speechless when she hears whom I'm playing next. She can't believe I've just been interviewed on Eurosport, or that my ranking will go up for getting to the semis, probably to eighth in the UK. She tells me a bit more about the holiday, and says she'll post me my air ticket.

'I bet Ivan's pleased with you,' she says eventually, and I look around me, puzzled. I see lots of fit young people in tracksuits milling about, and José and Kerry are laughing and messing around, sharing a sports drink with two straws. But I suddenly realize I haven't seen Dad since the end of the match.

'I don't know,' I reply. 'He's not here. I mean, he was, but he isn't now. Maybe his migraine came back.'

I hear Mum tutting in Kansas. 'Probably can't stand that you're in the limelight,' she says cattily. 'Perhaps he and your opponent have gone off to console each other in private somewhere.'

I think of how gutted Natasha must be, and feel sorry for her. I saw her briefly, giving her 'loser's debrief' to the TV cameras, and then she had vanished, sloping away with her racket bag over her shoulder. She was barely able to shake my hand after the match, trailing her fingers perfunctorily across mine over the net, not even bothering to attempt a smile.

Good riddance, I think, hoping I don't have to play her again any time soon.

'Well, I'd better go, Mum, I've got to get back to the hotel for some rest before the match tomorrow.'

'Take care, darling,' she says, as she always does. 'I'll keep everything crossed for you, you little star. You're the best, you know that, don't you?'

Not as far as Mark's concerned, I think. And then I think: But actually, in terms of tennis? Yeah, I'm getting there.

I lose the next day's semi, horrendously: six–two, six–one. I am no match for the world number three, who wipes the floor with me. But I don't really care. I'm pleased with my performance, my ranking's gone up, and even though I've been dumped, I haven't fallen to pieces, and I've had my best win in years.

On the plane on the way home I get to sit next to Kerry, who talks a lot about her physio, whom she fancies but who is married with twin sons, and who shows no interest whatsoever in her beyond the strictly professional. But at least I don't have to sit with Dad.

Dad and José sit in the row behind, talking tactics – or 'Tic-Tacs', as José once called them – and planning the arrangements for the next tournament.

It's endless, this treadmill. I'm so glad I won't be going to the next one; glad that I will be on holiday, like a normal person.

18

Susie

I couldn't believe we were really here – I'd never even been to Italy before. Living in Kansas so long, I'd missed out on so much that Europe had to offer. Kansas was very handy for anywhere else in the USA, since it was smack bang in the centre of the country; but not at all for Europe.

It was a 'singles holiday', which was all I'd been able to find at short notice, and all I could afford. I hadn't told Rachel that when I invited her; I thought it would put her off. And it probably would have done – the men in the group were, it has to be said, no great shakes. I hadn't had much of a chance to look them over while we were on the coach from the airport to the hotel, but as we picked our way through deep snow to a minibus waiting to take us up to the ski-hire shop, I studied them surreptitiously. More for Rachel's benefit than my own – there was no way I could face another relationship so soon. But perhaps meeting someone new would be just what Rachel needed to take her mind off Mark. They all looked a bit old for her, though. Frankly, they all looked a bit old for me too.

Our group, having been informed by the hotel manager that we had to collect our boots and skis right away, climbed gingerly aboard the minibus, which began to ferry us still further up the precipitous mountain road. I wasn't sure what the point of the urgency was, since all I wanted to do was to have some food, a hot bath and a sleep – I'd been travelling for twenty-two hours. Rachel had only flown over from London, but even she, seasoned traveller she was, looked a little jaded.

Although perhaps that was more to do with heartbreak. I thought how much less resilient the young seemed. She and Mark had only been together a few months, less than a year, yet she was acting like her whole world had crumbled. Her eyes kept filling up, and she'd turn to me, then turn abruptly away again. Surely she hadn't been in this sort of a state ever since the break-up? She said she'd been ill, but still . . . after three weeks, she ought at least to be able to function.

I felt awkward with her. I wanted to cuddle and console her but yet was conscious of this distance, unsure what she wanted of me. She clearly hadn't noticed that anything was amiss in my own personal life. I'd been with Billy for nine years, and *I* was managing to hold it together . . . 'You look fantastic, Mum!' had been her first words to me when we met at Verona Airport, and for some reason, I still hadn't been able to tell her about me and Billy. Perhaps I was afraid that she would think I was trying to steal her thunder. Or perhaps I couldn't bear to admit to my daughter just yet that another relationship had failed. Or maybe it was simply that there was too much distance between us now. She could comment on the new highlights in my hair, but not notice that I wasn't wearing an engagement ring any more.

After the excitement of our initial reunion, Rachel had been almost completely silent, and I could see that any socializing with the group would need to be initiated by me. I was about to introduce myself to the man in front, when he turned around in his seat and spoke first.

'So what do you two do?' he asked. He was friendly,

if a bit lecherous in the way he tried to look us both up and down. Not that he could see anything of our bodies, waist up, since our top halves were encased in all-encompassing puffy nylon like man-made pupae. Rachel looked better than I did, since she at least had trendy khaki snowboarding pants on, like weather-proofed combats. I was in what the ski-gear hire shop described as 'racing salopettes', which sounded glamorous but which were in fact skintight, thick, ugly leggings which flared out mid-calf, had two great fat built-in plastic kneepads and, to add insult to injury, braces attached to their ludicrously high waist. I could see the practicality of them as an item of sportswear, but they made me feel like Tweedledee and Tweedledum's unattractive little sister. If I'd had time to try them on in the store, I would definitely have gone for something different. Plus, when I stood up, the crotch seam felt as if it was going to split me in half.

However, at least the man couldn't see this, so I smiled encouragingly at him. He was probably in his late fifties, long-necked, balding and very lined, like a tortoise; although from what I'd seen of his body as we crunched up the path earlier, he was still lithe and skinny.

Rachel had completely ignored his question, and was gazing sullenly out of the smeary minibus window at the snowy mountain peaks, her jaw set in a hard line, lost in thought. I realized that this could be a difficult holiday.

'I'm – um – in the process of changing careers,' I replied, knowing I'd better tell him what I did first, since once he discovered that Rachel was a pro player, he more than likely wouldn't be remotely interested in me any more. 'I've been in real estate for some years, in the States, and now I'm thinking about becoming a life coach. I'm Susie, and this is my daughter, Rachel. She's a professional tennis player.'

'*Really?*' said the man, scrutinizing Rachel in the way people usually did when introduced to her: with the sort of attention implying I'd told him she was newly arrived from Jupiter. Rachel turned briefly, proffered a brief, tight smile, and went back to looking out of the window again.

'How fascinating,' he said, leaning further over the back of the seat. I waited for the barrage of questions to begin: Wimbledon? Success? Ranking? Etc. I always felt sorry for Rachel at being subjected to this inquisition every time anyone found out what she did. It was a bit like people finding out that I was an estate agent and instantly demanding to know how much commission I'd earned last year and what was the biggest house I'd ever sold. I'd hate it. But to my surprise, the man was looking at me. He had quite nice eyes, hazel with yellowy flecks in them. Pity about the appalling eighties-style ski suit, though, all red and grey and lime green in blocks. It was odd, after all this time, looking at men as potential partners. I wished I didn't have to. I only wanted Billy.

'I'm Robin. Nice to meet you. So what qualifies one to coach others in life? Your own success at it?'

Pompous ass, I thought, whilst simultaneously being amazed that he hadn't fallen over backwards with delight at meeting a real tennis player. But it was a reasonable question, if rather bluntly put. I thought bitterly of the rudderless morass of indecision which was currently my life: two failed relationships; a daughter I rarely saw and found it hard to open up to when I did; one career I'd disliked and another I hadn't even started (and to which I was, now that I thought about it, eminently unsuited); not to mention an inability even to decide on something as fundamental as which continent I ought to live on.

'Not really,' I replied shortly, wishing that he had talked to Rachel about her tennis after all. The minibus swept wide around a corner, and I clutched the back of his seat, narrowly avoiding grabbing his hand in the process. 'I have good interpersonal skills, and can empathize with others' problems.' I wondered if this was an accurate description. 'Although that's probably more true when I'm not tired, starving, and jetlagged,' I conceded, earning the first real smile from Robin. Actually, I felt rather embarrassed to be discussing my nascent career, when it was still so vague. I hoped Rachel was too lost in thought to be listening – it made me sound like such a lame-ass failure and I really didn't want her to think of me that way. I changed the subject.

'I'm not looking forward to the drive back down this mountain,' I said, as the minibus hurtled around another hairpin bend. 'It's bad enough coming up it.'

Rachel turned then, and laughed. 'Mum, you didn't think we were *driving* back, did you? We're skiing down.' She gestured towards the wide, glassy ski slope to our right. It was mid-afternoon, and dusk was already beginning to soften and blur the edges of the mountains. 'I heard the manager say so. It's to let everybody get a run in before dinner. Why else do you think they told us to change into our ski gear?'

I sat bolt upright, clutching the cold metal bar of Robin's seat back. '*What?* I can't do that! I've only had three lessons on a dry ski slope! I can't ski down a whole mountain yet!' Fear and exhaustion gripped me in a dual embrace of foreboding.

'Oh, you'll be fine,' said Robin dismissively. 'It's a blue run most of the way, I believe, except for one section that's red.'

Blue . . . red . . . in America, the easy runs were green. No, I couldn't do this.

I sank back in my seat. It was true that the information about the holiday and the resort had stated, in quite big print, 'Not suitable for beginners', but I'd assumed that surely I'd be able to pay for some tuition when I got here, and I'd brushed aside my qualms that

I wouldn't be proficient enough, mostly because it was the only group holiday that had any vacancies left, and I hadn't wanted Rachel to feel that I was holding her back. I'd wing it, I had decided, thinking that I was being brave and spontaneous. I had good balance and co-ordination, I was quite fit, and my dry ski slope lessons had gone very smoothly. How hard could it be?

But the Kansas City dry ski slope had been about fifty metres long, not the several *thousand* that we'd been steadily climbing up alongside for the past twenty minutes. Stray skiers were whizzing down at the sort of velocity that indicated they'd been fired out of a cannon rather than being propelled by their own body weight.

None of the rest of the group seemed unduly worried about the ordeal facing us, which struck me as odd too. I mean, weren't you supposed to warm up before hurtling down a mountain? They too had all come off planes and endured the long coach ride from the airport, with no rest or sustenance offered on arrival at the hotel, just this ignominious bundling into an ancient minibus. Yet they were all laughing and chatting tentatively to one another, the way you do when you meet a group of strangers with whom you'll be spending the next seven days. I was glad I had Rachel with me for company.

Across the aisle from Robin was a younger man whom I had initially spotted at Verona airport and identified as part of our group from his luggage tags. Although he looked in his early thirties, he had a helmet of iron grey hair with an arrow-straight side parting, the kind of hair-do favoured by retired army colonels. I thought that he must have some weird medical condition too, since he wore a rucksack with a clear plastic tube protruding from the top flap, which wound round to the front of his chest, and around the end of which was taped a piece of kitchen towel. Rachel later told me that this was merely a source of delivering water 'camelback' for the thirsty skier.

He saw me looking at him, and smiled, displaying far too many teeth all jostling for space, like piglets sucking at their mother's teats. 'Typical,' he said, thrusting a long leg out in front of me. He was wearing salopettes and Jesus sandals over his ski socks. 'I forgot to bring my callus-remover, and I just know the boots are going to make them worse.'

I smiled back at him, I hoped in a sympathetic way; although I suspected it probably came out more as incredulity than sympathy. As opening gambits went, this wasn't exactly gusset-dampening. The only other guy within my range of vision was a folliclychallenged Italian professor of philosophy, who had BO I could smell from three seats back, clearly not helped by the tight Lycra ski gear he wore. I could tell it was unlikely that either Rachel or I would be getting it on with any new men this week, unless there were some handsome waiters at the hotel. Still, at that moment, I was more concerned with how I was going to get down the damn mountain. Knowing my luck, I'd break my leg on the first attempt at a run, then Rachel would have her vacation ruined too, having to fly me home . . . I should never have pretended that I was anything other than a beginner.

Rachel caught my anxiety. 'You'll be fine, Mum,' she said, giving my arm a squeeze. 'I'll stay with you, don't worry. We can just take it really slowly.'

I laughed hollowly; it was my turn to feel tears smarting in my eyes. I looked away furiously. There was no way I wanted Rachel to see me cry. I missed Billy then, desperately and overwhelmingly. He'd never have done anything as daft as go skiing. Our holidays had always involved lots of lying around turquoise pools, Billy getting high, me sleeping and reading. It had often bored me stupid, though, now that I came to think of it. Wasn't that why I was here?

I didn't have to endure those holidays any more. I could do whatever the hell I wanted. Let Eva get bored and sunburned. *I* was going skiing. Although I'd have preferred to go skiing tomorrow. Not now. Not right down the mountain with no practice.

It struck me, not for the first time, how nebulous and unpredictable a beast my own self-confidence was. Had I always been like this? Wavering between certainty and doubt, bravery and cowardice? I wished I could be more like Rachel: she just went for it and worried about the consequences afterwards. I think she got that from her father.

'It's going to be dark soon,' I said, trying not to sound too chicken.

'That's why they hurried us,' Robin replied, not assuaging my fears at all.

We arrived at a cluster of buildings: bars, ski shops, gift emporia; and the minibus came to a sudden halt next to several large dumpsters.

'This must be the resort,' said Rachel doubtfully. 'It's very small, isn't it? We should have gone to Courchevel or somewhere.'

'Sorry,' I said. 'I'm not exactly au fait with European ski resorts. It was cheap. Maybe this is why.'

'I'm not criticizing you, Mum,' she replied, in what could only be described as a critical tone of voice.

We all queued up to be fitted with our boots and skis, and I thought: How strange to be standing on this icy path in Italy with Rachel and a bunch of strangers, like we were all waiting for a bus. Around this time, I ought to have been waking up in Lawrence with Billy's arms wrapped around my back and his breath warming my neck, wondering what to wear for work, or if there was time to make love *and* have a shower, or whether I'd have to head straight for the shower.

I'd thought we were fine, living out our futures together, taking the rough with the smooth, the mundane with the exciting. But it couldn't have been fine, could it? Eva had broken us up, therefore there must have been something seriously wrong with our relationship. How could I not have noticed what it was?

'Cheer up,' said the man in the shop, a hairy blond Australian, when I got to the head of the queue. He handed me a pair of boots in my size, but so ludicrously large and heavy I could barely lift them, then added, predictably, 'It might never happen.'

I made a face at him as I shoved my feet hard into the plastic casing, and allowed him to haul them shut. I felt as though I had concrete blocks on my feet – and that was before I'd even been given the skis.

Eventually we were all kitted out, and waddling in an ungainly manner back along the road towards the piste. My skis clanked together in my arms in an unwieldy fashion, and I felt sick with nerves. I couldn't even carry the damn things properly, let alone ski on them.

'Hold them like this, Mum,' Rachel instructed, showing me how to clip them together and carry them on my shoulder with my hand wrapped around their tips. When we reached the slope, the group dropped their skis on the snow and stamped on them to fasten them. Then they set off, flying away like chicks out of a nest, laughing and whooping. Their skill varied – Camelback Man just leaned over as if he was about to do a pike dive, and stayed in that position, shooting down the mountain immobile and lethal in his trajectory. Even I could tell that wasn't a technique recommended in any ski school.

Pretty soon only Robin, Rachel and I were left. I was teetering on the edge of my fear as if it were a knife blade on which I was trying to balance. I'd managed to attach the skis to my feet, and scissor my legs back and forth on the spot, but the idea of actually going anywhere on them was too frightening.

'Come on, Mum,' Rachel said kindly.

The piste looked so steep. Dusk had long ago swallowed up the rest of the group. Robin was trying to be chivalrous but I could tell he was getting impatient, shifting from foot to foot.

'Go, really, please,' I said, mortified. 'And you, Rach, I'll be fine.'

Rachel laughed. 'Don't be daft. I'm not leaving you to come down on your own.'

At that moment I saw the minibus, empty now save for its driver and a couple of crates full of our outdoor shoes, executing a reckless three-point turn, skidding around the icy road as if demonstrating an ice dance. The driver had a cigarette hanging from his mouth and was eating popcorn out of a large bag whilst talking out of the open window to one of the men in the ski-hire shop, but he could've been driving blindfolded for all I cared: the prospect of a lift down the mountain with him was still more appealing than the thought of skiing in the ever-encroaching darkness.

I stuck out my arm and yelled at him, like I was hailing a cab on Fifth Avenue, and he screeched to a halt by my right ski. Popcorn scattered across the dashboard as he leaned over and opened the passenger door for me.

'I don't want to hold you both up any more,' I said decisively to the others. 'I'm getting a lift back with him.'

Robin's look of relief was transparent. 'OK, see you later. Shall we go then, um, Rachel?'

'I feel like such a failure,' I said in an aside to Rachel, tears stinging my eyes again. At least now I could pretend they were due to the icy wind, but I don't think Rachel was fooled.

'Mum, so what if you're not as confident a skier as the rest of us? Who cares?' She kissed my cheek, her lips bloodless and cold. 'Look, I'd better shoot, if you're sure. See you back at the hotel.'

I watched her and Robin launch themselves off with

147

their poles, skating their legs wide in order to build up momentum, and then they were away, already vanishing in the half-light. Robin was a decent skier, but Rachel was effortless, with a smooth, hip-swaying rhythm of parallel turns which instantly assuaged my fears about her safety. She looked totally in control. I'd never seen her ski before, except in photographs. It was another part of her life I'd completely missed out on. Once more I got the feeling of a baby bird flying the nest – but my Rachel had flown long ago. I felt utterly depressed.

'Let's go!' called the minibus driver cheerfully in a German accent, flicking his cigarette butt out of the window. I managed, with difficulty, to release my skis and manoeuvre them into the back of the minibus, encumbered by the huge rigid ski boots, and slide clumsily into the front seat next to him.

'You did not want to ski?'

'No,' I said dully. 'I was afraid. I am not an experienced skier. In fact, I'm a total beginner.'

He turned and smiled at me, popcorn crumbs on his chin which I itched for him to dash away. He had thick sandy hair and eyebrows, and an interesting mouth. I wondered why I hadn't noticed him on the way up.

'And it is getting dark,' he said consolingly. 'What is your name? I'm Karl.'

'Susie,' I replied, feeling marginally better. 'Thanks for the lift.'

'No problem.'

'You're not Italian,' I said, cringing at the inanity of the comment. 'Do you live here permanently?'

'No, not permanently,' he said, taking a sharp bend so fast that I was thrown against his side. I looked for a seatbelt, but there didn't appear to be one. The feeling of uneasy trepidation this induced in me was not a new one, I realized. It was the same feeling I'd been living with ever since I'd seen Billy and Eva holding hands in the deli.

'My sister is married to Paolo, who owns the hotel. I help them out sometimes. But my main business is wine importing, in Germany and Italy mostly, sometimes England. And a little bit of selling magnets, you know, for health, also.'

Living in Lawrence, I did know what he meant. I was already au fait with the notion of utilizing magnetic forces to aid recovery after muscle damage. My friend Audrey was a great believer in it. She suffered from arthritis, and was always festooned with various different sized magnets which she swore alleviated the pain. I used to joke that if I didn't hear from her for a while, I'd have to come and check that she wasn't stuck to her refrigerator door.

'My friend uses magnets a lot for arthritis,' I said. 'She has a magnetic mattress on her bed.'

'*Ja, ja*, very good,' he said, nodding vigorously.

'Could I have some of your popcorn, please?' I asked as we hurtled round the next bend and the open packet skittered across the bench front seat, scattering more of its contents.

'Sure, help yourself.'

I took a large handful and stuffed it into my mouth. 'I'm absolutely starving,' I said. 'It's another reason I didn't want to ski. I've been travelling for almost twenty-four hours, and I've got no energy left.'

'I don't blame you. I too cannot do anything when I don't eat.'

He smiled at me again, and I decided I liked him very much. Too young for me, though. I wondered if he was single. He'd make a lovely boyfriend for Rachel.

'Do you stay at the hotel too?' I blurted.

'*Ja*, I live there for now.'

Right, I thought. Let Operation Matchmake commence. It was about time I did *something* for my daughter.

* * *

In the end, I was very grateful that I hadn't skied down. When Karl dropped me off, it was so dark that the headlights of his minibus illuminated my way into the hotel. Most of the group were already back, but a few stragglers were still clunking up the road from the bottom of the ski slope, silent and chilled-looking. I felt anxious when I didn't see Rachel among them.

'It's so dark,' I heard a middle-aged woman say, over and over, as she went into the boot room by the hotel's front door. The woman was wearing a pink ski suit, with greasy blonde hair pulled back with pink hair-clips, and the tip of her nose was exactly the same shade of pink, as if it was an additional accessory. 'They made us ski in the *dark*.'

No one spoke to me as they passed me, padding upstairs in their socked feet. I felt excluded, that I'd missed out on the bonding which had taken place as they felt their collective way down the ski slope. But judging from the look of shock on most of their faces, I was still glad I hadn't succumbed to peer pressure. I never had been particularly good at being part of groups. I preferred one on one. And so what if I didn't make any new friends this week? I had so much catching up to do with Rachel, I didn't need anybody else.

At that moment, Karl staggered through the hotel door, weighed down by the box of shoes for which most people had given up waiting. He beamed at me as if he'd known me for ever and was genuinely pleased to see me and, whilst I was still worried about Rachel, something inside me thawed a little. He was nice. It was good to know that there were genuine, decent men out there . . .

Although *Billy* was a genuine, decent man, so perhaps there was no hope for me. He had let me down so spectacularly that I felt I'd never trust anyone else as long as I lived. It would have been much better, I thought, if I'd always suspected Billy of a spot of illicit flirting; perhaps erotic text messages or the occasional one-night stand. Then I wouldn't have been so surprised. I would have expected nothing less of him; known that he could never be mine for ever.

'Mum!'

Thank goodness, I thought, snapping out of it. There she was, skis over her right shoulder, bursting through the doors pink-cheeked and exhilarated. Robin came in behind her, unsubtly admiring her backside as he manoeuvred his own skis through into the boot room. The boot room reminded me of school changing rooms: chilly concrete floor, faintly foot-scented, with damp slatted benches and high pegs.

'Hi, honey,' I said to Rachel, grabbing her round the waist for a hug as she passed me. 'I was just starting to get worried about you.'

'Oh, you do surprise me, Mother. What's to be worried about? Skiing in pitch dark on an icy run with no one else around is nothing to be *worried* about . . .'

It was the first time I'd seen her animated. She was her old sarcastic self.

'So you enjoyed it then,' I said, leaning on the door-frame and watching her and Robin trying to pull off their boots. I delved into the box of shoes and passed Rachel's Caterpillars over to her.

'Thanks, Mum. Yeah, it was fantastic. I'd forgotten how much fun skiing is,' she enthused, and I relaxed. The holiday had been the right thing to do after all.

Robin smiled up at me as he tugged at his left boot. His red ski socks made him look somehow vulnerable. 'Your daughter's quite the athlete, isn't she?' he said. 'We'd have been back much sooner, only she had to keep stopping to help me when I fell over.' I liked him a little better for saying that. I'd put him in the category of a man who'd hate to admit that a woman could beat him at any sport.

'Well, it's a good thing *I* didn't ski,' I said, smiling

back at them both. 'You'd both have been stopping every ten yards. We'd still be out there.'

'Fair enough,' said Rachel. 'But you'd better get ready. You're skiing tomorrow, and no excuses.'

Right. Damn. The smile fell off my face, like an icicle falling off the eaves of a roof. I realized I'd discovered the problem with skiing holidays, for me, at least. You had to ski.

19

Rachel

The best thing about skiing is the freedom of it. I can go fast, but it doesn't matter if I'm not the fastest. It's not a competition. I owe it nothing except the exhilaration of the experience.

I felt really miserable when the plane landed at Verona airport, even though I was looking forward to seeing Mum. It *is* lovely to see her, but however familiar her face still is to me, she's a stranger too. I didn't want to be sitting on a coach with her as she eyed up all the men; she's lucky to have a man already, I thought, what does she need to look at other men for? For a moment I felt resentful: I wanted to be going on holiday with *Mark*, not my mum and a bunch of people I've never met, and am not sure that I ever want to meet . . .

Mark and I talked about going away somewhere together. We were thinking of Northern Spain, or perhaps a mountainous Greek island. Somewhere rural and hot, without a tennis court; perhaps just ping pong or boules, or something else to quench Mark's insatiable thirst for competition. I would have let him make love to me, all night if he wanted. Even if we didn't make love, just to be in a bed cuddled up next to him till morning would have been so amazing. We hardly spent any whole nights together – Dad always quizzed me so relentlessly about where I was if I was out all night, and he saw Kerry every day on court, so I couldn't use her as an alibi more than once or twice. Plus I think Mark found it difficult to be in bed with me without doing anything.

It still makes me so bloody angry that I let Dad dictate the terms of my love life. I suppose because he runs everything else in my life, at the time it didn't seem all that weird that he had a say in whom I went out with too . . . Never again, though. If I ever manage to get another boyfriend, I don't care what Dad says, I'm doing it my way.

Mum and I are sharing a room. How weird is that? The beds are low and hard, with synthetic orange blankets tucked in too tightly, and the room so dimly lit that it will be difficult to read after dark. It's also stifling hot, until you swing open the window and then of course it's arctic.

'Have we ever shared a bedroom before?' I ask her when we are settling in after that initial run down the mountain. I'm standing in my thermals, having taken off my boarding pants and jacket, and draped my wet ski gloves on the heavy old radiator. Mum is fussing around, unpacking a vast cosmetic case on to the dressing table. Honestly, sometimes I feel like she's the teenager and I'm the mother: I only brought one eyeshadow and a lipstick and some Vaseline, and she's got enough crap in that vanity case of hers to turn the Statue of Liberty into a drag queen. The case opens out into several stepped layers, and each layer seems to be overflowing with little pots and tubes and pencils.

She laughs, in a tired sort of way. 'Have we? Let me think . . . not since you were a baby. It'll be fun! I bags this bed.' She presses down on the mattress of the bed nearest her, and it yields soggily. 'It was when we came back to England,' she continues. 'We stayed at Gordana's for a couple of years while Ivan was on tour. She was great with you: taking you out for walks in the pram, and down to the tennis club to show you off

to her friends. I don't know what I'd have done without her.'

That's right; I remember from before that Mum
always refers solely to Gordana, as if poor old Pops
doesn't even exist. Strictly speaking, it's *Pops's* house,
not Gordana's – he's the one who earned the money to
buy it and maintain it. But Mum has always adored
Gordana. In inverse proportion to the way she feels
about Ivan.

'I'm so looking forward to catching up with
Gordana. I've got so much to tell her,' she says, a bit
too wistfully, in my opinion. I wonder what she has to
tell Gordana that she can't tell me. But I suppose
Gordana's like that. She's just the best person to tell
your problems to – everyone does it. Except perhaps
Ivan, who, ironically, is the only one whose problems
she really *wants* to hear. She's the tennis club's agony
aunt, the Problem Guru. I feel a surge of love for her,
and pride that in our fractured little family Gordana is
the constant, the hub of a rather wonky wheel.

'What's this for?' I ask curiously, picking up a little
triangular wedge of sponge. 'Do you seriously need all
this junk?'

'It's all right for you, Rachel, you're young and
beautiful and you don't need any help. But you wait
till you get to my age, and *then* you'll see how vital it
all is,' she says gloomily.

'But Mum, you're only forty-four, and you look
great. I've got more wrinkles than you have!' I go over
to the mirror and screw up my face, fracturing the skin
around my eyes into dozens of fissures. Sighing, I flop
down on the bed instead.

'You certainly don't. Besides, any lack of wrinkles
on my face is due to Botox, not nature.' She instantly
blushes and looks horrified, as if she's momentarily
forgotten to whom she is speaking.

'*Mum!* You don't inject that poison into your face,
do you? I don't believe it!' I am far more horrified than

155

she is. I've always known she was vain, but because I also know how critical Ivan was, somehow I've never blamed her for it before. But she's with Billy now. 'Does Billy know?'

I can't get my head around Mum getting Botox. She surely couldn't do it for Billy's benefit – Billy is such a space cadet, he wouldn't notice if his fiancée grew a full beard.

Mum turns away and begins to remove immaculately folded thermal vests from her suitcase, placing them in neat piles in the top of the three drawers underneath the television. When she speaks, it sounds as if her throat is constricted.

'No. He doesn't. I didn't do it for him; I did it for me. It's no different to spending a fortune on facials and useless creams – except it works.'

'Can you even *get* Botox in Lawrence, Kansas?' I am curious. Lawrence, from what I remember of the time I visited it, is terrific if you're after a dreamcatcher, a tie-dye T-shirt, or any amount of paraphernalia featuring a stupid-looking blue bird, mascot of the Jayhawks football team (or basketball, or perhaps both); but I wouldn't think it would be bursting with beauty salons offering high-tech non-cosmetic surgery.

'Actually, I go to a little place in Kansas City,' she says, still not looking at me. 'Could we please drop it. I'm sorry I mentioned it.'

'Of course,' I say, clasping my hands behind my head and staring at the varnished wooden strips on the ceiling. I feel suddenly awkward. I don't know my mother at all.

20

Gordana

I am not accustomed to misfortune, and I am *never* unwell. I have always been attributing my good health to six, not five, portions of vegetable and fruits every day; regular tennis; frequent relations with my Ted – whether he likes it or not; a little echinacea when my nose tickles with the start of a cold; a lot of vitamin E for my skin. Although my face gets more papery all the time – I think I fight a losing battle there.

I have dabbled with other options in my attempts to retain relative youth and beauty, but haven't yet found anything which works as well for me. Elsie say that selenium is very good for decreased wrinkles and increased brain power, but I don't like it; it gives me taste of scaffolding poles in my mouth. And too much vitamin C makes me need the lavatory too often.

Anyway, I am healthy in mind and body, thank the Lord.

So I did not like to be sitting on that thin bed with my gown open like a flasher, even though the surgeon was a very beautiful man with brown skin and huge brown eyes and the gentlest hands. His name sounded like the word Rachel used for 'biscuit' when she was a toddler: *babish*. I decided to call him Mr Babish. It would not have been proper to look at his eyes while he touched me though, so I looked at a damp spot on the ceiling and hoped that my nipples were not getting hard from his touch. I was seeing him privately, of course, although it was a rather odd, crumbly local hospital where he held this breast surgery. I didn't think it would matter, just for the check-up, although I would rather not see damp spots on the ceiling when he was a private doctor and Ted would get a huge bill to pass to the BUPA. But never mind.

He asked me to put my hands behind my head like I was lying upright on a sunlounger, and it made me feel like some kind of old porn star. Ted is the only man who ever touched my breasts before. I don't think that Ivan's father ever did. *He* was only interested in getting to the main action area, and anyway in those days underwear was so awkward to negotiate.

I wonder what he is doing now, that useless spotty Paul Tyler. He joined the Navy, even though he knew I was pregnant when he left. I used to dread him turning up one day, knocking on the door and saying, 'Hello, son' to my baby; but I don't worry about that any more. Ivan always said he would punch him in the face if he ever met him, and I worry more about Ivan doing that and Paul Tyler telling the police and the police arresting Ivan. Then Elsie would have been right, and that would be most annoying.

'Ye-es,' said Mr Babish thoughtfully, rolling his fingers over the lump. It tickled. I felt a little embarrassed about my droopy old breasts, although he must see them all sizes and shapes. 'It's bigger than a pea or a bean, isn't it? It's more . . . oh, I don't know, cylindrical. Like a column.'

Doric or Ionic? I wondered, remembering the documentary Ted and I watched about classical architecture.

'A sub-cutaneous column,' he clarified, as if I'd spoken out loud. 'Thank you, Mrs Anderson.' Mr Babish drew out his hands. 'You can do up your gown now. I'll call the radiologist and we'll just pop you next door for a scan, check it out a bit further.'

Why do medical people always use the word 'pop'? The nurse kept saying it too: 'Pop your top off'; 'Pop up on the bed for me;' 'Pop your things in here'. I still think that English is very strange language.

'I'm sure it is nothing,' I said. 'I know I have lumpy breasts. A doctor told me that when my son was born.' I'd never forgotten that, actually. I did not wish to have lumpy breasts. It make me feel like the mattress on the spare bed.

'You did the right thing, getting it checked out,' said Mr Babish kindly.

I could hear hail against the window, and when I looked outside, it was half snowing, half hailing; they were neither flakes nor stones, too heavy for one and too light for the other. They sort of floated down past the window like they were unsure of where they should be going. Oh well. At least it was probably too cold to play tennis, which was where I'd told Ted I was off to; my usual Wednesday session with the girls. I wondered if they were being hardy this morning, wrapping up against the weather, playing in layers of scarves and hats and jackets, or whether they'd abandoned the idea and gone to drink big hot chocolates in the coffee shop round the corner. I imagined them in there: Esther, Liz and Lorraine, grumbling and laughing and gossiping. Maybe wondering where I am.

The same nurse came back and ushered me out to the waiting room, where some anxious-looking couples were sitting holding hands. So young, they were. I hoped they would all be OK. They looked so vulnerable. They all glanced up at me, and then quickly away. I wished Ted were with me. No. That's not true. I didn't wish that. I don't want Ted to be worried. He worry so much about everything else. I picked up an old tatty copy of *Good Housekeeping* and flicked through it without stopping at any of the pages.

'Shouldn't be long, Mrs Anderson,' said the nurse, who was a few years younger than me, probably, but with a lot more wrinkles and a very big double chin. Selenium would be good for her wrinkles, but she couldn't do much about that chin. 'We've just paged the radiologist – he ought to be here by now. Maybe he's been held up by the weather.'

There were no windows in this waiting room, but from what I'd seen out of the window in the examining room, the snowy hail – *snail*, I will call it – did not look as if it could hold anyone up.

'Oop!' the nurse said cheerfully. 'Here he is now.' All eyes in the waiting room swivelled away from me and towards a small, stooped Indian man, who nodded briefly at the nurse and hurry-hurried past us and out through another door.

Five minutes later I was lying on a different paper-covered bed, next to an ultrasound machine. The nurse was standing next to me looking very sympathetic – I suppose that was the face that she put on just in case. I wished she'd go away.

Mr Babish and the radiologist came back in again, and the door slammed loudly. I jumped, and was cross with myself for doing so.

'Sorry,' they both said. 'It always does that.'

The nurse squirted jelly on to my bosom, and the radiologist moved the scanner across it. A kaleidoscope of wavy grey tissue flickered across the monitor by the side of the bed. The nurse left the room and the door banged again. I jumped again, and the lines on the screen wiggled and dipped.

The inside of my breast looked like the surface of the moon. I couldn't see anything sinister or black, and waited for them to diagnose the column as a bad case of mattress-breast. Both men stared intently at the screen for a long time, as if they were concentrating on one of those 3-D pictures where another image is underneath the patterns. Eventually I realized what they were looking at: a series of small dark disc-shaped patches, denser than the rest of the fluid patterns.

'I'm not happy about that,' said Mr B 'We'll do a mammogram.'

I sighed. Still, it was all paid for. Better safer than sorrier. I was still not nervous, even then. Not even when the nurse came back (door banging once more) and ushered me next door to the X-ray machine. 'Good girl,' she kept saying as she squished my breast between two sheets of glass then compressed it to about one inch thick. It was uncomfortable but not painful. My poor old bosoms are so floppy these days that she could probably have rolled them up and stuffed them into an empty toilet roll if she had so wished. I tried to take my mind off it by thinking about Rachel and Susie on their girly holiday. I hoped they were having some fun. Rachel needs some fun. But the nurse was still annoying me.

'Please,' I said. 'You are younger than me, surely. I don't think I can really be called a girl any more.' Not by you, anyway, I thought.

The nurse looked surprised. 'I beg your pardon,' she said. I nodded, trying to look dignified – which was hard, bearing in mind I was standing there with one breast in exact dimensions of British Rail sandwich.

She left me alone again, taking the X-rays away for Mr Babish to examine. I dangled my legs over the side of the bed and thought perhaps I ought to say a small prayer. Although it might be too late for that now. So I said a prayer for Ted instead, that he would not become a widower and have all the women at the tennis club suddenly taking up golf and bringing him things in Pyrex dishes, even though we'd have a full-time housekeeper by then, not just that lazy Adele. I wondered if I should make sure she was not an attractive housekeeper, and then I thought: How selfish. I want Ted to be happy after I'm gone . . . Perhaps just not straight away after, though.

Mr Babish returned and smiled at me, such a warm, lovely smile. I glanced at his finger to see if he wore a wedding ring. He did, and I was relieved. I didn't want anybody except my Ted, but still . . . This man had just fondled my breasts, even if it was only in a professional capacity.

'Well,' he said. 'There's nothing showing up that's obviously cancerous, but I'm still concerned about that ultrasound. We'll just do a biopsy to give us a clearer idea.'

Now I wished Ted was here.

'How soon do I get the results of that?' I asked in a small voice.

'I will telephone you on Friday afternoon, hopefully,' he replied. 'Otherwise it will have to wait until Monday morning.'

Monday morning! That was five days away. I couldn't wait that long. I began to feel a little sick.

The biopsy was not pleasant, not at all. It was the sort of needle I imagine zoo-keepers using on their rhinoceroses, and even though my breast had already been injected with some anaesthetic, I felt invaded. The big needle's entry into my flesh hammered at me like a staple gun, and Mr Babish did it four times; the medical equivalent to pin the tail on the donkey, guiding it into the dark marbles of concern by watching on the ultrasound monitor.

I didn't even object when the big nurse held my hand and said, 'Good g— er, I mean, well done.'

'I haven't done anything,' I said, feeling a little sulky at these violations of my flesh.

'All finished,' said Mr Babish eventually, and the radiologist switched off the ultrasound. 'Did anyone come with you, Mrs Anderson?'

'No,' I replied, wiping the jelly off my chest with a wad of paper towels and refastening my robe. 'I drove myself. I will be fine.'

'Feel free to stay as long as you like, until you're sure you're fit to drive back again,' he said, concern in those melting doggy eyes. 'You may feel rather sore later.'

'Thank you,' I repeated. 'I am fine.'

I repeated those words again, over and over, all the way home. All that day and the day after and the Friday morning when I was waiting for Mr Babish to call, and the Friday afternoon when he did call, right in the middle of the Radio Four play. I felt cross that he rang just when it got to the important bit, when I was about to find out why the moody Frenchman called Marcel was so obsessed by a woman's necklace breaking in the Tate Gallery. Now I would never know, I thought as I picked up the phone.

Mr Babish announced himself by his real name, and it took me a moment to think who he was. I thought maybe he was someone calling to sell me some replacement windows. Then I remembered: Oh, Mr Babish. My lump.

When he told me that unfortunately it was cancerous, and I ought to begin treatment immediately, he would be able to schedule me in for a mastectomy in a couple of weeks' time, all I thought was: Oh, and I so wondered why that woman's necklace meant so much to Marcel. Then I went back to my silent chant because I couldn't think of what else to do: I am fine. I will be fine. I am fine. It will be fine.

'It will be fine, my darling,' I say to Ted, later that night. We are lying in our big bed, me with my three fat pillows to prop me up, him with his two smaller ones. We have our little bedtime routine: he makes hot chocolate, and then we read together for a while. He reads the sports section of the day's newspaper, and I read a novel. But tonight I cannot read, even though my reading glasses are on their chain round my neck and the book is open, on my knees. I don't know what page I am on any more.

I tell Ted. The newspaper rustles and falls from his hands, and grey skin grows on the mugs of hot chocolate that neither of us are drinking today.

'I will be fine. They catch it early, it's fine. Don't worry,' I say, laying my hand over his. 'In two weeks, he says, I will have the little op. Then some treatment. Then, we hope and pray, all will be OK again.'

He still doesn't say anything, just rolls his creaky old body towards me and gives me a big long hug. For some reason I think of that advertisement on the television, for a mattress, with a big hippo in blue stripy pyjamas on one side of the bed, and a teeny little yellow bird on the other. They were an odd couple, like us, but in bed together, happy.

'You make me happy, Ted,' I say, putting my reading glasses on top of my head like sunglasses, so he can't break them. 'I won't leave you, so don't you worry. You are stuck with me.'

I am not surprised he isn't asking questions. Ted likes to let things sink in first. We turn off the light and lie in spoon shapes to go to sleep, his big body solid behind me. But later, in the dark stillness of the night, I wake up again to find his back to me, his shoulders shaking with silent crying.

'Let's not tell Ivan and Rachel just yet,' I say, like we are carrying on the conversation from before. 'Perhaps not even until after operation. I don't want to worry them.'

Ted takes his handkerchief out of his pyjama pocket and blows his nose, still turned away from me. 'What about Susie? She wanted to come and stay when they get back from the skiing holiday. Do we tell her not to come?' His voice is stuffy and dark.

'No,' I say. 'I want things to be normal. I want to see her. Perhaps I will tell her, perhaps not. We will see.

It's good that she will be here, it will be nice for Rachel to have her close by. I don't know how long she wants to stay. I suppose if she stay a long time, then we have to tell her.'

We lie awake, I think, for the rest of the night, holding hands, not talking any more.

21

Susie

The weather was much worse the next day, with the mountains suffocating under thick grey cloud and relentlessly falling snow. It had been beautiful to see at first, the way it iced the tree branches and thickly frosted the bushes, but there was something almost sinister about the way it wouldn't stop. And it was a bone-chilling wet kind of cold, not like Kansas. Kansas was undeniably freezing in winter, but it was a different sort of cold; one that, to my disappointment, I could handle much better than this. I'd imagined it would be the other way round.

'Well, looks like we won't be skiing today!' I said cheerfully at breakfast over my dry roll and what appeared to be luncheon meat.

Our vacuous tour operator, whose name was Nadia, was sitting several places away on the long table. She looked up from the lone apple she'd been peeling and cutting into eighths, and laughed. 'Of course you will! If the lifts are open, which I'm told they are, you'll be fine to ski!'

That wasn't what I wanted to hear. I scowled at Nadia. Actually, Rachel and I had been discussing her, with much hilarity, the previous night in the bar after dinner. She was a beautiful English-rose-type girl, but so boring in her beauty that none of the men were even half-heartedly trying to chat her up. She was tiny;

anorexic, probably, with delicate little cheekbones and the sort of wrists you could snap in two. She had an unfortunately drony voice and a penchant for word misuse, which Rachel had pounced on instantly. At dinner, she'd stood up and made a speech about the resort, during the course of which she explained the procedure in case anyone were to 'ascertain' an injury, and how, on the slopes, it was best not to 'dilly' once the light began to fail, as it had that day. Rachel and I had had to smother our giggles. Laughing with my daughter had been the best feeling (albeit at poor old Nadia's expense, but still . . .)

I wondered why I hadn't thought of taking a holiday with Rachel before. I supposed it had just always seemed so difficult, with her tournament schedule and Ivan breathing down her neck. Perhaps Mark dumping her was a blessing for my relationship with her.

An hour later, blinking our way through the thick snow, Rachel helped me negotiate the chair lift ('Turn round! Look behind! Poles in that hand, grab it with that hand! Sit!' I felt like a dog being trained) and we were swinging our legs in the wet, cold seat of an open chair, on our way up the mountain. Everything was eerily silent, and we could only just make out the jackets of the people in the seat in front of us. Apart from the two splashes of colour of their ski jackets, the world was monochrome. You couldn't tell where sky ended and slope began.

'Is this really safe?' I asked, trying to sound brave although I felt petrified. My backside was soaked through and it was so cold that my lips would barely form any words. I wished I was tucked up in a warm bed with a good book.

'Well, it's not ideal, but it's not dangerous,' Rachel replied. 'Just follow me. I'll go really slowly, and we'll be fine.'

'You seem happier today,' I ventured, fiddling with

my jacket to try and cover a gap of bare skin on my wrist between sleeve and glove. It nearly caused me to drop one of my ski poles – I had to lunge for it, making the chair sway back and forwards.

'Mum! Be careful,' Rachel said, and I thought, was she always this bossy? I had that strange role-reversal feeling again. 'But yes, I am feeling better. A bit. I wish I was here with Mark—'

'Thanks very much,' I said, trying to joke but wishing that *I* were there with Billy.

She tutted, although whether in an amused or irritated way, I couldn't tell.

'Anyway, I think it's really good for me to have a holiday, a break from tournaments. I'm going to be really busy again in the next couple of months, and I know that's getting away too, but somehow I can never *escape* on tour. It's Mark's world too, that's why. I can't help seeing everything through his eyes – including Dad – and it does my head in.'

It's Mark's world and we all just live in it, I thought. I wasn't sure that I liked the sound of this Mark. He ought to have been living in Rachel's world, not the other way round. I pictured both their worlds: the endless flights, the endless matches, the endless debriefs and recriminations or congratulations.

Then I thought of Billy's world. Before Eva, his world had been big enough with just me at the centre of it: me, his pot, his garage, the cats. Then Eva had come along and casually plucked him off Planet Billy into a different galaxy, far, far away . . . How could she do that? She must have known that he belonged to me. But there must have been whole other continents of Planet Billy which I hadn't even known about, and ought to have done. Perhaps those uncharted territories held the key to Billy's dissatisfaction – for he must have been dissatisfied, otherwise nobody, not even Pamela Anderson (for whom Billy, to my disgust, had an embarrassingly soft spot) could have tempted him away. I remembered Audrey once saying, 'No one can break up a happy relationship.' I didn't want to acknowledge the truth of this, because to do so seemed to undermine our whole lives together.

I tried hard to think of other ways in which Billy might have perceived our relationship as unhappy, aside from my unwillingness to marry him. Not spending enough time together? We saw each other every day. Not enough sex? True, the frequency of our love-making had decreased quite a bit, but our sex life was still passionate, and far from dead. Drifted apart? Maybe. I supposed I'd been pretty obsessed with my job – but then again, so had he with his. We had, at various stages, talked about taking up more hobbies together, but neither of us had really pushed it. Or at least I hadn't, and Billy hadn't seemed to mind . . .

It must have been deeper than that. But if he didn't talk to me about it, how was I to know? I just kept going over it in my head, again and again, getting nowhere. It was easier to blame Eva. I hoped she couldn't sleep at night.

The thought gave me scant consolation, though. It only made me imagine that it was Billy keeping her up, not her conscience; Billy, doing that little trick of his with his hash-furred tongue which always made me scream and sent the cats shooting off the eider-down in panic . . . It seemed like a lifetime ago. I wondered if I'd ever sleep with him again.

'Do you think Mark met someone else?' I asked abruptly, through chattering teeth.

Rachel turned and looked at me indignantly. I remembered that expression of hers from when she was a little girl being told off: all frowny outrage and cross incredulity.

'No! I'm sure he hadn't . . . Maybe he has now though.' She slumped down in the chair, her skis swinging disconsolately, then straightened up again. 'Here we go. Are you ready?'

The top of the lift station loomed, a huge net spread out beneath it to stop the incompetent or premature skiers from alighting too soon. I gripped my poles as hard as I could and gritted my teeth as Rachel lifted the bar pinning us into the chair.

'Ready, steady . . . *now*,' she said, pushing herself off the seat and sliding gracefully down the small slope away from the lift. I tried to follow, but in my panic my skis crossed and the edge of the seat bumped into my backside, and I fell in an undignified tangle of poles, legs and skis at Rachel's feet. She helped me up, laughing, and I felt clumsy and embarrassed. She was my daughter, for heaven's sake, why should I feel so awkward in her presence?

Not for the first time, I questioned the wisdom of my having moved so far away when Ivan and I split up. At the time, I'd thought that they were so wrapped up in training and competition that she wouldn't have noticed if I'd moved to Mars, but perhaps I was wrong. I should've dug in my heels and waited in the wings for the time when I could become the pressure valve in her relationship with Ivan the Bully. Now was that time – but was it too late? How could I help her when I felt, at times, almost in awe of her?

I sometimes felt I had run away when I moved back to Kansas after the divorce. It had seemed the logical place to go: somewhere I still had friends, where I understood the life and enjoyed the laid-back social scene. Somewhere that I had some history, even just a year as an exchange student. But blood was thicker than watery American beer. I should have stayed in England.

If I'd stayed in England, Billy and I would never have got together. But perhaps, in hindsight, that would have been for the best. At least I wouldn't have gone through all this pain . . .

I brushed the wet, sticky snow off my body and tried to de-mist my ski mask, which had become dislodged.

Every time I tried to replace it, it steamed up again. I couldn't see a thing – not that there was much to see.

'Come on, Mum, I'm freezing,' Rachel said, in that impatient voice again. I peered at her through my misty goggles: tall, glamorous without a scrap of make-up, just a thick layer of Chapstick, and I envied her. I envied her youth and beauty and confidence. I envied the fact that, even though she couldn't see it yet, her broken heart would heal whole, and she'd love again, better. I envied her success and the independence I'd so selfishly bestowed upon her. My daughter the stranger.

After an interminable amount of fiddling, frozen-fingered, with my mask, I was eventually as ready as I'd ever be. The run down was narrow, but not too steep, as it wound around the side of the mountain. At least there were hardly any other skiers around, due to a combination of the unfashionable resort and the inclement weather.

'Let's go!' said Rachel jubilantly, and pushed herself off, skiing exaggeratedly slowly to enable me to keep up.

I followed, wobbly at first, then more strongly. I didn't have the hang of that pole-planting thing – I couldn't work out which side which pole went down – but it didn't seem to matter. I glued my eyes to Rachel's back, trying to emulate her rhythm and pace, keeping my moves as small as possible to ensure I didn't lose control and shoot off over the edge of the run.

It had stopped snowing, but visibility was still almost zero as we continued our slow progress down the mountain. My breathing was shallow and my heart thumping practically out of my Tweedledum salopettes, but I remained vertical, and this alone gave me the beginnings of jubilation. Rachel kept glancing back to make sure I was still following, and yelling encouragement through the thick silent air at me. I felt like a five-year-old.

No, that wasn't true, I thought, chastened, as a small group of pre-schoolers shot past me and out of sight, with their ski instructor bringing up the rear like a mother goose accompanying a very expeditious brood of goslings. I *wished* I felt like a five-year-old. Then I'd be able to ski without fear.

The piste steepened then, but became mercifully wider. I felt myself involuntarily accelerate, and tried to snowplough. Nothing happened. I tried harder, forcing my heels out till my knees knocked. It didn't seem to be having any impact on my speed at all. From behind me, I heard the heavy thwack and rumble of an approaching snowboarder, and I panicked slightly as I realized I couldn't stop. The boarder was getting closer, but hadn't yet passed me.

Then I made the fatal mistake of turning my head to try and see him. My balance, already shaky, was lost entirely, and my skis slid away from underneath me, as if the snow were a tablecloth someone had yanked off a fully lain table.

I heard myself shriek as top seemed to become bottom – although it was hard to tell, in that mono-chrome world – and I fell. But the thing which frightened me most was the panicked roar of the snowboarder, who was almost literally on top of me by then. I waited for the crash, the pain, the tangling and then untangling of limbs and equipment – I *heard* it, but I didn't feel a thing except the skid of freezing snow into my mouth and up my nose. How could I have heard it but not felt it?

When I sat up and shakily rubbed the snow off my goggles, I saw why. The snowboarder hadn't crashed into me. He'd swerved to avoid me, and had run straight into Rachel instead, who had stopped when she heard my cry. At first I couldn't even make out which person was which, as both went rolling and tumbling down the slope and out of sight in the fog.

'Rach?' I called in a quavery, thin voice which

didn't sound at all like my own. 'Rachel? Are you OK?'

Silence. I staggered to my feet, my ski-less boots sinking into the soft snow, and looked all around me, but all I saw was whiteness.

'Hello?' I shouted, as loudly as I could. 'Rachel!' I waited for a minute, thinking that she would be gathering up her skis and reorienting herself. One of my own skis was lying nearby, but the other one had slid away down the slope and out of sight. There was nobody around. I felt that I was the only person in the world; that Rachel and the snowboarder had simply dropped off the face of the earth. Panic rose in me, a kind of damp warmth in the cold air. 'RACHEL!'

I heard a grunt, downhill a way and to my right. I headed towards it, not stopping to collect my one visible ski, or thinking how on earth I would manage to get the rest of the way down the mountain ski-less, alternately wading and skidding through the deep snow. 'Hello, hello, do you need help? Rach, is that you?'

About ten feet in front of me, a figure finally hovered into sight. But it wasn't Rachel, it was the snowboarder. He was tall and broad, but young, a dazed, spotty teenager. His fringe was in his eyes, and his board was attached to one foot.

'Are you hurt?' I asked at the same moment I spotted blood oozing from a wound on his temple, splashing scarlet into the snow.

'Only this, I think,' he replied, in a heavily-accented Italian voice, touching his head lightly and getting blood on his glove. He looked pale and shocked. I delved into my jacket pocket and found a pack of tissues, which I handed to him.

'Did you see where my daughter went?'

He shook his head. I was beginning to get very worried indeed. I kept staring through the white, straining my eyes to see a figure climbing slowly back towards us; but there was nothing.

From behind, we both heard the sound of two more skiers approaching, and I waved my arms and yelled at them to stop. They were obviously a couple, in matching ski gear, middle-aged and proficient, and they swept to identically elegant parallel halts.

'Do you speak English?' I asked; but they shook their heads.

'Only very small,' said the woman.

The snowboarder said something in Italian, and they began nodding vigorously, expressions of concern on their tanned, lined faces. They looked so alike, as some couples do. Even in the middle of my anxiety, I wondered if Billy and I would ever have grown to resemble one another.

The boarder turned back to me. 'I have asked them for to see if your daughter she is . . . down,' he said, jabbing his thumb downhill. I didn't know if he meant 'down' as in fallen, or just 'further down', but I nodded too.

The couple skied off slowly, and I waited. I wasn't aware that I was holding my breath until the shout came, and then I let it out with a big gasp.

'Come,' said the boy, holding his hand out to me. 'They are not far down.' Together we edged sideways down the slope. It was such hard work, and I was so desperate to reach Rachel, that I felt like flinging myself on to my belly and body-surfing down. But he held my hand, even though he was still dabbing at the wound on his head, and in a couple of minutes we made out the shapes of the two skiers in their matching red jackets. The man was removing his jacket and placing it over Rachel's body. She lay face down, motionless in the snow.

My heart nearly stopped, and I cried out, the cry I should have cried when Billy left me; the cry I had been holding in for weeks now, keeping it trapped inside me, begging to be let out. I cried out so loudly that we were lucky I didn't trigger an avalanche.

Skidding the last few feet, I hurled myself into the snow next to Rachel, cradling her head to me, ripping off my glove and desperately trying to find a pulse with my cold fingers against her colder neck. One arm was twisted behind her back, as if the mountain had captured her and was getting ready to frogmarch her away somewhere; and her left leg was bent at an unnatural angle. Her trousers had somehow got torn all the way up one shin. Irrationally, I thought: what a shame, she loved those pants. At first, I couldn't feel a pulse. I had no idea what to do.

'Help,' I said, looking up at the three horrified spectators, tears flowing down my face in warm tracks of desperation. 'Get help, please, now.'

The snowboarder jabbered something, and the Italian couple hastily conferred. Then the man skied off without another word, flying away down the mountain, leaving his jacket under Rachel's head. The woman planted a little stockade of upright skis in a circle around Rachel, enclosing her.

I prayed then, to the God I knew I loved but didn't communicate with nearly enough. I prayed that he loved Rachel as much as I did, that there was nothing seriously wrong. That she'd get up in a minute, and be fine . . .

22

Rachel

My legs won't move.

Shit. I'm so dizzy, and my mouth is dry. It's that Natasha. She must have lobbed me and I fell over when I was running back to get it. That's it. She hates me. It's written all over her face. I can't understand why she hates me so much, I've never done anything to her. I've never even met her before – or have I? Oh Lord, I threw up, didn't I? With Eurosport filming it and everything. I wonder if they showed it on TV in England, if Mark saw it. He'll be here soon, at least. Kerry will have rung him and told him to come to me. This must be a Swiss hospital. It's dark and quiet, maybe it's night-time. Why do I feel paralysed if it's only a tummy bug? I've never been in hospital before. I don't like it, it smells funny and it's too quiet. But I've been feeling sick all day. I'm never drinking alcohol before a tournament again, no matter how much Kerry tries to persuade me ... Maybe I didn't throw up on court. Maybe that was later. I can't remember. No, I know – I was sick in the locker-room loo.

Oh. There's something on one of my legs. It feels smooth and cool, but aches inside, as if everything in there is liquid. My knee feels like a mint humbug. I wonder if I can play like this?

No, Rachel, you moron. Of course you can't play. There must be some kind of mistake. I can't really have broken my leg, surely I'd have remembered that when I was puking in the locker room? Perhaps there's been a mix-up at the hospital, like when babies get sent home with the wrong parents. They put my leg in this wrapped-up thing when they should be giving me antibiotics for my stomach bug . . .

But if it's a mistake, or a tummy bug, then why does it hurt so much? Where's Mark? Where's Kerry? I don't want to see Dad but I can't for the life of me think why, not right now. I feel too sleepy. I really need a drink of water.

There's a strange kind of noise somewhere around here. I wish it would stop. It sounds like someone mowing the grass, although it can't really be that. It's dark. No one cuts grass at night.

The noise is getting louder. It doesn't sound like a lawnmower any more, it sounds like a sort of creaky mooing.

I try to sit up, but I can't move. There's pain shooting up my leg. The mooing gets louder and louder, it's really annoying . . .

Someone is talking to me, her face looming into mine, but I don't recognize the words.

'I don't speak German,' I say. 'Water?'

The face is lined, and wearing a silly hat. The umpire?

'When's my next match? I think it's tomorrow. I'll be better by then, won't I?'

The umpire just smiles at me and pats my free hand. Her face vanishes and is replaced by another one.

'Rachel, darling,' says the other one, slowly and clearly. She looks like my mother, but it can't be. 'You are in hospital.' She snakes an arm around my shoulders, and lifts me up enough to take some sips of water from the plastic cup she's holding. Her hands are small, brown and veiny, like she spends too long in the sun. Maybe she is an umpire too.

'I know,' I reply, allowing myself to be lowered back against the pillows. 'In Zurich.'

'No,' says the one who looks like Mum. She even has a faint American accent like Mum. 'In Italy. You had an accident on the mountain.'

The mountain? I tut. Really, the administration in this hospital is appalling. They have all their patients' notes mixed up.

'I wasn't on a mountain. I puked after a match. They said it was a tummy bug. I have to be out of here by tomorrow. I think I won, so I'm in the next round.'

The face frowns, and tilts on one side. I frown too. Perhaps I didn't win. Or was it the next one I lost? Wait . . . Did I fall? Someone fell.

'I'm confused,' I say, in a small voice. 'I want Mark.'

'Try to sleep now, darling. It's just the painkillers which make you feel confused. Don't worry. It's going to be fine.'

I am gently pushed down again and, I have to admit, it feels more comfortable. I am getting really sleepy again, and trying to figure everything out is making my head hurt as well.

Must conserve my strength for the next round. I could win this tournament, I know I could. That's all I need; one big win. Get my ranking up inside the top 250. I could do it . . . I could be the outsider. It just takes time . . . I'm getting there . . . One foot in front of the other . . . Keep practising . . . keep hitting . . . keep your eye on the ball, Rachel . . .

23

Susie

It was the emotional equivalent of being freezing cold, too cold to form words. That was how my heart felt. I don't remember how long I knelt in the snow by my unconscious daughter, but it was ages before I even realized that my salopettes and thermals were soaked through. Mountain rescue arrived, a flurry of men in red jackets, and after they'd examined Rachel and put a neck brace on her, they moved her on to something which looked like a sleeping bag with a tent around her head, and I watched her being dragged away down the mountain on ropes, pulled by one skier. Then I was whisked away too, on the alpine equivalent of a jet-ski, but my eyes were shut tight and my arms wrapped around one of the red-jacketed men.

They let me go in the ambulance with her, and, mercifully, she had by then regained consciousness. She had done something to her knee: they cut her trousers off and we watched it swell out before our eyes, like a loaf rising; and she had concussion from hitting her head on something as she went down, probably the edge of the Italian boy's snowboard. I thought her arm would be hurt too, after seeing it twisted like that, but they said it didn't seem to be.

They gave her something for the pain, but she was moaning and muttering, something about not wanting a stretcher, asking where Kerry and Ivan were, and saying that Mark would ring her soon, now the match was finished. I remembered her being sick after that win in Zurich, when she was on the phone to me. She must have got confused and thought that she was still in Switzerland. Still, I thought it was better for her not to really know what was going on, not yet. I couldn't bear to think about it myself either. Nor about what Ivan was going to say . . .

The hospital was thirty miles away. I stayed with her, or hovered outside thick flappy double doors, while they X-rayed and CAT-scanned her. She was so woozy from concussion and painkillers that she was barely aware of what was going on, so the surgeon came out and showed me the X-ray of her knee. It was just the way you always see in hospital dramas on TV: the delicate fingers pushing the black film against the light box, the purple ghostly image of shattered bone lit up, the earnest explanations.

'It is a significant fracture of the tibial plateau,' said the surgeon, in precise but heavily accented English. He had a hank of black hair flopping across his left eye which gave him a far more youthful appearance than his baggy face suggested.

'What does that mean?' I asked anxiously. For a moment I wondered if he was misusing the word 'significant', and what he actually meant was something else, something like 'minor'. But then he said, 'I am going to operate on it tomorrow. It will take three hours. I must screw in a metal plate, and make a bone graft from your daughter's hip, to help repair the bone. See here, underneath the kneecap, where it is all smashed. I must put in new bone, how you say it? Mashed up, to fill in the gaps.'

I felt sick. I'd somehow thought that even if it was broken, they could just bung her leg in plaster and tell her to put her feet up for a couple of weeks. This sounded positively Frankensteinian.

'How long before she plays tennis again? She is a professional tennis player.'

He tutted and shook his head. 'Well then, this is not very good. She must not put any weight on the leg for three months. We say usually it takes one year for a full recovery.'

I sank on to a plastic chair and put my head in my hands. One year . . . poor, poor Rachel. Oh God, this was all my fault. Ivan was going to *kill* me.

'They're going to operate tomorrow, my darling,' I said to Rachel some minutes later, once I'd finally been able to gather my composure enough to go back and talk to her. Talking itself was increasingly difficult, as if I was back there in the snow. My legs still felt frozen even though an English-speaking nurse had lent me some dry blue hospital scrubs, which I was now wearing, with just my ski socks and no shoes. (Where had I got changed? And where was my wet ski gear? I had not the faintest idea.) I just kept lightly stroking the hair back from her forehead as her eyelids fluttered open and closed.

Later, the nurses made up a camp bed for me next to Rachel's bed, but I don't think I managed to sleep for more than half an hour. I had to be there if she woke up. I couldn't bear to think of her, confused and in pain and believing that she was alone, so I kept getting out of the bed and stroking her forehead again.

She was so pale, but at least looked peaceful. I had a flashback to when she was a little girl, when I used to check on her before I went to bed myself. She'd never been a peaceful sleeper, though: after even just a couple of hours' sleep, her nightdress would be twisted indecently up around her middle and her duvet would be making minimal contact with the bed, having mostly slithered on to the floor. She was usually squashed up with her nose touching the wall, and a plethora of cushions and soft toys taking over the space in the middle of the mattress that was right-fully hers. It looked weird to see her now, so straight and still like that. At least they had put her knee into a temporary plastercast, just around the back of her leg, so it was immobilized.

'I'm so sorry, Rach,' I kept whispering in her ear, dreading on her behalf the pain and incapacity and misery she still had to come. I felt as if I'd done nothing but apologize to my daughter. And this was the biggest thing yet I had to apologize for.

They operated on her knee the following afternoon. For me, the day passed in a sludgy blur of waiting, drinking bad coffee and having small chats with various medical personnel who spoke English in vary-ing degrees of proficiency. I decided not to ring Ivan and Gordana until after the operation, so at least I could report on her progress (and, if I was honest, not have to call them again to tell them how it had gone. I was dreading making the first call).

Rachel herself was very quiet after she came round. She did at least know that I was there, and what had happened, but she barely said a word other than to ask for more morphine. The rest of the time she just lay there, her leg in a strappy brace with a big dressing over the incision, with an expression of confused dis-belief on her face. I was so tired that I could barely keep my eyes open, but I tried – to no avail – to cheer her up. I couldn't bear to tell her that she wouldn't be walking for three months, let alone playing tennis again any time in the near future.

Later that day, while she was having a nap, a face appeared at the porthole cut into the door of her room. A familiar-looking man was standing there, smiling hesitantly at me. I wondered who the hell it was for a moment, and then remembered: it was the popcorn-eating minibus driver from the hotel. Karl. I left the room to greet him, inexplicably relieved at the sight of him standing there, his van keys dangling from his thumb and a small bunch of cellophane-wrapped flowers tucked under his arm.

'Mountain rescue contacted the hotel. Nadia should have come, but her ski boots have given her a very bad blister. I wondered if there was anything I could do to help. Perhaps you would like a lift? Or I could get you some change of clothes,' he said. 'I am sorry about your daughter. Is she OK?'

'Who's Nadia?' I asked vaguely, wondering why I asked, since I couldn't care less. I was feeling rather dizzy. I must have got up too quickly. Or else it was lack of food – I was starving, but had only managed little snacks here and there since I'd got to the hospital.

'Your holiday rep,' he replied.

Oh yes, I thought, her. Only she could cite a blister as a reason for not carrying out her job. I was so tired that I could hardly bear to speak, but I forced a few words out.

'Rachel's going to be OK. She's got a bad fracture just below her knee, and concussion. She'll be here for a couple of days and then they'll fly her home.'

'And what about you? Are you OK?' He bent his knees and his head a little as he spoke, bobbing down so that he could look into my eyes at the same time. I couldn't reciprocate. There was such compassion in his voice that I was worried I might break down. 'I thought you might like a lift back to the hotel. To get some things perhaps.'

'Well . . . I'm not feeling too great, actually . . . but all the same, I think I can manage. I don't want to leave Rachel. It's very kind of you to offer, though.'

'Not at all. Nadia should be here really,' he said without rancour. 'But I think you should come back with me. You need a rest also, I think.' Alt-zo, he pronounced it.

A passing nurse, the one who'd lent me the scrubs,

183

stopped in the corridor. 'Mrs Anderson, your friend is right. It is important that you have a good night of sleep tonight. You had a shock too. Rachel is still sedated. You can come back tomorrow. I get your ski gear for you.'

I still wanted to tell them both: No, I don't want to go back to that empty twin room, with Rachel's stuff strewn over it, and no Rachel to chat to. I was just beginning to enjoy the experience of sensing her drift off to sleep in the identical bed beside me; my daughter, with me again . . . and now this.

But I felt too jetlagged and exhausted to argue. My skin felt itchy with grime and fatigue. For the first time, I realized what I must look like: yesterday's make-up, my hair untouched by a brush, no lipstick, wearing the unflattering hospital scrubs . . . I wanted a steaming bubble bath, some cleanser, my own clothes, a large alcoholic drink, and a hot meal.

'It's not Mrs Anderson, actually,' I said wearily. The staff had been calling me that since we arrived, but I hadn't had the energy to inform them that I went back to my maiden name after Ivan and I got divorced. 'But OK. I'll go, and come back to the hospital tonight. I need a change of clothes and my washbag. And I have to make a call to Rachel's father.'

Ivan was going to be so, so furious. He'd instantly blame me. But then, I thought, why wouldn't he blame me? It *was* my fault.

I looked through the porthole. Rachel was awake again, lying still, her big brown eyes gazing out at us without curiosity, in a sort of stunned vacancy. I pushed open the door and Karl followed me in.

'Hello, Rachel,' he said softly, proffering the flowers. 'I am sorry about your accident. I brought you these.'

She smiled faintly, looking more normal. 'Thank you.'

'You remember Karl, from the hotel,' I said, taking the flowers and laying them on Rachel's locker. The

184

nurse could put them in water. 'He's kindly offering me a lift back to get some stuff. I won't be long, though, Rach, I'll come back later and—'

'Mum. Come back tomorrow. All I want to do is sleep.'

'Are you sure?'

She nodded. I wanted to object, but I was so exhausted that I wanted to cry. The nurse came back in carrying my ski boots and a green plastic hospital waste bag containing my ski clothes. I thanked her, then turned back to Rachel

'Right then, angel. Ring me if you need anything, you promise? Even if it's a chat in the middle of the night. Anything. I'll keep my mobile on all the time.'

'I'll be fine.'

It began to snow again during the journey back to the hotel. Thick white flakes batted the windscreen and the van tyres slipped on the road, several times. Karl didn't say that he was concerned, but he leaned further forwards on his seat. Several times his hand twitched towards the windscreen as if he wanted to brush the snow away faster than the wipers were, but then remembered it was on the other side of the glass. He seemed much tenser than he had done the other day when he brought me back down the mountain. Although he had the sort of ruddy complexion which never paled, his cheeks looked a little blotchy.

'I will stop and put the chains on, if the snow worsens,' he said in his precise voice.

'Worsens'. That was an odd word. I remember Gordana getting stuck with it once. It was when Ivan and I were first together; probably one of the first times I'd ever met her. She'd been frowning at a tube of some kind of antiseptic cream – Germolene, or something similar. ' "If rash occurs, or worsens, cease application",' she'd read out loud. 'What are worsens?'

Ivan had laughed at her, and I saw rage flare briefly into her cheeks as she glanced at me and then away.

Gordana hated anyone to think of her as a fool – not that I did, of course. It was a perfectly understandable mistake, especially if English was not your first language.

'This is the second time you have rescued me,' I said, trying to sound light-hearted when it felt as though someone had filled my chest cavity with lead. 'Wish you'd been out on the mountain with us. Perhaps I wouldn't have caused the collision then.'

'Caused it?' said Karl. 'What do you mean?'

'It was my fault,' I said miserably, looking away from him out of the window. But I couldn't see anything except snow swirling out of darkness and the occasional yellowy wobble of headlights from on-coming vehicles. 'I fell over because there was a snowboarder coming up fast behind me, and he swerved to avoid me and crashed into Rachel.'

Karl shook his head. 'Not your fault, then. On the mountain, you are only responsible for the person in front of you. The person behind you is their own responsibility. It was the snowboarder's fault.'

'Thanks,' I said.

Karl shrugged. 'No need to thank me. It's the rules.'

I still felt wretched, however. Perhaps where Rachel was concerned, my default emotion was one of guilt and self-recrimination. I wondered what I as life coach could advise for that? I had absolutely no clue.

We were silent for the rest of the journey. Karl kept glancing anxiously across at me, but I just couldn't summon up the energy to make small talk. I wished I'd stayed at the hospital. I was a terrible, terrible mother. Even if I didn't cause the accident, I had abandoned Rachel – again! – when she needed me.

24

Susie

We eventually made it back to the hotel at eight o'clock, and I hauled myself laboriously out of the minibus in my borrowed blue scrubs and undone ski boots, the only footwear available to me. I left them in the boot room and padded up the stairs to the elevator and bar area, feeling as if I'd aged about twenty years since the previous day. I could hear the laughter and chat of the rest of the group in the dining room; they didn't have a care in the world. I felt a sudden, unwarranted resentment towards them. In fact, I never wanted to see any of them ever again, nor ever strap a ski to my foot again either. This holiday couldn't have been more of a disaster.

'Your group are having dinner. Do you want to join them?'

I'd rather saw my own arm off with a rusty breadknife, I thought. 'No, I won't, thanks. I'm going to hit my room and have a long bath and then I think I'm just going to bed. Thanks so much, Karl, for everything.'

As I waited for the interminably slow bath to fill, I bit the bullet and called Gordana to tell her what had happened. She was out, so I spoke to Ted, for which I was, afterwards, grateful. He was so calm, where Gordana would have been hysterical. He just got the facts and the information he needed, with no implied judgement or apportioning of blame. He sounded so sad, though, sort of weary and resigned. He said he and Gordana would ring Rachel at the hospital, thanked me for phoning, took my number at the hotel, and said how much he was looking forward to seeing me when I came over. We must both come and stay with them when we got back, he said.

Gordana was so lucky to have him, I thought later as I lay in the bath, bubbles up to my drooping eyelids, the scent of cheap hotel bath foam in my nostrils (not particularly nice, but better than the smell of the hospital). Bet *Ted* would never run off with a PhD student. He was devoted to Gordana, even though she could be difficult at times . . .

Tears of self-pity and exhaustion slid down my cheeks into the bath and I cried until all the bubbles had subsided around me. At least crying was better than the alternative though, which would be to make some ill-advised and extortionately expensive telephone call to Kansas, in the hope of a few nuggets of sympathy from my cheating son-of-a-bitch fiancé . . . I had to retain at least some pride. Plus, if I rang him now, he'd know what a disaster the holiday was, thus defeating the object.

In the end, as the water chilled around me and the hot tap refused to yield anything warmer than tepid, I told myself not to be so self-pitying. The holiday could, actually, have been far more disastrous. Rachel could have been permanently paralysed, or even killed, but she would – eventually – be fine. Ted had been lovely on the phone, and I'd got away with not having to speak to Ivan, or even Gordana. I hated the thought of upsetting Gordana. Everyone here had been so nice, especially that Karl.

I fell asleep. When I awoke, some time later, so disoriented by the sound of the extractor fan in the bathroom that I thought I was still on the aeroplane, my fingers had turned into prunes and I was covered in gooseflesh. I let out the bath, dried myself perfunctorily, staggered over to the bed, and climbed into the cold sheets, shivering violently before falling back asleep again. Sleeping was the easiest way to resist the temptation to call Billy.

I had hoped to sleep until the next morning, but hunger woke me a second time, at almost half past midnight. I tried to ignore it, but it was like trying to ignore my grief at Billy's affair – impossible. I realized I hadn't eaten anything not out of a vending machine since the bowl of *pasta e fagioli* soup Rachel and I had shared at noon thirty-six hours ago, in one of the restaurants by the side of the nursery slope.

I couldn't do anything about Billy leaving me, but at least there was an easy solution to the problem of my stomach rumbling. I got up and searched my room for something to eat, but there was nothing, not even the half-finished fruit bar I'd thought I had in my carry-on bag from the flight. I pulled on a sweatshirt, jogging bottoms and ski socks and made my way cautiously downstairs, thinking that if anyone was still in the bar, I might have to run back up to my room and put on some make-up.

Ridiculous, but there it was. I was so hungry that I could puke, and yet I still balked at being observed, by a bunch of semi-strangers I'd never see again, without my mascara and foundation on? I berated myself for my vain foolishness.

Luckily, when I got downstairs, the hotel bar was dark and quiet, with just a soft yellow landing light burning in the reception area. I hoped they didn't lock the kitchen at night. I was just heading towards the dining room to find out when a voice called my name. I jumped guiltily. It was Karl, standing in the darkened doorway of the bar, smiling at me.

'I was just about to go to bed. Your group are the lightweights,' he said. 'Usually the groups stay up drinking till quite late. Are you all right?'

'I'm really hungry,' I said, looking apologetically at

him with my bare, un-made-up face. But to my relief, I found I didn't care as much as I'd thought I would. In fact, I didn't care at all. 'Are there any peanuts or snacks behind the bar? Or could I make myself a sandwich in the kitchen?'

Karl slapped his head in an exaggerated way. 'Of course, I should have thought,' he said. 'You must be starving. I will get you something. Please wait. Sit in here.'

He ushered me through to the bar, which was in darkness except for embers glowing in the huge fireplace. I appreciated the fact that he didn't switch on the overhead lights. After the artifice of the hospital, the fake air, unnatural chemical smells and harsh strip lights – it was relaxing to sit in the soft darkness of a empty bar, so recently inhabited by the gossip and chatter of people who'd put their cares behind them for a week of escape in the mountains. It seemed strange that Rach and I had, up until today, been two of those people.

'I will give you a brandy to drink while I get you some food,' Karl announced, slipping behind the bar and pushing a large glass hard up against an optic. I didn't argue. I leaned back into the squashy leather cube armchair nearest the fire, feeling it envelop me like a hug.

'Thanks,' I said as Karl brought over the glass and I took a mouthful, calmed by the bronze burning in my throat. I leaned back and put my feet up on the stone hearth.

The fireplace was vast; able to accommodate five or six crouching men. The grate had wrought-iron dragon heads at each corner, which I hadn't noticed the night I'd been in there before, even though I'd been gazing into the flames then. It was a very medieval-looking fireplace, but somehow fitted with the seventies appearance of the rest of the bar. I closed my eyes, although the brandy had cleared the sleep out of my head, rather than further befuddling it.

When I opened them again, Karl had left the room and I was alone. The only movement around me was the snow, still falling thick and steady against the windows, and the occasional faint crash of burned logs in the grate as they collapsed into ashes. I was still tired, but not sleepy. It was twelve-forty-five, so what would that be in Kansas? About dinnertime, I calculated. I hoped Audrey had remembered to feed the cats. Billy would probably know by now that I'd gone away. I'd hoped that I'd swan back again – assuming I decided to go back – full of confidence and rediscovered *joie de vivre*, a tanned face with white goggles marks and newly-taut thighs, and casually drop into the conversation that I'd just been skiing in Italy.

I hadn't wanted him offering to keep an eye on things. I'd changed the locks, anyway, so that when he found out I was in Europe, he and Eva wouldn't be able to sneak in and use the sauna or sleep in our bed. Not that I really thought he'd be that mean.

I hated hating him. It felt so alien to me. How can you suddenly hate somebody for whom you've had nothing but love for nine whole years? It was easier to hate Eva – although, rationally, I doubted that it was any less her fault than his.

I wondered how it had started between them. She was an academic. He most definitely wasn't. Perhaps she'd brought her car into his garage to be fixed. Perhaps all he was to her was a bit of rough, a minor distraction from the stress of writing papers on existentialism or whatever. Had Audrey said she was doing a PhD in philosophy? I couldn't remember. Maybe it was geology, or anthropology.

She'd get bored of him, I thought, as I'd thought on many occasions. The novelty would wear off . . .

But what if I was wrong; what if she didn't? Worse – what if he asked her to marry him, and they didn't wait like we had, but plunged right on in there? Perhaps that was all he'd ever wanted: a bride-to-be who wasn't afraid to set the date? I felt a terrible lurch of anguish. Perhaps he'd been trying to tell me this, and I hadn't been listening.

'Are you all right? What are you thinking about?'

Karl reappeared, bearing a large plate of ham and cheese, three bread rolls, and some pickled beetroot in a bowl.

'I am not sure how brandy and beetroot will mix together,' he added, 'but it is the only salad I could find left in the kitchen. It seems your group dislikes late nights *and* beetroot.'

I smiled. 'Thanks, um, Karl. That looks great.' I had planned to ignore his previous question, but something about the way he was looking at me, with those sandy eyebrows and kind face, made me want to talk. And eat, of course, but I could do both. Multi-tasking, didn't they call it?

'I was just thinking about my partner. My soon-to-be ex-partner, I suppose. He met another woman. They're living together – well, I think they are. At the moment I hate them. Or at least I'm really trying to, because it seems like the easiest thing to do. I didn't even see it coming.'

I blushed, but now I'd started, I couldn't stop. In between mouthfuls of the rolls I filled with cheese and beetroot, I carried on. It was easier to talk about Billy than it was to talk about Rachel. (Funny, I thought, how when Rach was here, it was easier to talk about anything else except Billy . . .)

Karl uncapped a beer and swigged thoughtfully at it, coming over to perch himself on the low stone hearth, while he watched me eat and listened to me talk. He didn't say anything, but every time I stopped to draw breath or chew – once, I made the mistake of doing both simultaneously, and had to take a big swig of brandy. Karl got me a refill immediately – he'd nod and frown sympathetically, urging me to continue with subtle encouragement. His legs were long and solid, chunky like a lumberjack's. He wore rumpled cords and a baggy sweater, and I half expected him to extract a pipe from his trouser pocket. But he just propped one leg up on to the hearth and continued to listen.

I told him everything, right back to when Billy and I first got together, and further: I told him about Ivan, and how screwed up he was, and impossible to live with. I even confessed that our sex life had dwindled into nothing by the time Rachel was at school . . . something I hadn't ever admitted to anyone before, because it always somehow felt like a failing on my part. Billy and I had been fine in that department; right up to when Eva came on the scene. And I told him how I'd never really been able to settle, because I didn't feel I belonged wholly either in England or Kansas.

I talked a lot about Gordana, and how she could be difficult, prickly and too strong-minded, but that she loved Rachel and Ivan so deeply. Their success was largely down to her ambition for them, some of which they had inherited from her, some of which was manifest in the way she'd pushed them. I had so much respect for her.

I did end up telling him about Rachel, too; how her career was successful – but not successful enough for any of them, neither for her, nor for Ivan, nor Gordana.

'If I was the eighth best tennis player in the country,' I said, trying to wipe beetroot stains off my fingers on to a paper napkin, 'I really think I'd be so pleased. I mean – out of all the millions of people in the world! I think that's awesome. But then that's probably why I don't do anything competitive. I just don't have that drive, not like they do. Rach isn't as . . . hard about it as Ivan and Gordana are, but she still wants it, so badly. She was so close to her big break, I know she was. But not this sort of a break . . .'

I had to stop and turn away, so Karl couldn't see the emotion on my face. Snow was still brushing fatly against the windows. It looked beige and benign, so far from cold that I'd have been surprised to go outside and feel its chill against my face.

'She's on the verge of real success, we're all sure she is,' I said, reverting to the present tense because telling Karl that Rachel 'was' so close to success just seemed so defeatist. 'It's all she's ever wanted, since she was tiny. She's worked so hard for it, for years and years and years. And now, one split second's bad timing on a mountain, it could all be over . . .'

I gritted my back teeth, willing myself not to cry. I really didn't want Karl to see me cry.

'Is it really what she has always wanted? Or is it what her father and her grandmother wanted?' Karl asked, diplomatically ignoring my battle with composure. I was grateful for that – the slightest hint of solicitude and I'd have collapsed in a weeping, dribbling heap on the floor.

'Both,' I said. I wished I could have blamed Ivan, claimed that he pushed her to want it and work for it the way she had, but I couldn't. Rachel wanted it just as much. If anything, Ivan was threatened by Rachel's success. He couldn't bear the thought that she might get further than he had.

I told Karl this, and he smiled faintly.

'Men have much pride,' he commented, leaning back against the side of the fireplace. 'My brother-in-law cannot stand it when my sister beats him at Monopoly.'

Good grief, I thought, how rude of me. I've been banging on for hours about my life, and I haven't asked him anything about his. I so hated it when people did that to me.

'So how come you ended up here living with your sister and her husband?' I asked, rather too bluntly. I'd hardly seen anything of them, actually, only when we'd checked in, and when his sister had changed a dead lightbulb in our room. She looked like Karl: tall and blonde and pleasant.

Karl merely smiled and rolled himself a cigarette. He lit it, and the sweet smell of the smoke reminded me of Billy. 'I would like to tell you about that another time,' he said. 'If you don't mind, of course. For now, I am interested in Billy and Ivan and Gordana. Tell me some more.'

So I continued to talk, and Karl continued to listen, his head on one side, his eyes half closed although I could tell he was taking it all in. I kept thinking of Rachel on her own in a strange hospital, but I let my words brush away the image. I told him about our life in Kansas; and about why I'd moved back there a second time – as far as I could even articulate it. I told him about my idea of training to be life coach – 'if they'll have me,' I said miserably. 'I'm not exactly a good example, am I?'

Karl waved his beer bottle at me reproachfully. 'You must not say that. In fact, to be a good life coach you must be sympathetic with the experiences of others. You have had many life-changing experiences lately. These will benefit you, not hinder you.'

He was so nice. Not that I wanted to compare, but neither Ivan nor Billy would ever have said anything like that. Ivan was too self-obsessed and Billy too oblivious.

'Thanks,' I said. 'May I have another brandy?'

'Sure,' he replied, unfolding his legs and sauntering back over to the bar. I noticed that he put some Euros into the till for my drinks, which embarrrassed me. 'Please, put the drinks on my room,' I called. 'Have one yourself.'

'My drinks are free,' he called back. 'And tonight I treat you.'

'Thanks,' I repeated, gratefully accepting my third brandy.

I didn't go back up to bed until almost three o'clock, but since my body clock was still just about on US time, it made no odds. The best thing was that the awful panic of the day had subsided. There was no point in fretting about Rachel's career, and she herself was going to be fine. Nobody had died. It wasn't my fault (although I had trouble holding on to that one for more than a moment). I'd even made a new friend. I went back to sleep feeling much better.

The next morning, spaced out with jetlag and headachy from too much brandy at a high altitude, I awoke to the sound of the telephone: a shrill, old-fashioned ring. I thought I'd escaped the wrath of Ivan, but I was wrong.

'I've just heard . . . how could you let this happen?' he screamed without preamble when I picked up the receiver. 'Do you realize what you've done? I called the physio to ask him about fractures of the tibial plateau, and it's an incredibly fucking serious injury! She won't play for months, maybe never again professionally! What the hell were you thinking, inviting her on a flaming skiing trip, when she's on the edge of the big time? She only went to piss me off, you do know that, don't you? And now her career's probably ruined, thanks to you!'

I rolled on to my back against the pillows, holding the receiver as far away from my ear as I could, but still hearing the indignant squawking. 'Susie? *Susie!*'

'Ivan,' I said, calmly, although my hand was shaking so much that I had to hold my elbow with my other hand to steady it. 'Rachel is a grown woman. What she decides to do on holiday is entirely her own business. I didn't force her to come with me. She loves skiing – and she loves it because *you* taught her! You've taken her skiing a couple of times, why is this any different? You're not being fair. It's just one of those things; accidents happen. She could have tripped off the kerb at home and done the same thing. This isn't helping any of us.'

Despite my words, however, the guilt inside me was horrendous, bubbling up inside my gut like an evil sort of stomach acid. I felt dizzy with it. In my head, I kept chanting Karl's words about it not being my fault. It was the Italian boy's fault, not mine . . . But it was still down to me that Rachel had even been there on the mountain. I felt like losing the calm, rational, defensive voice and screaming back at him: 'I know! I feel terrible! I'm sorry!'

I got off the bed and pulled aside the orange curtain to look out of the window. The snow had stopped, but overnight it had drifted into glittering peaks and mini ski slopes on the terrace outside. It was so bright, and perfectly flawless under a clear blue sky, coating the ground and hanging heavy on the fir trees, a good six inches of it along each individual branch.

Ivan was still ranting. What had I ever seen in him, I thought, trying to block out the words and wondering if I had the nerve simply to hang up. His voice was polluting the perfection of my view. In the end, I managed to interrupt, by some miracle keeping my voice calm, if sarcastic.

'Listen, Ivan, I appreciate your concern. It was sweet of you to call, but I'm afraid that I need to get on now. I need to get to the hospital and see how our daughter's doing. She's asked me to take her washbag in for her. I'll tell her that you sent your love, shall I? She'll be touched. Bye, then. I'll let Gordana know when we're coming home – in about three days, they think. Thanks *so* much for ringing . . .'

It took me ten minutes before I stopped shaking enough to do up the buttons of my shirt.

I checked out of the hotel and allowed Karl to drive me back to the hospital with Rachel's and my bags in the back of the minibus. The hotel owner – Karl's brother-in-law – had made a reservation for me at another hotel, two minutes' walk from the hospital.

'Will you still require a ski pass?' he'd enquired, and I'd laughed hollowly.

'No. Thank you,' I said, certain that I'd never set skis on piste again.

I didn't bother to say goodbye to the rest of the group. Apart from our encounter with Robin on the way up the mountain, and the first evening spent with them, we hadn't really got to know them at all. It was only Karl whom I was sorry to leave.

'I can't thank you enough,' I said when he dropped me off outside the hospital, having already waited as I checked in at the new hotel. He shrugged.

'It's only a couple of lifts,' he said.

'I don't mean for the lifts – although I'm very grateful for those too. I mean what you did for me last night, letting me talk like that. It really helped. I didn't want to be on my own.'

'It was a pleasure,' he said, inclining his head in a slight bow. He had lovely eyes, I thought. He was a lovely man. Far too young for me, of course.

'I am often in England on business. Could I have your address, if you will be there for some weeks? I would like to keep in touch and hear how Rachel gets on. And if you become a life coach. That is most interesting also.'

There it was again, that 'alt-zo'. I noticed with vague interest that it did something funny to my insides. I delved into my bag and tore a page out of my notebook, on which I wrote Gordana's address and phone number.

'This is my ex-mother-in-law's number; Rachel's grandmother. I won't be there all the time, but she'll know how to get hold of me if I'm not. I'd love to see you over there – I'll buy you lunch, as a thank you.'

He smiled and kissed me lightly on the cheek. 'I will keep you to that,' he said, and hopped back into the driver's seat of the van. With a grinding of the clutch and a squeal of the accelerator, he was gone, and I felt his loss with a brief, almost pleasurable pang of anticipated nostalgia. I was sure he wouldn't look me up at Gordana's – or at least not before I'd gone back to Lawrence, anyhow – but I didn't mind. There were some people who only flitted into your life for the briefest of moments, and that was how it should be. Any more than that would spoil the experience.

I didn't even know his last name, I reflected, as I hurried into the hospital to see how Rachel was. I could always contact the hotel and find it out, I thought, knowing that I wouldn't bother.

25

Gordana

So Susie and Rachel are coming to stay. I must say, despite these bad circumstances for me and for Rachel, I am almost excited. It will be nice to have something else to think about, and I hope too it will stop Ted giving me these anxious looks. We don't talk about it much – what is there to say? I have told him the facts. There is a way of telling facts which makes it sound not quite so serious, and this is how I tell them. But he still keep giving me the nervous looks, as if I am a small pan of milk which will boil over at any moment. He took me to my appointment at the Marsden: more tests, more information and chit-chat I didn't really wish to hear. Ted shook hands with Mr Babish like they were two business associates meeting for lunch. Mr Babish explained the tests and gave us leaflets which I have hidden in the back of the bathroom cabinet. The operation is next week.

I can't remember the last time Susie and Rachel were in our house for more than a lunch or a flying visit. It used to make my head spin around, to think about how busy Rachel was all the time. Even when she wasn't at tournaments, she was either training or working out in that gym six days every single week. But if she has any hopes of becoming a champion, it's what she must do. I am so worried about her now. What will she do without her tennis? Maybe she will just slow down and stop altogether. The thought of that is terrible; it makes me want to cry. She is young, and beautiful, and always on the move. She will hate so much that she has this accident now. And Ivan so cross too.

In secret I often felt sorry for her, especially as a child, when she cried with exhaustion or defeat; but I always told her to keep going, work harder, don't stop. It's what I had to do with Ivan also. Even one hundred per cent commitment will not be enough. One hundred and twenty per cent is what's needed, minimum.

I hate to admit it, but perhaps this accident is her body telling her something: to slow down. It would be very sad if this is the case, but we must be philosophical about it: Rachel will not succeed where Ivan failed. I will just have to try and come to terms with this. Even though somebody crashed into her, her injury may be a result of her body's complaints at how hard we push it all these years.

I haven't seen Susie for a while. Ivan was cross when I said she was going to stay with us, but that is just tough. He is furious about Rachel's accident, but I suspect he enjoy any reason to be furious with poor Susie. It was not her fault. Rachel chose to go skiing; her mother didn't force her. Ivan doesn't have to see her if he doesn't want to. I know I have soon to tell Ivan about my lump, but I still have not decided whether to wait till after the operation.

I wonder why Billy has not come over too, at least for part of the time? When I ask Susie on the telephone, the way she said no, like a gulp, made me think that perhaps this is more the reason she decide to take a skiing holiday in Italy instead of Canada or Colorado.

I only once met that Billy of hers. He seemed very relaxed, and he laughed at things which weren't particularly funny. I couldn't help thinking there might be something a bit wrong with him. I don't know why I wonder if all is not well. Just a feeling. I know Susie better than she thinks. She will tell me when she gets here.

I have always liked Susie, once I got over the shock of Ivan getting her pregnant. She has a direct sort of a way about her which is refreshing. I think it's a shame that she and Ivan broke up. I know I was against it when they first started, so young, and with a baby, but that was just because I didn't want my Ivan to feel trapped, with his career so important to him. But I think Susie helped. She kept him . . . what is that word which always make me think of camping? *Grounded*, that's it . . . in a way that I could never have done. She stopped him sleeping around with many tennis groupies; she travelled everywhere with him.

Also she encouraged Rachel to start playing tennis, at the age of three. People think it must be because of Ivan that Rachel took it up, but it wasn't, it was Susie. I remember seeing them out on court, for hours, here or at the club, hitting a pink foam ball over the mini-tennis net, Rachel with her little racket, with so much concentration.

She enrolled Rachel in mini-tennis classes as soon as she turned four. The other children were older, but they would chat and giggle and stop to examine a worm on the court, or whack the ball far away, but Rachel could hold a long rally by then. So Susie got her moved up to the classes for the six-to-eight-year-olds, and then the ten-year-olds . . . Nobody could believe it, except Susie. And me and Ivan, of course.

I think that, just as Susie helped Ivan's career, she also helped Rachel's; even though she says she felt left out of it, that Ivan pushed her away.

It will be good to catch up with her. I've been getting their rooms ready this morning; I'm putting Susie in the Blue Room, the biggest of the en-suite spare rooms, the one with the view over the front garden and then out to the parkland across the road behind. Susie likes that room. It was where the three of them lived when they came back from Kansas, for a year, when Rachel was a baby. She slept in a cot by the window.

I remember one morning Susie came and found me when I was putting on my make-up in my own bedroom. 'Come and look, Gordana,' she said. I came, hoping I would remember that I had put mascara on only one eye so far. Rachel was lying in the cot, very still except for her eyes, which had focused on the leaves of the big plane tree outside the window. It was a windy day, and she was concentrating on a branch which swayed back and forwards, making the leaves dance and jump, and her eyes went back and forth, back and forth, wide open with wonder.

'She looks like she's watching a tennis match, doesn't she?' said Susie, and we laughed together. I don't know why I always remembered that.

Rachel was such a delicious baby, I could have eaten her up. I loved having them both living here. I say 'both', because I don't recall Ivan being around that much, and of course it was long before Ted retired, so he was out all day, running his jewellery shops. It was just us three girls, and we had so much fun. I taught Susie to play tennis – she wanted to surprise Ivan one day. I don't know if she ever did. I doubt it, somehow. Ivan never had the patience to play with anyone unless there was something in it for him: money, or a good match, or reflected glory.

My garden looks beautiful at the moment, with frost on the bare branches of the beech trees, although the lawn is leaving something to be desired. I'll have a word with Manuel; tell him to rake the rest of the leaves off it before my guests get here. He should have done it two weeks ago.

I always think of Manderley when I stand at the window of this room, as if Mrs Danvers will glide in and appear at my shoulder. Not that our house is as impressive as Manderley, and there's no sea view to watch; but still. *Rebecca* is my favourite book. It is the first one I ever read in English.

That reminds me, I must talk to Ted again about getting a housekeeper – a non-sinister one, of course. He has no idea how much work is involved in running a house like this, even with the cleaner and a gardener. I could do with some nice organized person with cheeks like apples to come and take over, especially when I am recovering from the operation, and having the nasty treatments. I don't want Susie pushing her finger along the mantelpiece to see how dusty it is – not that she's likely to, I suppose, I don't think she notices that kind of thing. Ivan's Anthea would, without any doubts. She doesn't keep her own house clean, but she would look down her nose if mine wasn't. I hope Ivan's Anthea will never come to stay.

Ivan is dropping Rachel off. Susie will come separately – she spent last night with an old friend of hers from Kansas. She and Ivan made careful plans so that their paths didn't even cross at the airport when Ivan was picking up Rachel. It's ridiculous that they still can't talk, after all this time. Surely past is past. But I'm glad she's not coming just yet. That way, I can insist that Ivan come in for coffee when he drops Rachel off here.

I want to ask him how things are going with the tennis club. I think not very well, because lately Ivan look even more worried than usual. I'm sure his hair is disappearing even faster, and the bits he still has are getting quite grey. The girls say they haven't even seen him down there for a while, which is a worry. I hope he has not lost interest in it, after all this effort. Worse, I hope that the Immigrations people have not been giving him a hassle again.

It's difficult. Ivan need a big success with his academy, or at least with one of his players. Preferably Rachel, of course. I only lent him the money because the academy would benefit Rachel's career. I hope he will not have problems paying me back. Well, I suppose that flying to tournaments all the time is very expensive, if Rachel doesn't win. The LTA pays José's wages, but not his travel expenses, or Ivan's, of course.

It has been quite a long time since I saw Rachel play. I think the last was when she got through to the finals of that tournament in Bournemouth some years ago – lovely day, for us anyway. We had gorgeous lunch in that hotel in Boscombe, with the best prawn salad I ever had. But poor Rachel; by the time she was a set down to that Slovakian girl, such a skinny little thing, she was ready to throw her racket to the ground. Ivan would have done it, at her age, but Rachel always had a better control of herself. She was so upset, though, she couldn't even talk to us afterwards. I'm sure it wasn't helpful that Ivan was shouting at her. I think he made her cry that day. Sometimes my boy is not very sensitive – and he of all people should have understood.

Ooh, here they are now – but with brown leaves still all over the lawn! Look at her, my poor darling, waiting in the front seat while Ivan unfolds a wheelchair for her. Better run down and welcome them. I will just put on some lipstick while Ivan gets her bags out of the boot . . .

'Hello, Gordana, thanks so much for having me,' Rachel says when I open the door. She's such a lovely girl, although why must she always wear those terrible tracksuit bottoms? I bend down and hug her carefully. Usually she almost crushes the breath out of me, but in the wheelchair with her leg sticking out straight, she can only lean into me.

'Hello, darling; hello, Ivan, other darling,' I manage to say, kissing them both and then wiping my smudgy lipstick prints from their faces with my thumb. 'It's wonderful to see you. How do you feel, Rachel? We've been so worried about you. Do you have to be all the time in this wheelchair?'

'I'm not too bad, Gordana,' she says bravely. 'And no, I'm meant to be on crutches. I've got to get back on my feet as soon as I can. They just gave me a chair for the travelling and all.'

Ivan takes a pair of metal crutches out of the boot and offers them to Rachel, but she shakes her head. 'Think I'll be a wimp and stay where I am for the moment, thanks, Dad,' she says, without smiling at him.

'Is it hurting, my darling?'

'It kind of aches, but weirdly my hip hurts more than my knee, in the place where they took the bone graft.'

They both look very bad. Ivan is weary, and his stubble scratches my cheek. Rachel looks worse: grey bags underneath her eyes, skin pale and blotchy, and all her hair greasy at the roots, scraped back away from her face with a thick rubber band – not even a scrunchy or a bobble, just the sort of rubber band the postman uses to keep bundles of letters together. And so scruffy, with those awful baggy, stained sweatpants. I know she's just come out of hospital but it would seem to me a good time to wear a skirt, now she won't need the sports clothes for a while.

I hold the sides of her arms and look into her pale face. Her triceps are hard like iron, like a man's. She never wears make-up normally, able to get away with the fresh bloomingness of sport and youth; but her face is crying out for it today. I want to get her a make-over so badly that my fingers itch to start putting sparkly eyeshadow on her poor dark eyelids. My heart sinks to think what other bad news I must soon give her.

'I'm so sorry, darling,' I say. There was little else I could say. 'Come in, I will put some coffee on. Do you like my shoes? They're new ones: Bruno Magli.'

Rachel hardly glances down at them. 'Yeah. Pointy enough to clean your ears with. You're as bad as

Anthea, Granny, she's always name-dropping designers and labels and all that. Unless it's Nike or Adidas, it doesn't mean a thing to me.' Her voice sounds flat and tired, even though she is trying to be jolly.

Even so, I am very slightly affronted. I look to check that Ivan isn't listening – he isn't, he's gone into the downstairs toilet – and whisper: 'Please don't put me in brackets with that woman, Rachel. And *please* don't call me Granny, you know I hate it.'

Rachel rolls her eyes and allows me to wheel her into the kitchen, where she parks herself at the kitchen table while I make a pot of filter coffee. 'Where's Pops?' she says, looking around for him. Rachel loves Ted.

'His exercise for today,' I reply, pouring cream into a jug. 'He goes out for the paper every morning.'

I set out three cups and saucers.

'Not for me, thanks Mama,' says Ivan, who has rejoined us, already looking at his watch. 'I need to get back. Squad practice.'

'You have time for one coffee, Ivan, while Rachel gets herself sorted out,' I say firmly, in the voice with which I used to tell him he was not permitted to watch television before school. 'You're in the downstairs bedroom, Rachel darling, so you don't have to manage the stairs. Perhaps you could go and settle in for a while.'

'Oh . . . right. Can you believe they wouldn't let me fly home until I could go upstairs on my crutches? Italian sadists. I'm making the most of this chair while I've got it. So I'm glad I'm on the ground floor. I'll go and get settled then, shall I?'

Rachel swivels around and wheels herself out of the room, after taking a mouthful of coffee. I feel bad, sending her away like that, but I do really want to speak to my son. Although he seems to have other ideas.

'No, Mama, I don't have time,' he says with exasperation.

'Darling, I want to chat to you for a bit! Surely that is not too much to ask for?'

'Sorry. I have to go. Rach, it's OK, come back and finish your coffee. I'm off.'

He is impossible! I pat at my hair, to try and disguise my irritation. 'If you must,' I say, crossing the room and brushing some lint off his sleeve with my palm, like a slow-motion slap. 'But you know I will catch up with you soon, don't you?'

He grunts, and Rachel wheels herself back in again, looking awkward. It is odd seeing her face at chest level instead of above me, as if she has shrunk.

'Bye, Rach, have a good time.' Ivan moves a little way towards her, as if he wants to hug her, but she squares her shoulders against him and looks out of the window.

'Yeah. Thanks. Bye, Dad. Thanks for the lift.'

I put my hands on my hips. 'And now what is going on with you two? You are not speaking!'

'I'll tell you later,' Rachel mouths at me.

Ivan ignores me altogether, picking his keys off the table where he had briefly placed them, and stuffing his hands in the pockets of the jacket he hasn't even bothered to take off inside the house.

'Don't worry, Mama, I'll see myself out.' He sneezes explosively, making everyone jump. 'Sorry. Getting a cold.'

'Take echinacea and vitamin C, darling, and it'll be gone in no time,' I counsel as he pulls a large handkerchief from the depths of a pocket. A red envelope falls out on to the floor.

'You dropped something,' I say, picking it up at the same time that Ivan lunges for it. It is addressed to Rachel. 'Oh, Rachel, it's for you.' I hand it across to her, and she takes it, examining the writing.

'What's this?'

'Almost forgot,' Ivan says in gruff voice, stopping in the doorway and not meeting her eyes. 'I – er – think it's a get-well card.'

'Oh,' says Rachel with surprise. 'Who from?'

Ivan continues to look at the spot on the floor where the card has fallen, so intently that I follow his gaze, thinking that he must have seen something which Adele has overlooked in her daily washings, a sticky patch of spilled orange juice or a small dustball; but it is perfectly clean.

'It's . . . it's from Natasha Horvath.' He clears his throat noisily.

I look at him sharply. I know that name. Rachel does too – it is the girl Rachel was playing in Zurich.

'That's kind of her,' I say as Rachel rips open the envelope, pulls out the card and opens it. The card itself isn't very nice. It's a cheap, shiny one, with a podgy cartoon teddy bear with his leg in a bandage. Inside, in small, curly and recognizably East European handwriting – it's as easy to identify as American cursive, we all had to learn it at school – Natasha has written: 'Sorry about your accident. I hope you will recover soon. With good wishes, Natasha Horvath'.

'I'll be off then,' says Ivan awkwardly.

'Wait a second,' Rachel says. 'How come you've got this?'

'What do you mean?' Ivan sounds aggressive.

'What I said: why is she sending me a card? And how did she give it to you to give to me?'

Ivan rubs his little balding patch and shrugs his shoulders. He is so tense that they don't shrug very far; as if there is somebody pressing down on them. I must know what he and Rachel were having the cross words about.

'It's no big deal, Rachel. I think it's very nice of her. She was at the club yesterday. One of her friends is training with me for six months. Anyway, people were, you know, talking about your accident.' He

209

laughs nervously. 'She gave it to me soon after that. Must have gone to the newsagents and got it straight away.'

'Oh. Right. Yeah, that was nice of her. But I'm just surprised that she'd send me a card. She seemed to hate me so much.'

'Of course she didn't bloody hate you, Rachel, that's just your paranoia,' snaps Ivan, looking at his watch again. 'Anyway, take it easy. Rest your knee, keep on with the painkillers when you need them. I really must go now.'

With a quick kiss for Rachel's cheek, then one for mine, he is gone. Rachel looks at me, frowning. She is so like Ivan when she frowns. She has inherited all his wrinkle patterns – or crinkles as she called them when she was a little girl. 'Look, Daddy, I can play guitar on your crinkles,' she once said, strumming at his forehead with her finger. He was not pleased. And then for a long time I was confused and thought that the actual word in English *was* 'crinkles'. The lady at the Clarins counter laughed at me when I went in and asked for anti-crinkle cream.

'What are you frowning about?' I ask her.

'It's just a bit weird, Dad mentioning he's coaching someone for six months. When I talked to Kerry this morning she said that she hadn't seen him at the club for ages; and if he was coaching again, he ought to be there every day.'

I do not think this is so weird. 'Well, yesterday he was there. Kerry is not there all the time either, is she? I think she just has not seen him.'

I smile to myself as I pick up the dirty coffee cups, remembering Rachel's little fingers on Ivan's crinkles. It only seems like last year. Time rushes too fast.

26

Susie

'Susie, are you sure you don't want a nap or something? You look wrecked.'

Corinna lit another cigarette, although the last one was still smouldering in the ashtray. In the old Lawrence days, her nicotine habit had always given me a good excuse for time away from Ivan – he couldn't bear her constant smoking, and so had never made a fuss about coming too when I said I was going to visit her. Although he used to complain when I came back reeking of smoke . . . but then, six months into our relationship, he'd found fault with pretty much everything about me.

'No, I'm fine. We only came in from Italy, it's not like I'm jetlagged any more,' I said, even though I felt totally jetlagged. I leaned back in Corinna's red leather armchair and yawned wearily. The chair was too slippery to be comfortable, and the back of it so steep that my neck felt ricked, but I was so tired I felt I could have slept on a runway.

Rach and I had got back that morning, and Ivan picked Rachel up at Heathrow. We were to meet again tomorrow at Gordana's in Surrey, and she would spend the next few weeks there convalescing. I wasn't sure how long I'd stay – perhaps a week. It had been ages since I'd seen them, and although I really wanted to confide in Gordana, I didn't wish to outstay my welcome.

I couldn't even face seeing Ivan at the airport, so I'd kissed Rachel goodbye in the Blue Channel of Customs, before the electric doors into Arrivals, and had loitered behind while she wheeled herself through, a porter carrying her suitcase, waiting a discreet amount of time until I was sure they'd be gone. I was dreading bumping into him at Gordana's.

Somewhere deep inside the tight coil of stress in my body, it felt as if there was a vacuum, a dull empty throb at the realization that although I wasn't even all that keen on going to Gordana's, I had no choice. I didn't have anywhere else to go. I didn't want to go back to Lawrence yet. I wasn't sure I could ever be there again without Billy. Perhaps I would ask Corinna if I could come back and stay with her for a bit longer.

Two large cardboard boxes sat on the polished leather floor in front of Corinna and me, boxes of junk I'd asked her to keep for me when Ivan and I first split up back in '95. I'd stayed at Corinna's then too, for a couple of weeks, whilst I'd made the arrangements for my new life back in Lawrence; and she'd agreed to keep the boxes for me until I got settled over there, when I'd send for them. Of course I never had.

At first I kept putting it off, then I realized I couldn't even remember what the boxes contained, which meant that more than likely I'd be able to live without them in my house in Kansas. Plus, Corinna hadn't wanted the hassle of shipping them to me. It had been much easier to store them, unseen, in her loft, while she went about the business of transforming the dingy flowery-wallpapered cottage she'd just bought into the design masterpiece in which she currently resided.

Now, though, I was vaguely curious to see what was in the boxes, and I'd asked Corinna to look them out on my arrival . . . once I mustered sufficient energy to open them, that was.

I felt totally drained. Although I'd only been out on the ski slopes that one disastrous time, all my muscles ached as if I'd been in a car crash. I would have loved to take up Corinna's offer of a nap – ideally, go to bed and sleep for a week, but it was only three in the after-noon, and it seemed rude when I hadn't seen her for so long.

'It's just that this is the first chance I've had to draw breath, really, since all the dramas of the accident, and the hassle of getting Rachel back from Italy. She's been so nice about it, but I can't help feeling that it was my fault she got injured. I can't stop thinking about it: what if she can't play tennis ever again, professionally, I mean? And it's my fault? God, Corinna,' I said, the words beginning to pour out once I had someone to confide in, 'I knew I was a crap mother, but now this? First time I see my daughter in years, and I cause her leg to be totalled, possibly at the loss of her career. The one thing she really had going for her . . .'

Corinna blew out a long, thoughtful cloud of smoke, like a jetstream.

'You aren't a crap mother. You just had a crap husband, that's all. If it wasn't for Ivan the Terrible, you'd never have left Rachel, would you?'

She and Ivan had always disliked one other. He used to refer to her as Peroxide Monkey-Girl, although a few times I'd caught him staring at her, surreptitiously and lustfully. The nickname was harsh, I thought, since she'd actually been very pretty back then. She hadn't aged all that well, in the intervening years since she'd been my spiky-haired, slim room-mate in Lawrence.

Corinna was a freelance journalist now, but she seemed to spend most of her time improving her small North London terraced house. Its interior was like something out of a design magazine, all sharp angles, interesting textures and subtle shades. I wondered if this was somehow to compensate for the way her own angles had blurred into plump curves and deep wrinkles. Her designer wall lights appeared to stay up by themselves, but her breasts were distinctly gravity challenged. Her hair, once so crisp and spiky, was limp and somehow colourless, and her eyes reflected a loneliness that she never admitted to.

Since her first serious relationship at twenty-one, with Calvin, the rasta she'd met at the party where Ivan and I first crossed paths, she had had a string of unsuitable lovers: the married, the commitment-phobic, the alcoholic, the sex-addict . . . Her emails to me from London to Lawrence detailing her latest catastrophically unsuccessful affairs were always entertaining, but tinged with a deep sadness that even the austerity of the medium of email couldn't disguise.

It was good to see her again. I felt awkward about feeling sorry for her, although she probably felt the same about me.

'Don't beat yourself up,' she said. 'It was an accident. Everyone knows skiing's risky. Some might say she should never have gone. I can't believe Ivan was happy about her going – and who knows, if she can't play again, maybe it's the best thing that could happen to her? You were always saying how depressed she'd get that she would soon have to retire, without hitting the big time.'

'Yeah, but it ought to be her decision. Not because her crap mother caused a pile-up on a ski slope.'

Corinna shrugged. 'Whatever. Shit happens. We deal with it. I mean, it wasn't your decision that Billy went and shacked up with another woman, was it? And *you're* dealing with it. Well, in a manner of speaking you are . . .'

Her directness made me wince, but I could see what she meant.

'I still haven't told Rachel about that.'

Corinna gazed at me in astonishment, smoke leaching out of her mouth and nose. 'You've been with your daughter for over a week and she hasn't even asked what's going on? Why does she think you're going to be staying away from your man for so long?'

I chewed the inside of my lip, an old habit. 'Because of her injury, I guess. She knows him well enough to know he'd never want to go skiing, so she didn't think it was weird that I went without him. I didn't want to worry her.'

'And she hasn't guessed that you're not OK?'

'I *am* OK.'

'No you aren't. You're totally down on yourself, full of self-pity and self-hatred, which isn't like you . . . In fact, you're in a complete state.'

'I'm just stressed from Rachel's accident, that's all, and feeling guilty about it,' I protested.

'Guilt,' said Corinna contemptuously. 'It's the most redundant, unconstructive, damaging emotion there is.'

'Oh great,' I replied, ripping brown tape off the flaps of the box nearest me. It had long ago lost its adhesiveness, and seemed to float away from the cardboard it had once bonded to. 'Now I feel guilty for feeling guilty. Thanks, Corinna.'

She laughed. 'What's in the box, then? Anything you can't live without, or are we taking a trip to Oxfam before you leave tomorrow?'

I peered inside. It was full of books: damp, yellowing, dog-eared paperbacks, mostly set texts for my degree, plus a few tennis-related ones of Ivan's which I must have absent-mindedly stuck in there by mistake in the course of my hasty packing. I lifted out an armful: *Collected Short Stories from the South Pacific*; *Wide Sargasso Sea* by Jean Rhys; *Ways of Seeing* by John Berger; *The History and Theory of Art*.

'Oxfam, I think,' I said, digging in again. The books smelled musty; almost pulpy and decomposing. I could so clearly remember buying them from the campus bookstore at KU, an impressively smart and well-laid-out basement shop in which I used to spend a lot of time – not least because I often saw the town's most famous resident, William Burroughs, browsing hunch-shouldered in an over-large overcoat amongst the tables near me.

The books had been crisp and new then, and their spines ramrod straight and unbroken, full of promises of what they'd teach me in their closely guarded pages.

It was strange, how different my two spells of living in Kansas had been. The first time I'd been a student, an insecure pretty girl with an overbearing boyfriend and too many papers to write, nothing deeper to worry about than Jean Arp's navels, which band were playing that night at the Emporium, or whether Ivan really did love me.

The second time, I felt like a completely new person. I'd thrown off the shackles of Ivan's self-centredness and I was free: free to choose not only the person I wanted to be with, but the person I wanted to become. I had gone back there because it seemed like home – and then I'd become Billy's fiancée, and it felt even more right.

'If Oxfam will even take them. Maybe we should just chuck 'em away,' I said briskly, my eyes watering annoyingly.

'I'll have that one, it's a classic,' said Corinna, reaching out and picking up *Ways of Seeing*.

'These tennis ones can definitely go.' I scooped up four or five hardbacks with titles such as *Topspin!*, *Tennis: It's All in the Mind*; and *The Story of Rod Laver*.

Something fell out from between the pages of the Rod Laver autobiography, a large black and white photograph. It had evidently been in there for some time, because it was dry and brittle, and the edges were slightly yellowing.

I picked it up and studied it. It was an official press shot of a very young blonde female player, standing on tiptoes on court, beaming and holding aloft a small trophy. Ivan was in the photograph next to her, beaming equally widely. He was clapping, and something in

216

his expression conveyed utter pride. More than pride; admiration. Lust, possibly, too.

I examined Ivan's apparel (a shellsuit, ugh) and his facial hair (sideburns), and decided the photo was probably taken some time during the mid-nineties – Ivan hung on to those ridiculous sideburns for years, until after we split up. He only cultivated them after he began to go bald, in a somewhat futile attempt at proving he could still grow hair, even if not in the preferred location. So the photo couldn't be more than about ten years old, although it looked older. He'd had a full head of hair throughout the Eighties.

I flipped it over to see if there was a date on it. There was, in faint grey print at the top: '02/06/95', but it was the handwritten message underneath which made my voice catch in my throat as I tried to speak.

'What is it?' said Corinna, alarmed at the sight of me.

I cleared my throat, too loudly. 'It's . . . probably nothing.'

June 1995, the summer he was coaching at that academy in Hungary, with Rachel. I looked at the photo again, as if somehow I had mistaken this skinny blonde for my tall, dark daughter, who, even at thirteen, was ten stone of pure muscle. No. Definitely not Rachel. And she certainly would never have written what was on the back of the photo . . .

'What?'

'Um . . . what do you make of this? "Dearest Ivan, to the best coach ever in the world. You teach me so much things and not just about tennis." Five, no six exclamation marks . . . "Nobody tell me it could be so great. All my love, Tasha". Kiss kiss kiss kiss kiss, all in capitals.'

Corinna stared at the message. 'It might be innocent,' she said doubtfully.

I snorted. 'Sure.'

'Look at her, she's only a kid. Perhaps she had a crush on him. Must happen all the time.'

'Yeah. But looking at Ivan's face in this photo, I'd say it was him who had the crush on her . . . And it was when we were still married . . .'

Outrage drained out of me as I felt suddenly overwhelmed by betrayal: the revelation that Billy was probably not the first partner who had cheated on me. From where I was kneeling in front of the boxes, I slowly bent forwards until my forehead touched the floor, wrapping my arms around my head. I hated Ivan more than I'd ever hated him, so why did it hurt so much? It shouldn't make any difference, what Ivan had got up to when we were married – and if Billy and I had still been happy together, I couldn't have cared less. But Billy was gone, and I didn't even have the comfort of complaining to him about Ivan's betrayal, because Billy's own betrayal was ten times worse. I'd loved Billy, and trusted him. Ivan, I had always half expected it of. But not Billy.

Corinna tentatively rubbed my prone back. 'You don't know for sure,' she said again. 'Surely he wouldn't have kept the photo if he thought it would incriminate him.' She didn't sound as if she was even remotely convincing herself.

'He'd hidden it in that book,' I said, with a muffled voice. My nose was pressed against the weird leather floor, and it smelled like a big new shoe.

She sighed. 'Maybe you're right. I'm not sure if I should tell you this,' she continued, and I unwrapped my arms from around my head – despite not being sure if she should tell me, either. 'Do you remember the Harmonic Convergence, that summer in Lawrence, a couple of weeks before I flew home? Some hippy thing, meant to herald the start of a New Age, or some such nonsense. We all got up at five in the morning and sat on Calvin's balcony to watch the dawn break. But we all felt really ill because we'd spent the day before drinking all day – all except Ivan, of course, Mr "My Body is a Temple". I can't remember why, some gig or other – no, I know, it was the Fiddling and Picking Contest in South Park, do you remember?'

I frowned. A Fiddling and Picking Contest – no wonder we'd all got drunk. I had a vague memory of sitting on a rug in a park, worrying about whether there were chiggers in the grass waiting to dig their way into my ankles and give me whatever disease it was that they imparted, and watching men in dungarees with too much facial hair showing off with banjos. It had got unutterably tedious after the first half-hour – I mean, I liked 'The Devil Went Down to Georgia' as much as the next woman, but I didn't want to listen to it all day.

'Oh yeah. Vaguely. I can remember the Harmonic Convergence better – mostly because absolutely nothing happened. I'm not sure what we were expecting, though.'

'Well, I had such a bad hangover that I only managed to watch the sunrise for about five minutes, and then I decided to go and have a bath, so I left you all to it. There was that hippy chick, Heather, who was trying to get you all to chant, remember? I thought I'd throw up if I opened my mouth. Anyway, I'd been lying in the bath for a couple of minutes and suddenly the door opened and in comes Ivan. He apologized, but he was staring right at my tits, you know? I thought he'd leave straight away, but he didn't. He sort of leaned on the doorframe and carried on staring. I covered myself up–' Corinna demonstrated, putting one arm across her breasts and the other across her crotch, like Venus '–but then he came over and knelt down by the bath. "We should make love some time before you go back home," he said. "You've got lovely breasts." Then he reached out and touched my chest.'

'What did you do?' I said, in a very small voice.

'Splashed him in the face and told him to fuck off out of it,' she said briskly, lighting another cigarette. I noticed the nicotine stains on the side of her fingers, so tainted-looking. In my head, I compared this tough, yellow skin with the tender white of her youthful breasts sticking out of the water, luring Ivan towards her like a siren. I hated myself for feeling furious with her, instead of him.

'Why didn't you tell me?'

'I was going to. But I left soon after that, and the next time I saw you, you were up the duff, and you were so happy I didn't want to wreck your buzz. Seemed a bit pointless.'

'I wonder how many times he cheated on me?' I looked at the letter in my hand. 'I wonder how many times *Billy* cheated on me?'

Corinna patted my shoulder and blew smoke in my face, affectionately. 'Ivan, lots of times, probably. Billy? From what you've told me about him, I'd put money on this being a one-off. His head's been turned, that's all. He'll work out which side his bread's buttered on, and come running back, you wait and see.'

I looked again at the back of the photograph, at the girlish, excitable handwriting. 'What's her name? Oh, Tasha. Poor little Tasha. He probably shagged all the girls he coached. I could get him put away for this.'

Corinna laughed hoarsely. 'Go for it, honey. Get your revenge.'

I sighed. 'No. Of course I wouldn't, for Rachel and Gordana's sakes. He's scum, but they don't deserve that.'

'Well, if I were you, I'd keep hold of that picture. It might come in handy at some point.'

'Yes,' I said thoughtfully, sliding it into the side pocket of my handbag. 'I don't know how, but it might. Oh Corinna, it shouldn't even matter, not after all this time . . .' My voice cracked and I put my head in my hands again.

She stood up briskly. 'But it does. I know. Right, there's only one thing for it. We're going to relive our student experiences.' She flung me the TV remote. 'Choose your movie. I'm sorting out the refreshments.'

We didn't mention Ivan or Billy again that night. Instead we drank Kahlua, ate home-made popcorn, and watched a vacuous movie on Pay Per View. It was like 1980 all over again. But somehow I couldn't stop thinking about that young girl, Tasha. What had I been doing when Ivan was, in all probability, off sleeping with her? At home with Rachel, most likely, feeling trapped but being loyal. Supporting Ivan's career.

And look where *that* had got me . . .

27

Gordana

I must make some bread – I meant to do it earlier but I was so busy getting ready for my guests. But I think it is important always to have fresh bread. I take the ingredients out of cupboards and start weighing flour.

'I can't believe you've still got this!'

Rachel has found an old copy of *Tennis Now* magazine stuck in between the cookbooks. It is the one with her picture on the front cover. She pulls it out and wheels herself back to the table to study it.

'I forgot it was up there. How serious you look!'

For a moment I take my eye off the flour I am measuring, and a great lump falls out of the bag and lands splat into the bowl. It makes a big white cloud above the wobbly dial, and some flour dust settles on the cover photograph, which is of Rachel serving. She is stretching up high to the ball, with wide concentrating eyes and big muscles in her arms.

'It's an awful picture,' she says, wiping the flour off it, and I must agree, it is not the best. 'Look at my *boobs*. That one's about six inches higher than the other one! I look positively deformed!'

'Perhaps it is your sports bra, darling,' I say, going back to my bread-making, a bit distracted because from the window I see Ted and Ivan talking in the drive. They have their backs to me. Ted is wearing the expensive overcoat, with cashmere, I bought him last Christmas. It is lovely coat, but on his short body it makes him look a little bit like an Oxo cube. Then they move out of sight, back towards the house. As I put the bread machine on, I wonder why Ivan is not leaving as he said he must. Something about the way their heads are down makes me think this is not normal chit-chat.

'No, it's just the angle it was taken,' says Rachel, although now I am not paying so much attention.

'Back in one minute, darling.' I wipe my hands on a tea-towel and leave Rachel turning the magazine around to look at her photo from a different angle. I want to know what Ted and Ivan talk about.

I have a 'hello, sweetie' smile for Ted on my face, and I am looking at the huge vase of pussy willow on the plinth in the hall and thinking: I must arrange those again so that they don't all stick out in one direction like that, as if they have blown there in a strong wind, but then the smile falls off.

Ivan is leaning against the side of the open front door, his back to us, his elbow against the doorframe and his sleeve over his eyes. He is quite still. But it's Ted I'm worried about first. He looks like I haven't ever seen him look: grey like porridge, like something has upset him bad. His eyes are big with panic. He puts a hand on his chest and I think: Oh no, no, he is having the heart attack. We can't both die! I rush to him, wondering if somehow the news of my illness has only just hit him. I hope he hasn't told Ivan. Perhaps that's why Ivan looks so upset.

'Ted, Ted, what is matter? Darling, sit down here, on stairs. Do you need ambulance?'

He shakes me off, but sits down on the third stair anyway. 'No, no, I'm not ill.' But his voice sound funny, gaspy, shocked. He look at me like I have grown extra head. The newspaper is on his lap.

'What then?'

Rachel wheels herself out of the kitchen. 'What's going on? Pops?'

Seeing Rachel seems to make him worse. He lifts his glasses and rubs his hand over his eyes, squinching his thumbs into the corners. Me and Rachel wait, with horror. This is something very terrible.

He pull himself up with a big effort, holding on to banister. 'Let's go and sit down in the kitchen,' he says. 'Hello, Rachel, my darling,' he adds, bending to kiss her head, but without the smile he always has for her.

'Come, Ivan,' I say, tugging my son's arm away from his eyes. I half expect to see tears, but he is not crying. His eyes are blank, but then they flicker with rage.

We arrange ourselves around the kitchen table, me and Rachel with dread, Ted still looking horrified, Ivan looking shocked and also furious. The bread machine suddenly stops kneading the dough, and there is deep silence for the bread to rise into. The only other sound I hear is the kitchen clock ticking, and a distant noise of someone cutting branches off a tree. I feel ill.

Ted puts the newspaper in front of him. Slowly he opens it, and turns to the second page. Clears his throat. Stops. Clears it again.

'I, er, had a quick flick through this on my way back from the newsagents,' he says. 'You know the way I always do when I'm walking back.'

I frown at him. I always tell him not to do this, in case he walk into lamppost or trip over kerb, but he doesn't listen. I brush a small smudge of flour off my skirt.

'I wanted to see what was happening in the golf, but . . . something caught my eye . . .' He bit his lip and squeezed my hand with his trembly one.

At first I couldn't see what he showed us. All I saw was headlines like 'HOUSES PRICES FALL FURTHER' and 'BLAIR TRIES TO END RIFT RUMOURS'. What sort of a rumour is a rift rumour, I wonder? But now does not seem the time to ask. I try to think what else it might be. Perhaps something is wrong with our investments. Ivan leans back on his chair, looking hard in the other direction, like he doesn't want to see it at all.

Rachel sees it first. She gasps, and her hands fly to her mouth, pressing hard as if to stop her speaking.

Then Ted's shaky finger points at another headline: 'EX-BRITISH TENNIS STAR CHARGED WITH POSSESSING IMAGES OF CHILD PORN'.

'Give me that!' I shriek, dragging the newspaper over to me. Rachel does not move; she is like statue. Ivan tips his chair legs back on to all fours again and buries his head in his arms on the table.

Ivan Anderson, 44, from Surbiton, Surrey, was arrested last month on suspicion of offences under the Criminal Justice Act of 1988, specifically of possessing indecent photographs of children . . .

Oh no, please God, no. Elsie was right all along. Bloody Elsie. I skim the paragraphs as words like black fleas jump all over me:

Police seized computer equipment from Anderson's house in a dawn raid . . .
Conditions of bail allowed him to travel abroad for his job as a professional tennis coach, but not to attend the club he owns, the Ivan Anderson Tennis Academy in
. . . appeared before magistrates in Kingston, and has been bailed to reappear at Kingston Crown Court at a later date . . .

I hear myself groan, long and deep. This will finish us all. And the lump in my breast throbs then, for the first time, like it is a lump of screwed-up newspaper with these evil untrue words printed on it, which some mean person has stuffed into my bosom and sewn in there when I am asleep, where it will fester and grow more poison to put through my body . . .

'Mama,' Ivan says then. He gets up and stumbles towards me, and holds me so tight that it is not comfortable and I must make his arms looser because he's making my own arm squash against my evil lump.

The lump he doesn't even know about yet, and I was going to tell him soon, and, oh Lord, how can I tell him now? How can I tell him and Rachel and Susie with all this going on?

'It's a mistake. I didn't do it, I swear. I promise you, Mama, I've never downloaded . . . that sort of stuff on to my computer. I don't even know how to download anything, you know what I'm like with computers. It'll all get sorted out. It'll be OK.'

'You don't know that,' I say, and to my shame I push my boy away from me and leave the room. My heart is beating very fast and I feel my face get red and hot. I go into the downstairs loo and sit on the toilet seat. The walls around me are all covered with framed photos of Ivan or Rachel playing matches, collecting trophies, signing autographs, meeting other famous players. It is our little Wall of Fame.

I am scared, far more scared than by what Mr Babish told me about my lump. A lump is a lump, it's my body, and I will *make* it go away. I will not let its poison stay in my body after it's taken out. Surely I am in control of that.

But this . . . I can't do anything for this. My poor Ivan. And I pushed him away.

Ted comes then, opening the door and squeezing himself in sideways. It is a tiny bathroom, with one of those corner basins which only lets you wash one hand at a time, and Ted's tummy is quite big these days from too much port and Stilton after dinner. He only just fits, with my knees in his way. I stand up, and we are face to face, as if we are about to dance.

'Let's try and keep calm,' he whispers, although his forehead is covered in sweat. I hand him the little pink towel with scallopy lace edges and he wipes his head with it. 'We don't know the facts.'

'Yes we do,' I whisper back. 'Those are facts, in the newspaper.'

'But it doesn't mean those facts are true. We have to believe what Ivan says. And he's got a point – he knows almost nothing about computers. I personally would be surprised if he even knew how to send an email.'

'Why didn't he tell me?' I say, louder, leaning back against the wall. 'Why did he not tell his mama, before it's in the paper for everyone to see? Instead he tell me lies about Immigrations people. And he tell Rachel lies about Jehovah's Witnesses!'

Ted puts his hand on the side of my waist, but I snatch it away.

'For goodness' sake, why are we in this toilet? It doesn't matter if they hear us.'

He opens the door, which means for a moment I must stand behind it like I'm hiding, and then we both come out again. I am still holding the pink towel, which I put straight into the washing machine. I must not forget to replace with fresh one.

Rachel has gone from the kitchen. The back door is open, and she has hopped on her crutches into the garden. She sits down on the iron bench on the patio and I can see she is crying. Ivan is leaning against the kitchen counter, with his hands in fists and his head low.

I take some deep breaths. I must be strong for my family. They don't even know what other bad thing I must tell them soon.

'We have family conference, all of us, now.'

'Even Susie?' Ted asks doubtfully. 'She's coming this afternoon.'

'No bloody way,' says Ivan. 'I don't want her involved.'

'OK, darling, I will ring and tell her to come tomorrow instead.' Shame, I think. It would be good to have Susie

227

there, she could help. But at the moment it would be like pouring petrol on to a big fire, with Ivan so cross already with her.

'What about Anthea?' he asks.

'I don't think so, darling, if you don't mind. She is not family. No, the four of us. We decide what to do. We will work out how to fix this. We will support you however we can.'

I go over to my boy and hold him. My head only reaches up to his chest, and I feel his heart beating hard into my ear. 'I'm sorry I pushed you away, Ivan darling. It was just shock. Of course I believe you. I know you would never do such a terrible thing.'

'Thanks, Mama,' he says in a small voice. 'I don't think Rachel's as convinced though.'

'I'll get Rachel in,' says Ted, as if Rachel is a dog who's running around the garden off her lead.

'Thank you. Please tell her to phone Kerry and ask her if everyone knows yet, if they all talk about it at the club. We need to know what is going on there. We make some plans.'

I try to sound calm, like the plans we can make will sort it all out. But the truth is, I don't even know where to begin.

28

Rachel

I can't believe it. Dad wouldn't do anything like that! He's worked with kids for years, ever since he became a coach. He knows the implications; how careful you have to be – for God's sake, he won't even be alone in the clubhouse with an underage kid, male or female. If one of his Juniors gets stranded without a lift home, he'll take them himself, but only if another adult accompanies him in the car. I've heard him saying a million times that you have to cover yourself at all costs, he's seen what even the most spurious of allegations can do to a coach's career. There was that guy in Essex, a colleague of Dad's, who got taken to court for fiddling with little boys. Even though he was cleared of all charges, he still lost his business, because his reputation was in tatters. It just takes one peeved teenager with a grudge, Dad says – perhaps someone who wasn't picked for a squad, or who got shouted at for being lazy; anything really – to complain that their coach 'touched' them inappropriately, just to cause trouble, then before you know it, it's tribunals, maybe court proceedings, and bingo! Instant career death and shame, even if only by implication. Surely nobody will believe that Dad, who is so conscientious, has been downloading filth off the Internet?

They might. Oh, what will they be saying down at

the club? Poor Gordana. How are we going to show our faces? A hot piece of gossip in the Intermediate and Midweek sections would be somebody wearing a top on court with a zip and hood, instead of the regulation sweatshirt; or bringing a soggy quiche to the Committee Meeting lunch. This will blow their minds. For the first time, I'm glad I'm injured and off the circuit. At least I don't have to face anybody.

But the club is practically our second home . . .

Pops just called me from the kitchen door, asking me to phone Kerry, and I will, but I need a minute first. I needed to get out in the fresh air.

It's cold out here. I can see my breath, in small anxious clouds, as I breathe fast. I've been sitting on a bench on the patio, but I've only got a thin cotton top and jeans on, so I get up and walk around and around the garden on my crutches, leaving little dents in the grass, muttering furiously to myself and stopping every now and again to get the tears off my face by hunching up my shoulder and wiping them on the top of my sleeve. My knee is absolutely killing me, a deep, throbbing pain radiating through the rest of my body, into the already sore place on my hip, down to my swollen ankle, but I don't care. Somehow, I want to feel this physical agony, because I can't bear the pain of how I feel about Dad and what he's been accused of doing.

What will Mark think? He'll probably believe the worst: that Dad did it. Maybe he's even gloating; telling his team-mates: 'I knew he was a dodgy git, you can just tell . . .'

I haven't heard from Mark since my accident, despite leaving him a voicemail message saying I was bound to get really bored stuck at my grandparents', sitting on my backside all day convalescing, and wouldn't he just pop round, as a friend? I am hurt that he hasn't responded immediately, but afraid that he won't at all. Now he's even less likely to, isn't he? I think about him all the time.

I feel so alone. There's something wrong with Gordana – apart from this, I mean. She has been so distant lately, and I can tell it's making Ted fidgety. Perhaps she knew about it all along and kept it quiet – although she seemed as surprised and shocked as we did. I want Mum. I want Mark. I want the mindless rhythm of hitting tennis balls over a net to clear my mind of the picture of that newspaper headline, or the image of the thrilled and appalled clusters of gossips in the clubhouse.

But what if Dad did do it? What if all those elaborate efforts to 'cover himself' were for a reason, because he did have something to hide? It's not as if he didn't have the opportunity, if he decided that young girls – or boys – were his particular bag. I think of all the hundreds of girls he's coached over the years, our smooth muscly tanned legs, our short skirts and tight tops, our sweaty bodies jumping around and panting with exertion. I remember the way he looked at that Natasha Horvath before that match.

My breath is coming even faster and whiter around me as I swing along on the crutches. Out of the corner of my eye I can see movement through the kitchen window, and I know I ought to go inside again, but I don't try to focus on who it is or if they're calling me in. The tears in my eyes make the house waver and swim like a mirage.

What is this going to mean for all of us? Especially Gordana, the erstwhile proudest mother in the Home Counties. And it's not going to do my own career any favours either, is it? Suddenly I stop feeling cold and start sweating with pure outrage. Guilty or not guilty, Dad seems to have a knack of ruining everything for me. I'm not sure how any of us are going to get around this one . . .

29

Gordana

Finally Rachel comes back into the kitchen, hopping and crying. She needs both hands for her crutches, and her nose is running. She said earlier she is meant to be on her feet as much as possible and not in the wheel-chair, but I push it towards her and she sit down gratefully. She look exhausted. I pass her a tissue and she blows her nose with a big noise. She will not look at her father. Somehow, her being in this wheelchair, so pale and with pain, makes it all seem so much worse.

Rachel so badly injured, Ivan maybe soon in jail, I perhaps soon . . . Well. I don't need to think it. But what a state we all are in, all at the same time! Now we just need Ted to discover that his prostate is up the blink – on the spout – whatever the expression is – and that Susie – I don't know. I hope nothing is wrong for Susie either . . . Bad things come in three, though, so I pray this is it for now.

'Right,' I say, putting my hands on my hips and try-ing to sound like I am in control. 'We must not panic. We must be strong. Ted, please get out the brandy; this is a big shock for us all.'

Ted leaps up and gets busy with the Waterford crystal, fetching in the decanter from the dining-room sideboard. We all have a small glass, except Rachel, who says it would not mix with her painkillers.

'Ivan,' I continue, 'you must keep a low profile. I expect since this story is now out there, all sort of unpleasant people will probably try to make you talk to them and give you a hassle. Journalists and so on. How did the newspapers find out these secret things when your family don't even know them?'

Ivan has his jaw set tight, staring at the table. 'I have no idea. Somebody could have leaked it. Now everybody will know and think I'm a paedophile. Perhaps your "friend" Elsie. They'd have given her cash for the story.'

Rachel sniffs, I think just because she has been crying, but Ivan is too sensitive and believes her sniff is saying something else.

'I'm not a sodding paedophile!' he yells at her suddenly, making us all jump. 'This is . . . not fair! Some evil bastard's set me up. I never downloaded anything, ever. I've never paid for porn. Is it really too much to expect my own family to believe me?'

Rachel bows her head, tears running down her cheeks again. Say you believe him, darling, I beg her inside my head. He is your daddy. He would not do these things.

But she say nothing.

'We believe you, Sonny Jim,' I tell him softly. Ted clap him on the shoulder in a manly way of agreeing with me.

'So, now, please tell us what happens. Do you have to go to court and prove you are innocent? Do you have a good lawyer? What happens next?'

'Yes, I have a good solicitor,' Ivan says, sounding like his voice comes from a long tunnel of exhaustion. 'He managed to get me bail so I could go to the Zurich tournament with Rach. But I'm not allowed at the club – well, you read it in there.' He jabs at the paper. 'Imagine: banned from my own club.'

He downs his brandy in one big gulp, and pours another one with a shaky hand. It is not like my boy to

233

talk and talk, especially under pressure like this, but we all – apart from Rachel – have our sympathetic faces on, and I guess this is a secret he has been holding inside him for a long time now. I hope this is not going to make him start drinking too much every day.

'Does Anthea know, darling?'

He nods miserably. 'She's been supportive . . . I suppose. I think she's in shock too. But she says she believes me. It's hard for her too. You know how worried she is about what people think of her. Guilt by association, and all that . . .'

I see Rachel roll her eyes and shake her head. For a moment I feel angry with my granddaughter. She is mocking Anthea, but at least Anthea believes Ivan.

Still, Rachel is in pain, I can tell. I must make some allowance for her. The poor girl hasn't even had time to get over the shock of her accident yet, let alone this too.

'So what has happened so far? Have you been into the court yet?'

Ivan drums his fingers on the table, talking to a bit of kitchen ceiling and not to any of us. 'I appeared at the magistrates' court in Kingston, just after we got back from Zurich, to ascertain if I was going to face criminal charges. They decided I was, and bailed me to appear at Kingston Crown Court. I don't have a date yet, but it'll probably be in another couple of months. If I plead guilty then, they'll sentence me.'

He glares around the room at us, like we're the jury declaring him guilty. 'But there is no way I will ever plead guilty to something I didn't do, so I'll plead innocent. Then they'll set a date for the actual trial. It's going to take months and months to sort through all the computer stuff, let alone waiting for the trial. It's a complete nightmare. Sometimes I just want to . . .'

He stops, and I feel my lip trembling with fear and pity for him. My poor baby. He doesn't even know there is more bad news to come. Although perhaps my little bit of bad news will not seem quite so bad now.

He takes a big deep breath. His voice sounds flat and muddy. 'This is it for me. I've had it. I thought if I kept it quiet enough, I might escape with my reputation, once they found me not guilty. But now it's in the papers, I've got no chance. José's already had to hire another coach to look after my squads – they think I'm on sick leave. All the juniors' parents will take them out of the academy, of course, because mud sticks. I expect all my squads will go elsewhere too. The club will close. I'm finished.'

Ted refills our brandy glasses. 'You don't know that, Ivan. You're a brilliant coach, old chap. I'm sure more than you think will be loyal to you. And the truth will out. There's no way you'll be convicted. You'll be found not guilty, you'll see.'

'If I can only find out who set me up, I'll kill him,' said Ivan with such anger that I was afraid for him all over again. 'All that work, all that money. All my dreams, for nothing. One nasty vicious little lie, and it's all over.'

He kicks the leg of my kitchen table hard, and Ted has to reach for the decanter to stop it wobbling over. I would have been very upset if that had broken; it was a wedding present.

'Don't kick, please,' I say sternly, and it's like Ivan has shrunk to seven years old again. Only in a heap more trouble.

Rachel hasn't said anything this whole time. She is so white that I think she might faint. I fetch her a glass of cold water, and she nods thanks to me, her eyes pink and her face spaced-out, no tears left. It is awful, just awful, to see her like that, especially in the damn wheelchair.

At least Ivan is still angry – but as usual he is too angry. He acts like it is our fault that this has happened. He glares at each of us, even me and Ted who are supporting him. I would suggest those classes you can do called Anger Management, but he might hit me.

'Darling, please, we are trying to help you. You can stay here with us, if you like.'

'Thanks, Mama, but haven't you got Saint Susie coming tomorrow?' he says sulkily. 'Besides, I know you don't want Anthea here, and I can't very well leave her, can I? We might go away for a bit – not abroad, I'm not allowed to any more. Maybe just B&B round the UK. I can't handle the thought that there might be journalists or TV cameras outside the house.'

'Darling, please keep your calm with the reporters,' I say anxiously, all the while thinking he is living in Cuckooclockland if he believes there won't be reporters. 'You have to remember that everything will be one thousand times worse if you get angry with them, you know that, don't you? Just say "no comments" in your politest voice. You will do this for me, you promise?'

He tut-tuts. 'I'm not a total moron, Mama, I do know that.'

Ted speaks up. 'Dana, they might ring here, too, if they find out our address, you know. Or try to talk to Rachel – but at least you won't be at home, Rach. We have to agree that we'll all just say "no comment" if anyone asks us any questions. Or just say nothing at all.'

'Can't you just say "he's innocent"?' asks Ivan. '"No comment" sounds like you think I'm guilty.'

'Well, it's better to say nothing, even though we know you're not guilty, son,' says Ted quickly. 'If you say anything else, they think they can get you into a conversation, and that's what you want to avoid. Heads down and walk away, that's what I advise.'

'That's what we agree, then,' I say, patting Ivan's leg. 'Darling, do you need money to pay your solicitor?'

Ivan has that furious look again, like someone has pushed him into a corner with a big pointy stick.

'No, Mama. I can manage. For now. I already owe you enough, I don't want to owe you more.' He hates to talk about money, especially when he doesn't have it.

Rachel lifts her head up then. 'I'm not feeling too good,' she says. 'My leg really hurts. I'm going to lie down for a bit. Could someone push me, please?'

How am I ever going to tell them? I must wait till Rachel's better, and Ivan's calmed down, or been to court, and this is sorted out . . . But by then, I will have had my operation.

Oh, it will never be a right time.

I must tell them now, while they are both here. Get it over with. I take huge deep breath. Poor Rachel; she will have to wait one more minute for her lie-down. 'There is something else . . .' I begin. It hurts very much to see the anxious faces of the ones I love the most.

30

Susie

I'd known who Billy was, right from when I lived in Lawrence as a student. He led a different sort of life to Ivan and me, with our lectures and papers, and Ivan's regular training. Billy was a local, one of the granola hippies who hung out on the stoop at the Crossing, a bar which was little more than a timber hut on the edge of campus.

There was always live music on in there, and regardless of the style or genre of the band, the granola hippies were attracted to it like moths to light, gyrating away to the music as if they were at Woodstock. It was quite funny to watch hippies dancing to the Lonesome Hounddogs, Lawrence's own cow-punk band. In general, the hippies disliked the students, and looked upon them as noisy inconveniences clogging up their bars, although to be tolerated because their presence did mean that a lot of good bands came through town.

'Granola hippies are the real hippies,' said Raylene on a warm day in the spring of 1980, as we sat on the stoop watching the hippies dance, 'I mean, the ones with principles and all. All the other ones just say they're hippies because they can't be bothered to wash. I'd rather sleep with a granola hippie any day.'

'Have you slept with many of them?' I enquired, taking a slug of my Corona. The lime which had been

238

wedged into the bottleneck stung my lips, so I licked them carefully, tilting my face up to catch the sunlight. When I looked up, one of the hippies was grinning at me. He wasn't dancing, like the others, but was playing hackysack by himself, deftly doing keepy-uppies with a little coloured beanbag, bouncing it off his knees and toes and sometimes behind him on his heels. He kept glancing slyly over at me. He had bright green eyes and dimples, and a sweet, babyish face which made determining his age completely impossible.

'I've had them,' said Raylene, gesturing towards a group of older men near him, all grizzled white hair and leathery skin. 'Phil, Roger and Shag. Shag has the most awful breath, but Phil was awesome.'

I marvelled at the way that Raylene boasted about her conquests. Then I thought of something. 'Are you serious about their names?'

'Sure, why?'

I giggled. The beer had gone to my head in the warm sunshine. 'So you've been shagged by Shag, rogered by Roger and filled by Phil?'

It was lost on Raylene though, as many of my British expressions were.

'And who's that?' I asked casually, jerking my head in the direction of the green-eyed younger one playing hackysack. Not that I was interested or anything – I was happy with my Ivan.

'Billy Estes. He's *real* cute – for a hippie. I had him, too, and his brother Tom.'

'Tom Estes? What's the deal with all these weird names? T. Estes. Didn't his parents realize when they had him christened?'

Raylene looked at me blankly.

'T. Estes. Testes. Testicles,' I explained.

Billy waved at me. I waved back. He *was* cute, if you overlooked the grimy torn T-shirt. Lawrence men often dressed like Third World refugees: collapsing sandals

239

and ragged shorts which looked as if they'd never seen the inside of a washing machine.

'He looks quite young,' I said, trying not to sound disapproving. I felt quite envious, actually.

Raylene shrugged. 'I like 'em fresh,' she said. 'Makes a nice change from the oldies. I reckon he's about twenty – he and his brothers have lived here all their lives. Known 'em all since they were preschoolers.'

'Oh,' I said politely, biting my lip to prevent myself adding, 'Not in the biblical sense, I hope.'

I had soon learned that there were few males in town with all their faculties intact for whom Raylene hadn't unlocked her mailbox, but she was refreshingly up-front about it. In fact, I had been wondering for some time if perhaps the only reason she had remained friends with me was because she had her beady little eye on Ivan. My room-mate Corinna and I weren't very nice to Raylene sometimes, making sly digs about her several boyfriends a week. As an insurance policy, I told Ivan that she had herpes, which wasn't very charitable of me.

Ivan and I had been sleeping together for some time now and, although I was crazy about him, I had to admit that the experience wasn't entirely satisfactory. I know they say that size doesn't matter but, as most women will concur, unfortunately it does. I wondered if that was the reason Ivan had held back from me for quite some time, although he didn't seem self-conscious about it. He was an enthusiastic lover; rather too enthusiastic, if the truth be known. Perhaps it was overcompensation, but the tender, lingering kisses he'd bestowed upon me in the months of our cautious courtship became full-on writhing assaults once we hit the sheets. He'd snog me so hard that he practically dribbled into my mouth, and he sweated copiously while we made love.

There was also an undercurrent of something more sinister, which bothered me. I didn't have the sexual experience to be able to articulate exactly what it was, and I thought perhaps I was just being over-sensitive, but he was into role play, to the extent that I some-times wondered if it was because he wished I were someone else. He used to get me to dress up as a French maid, or a naughty schoolgirl –he was always trying to spank me, which irritated the hell out of me – and he'd get a sort of glazed, frantic look in his eyes. Whatever it was, it didn't feel like love; not when he was contorting my limbs into strange positions and telling me sternly I'd been a bad girl.

But he was only my second lover, and I couldn't say that the first (my sixth-form boyfriend) had been any more proficient. He'd certainly been less imaginative. When I tried to quiz Raylene, with all her vast experi-ence, to find out if it was normal to feel vaguely unsettled, even when one's partner seemed com-pletely happy and sated, she roared with laughter.

'You're complainin'? Honey, you're lucky he don't just lie on top of you and hump away for hours, like most of 'em do. You got a good one there.'

I decided that she was right. Things were OK with Ivan. Most of the time I adored him, and, as Raylene said, 'Hell, no one's perfect. He's hot.'

She was right, I thought, turning away from the sight of cute Billy and his beanbag and gathering up my backpack. 'Anyway, I'd better go. I'm meeting him after his Economics class. See you later.'

'See you later,' said Raylene, waving prettily at either Shag, Roger or Phil, who all waved back. I tried to imagine being in bed with any of them, and it made me shudder. Bet at least one of them had white hair all over his back. Then, disloyally, I pictured myself in bed with Billy, stroking that soft nut-brown skin of his. He smiled at me again when I passed him on the way back to campus, and I felt his eyes bore into me as I walked away. I bet he wouldn't make me dress up in cheap nylon frills, I thought. Those green eyes ... Not as nice as Ivan's brown ones, though, I decided hastily, forcing myself not to turn around.

But was it possible to be attracted to someone when in love with someone else?

31

Rachel

When Gordana told me and Dad that she had a lump in her breast, I don't think it really sank in at first, with either of us. She didn't say she had cancer. She didn't say she'd have to have treatment and a mastectomy – typical of her to underplay it – and somehow, even though we both knew what would be involved, it took the sting out of the initial revelation. I think Dad is so preoccupied by his situation, and my bloody knee was hurting so much, it was as if we couldn't take any more bad news.

Even so, Dad managed to react as if she had made this announcement solely to complicate his own life further. He swallowed a bit and seemed to turn a shade greyer than he'd been before. Then, after giving Gordana a quick, wordless kiss, he left, muttering something which I think was supposed to be sympathetic, but I couldn't make out any of the words. We sat listening to his car tyres squealing away up the gravel driveway. It was as if he were fleeing the scene of the crime.

Gordana tutted. 'I wish he would not do that. Now I must get the gravel raked again.'

'Perhaps this will give him another focus,' said Pops sadly. 'Rachel, beautiful, are you all right?'

I nodded dumbly, gazing at Gordana.

'Would you like to go and have a nap now?'

I hesitated. It seemed that something more was called for under the circumstances than me rolling off to bed . . . but I had nothing else to offer.

'I'm so sorry, Gordana,' I said, my voice wobbling. 'If there's anything I can do, just let me know . . . You'll be OK, though, won't you?'

'Of course I will! It's just an operation. I will be fine. Thank you, darling.' I accepted the hug she gave me (*She* comforted *me*! Shouldn't it have been the other way round?) and then allowed Pops to wheel me out of the kitchen and into my room, where he helped me on to the bed as if I were the OAP. We both seemed dazed, speechless with worry and our individual pain.

I refuse to believe that this is anything which could in any way get the better of her. The mere thought is preposterous. At the time, though, I couldn't say anything much. I felt too emotionally drained.

'She will be OK, won't she?' I repeated plaintively to Pops. He sat heavily down on the bed, and I noticed his brown speckled scalp beneath the thin strands of white hair. Like a warm brown egg, I thought. When he raised his head, there were tears in his eyes. I couldn't cry. I mustn't cry, I thought, because if I started, I wouldn't be able to stop.

'Oh, I hope so, Rachel,' he said fervently. 'I don't know what I'd do without her, you know.'

Then he left the room and I was alone, the only sound in my ears the sound of my knee throbbing pain around my body. I let its nasty singing hum take over the worry in my brain; chase out the fear for another day. There was no room for it today. No room for anything except the escape of sleep.

Somehow I didn't expect Mark to turn up quite so soon, but the next morning there is a message on my mobile phone from him, saying that unless he hears otherwise from me, he'll be over to see me at Ted and Gordana's this afternoon at three. With a present for me. I'm almost surprised; I'd convinced myself he wouldn't come anywhere near us after Dad's scandal. Perhaps I have underestimated him.

He certainly seems excited about this present. I wonder what it is? Why is he bringing me a present at all? I suppose it's his attempt to be supportive – and not before time, either. The sound of his voice gives me a very strange feeling in my throat: a soaring sensation which I instantly suppress, overriding it with the old caution telling me not to let myself get hurt again.

Mark's absence when I really needed him; his lack of response to my plaintive messages (I left a couple more, to my shame) on top of him finishing with me – on my birthday, lest we forget – has left me feeling distinctly . . . damaged.

'*Damaged*,' I say out loud, putting my phone back on top of a nest of shiny mahogany tables next to Gordana's huge chinzy sofa, into which I have just gingerly lowered myself. The room feels as though it holds its breath in anticipation of Mark's visit. Where will he sit? Should I bring him in here to sit among the fat, shiny striped cushions, or ought we to go into the more informal kitchen? Perhaps I will open the front door to him and he'll carry me wordlessly up to a bedroom . . . The thought arouses and terrifies me in equal proportions. Am I ready, finally? And even if I am, will we be able to manage it with my knee in a brace, sticking straight out in front of me?

I hadn't realized Gordana was passing the room at that moment. She comes in. Since her revelation, she has made a big effort to look as if everything is normal. The only thing she asked was for me not to be upset. 'I have a problem. It will be fixed. If it is not fixed, *then* you may be upset. Not now though. Now we have other things to worry about.'

I guess she's right. She's having an operation to remove the tumour, and while we can be concerned at the discomfort she'll have to endure, it is a means to an end. We *may* have nothing at all to fear, once the treatment is over. I shiver. Everyone knows that the treatment is horrendous, and I can't bear the thought of her going through that pain.

'What's damaged, darling? Do you still have the receipt?'

'Oh. Nothing. Only me; and I don't have a receipt for me. If I did, I'd have taken me back and changed me ages ago.'

She laughs and ruffles my hair. 'Darling, *I* wouldn't change you for anything, even if you were still under guarantee.'

I lean my head back and look up at her from the back of the sofa. I just don't know how she manages to be so breezy, with the double whammy of Dad's . . . little problem, on top of the prospect of major surgery for a life-threatening illness in a few days' time. We haven't heard from Dad since yesterday. When I awoke from my nap last night, Gordana, Ted and I watched television with great trepidation, but there were no reports of Dad's arrest in the main news, or the local news.

Classical music swells softly around us from hidden speakers, something melancholy and familiar, full of foreboding.

'What's this music? I recognize it.'

'It's Samuel Barber, "Adagio for Strings".'

For a moment, I am none the wiser. Then I realize how I know it: it is the music that the BBC used to accompany their coverage of 9/11. As I listen, I see again the planes' impact, the fireball against a clear blue sky, then the great grey clouds of dust, people running and falling. Another great way to put my problems into perspective.

'Your knee will soon be better, darling.'

'I know,' I say. 'But actually, I wasn't talking about broken bones. I was talking about how Mark made me feel. He's coming over this afternoon, with a present for me. What do you think it will be?'

Gordana comes around the sofa and sits next to me, opening and reading a pile of post which she has just been out to collect from the mailbox at the top of the drive.

'I don't know. Do you think perhaps it's an engagement ring?'

The thought has crossed my mind, actually. I try to imagine the scenario: beautiful, penitent Mark, turning up here with hair cut short especially for the occasion; the way I like it, when he gets it shaved up the back like a squaddie and I can rub my hand up the back of his head and feel the soft hairs tickle my palm. He might even put on some proper trousers instead of tracky bottoms; perhaps the sexy combats I bought for him. He'd look at me with those huge, delicious eyes before dropping to one knee and handing me that tiny black box with a popper on the front, the sort of box which only ever contains one thing. What sort of ring would he buy me? A gorgeous antique emerald; a big fat diamond (unlikely – he couldn't afford it); or a jewellery chain store special, something unassuming and boring that I'll have to wear for the rest of my life even though I don't particularly like it?

Wait. Am I thinking that, in the unlikely event it is an engagement ring, I will automatically burst into tears, hug him, and scream: *Yes, yes, yes*?

Yes. In fact, I almost certainly would.

'Ahhh. That is sweet,' says Gordana, opening a get-well-soon card from her friends in the Midweek section of the tennis club. 'They say they will miss me, look, and I must be better in time for the championship tournament in summer.'

I look at their neat, repressed signatures and bland exhortations: *Keep your chin up, Gordana! Thinking of you!! Take care now!* All with exclamation marks covering up their embarrassment.

'I'm sure it won't be an engagement ring,' I say dolefully, watching her prop up the card on the identical nest of tables on the opposite side of the sofa. 'If he couldn't live without me, I'm sure he'd have realized it sooner.'

Gordana nudges me with affection. 'Well, you never know,' she says. 'Just don't give him too much of an easy ride, will you? I know you can't resist him, but he has not treated our little Rachel the way he should have done, has he?'

'I *can* resist him,' I reply haughtily. 'I've managed perfectly well without him for a month.'

Gordana harrumphs, and hauls herself off the sofa. '"Perfectly well?" That is questionable,' she says. 'Anyway, I will make myself scarce when he comes, and Ted will be out till later. You have the place to yourselves.'

Good, I think, in case the 'carrying upstairs to bed' scenario becomes a reality. I have a sudden, unwelcome vision of him accidentally dragging my broken leg along the banisters on the way up the stairs, bang, bang, bang, in his enthusiasm to get me into a bedroom before I change my mind again, and it makes me wince.

'Please, don't tell him about my little op on Monday, will you? The girls at the club know, but I have told them to keep it a secret. Not that I believe that is possible for one minute, but . . . at least this secret isn't in the national newspapers.' She kisses the top of my head. 'And remember: your heart has been as broken as your knee, so be careful, won't you? You are just on the mend, in all ways.. Now I must go and start to think about packing. How many nightdresses do you think I will need?'

She sounds as if she's off for a fortnight aboard a luxury cruise liner, not a small room in a big hospital to recover from having a breast removed, or, as she calls it, her 'little op'. I love her so much.

* * *

Mark duly arrives, right on time. As I heave myself on my crutches along the black and white parquet hall floor to open the door, I feel so nervous that my tongue is making dry little sucky sounds when I try to unstick it from the roof of my mouth.

Suddenly I can't even picture his face, let alone remember how close we'd been. It feels as if our intimacy has passed its expiry date. When I open the door I have a sudden urge to shake his hand and say, 'You must be Mark. Pleased to meet you, I'm Rachel.'

Instead we gaze at each other, me shyly, him in a kind of appraising way. It all comes back to me in that one look. He hasn't had a special haircut, though, and is wearing his usual baggy black sweatpants and a beige hooded sweatshirt with a tea stain down the front. He always has been what Pops calls a 'mucky pup'.

'Hi,' I say.

'Hi. You all right? You look . . . Well, you look fine, apart from the . . .' He gestures to the large and obtrusive brace on my leg, under the frayed shorts I decided to keep on. It's so hot in this house, but I'm not going to dress up for Mark. He probably wouldn't notice if I did, anyway.

'I'm fine. At least I will be, soon.'

'Great. That's great. So – can I come in?'

I stand aside to let him in. He doesn't appear to be carrying any presents with him, nor is there a ring-box-sized bulge in his sweatpants pocket.

'Did you find it OK?' I enquire politely.

'Oh. Yeah. I printed directions off the Internet. Way too many windy country lanes round here, though. Thought I was gonna get lost anyway.'

I am impressed at his hitherto well-disguised resourcefulness. Mark has always been hopeless at getting himself to the right place at the right time without the incentive of prize money or beer.

I show him into the kitchen (I have decided against the stuffy dead atmosphere of the living room) and study him. Now that he's in the same room as me, I remember his scent and the feel of his arms clasped around me, holding my shoulders in a tight grip with those big biceps of his . . . He seems a little edgy himself, shifting from foot to foot, looking repeatedly out of the kitchen window at his car.

'It's still there. Nobody's nicked it,' I say sardonically. 'Cup of tea?'

'Yeah. Yeah, sorry. Tea would be great, thanks.'

He finished with you, I remind myself. 'So. To what do I owe the pleasure?' I enquire coolly after I've filled the kettle and started making the tea.

'Rach,' he begins, a little break in his voice which makes me think: Crikey, he *is* going to propose. 'I just wanted to come and see you to say, you know, sorry. I ought to have got back to you straight away. I'm sorry I didn't return your calls and all that. I feel like a shit, actually. But . . . well, I'm not sure how to say this . . . but . . .'

'What?' Oh no, I thought, please God not more bad news. I can't handle it. I'm almost expecting him to tell me that he, too, has contracted some sort of life-threatening disease, or been exposed as a notorious diamond thief, or something as implausible as my dad being arrested for possessing kiddie porn.

'I met someone else,' he says, looking out of the window at his car again.

I swivel round as fast as I can on one leg, but the car appears to be empty except a large box on the front passenger seat.

'Oh.' I digest this with interest, testing myself for an emotional reaction. It hurts, undeniably, but above all I feel kind of numb. Perhaps it will hit me later.

'But, Mark, we finished weeks ago,' I say, as if it is perfectly understandable that he'd already be in another relationship. 'Why shouldn't you meet someone else? I assumed there was no chance for us anyway. Was I wrong?'

'Um. Well. No, not exactly, but . . .' He pauses, then blurts out, 'You *hurt* me, Rach. I thought we had something really good going. I was really upset when you said . . .' He turns away and leans against the kitchen table. I am puzzled, and shocked.

'So was I. I didn't want us to break up, you know. You didn't have to do it.' All my old passion for him returns, and I am furious that I've lost him to a new woman. 'So did you really come all the way out here to tell me you'd met someone else already? Who is she, by the way?'

'No. I came to say I'm sorry for the way it ended between us, and for all the troubles you're having with Ivan, and all that . . . I know that he and I don't see eye to eye, and well, whatever he's been up to is none of my business—'

'He hasn't been "up to" anything!' I flash back, hotly. 'He didn't do it; someone set him up.'

'Yeah, sorry, sure. But it must be a nightmare for you and Gordana, on top of your accident.'

You don't even know the half of it, I think, picturing Gordana in hospital, anticipating her bald, wan with lethargy, the skin stretched tightly across her cheekbones. It's an image which kept me awake last night.

He has ignored the last part of my question. 'So who is she?' I repeat. He looks shifty, and scratches the stubble on his chin.

'It's, um, Sally-Anne.'

I grit my teeth. Bloody Sally-Anne Salkeld. I might have guessed. He only knows her through me – she's in the same squad as me and Kerry. She's been after him for ages, not appearing to let the evidence of our involvement bother her. She's a loud, horsey, blonde Sloane with a flash car – personalized numberplate, natch – who thinks she's better than everyone else. I

251

feel like slapping Mark around the head. But since I've been playing it cool, I make a gargantuan effort to keep it up. I make myself put it all in perspective by thinking about Gordana again, and what she is going through.

'Well!' I say brightly, forcing my lower lip not to wobble. 'I'm very happy for you both. So what's this present, then? You really didn't need to get me a get-well present. I'm over the worst. It's just a matter of time now.'

'I know. But it's the sort of present I couldn't give you until you were much better,' he says, the spark back in his eyes. He is practically hopping from foot to foot now, as if the gift will wipe out all the bad feeling between us.

'Come on then, where is it? The suspense is killing me.'

'Back in a minute.' He shoots out of the kitchen and I hear the front door open. I watch him run over to his car. I've always loved to watch him run, he's so agile and sexy when he moves. He carefully extracts the large box – giving me ample chance to admire his tight rear view – and carries it gingerly back to the house. Now I am really mystified.

He comes into the kitchen and puts the box on the floor. It has a big red ribbon tying the top of it closed. Something inside is scrabbling around and making funny little noises, and my heart sinks. The silly prat has bought me a *pet*.

'It's a mental present, babe, wait till you see it,' he says excitedly. 'I just felt so sorry for you, what with your career being over and everything—'

'What do you mean? I'm probably going to be fine,' I snap at him. 'I just won't know for sure until I can start walking again.'

This is not going well. I don't want a pet, unless it's something completely low maintenance, like a tortoise. But the way the box is hurling itself around the floor makes me think that unless it's on serious amphetamines, this is no tortoise.

'Oh, right, sorry . . . Anyway, I thought: What would really cheer me up if I was you?'

Now I'm beginning to suspect he's bought me an Arsenal season ticket, and whatever is in the box is merely a decoy.

The box skids about a foot along the kitchen floor and the strange noise turns into unmistakable yelps.

'You haven't . . .' I begin incredulously.

'I have!' He beams, ripping off the ribbon and delving into the box to lift out a squirming, yapping – admittedly very cute – puppy.

'It's a dog,' I say, stupidly.

'Isn't he awesome! He's called Jackson. He's an Alsatian.'

'It's a *dog*,' I repeat. Mark is grinning from ear to ear, and in fact, at that moment, is the spitting image of Jackson, who is madly trying to lick his face. Something bubbles up inside me, an emotion I had not anticipated: pure, red, rage. 'You – stupid – thoughtless . . .' I can't think of a suitable noun, so I change the subject: 'Are you sleeping with Sally-Anne?' I yell, and burst into tears.

Funny, isn't it, how I can hold it together when my beloved grandmother tells me she has cancer, but I can't cope with my ex-boyfriend having sex with another girl?

32

Gordana

Dear Lord, I know I complain sometimes – well, often – about stupid things like Manuel not raking leaves and Ted snoring and the fact my singing career never got off the ground, and I know I don't come to see you in this beautiful church as often as I should . . . and I'm sorry, Lord. I don't know why I don't come so much these days. It is so good to be in here. It's warm and still and the colours of the windows are soothing like throat sweets and even though outside it is so windy, the flame of this candle is constant and straight and somehow brave like I know I must be. People think I'm brave but you know I'm not, Lord. Just because I have a good figure and nice clothes and am married to a good, kind, rich man, somehow that make people think I'm strong as well as lucky. Although I suppose now they do not think I'm so lucky, with my son in such a disgrace for this dirty crime. Oh, I pray it never gets back to the cousins in Korčula. It's bad enough that the Midweek ladies know. Well, everyone knows. Even the postman gives me funny looks now . . . anyway, I must not fret about it. I cannot help that.

I am strong and lucky in many ways, I know – but I am scared, Lord, I am so, so scared. I curse myself for ignoring the evil lump. I knew it was there, why did I not go to see Mr Babish and his gentle hands weeks ago? How could I be such a coward? I suppose I was thinking: never mind, I've had a good life, I am officially Old Aged Pensioner although I feel like a teenager. I have been lucky, but if my time is up, it's up, and there's nothing I can do about it.

I feel so guilty for that, Lord. It's my life, but I have others to consider. I am still a mother, and Ivan still needs mothering, especially now, whatever he might say. I can't leave him to cope with all this on his own. Rachel needs me; she has been through so much and although she does not talk about it, she must know that she might not play again, not professionally. She needs her family. God knows – sorry, *you* know – that we have not been so good at sticking together before, and now we must. I must hold us together. I wish I had enough arms to pull everyone in, all these people who can be difficult but who I love more than nice houses and clothes and success, despite what others may think. OK, so I married Ted because he said he would look after me; he was my escape. But now I want to look after him. He has loved me all these years and I am selfish enough to think I don't care if I die? I knew I was selfish, Lord, but I didn't realize how selfish . . . It makes me weep. I love him dearly.

I am glad there is nobody else in here. I don't like anyone to see me cry. I will not cry after the operation. I will tell myself that it doesn't matter if I lose my dignity and my hair, and if I'm sick all the time. Apart from sea-sickness on that unfortunate dolphin-watching expedition in Spain, I have not vomited for seventeen years; not since the bad mussel in Bayeux. But I am strong. I will cope with the chemo and everything else. I will let them stick in their needles and their toxins, just so that Ted will not be left alone, and Ivan and Rachel will not have something else to be sad about.

Besides, I am not ready to go yet. I want to see Ivan cleared of all these nasty charges. I want to win the

Veterans Club championship. I want to sing in a night-club. I want to teach Ted to do Ceroc – tricky, with those stumpy little legs of his – and to go on cruise around the fjords in Norway. I want to see Rachel married to a kind, loving man who adores her (not Mark, I suspect) in a big wedding I can organize with Susie, and we can wear the biggest, most outrageous hats we can find. I would like to watch Ivan walking with her down the aisle.

And while we're on the subject of weddings, I would love to see Ivan married again too. Just not to that Anthea; I'm sure you agree.

I won't do bargaining with you, Lord, I expect you hate that. So I will just say: Please, consider to let me stay a bit longer. Ten or twenty years, perhaps. I am too busy to go now.

33

Rachel

Mark gapes at me in genuine astonishment. 'Don't you like him?' he asks, holding the puppy at arm's length to avoid the frantic licking.

'It's not about whether I *like* him or not,' I sob, turning away, my shoulders heaving. 'And are you? Shagging her?'

'I don't see that it's important,' Mark says defensively.

'Why not? It is to me. I bet you any money if we'd been sleeping together, you wouldn't have broken up with me.' I grab a tissue from the box on the windowsill and blow my nose, but can't stop crying.

'I'm sorry, Rach. I shouldn't have come. But I really thought you'd like the dog.'

So they are sleeping together. Of course they are. Why wouldn't they be, for heaven's sake? It's what most normal couples do, unless they have religious or health reasons why they shouldn't. I stop asking him. It's obvious. Might as well just talk about the damn dog instead.

'What possessed you, without even asking me first?'

The puppy widdles luxuriantly, and it's Mark's turn to yelp as dog wee splatters all down the front of his jogging bottoms. I tut angrily and unroll several sheets of kitchen towel, which I drop on the sparkling white tiles to soak up the puddle. Gordana would have a fit if she saw the mess.

'You always said you wanted a dog,' he says, sounding defensive. 'And Gordana said you need to start doing lots of walking, so I thought it'd be perfect.'

I drop more dry kitchen paper on top of the sodden yellow sheets, and wipe them around with my good foot.

'Mark, you prat,' I say, tears still flooding down my face, 'I *can't* walk! I can't even put weight on my knee, not for three months! She didn't mean I was actually walking yet, at least not without crutches.' I brush the tears away angrily; I so hadn't wanted to cry in front of him. But they are tears of pent-up fury; frustration; grief – for me, for Mark and me, for Dad, and most of all for Gordana and Ted.

'A bloody dog is a huge commitment for anyone – I mean, how long do these things live for? Ten, fifteen years? You need to spend a couple of hours every single day walking them. And even when I'm back on my feet, who's going to take it – Jackson – when I'm away at tournaments? Plus I don't even *live* here, remember? I live with Dad and Anthea, in a house which doesn't have a nearby park, and I don't drive, so I won't be able to take him to one. Anthea hates dogs. She's probably allergic to them. The house is far too small for anything bigger than a gerbil to live in comfort with us three. And Anthea sure as hell won't want to look after him when Dad and I go away.'

It's the look on Mark's face which finishes me off. He's gone from pleased to defensive to – and this is the worst one of all – pitying. He pities me.

'You don't think I'm going to play again, do you?' I ask abruptly. Mark puts the puppy down and it immediately shoots under the kitchen table, crouches down, and defecates on the floor.

Mark spreads his arms wide and shrugs his shoulders. 'What do I know?' he says, as the offensive aroma of wet dog poo fills the air. 'It seems I can't do or say anything right. I thought he'd give you some 'stability. Something you could, you know, bond with.'

'What – now that I don't have a boyfriend any more? You don't want me to be lonely, so you buy me a dog instead, while you and Horse-Face Salkeld shag your way round the world? Unbelievable.'

I shove the roll of kitchen towel and a pair of rubber gloves at him, and go in search of air-freshener in the cupboard under the sink. '*You* clean that up.'

Mark obliges, humbly crawling under the table. 'I'm sorry, Rach. I really thought you'd love him. And he wasn't cheap, either – he cost me three hundred and fifty quid, you know!' I hear him gag slightly. 'Man, that *stinks*!' he comments in a choked voice.

'I am touched, Mark, honestly. It's just that it's so . . . *ill conceived*. I can't possibly keep him. You'll have to take him back.'

At that moment the puppy capers around the table, barking excitedly at the sight of Mark on his hands and knees down there.

'He is kind of sweet,' I admit, almost managing a smile.

Mark emerges, holding a wad of paper towel at arm's length, his head turned away in disgust. 'Where's the bin?'

'Take it outside, by the back door. But don't let the dog out.'

'Pick him up then, otherwise he'll make a run for it.'

Mark vanishes, and the dog and I are left alone, staring at each other. Jackson puts his head to one side and whines appealingly at me.

'Oh please. Don't start all that.' But I gingerly scoop him up and stroke him, wondering how clean a recently defecating puppy's nether regions are, since they're resting on my forearm. Jackson squirms joyously and licks my neck. It reminds of the way Mark used to lick me.

'Hello, you,' I say crossly, tickling him under his chin.

Mark comes back in, peeling off the Marigolds. 'You don't really want me to take him back to the shop, do you?'

I remember a book Mum used to read me as a kid: *The Diggingest Dog*. It was about a dog who'd lived in a pet shop all his life and, because of the hard stone floor, had never learned to dig. When he was finally purchased, by one Sammy Brown, he finally cracked the art of digging, and proceeded to dig up everything he could; in fact, he dug up the whole town, shops and roads and all. Jackson cuddles into me, flopping his big paws over my arm.

'Don't get too comfortable,' I warn him darkly.

At that moment Pops's car edges slowly up the drive – he always drives at speeds of less than thirty miles per hour, because he's terrified of scratching or in any way damaging his car, a beautiful caramel-coloured vintage Jaguar so shiny that I could have plucked my eyebrows by peering at my reflection in the bodywork. (Not that I ever did pluck them. Mark used to call me 'Brooke', after Brooke Shields, because of my bushy eyebrows).

We watch my grandfather laboriously climb out and approach the house. He looks anxious and pale, and my heart goes out to him.

'You haven't met Pops before, have you?' I sniff the air suspiciously, to make sure the smell of Jackson's misdemeanours has been sufficiently masked by liberal sprays of forest fruit air-freshener. It hasn't.

'No. So that's Gordana's old man? Wow, he *is* an old guy too, isn't he? Bet she wears him out!'

Mark and I used to laugh and joke about Gordana and her Midweek friends, but I can't countenance any teasing of her at the moment. 'He's not that much older than her. Don't be so rude.'

'Sorry,' Mark says. 'Can't do anything right, can I?'

Pops comes in the back door and stops, wiping his feet meticulously on the doormat. It has an image of

260

three kittens somehow stamped into its bristles, and I think how much this house reflects Gordana's taste and not his. I wonder if he minds wiping his feet on kittens. He raises his eyebrows at the sight of Mark and the puppy. Then he holds out his hand and advances towards us.

'Hello. I'm Ted. You must be Mark. Very kind of you to visit Rachel. Is this your dog? What a lovely puppy!'

'Good to meet you,' says Mark, giving him the firm handshake and eye-contact he does so well with umpires after tennis matches. Particularly matches he's just won. 'This is Jackson. He's a present for Rachel.'

Pops's white eyebrows shoot up his forehead again. He glances at me, taking in my tear-stained face, and I roll my eyes and shake my head. 'A present? Well . . . well. That's certainly . . . quite a gift.'

'I've told Mark I can't possibly keep him,' I say firmly. 'I won't be able to take him for the sort of walks that he needs, and Anthea would have a fit if I took him home with me.'

'May I?' asks Pops, scooping the dog out of my arms and into his own. 'Hello, old chap, you're rather nice, aren't you?' He scratches the puppy's head, and Jackson wriggles and pants with bliss, frantically licking Pops's hand. 'That's a shame. Why don't you at least ask Anthea if she'd mind?'

'Pops! Back me up here, can't you? I don't want a dog! Not right now, anyhow. It's too much of a commitment.'

But Pops appears to be besotted. He and Jackson are gazing into each other's eyes. 'Always wanted a dog,' he says dreamily. 'Can't imagine what Dana will say, though . . .'

34

Susie

I should have returned to England when Corinna did,
at the end of the academic year at KU, but I just
couldn't take the risk of going back without Ivan,
whose scholarship still had a year to run. Out of sight
was, I was sure, out of mind as far as he was concerned, and I did not want to lose him. He drove me
crazy, but I loved him.

So I dropped out of my degree course altogether, and
stayed in Lawrence. (There were no Immigration
issues, thanks to the lucky happenstance of my mother
giving birth to me when she'd gone with my father on
a term's sabbatical to Yale. I had joint nationality,
which meant I could come and go at will. In hindsight,
I sometimes wondered if that was really the blessing I
used to assume it to be.)

I finished my dissertation, just to prove to myself I
could; and then got a job cleaning houses. It was hard,
menial, and back-breaking, but in a weird way I
enjoyed it. No longer having to study came as quite a
relief – my dissertation was entitled 'Gertrude Stein:
Method, Aim and Influence', and by the time I was
done with it, my mind felt utterly scrambled by the
nonsensical dadaist poetry of 'Tender Buttons'. It felt
gloriously uncomplicated to scrub floors, then come
home to Ivan.

Ivan and I had a free apartment for that second year,

which meant that I didn't need to earn more than pin money for us. A friend of his had gone to Europe and wanted somebody to cat-sit his tabby, Barker, a commitment we undertook willingly. The apartment was small for two of us and a lively cat – a studio, with an irritatingly unpredictable heating system – but it was at the top of Mount Oread, and it had a balcony and wonderful views out across the plains to the endless horizons. Not to mention a bird's-eye view of the bar opposite, my local, the Crossing.

On my day off, I could check who was there, congregating out front on its shabby deck, and nip down for a beer if there was anyone interesting about. Billy, for example. For some reason, I often popped over when I saw his pick-up truck parked outside the Crossing, if Ivan was training or away at a tournament. I convinced myself I didn't *fancy* Billy, or anything so base or illicit; but he was good company and, because he was the local pot-dealer, he was always surrounded by people who I thought – at the time – were interesting. (They became considerably less interesting after several years of them walking uninvited into our house at all hours – but that was all still in the future.)

The day of the big storm, however, in January of 1981, I didn't go over to the Crossing. I stayed up on our balcony, relishing some unseasonably hot sunshine, and waiting for Ivan to come home after three days away at a tournament in Dallas. In the pre-mobile-phone era, all I had to go on was a brief call on the answerphone to say he'd be back 'some time' that afternoon.

It was ridiculously warm for the time of year. People were sitting outside the Crossing in sandals and shorts, despite the fact that just two days earlier it had been snowing. The temperature was over seventy degrees – and it felt twice that inside the apartment, since I had been unable to turn down the heating.

My muscles ached from washing windows and

polishing woodwork all week, and I felt too tired to go and do anything; so I just stayed on the balcony nursing a cold beer and reading Tom Robbins' *Even Cowgirls Get the Blues*. Barker was next to me, stretched out to about two feet in length along the balcony rail, his furry flanks rising and falling as he dozed.

Down on the Crossing verandah there was an impromptu jam session taking place: someone was thumping a bass home-made from an upside-down washpot, broom handle and string; someone else played twelve-string guitar; and a woman I didn't recognize with wild red hair was singing, just about in tune. People in Kansas knew how to make the most of a bit of unexpected sunshine, especially when it was obvious that there was a storm brewing, and at any minute we'd all be plunged back into winter again.

Billy was there, and I watched him unseen, admiring the way he was so much at ease with everybody, the way his face looked so relaxed that, even at a distance, I felt my own face relax into a smile too. He even had a kind word and a clap on the shoulder for the local town outcast, an unusually pungent and gloomy alcoholic whose real name I could never remember, but whom I had christened Eeyore for his grey pallor and miserable demeanour. That afternoon, the pre-storm air was so heavy and still that I quite clearly heard him, Eeyore, asking Billy for a quarter for the phone. Billy obliged, and Eeyore weaved slowly across the road to the phone booth near the door of our apartment block.

I saw Ivan's cab pull up then, his familiar racket bag on the back seat, and the sensation of relief that he was back safe and sound flooded through me. I watched him delve around in his tracksuit pocket for the fare, and I noticed that he didn't once look up to see if I was there waiting.

Eeyore's voice floated up to me. He had put his quarter into the phone, but he didn't appear to have dialled a number. 'Hello?' he said authoritatively. 'Yes. I wish to make a complaint. I have dirt on the back of my pants and . . . yes . . . my stomach is too large. Thank you.'

He nodded with satisfaction, hung up, and began to weave back towards the Crossing, just as Ivan finished getting his stuff out of the cab and was walking up the path towards the apartment door. They collided; Ivan's big racket bag caught Eeyore's shoulder and knocked him clean off his feet.

'Watch it, dude,' I heard his reedy nasal voice protest as he staggered to his knees. I waited for Ivan to apologize and help him up, but he didn't. Instead I heard a muttered imprecation, and then the outer door of the apartment building slammed. Eeyore, grumbling and furious, made it back over the road to the bar, where I saw Billy greet him with concern.

'Are you all right, man?' he said, and I swear he looked up at me then, catching my eye as I stood up to meet Ivan. His naturally sunny expression was gone, and something which could easily have been disapproval, or perhaps pity was there instead.

Don't be so paranoid, Susie, I told myself. But nonetheless I felt ashamed.

'How did you get on?' I asked Ivan when he came into the apartment, sweaty, unshaven and as malodorous as the unfortunate Eeyore. 'Phew, you need a shower.'

'I know,' Ivan snapped, ignoring my question about the tournament (although I should have known better than to ask. He'd have been away longer than three days if he hadn't been knocked out). 'I've been in that bloody cab for over an hour. What the hell's up with this weather? It was freezing when I left. Turn the heating down, can't you?'

'I can't. It's stuck again,' I said mildly. 'I'll run you a cool bath, shall I? Then we can have some beers outside.'

Later, once Ivan had washed off his travel grumpiness, we went out on to the balcony, marvelling at the
novelty of being able to wear shorts in January. We sat
watching the sky turn to a dark greyish-purple colour,
part storm, part evening, and laughed with awe as
lightning forks zigzagged closer and closer. The smell
of rain filled the air, signalling that the unseasonable
sunshine would soon be forgotten again. Billy had
gone from the Crossing, and the music had moved
inside, but a few hippies were still out there, their
faces tilted upwards in readiness for the rain.

Barker's tail whipped nervously from side to side,
and Ivan stroked him absent-mindedly.

I hadn't intended to bring up the incident with
Eeyore, but seeing him still over on the Crossing
verandah, sitting on his own in a corner, made me feel
sorry for him.

'Ivan,' I began, 'what happened with that man, you
know, the drunk who was making a phone call when
your cab arrived?'

Ivan shrugged. 'Like you said, he's a drunk. He
bumped into me and then fell over. End of story.'

'You could have helped him up,' I said. 'It was your
racket bag that knocked him over.'

He glared at me, his face lit by a lightning fork with
something akin to malevolence. 'Why are you asking
me what happened if you think you already know?
What did you expect me to do? Kiss it better and bring
him home with me?'

Billy might have done, I thought, but I didn't say so.
'You could have said sorry,' I said, getting up abruptly.
'Want another beer?'

Thunder crashed above us, making us both jump
and Barker growl, his fur standing up on end. He shot
indoors and under the sofabed. Ivan grabbed me
around the waist. 'Beer later,' he said, dragging me
down towards him. 'You now.'

He kissed me hard, less sloppily than usual, and I

felt lust stirring within me even though I was still annoyed. I was further incensed to realize that I was only as annoyed as I was because Billy had witnessed the incident.

'I missed you,' I said, truthfully, deciding to try and forget about it.

'I missed you too,' he murmured as the first fat drops of rain splashed on to our faces, at that stage still as warm as a Spring shower.

'Sorry you didn't win.'

I felt him shrug through my embrace. 'Can't win 'em all.' He rubbed the sides of my bare thighs, inside and out, with his big hands, then slipped his fingers up inside my brief shorts.

He was lovely when he was clean, I thought, although even just twenty minutes after his bath, he was sweating again. The rain began to fall harder.

'I'm so glad it's raining,' I whispered. 'Let's make the most of being outdoors. Let's take off all our clothes and stay out here. It'll probably be snowing by tonight.'

'Too bloody hot in that apartment anyhow,' Ivan agreed, stripping off my sleeveless top. I wasn't wearing a bra. I glanced over to the Crossing to make sure nobody was looking, but the rain had sent everybody running for cover, except for a few hardy – or, more likely, stoned – souls who had skipped out into the street to yell and dance in the rain. Besides, it was coming down so heavily now that visibility was almost zero – which was just as well, considering I was standing outside, topless.

Ivan squeezed my breasts, his eyes glazed with lust and a crafty little smile on his lips. The shape of his face was beautiful, I thought.

The noise of the rain was deafening below on the sidewalks and against the balcony floor, dashing off it in spikes which pricked my bare skin and made me shiver. It's *January*, I thought incredulously. I felt like a sponge, heavy and sodden, soaking up the water. I lifted Ivan's T-shirt over his head and threw it into a corner of the balcony. Then I ran my wet hands over his body, pushing him down to the wooden floor; smiling at the whiteness of his torso against the year-round tan of his arms and into the V on his chest. Ivan resisted my push. Instead, he sat up and quickly removed his shorts and underwear.

'Nobody can see through these gaps, can they?' I asked anxiously, referring to the narrow spaces between the wooden slats of the balcony wall.

'No. Now get yours off,' he commanded, slapping my backside hard, still grinning.

'Ow!' But I complied immediately, and as I wriggled out of my own shorts, he smacked me again, this time on my bare flesh. The slap made a sharp crack audible over the rattle of the rain. 'Stop it!' I put my hands behind me to cover my bottom, laughing and hopping around naked, squealing at him, half in fear, half in excitement. For once it didn't irritate me.

Now he yanked me roughly down on top of him on the wet floor, and I lay full length on him, enjoying the sting of the slaps and the lash of raindrops across the back of me.

We began to make love. Through the gaps of the balcony wall I could just about make out the people dancing below on the street, and hear their whoops and splashes. I lifted my head and chest and arms and legs and allowed myself to surf and slide on him, pinioned in one place only. I no longer felt cold.

After a few minutes he pulled out of me and rolled me over on to my stomach. The wet wood was slippery beneath me as he got hold of my waist and lifted me up until I was on my knees and elbows, entering me from behind, holding on to the top of the balcony for support. I could see Barker peering disgustedly out at us from inside. But then I shut my eyes to relish the sensation, and the wonderful freedom of air on my skin at a time of year when it would usually be wrapped up in woollens.

Ivan loved this position. I suppose most men do, but I got the impression that given his own way, he'd have always done it like that. I think because it distanced him, meant that he didn't have to pretend to feel closeness; he could just pump away and think about his backhand volley, or whatever.

Perhaps that was unfair. And that time out on the balcony did seem different. Maybe it was the novelty of the alfresco act, or the pleasure of the rain, but I thought we were really connecting in more than just a physical way. He always did that to me – just when I'd decided he was unbearable and I was worth more, he redeemed himself somehow.

I realized then that something else was different, and turned my head.

'Ivan,' I said in a slightly panicked voice, 'you're not wearing a condom.'

'I know,' he panted, 'I'll pull out. You're due on, anyway, aren't you?'

That was the other thing about Ivan. He had an almost spooky awareness of the progress of my cycle. I was convinced that he must have a detailed wall-chart rolled up in a cardboard tube somewhere, on which he plotted the course of my ovulation, PMT and menstruation in order to avoid either fertilization or confrontation, depending on the time of the month.

'I'm going to bend you over the edge of the balcony,' he said, dragging me to my feet again.

I protested, pushing my sodden rat-tailed hair out of my eyes. 'What? No! What if someone sees? You'll get us both arrested.'

'No one can see through this,' he said. 'Now get over there.' He grabbed my elbow and steered me over to the balcony wall. The hippies were still dancing in the street, but I could barely make out their shapes through the rain. Thunder boomed above us, and he pushed me between the shoulders to make me bend over. Pressing down hard on my back to keep me in place, he entered me again, and I felt, through the embarrassment of dangling bare-breasted over a balcony's edge and the blood rushing to my head, twitchy waves of orgasm begin to wash through me. I couldn't prevent myself shrieking out into the rain, and I heard Ivan yell too as we were both swamped and helpless.

The temperature began to drop noticeably as we lay in each other's arms on the balcony floor, until all of a sudden it felt like January again.

'Let's go inside. I'm freezing,' I said, and we staggered back to our feet. 'You didn't pull out,' I added, trying not to sound accusatory.

He glanced sideways at me, almost sheepishly. 'I know. Still, I'm sure it'll be OK. You ovulated two weeks ago.'

'I hope you're right.' I opened the balcony door and the heat from inside hit us, finally welcome. 'Oh well, if I'm pregnant, we could always call the baby Storm. Or Rain. Good old hippie names.'

'Don't even joke about it,' he snapped suddenly, ruining the mood. 'It's not funny.' He walked naked over to the fridge for another beer, leaving wet footprints on the floorboards. I was pleased to see a nasty-looking splinter embedded in one of his buttocks. Ha, I thought, serves him right. Hope it hurts so much that he's begging me to tweeze it out for him.

Then I felt a tiny strange flutter in my lower abdomen, an almost subliminal impression of movement, of development. It was a split second's prescience, but I kept it to myself.

The temperature continued to drop that night, and for the few days following it. By the time the next sunny day came around, I was already seven weeks pregnant.

35

Gordana

So many machines in our lives already. Usually I understand how they work: coffee machine, ticket machine, ball machine, sewing machine. In here, I don't understand how any of them work, but I'm surrounded by them. I have been in them, on them, next to them: X-ray machine, mammogram machine, MRI . . . The MRI doesn't hurt at all but it scares me: the thudding boom-boom in an enclosed space, the throbbing of a giant artificial heart, much stronger than mine. They have injected me with something radio-active for 'tracking'. Perhaps it make me glow in the dark, so they can keep an eye on me. All in one day: needles and machines. And then Mr Babish draws all over my chest with a black marker. I feel foolish, and am surprised that I do. What does it matter if I am being drawn on? This man's going to save my life. But I look like one of those maps Ted brings on long walks, with the dotted lines showing us where are the hills. As if we can't tell. The hills are the bits which are hard to walk up, I tell him. Anyway, I have grade three tumour. It is three centimetres wide, and Mr Babish says it's about seven weeks old and growing fast. He makes it sound like a foetus, an evil little baby in the wrong place.

It's all very tiring, if I let myself stop to think about it.

Ted's with me. He holds my hand and talks about this blasted puppy. It's the only time he smiles, so I suppose we must keep the wretched thing. It will be a good way to make Ted take exercise. But I tell him, as they wheel me off into surgery, that he has to promise he will clean up all the little mistakes. I do not wish to find dog mess under my sofa. And if that puppy eats any of my shoes, it will have to find a new home.

Ted smiles again, with those teeth of his. He'd look like Dracula, if Dracula was a kindly count. His crooked smile was the first thing I ever noticed about him, when he turned up on my parents' doorstep, at the wrong party. That was a very long time ago now. I was young and stupid then, and so grateful to Ted. I'm still so grateful to him.

I hope the puppy doesn't try and jump up on me when I come out of hospital. Lord, it makes me weary just thinking about going home again: there is not only the puppy, of course, but I need to keep an eye on Ted, and Ivan. There will be court appearances and journalists and all sort of nightmare things. Ted already looks like his heart is beating fast, all the time, and even when he's smiling, he's grey.

Rachel is a lot better, but I still worry about her. Ivan, I think, is about to explode at any moment. Susie will be at home too, and I am fond of her, but she wants to talk to me all the time, to tell her what to do with her life, like I'm some kind of expert. I can't do that any more. I will have to tell her she must decide.

These people must learn to look after themselves, I think. Let me get today over with, before I start worrying about getting home. First things first.

I feel a needle in my hand, am told to begin counting backwards, and I give myself permission not to think about it all. Ted's white hair wavers into a misty cloud, and then his face become a blob . . .

* * *

272

I wake up again, and Ted is with me, his head still a little blurry. When I reach out to touch his face, I'm surprised to find it wet.

'Have I only got one breast now?' I ask, and then I go back to sleep again before he tells me yes or no.

Next time I wake up, Ted has gone, but Rachel and Susie are both there. I wish they weren't. I don't want them to see me disadvantaged like this. I hope I am decent. I remember the time I came round from the anaesthetic after having my wisdom teeth out: Ted came to visit me and I could see he was embarrassed, because (he told me afterwards) my pyjama top had ridden up and was exposing my breasts, but I hadn't even noticed. He could have told me!

But now of course there is no chance of me exposing my breasts. I don't have breasts, plural, any more, and whatever raw unpleasantness is down there is all covered over with many bandages.

'Pops has just gone to put more money in the parking meter,' Rachel says, stroking my hand with hers. Her hand is like a man's: short, square nails, large, dry-skinned. 'How do you feel? Are you in pain?'

I smile at her. I always had such high hopes for her.

'I feel fine. No pain,' I say, automatically, although in actual fact I am rather uncomfortable. I feel as if I am lying on my front, on a bed of nails, which is strange, since I am propped up with my back against pillows. But it isn't exactly painful.

Ted comes back in the room, looking happy. 'Darling,' he says, reaching down and kissing my forehead. 'You look much better. Good news. I just spoke to Mr Babish' – we had all taken to calling him that – 'and he said that only three of the twelve lymph nodes he removed from under your arm were affected, just with a little speck. He doesn't think it has spread anywhere else!'

He is crying again. In fact, they are all crying.

'Oh please,' I say. 'What are you crying for? I told you I was fine.' The room I'm in has dark orange-coloured walls, almost terracotta, with patterned brown and orange curtains. 'I think I may do the kitchen this colour,' I say, and close my eyes again.

Mr Babish comes to see me himself soon after that. I make Rachel and Susie go home, telling them I don't want that puppy causing the mayhem in my house without anybody to supervise it except Adele the cleaner, whom I am paying extra to dog-sit in the evenings so Ted can visit; even though she will probably feed it banoffi pie and then not clean up when it is sick. She is not terribly bright, bless her. I will use the same puppy/mayhem excuse on Ted later too. He looks like he needs an early night. Anyway, I don't like all this fuss. And poor little Rachel has had quite enough of hospitals lately too.

Mr Babish tells me and Ted that, although it is very good news that the cancer hasn't spread, I am still at high risk of it coming back. I must have six months of chemotherapy and five weeks of daily radiotherapy. Five years was how long the possibility of recurrence would be highest for. Again, I feel tired. Five years is a long time to worry.

'Then don't worry,' says Ted. Funny – I hadn't realized I said that out loud. 'Just focus on the next seven months. We'll do something really special at the end of it.'

'You are so practical,' I tell him. 'That's why I love you.'

'We'll start your course of intravenous chemo in a fortnight,' said Mr Babish briskly. 'You should be able to lead your life fairly normally in between sessions, with perhaps a little nausea for a couple of days after each treatment. If you are tired, rest. If you have the energy, you can be up and about.'

'Can I play tennis?' I ask, quite seriously, but Mr Babish laughs. 'Tennis? Well, I'm not sure you'll have the energy for that.'

274

I feel cross. He'd just said I could lead a fairly normal life! Seven months without tennis is not a fairly normal life. Plus Elsie is taking lessons from that hunky new coach Ivan has just hired. It will be disaster if I come back to the tennis club and she can beat me. This is most annoying.

'We will talk about the radiation nearer the time,' he continues. 'I'll make sure you have the information you need about that, but the main thing to remember is that it's almost always painless. The most awkward part of it is that you need to do it every day, five days a week, for the duration. So don't book any holidays for that time.'

'We won't,' says Ted, who was alternately beaming and crying. What was I going to do with him? Great big wet blanket, he is.

'We have an expensive holiday afterwards, please,' I say firmly. 'I fancy a cruise. Or perhaps a party. Yes! We will have big party for our anniversary.'

'Whatever you want, my angel,' he replies, stroking my hair. Which remind me. It need setting.

'What day does the hairdresser come round?' I demand, and for some reason both Ted and Mr Babish laugh.

36

Susie

I told Rachel about me and Billy last night, on the way back from visiting Gordana. I couldn't quite believe that it's taken so long to get around to it, but she was very understanding. I think she's so traumatized by her accident and by Gordana's illness and Ivan's arrest that my news sort of pales into insignificance for her.

After we left the hospital, summarily dispatched by a rather disgruntled Gordana, we decided to grab something to eat on the way home. Neither of us fancied going back to Ted and Gordana's empty house, and the puppy was being babysat by their cleaner, so we didn't have to hurry back to walk him.

I've been allowed to drive Gordana's little Polo while she's incapacitated – very generous of her, since I'm none too confident with a stick shift, on the wrong side of the road – so I took Rachel for a little drive in search of a restaurant, and we ended up in a country pub which had some painted rosettes on a board out-side, and signs announcing that it was in the *Good Pub Guide*. We were shown into a tiny front room, with just five tables, and a careworn woman smelling of ciga-rette smoke brought us two menus.

I was starving, as per usual. Why did stressful situ-ations always induce hunger in me? It was most irritating. Just think of all the weight I could have lost by worrying instead. I hastily ordered a bottle of house white before the waitress vanished again. I needed a drink.

Speaking of looking worried, Rachel had a very long face.

'Are you all right, honey?' I asked, reaching out for her crutches so that I could lean them against the wall, safely out of tripping distance.

She gazed with unseeing eyes at the menu and sighed wearily. 'I don't know,' she said. 'This all seems . . . too much.'

'I'm sure it does. First your accident, then Ivan, now Gordana. It's a lot to take in. But it looks like she'll be fine. You know how tough she is, and fit too. She can beat this, I know she can.'

The waitress brought our wine in an ice bucket, already uncorked. She didn't deign to show it to me, ask if I'd like to taste it first, or pour it for us, but I couldn't be bothered to complain. I just needed a drink. I filled both our glasses, the bottle dripping water all over the table as I lifted it out of the bucket, its ice long melted. Rachel was studying a series of seven plates hung in an arc on the wall by our table. The first one had a green apple painted on it, with the word 'Pomme' inscribed above. The next was an apple with a bite taken out of it, and 'pomme' became 'pomm . . .' and so on, until the second from last was an apple core, and the last, a few painted pips.

'I wonder when I'll have a place of my own,' she said wistfully, taking a sip of her wine. 'I'd like some plates like these, for the kitchen. They're sweet.'

'I'm sure Gordana and Ted would lend you money for a deposit on a little flat somewhere,' I said, downing about half my glass. 'You know how canny Gordana is with money. I would, if I had it.'

'Thanks, Mum. I don't know – I've always assumed there's not much point in me buying a flat when I'm hardly ever there. But I don't want to live with Dad for ever, and Anthea hates me being there. I've got to think about it sooner or later.'

'You could always live with Ted and Gordana. And the lovely Jackson,' I added, to try and make her smile.

'I don't want to. I don't want to be the guest all the time. I want some independence. I'm fed up with Dad running my life for me!' She raised her voice slightly, and people at the other tables glanced over.

I removed my peach linen napkin from where it was arranged in a fan shape in my water glass, and spread it over my lap.

'I know. But I suppose you can't really make any plans until you find out . . .' I gestured awkwardly towards her leg.

'It'll be fine,' she said stubbornly. 'That was the whole point of the operation – to make sure I regain full use of it.'

I sighed. 'But, Rach, are you sure that's what you want? I mean, you'll have to do tons more physio to get back to your old flexibility. You'll have to work really hard to regain your fitness. It's going to be a while before—'

Rachel glared at me so ferociously I was almost scared. 'Mum! Do you think I haven't gone over this a million times? I'm twenty-three, but I know I haven't got as far in tennis as I can go yet . . . and anyway, what else would I do? I don't want to follow in Dad's footsteps any more.'

I attempted to think like a life coach. 'Well, what do you like doing? Aren't there lots of other things in tennis you could do – marketing, for instance? Or you could be a personal trainer, maybe? I know – how about running a club? You could go and run Ivan's club for him . . . No, sorry, scratch that. Mad idea.'

'Yeah. The fact that Dad's not allowed in his own club makes me not want even to show my face down there, let alone take it over. He's ruined everything.'

She was becoming petulant now, reaching down and scratching at the bandage under her loose jersey trousers.

'Oh Rach, that's a bit harsh,' I said, wondering why I was defending Ivan. 'He's only banned until the trial. I'm sure it'll all be OK again after that.'

She exhaled, in the exasperated sort of way that only a daughter irritated by her mother can.

'I need to decide what to do with my life, too,' I said suddenly.

Rachel jumped at the chance of changing the subject. 'Oh yeah. You mentioned the life-coaching thing. Are you still thinking about that? Why don't you want to be an estate agent any more?'

Here goes, I thought, taking a deep breath. Might as well tell her. I hoped she wouldn't be angry that I'd taken so long about it.

'Things have changed for me, Rach. I didn't tell you before – well, I couldn't at first, and then you had your accident, and there never seemed to be a good time for it . . .'

'What?' she said, just at the moment the waitress came back to take our order.

We scanned our menus perfunctorily, and I ordered seabass, because it was the first thing which caught my eye. Rach ordered a steak. As the waitress laboriously transcribed our requirements on to her pad, I found my mouth was dry and my heart thumping. Hold it together, Susie, I told myself. I was annoyed that I felt so uptight about confiding in my daughter – surely she should be the easiest of confidantes? I refilled and drained my glass.

'Steady on, Mum, you're driving,' Rachel said. The waitress finally went away, having taken so long to write down that Rachel wanted her steak medium, with a rocket and parmesan salad, that I began to suspect she had been executing an intricate border of flowers around the edges of her pad to illustrate our order. But I didn't mind. It all put off the dreaded moment.

'So? What's changed, Mum? Has Billy lost his job? Are you two thinking of moving?'

I twisted the bare skin of the third finger of my left hand, seeing the faint white stripe where my engagement ring used to be. 'Haven't you noticed something different about me?'

She didn't follow my gaze. 'Well. You do seem a little down. But I thought that was just because our holiday got spoiled, and now Gordana's news . . . Is there something else?'

I wanted to laugh at the understatement of it. Yes, there was something else. I nodded towards my ring finger, and finally the penny dropped.

'You're not wearing your ring,' she said cautiously. 'Why not?'

'Why might a woman stop wearing her engagement ring?'

She narrowed her eyes. 'I thought it was because you were afraid of getting your opal damaged, or losing it.'

A fair point. Billy had bought me a beautiful old opal ring from Quantrills Antique Mall and Flea Market in Lawrence, but it was so fragile that I was always having to take it off to stop it getting soapy, or bashed. One terrifying time, the opal itself had clunked out of its setting when I'd been washing my hands after using the loo at a service station, and I'd just managed to catch it before it rolled down the sink plughole. In the end I only wore it on special occasions. I missed it, all the time. I missed the way I felt when I looked at it, the way the colours flashed crimson and green and turquoise, deep inside the stone. I'd thought it reflected the way Billy felt about me. The thought of never wearing it again broke my heart.

'But I would never go away anywhere without it, would I?'

Putting it this way, it sounded like I was criticizing her for not having asked me why. Perhaps I was.

'What happened, Mum? Have you had a row? I thought you hadn't been on the phone to him much. I didn't like to ask . . .'

I dropped my voice so the other diners were less likely to be privy to my confession. 'I haven't been on the phone to him at all, Rach. He left me for a PhD student called Eva. They're living together.'

Rachel clapped her hands over her mouth in horror, and fresh tears came to her eyes. 'Oh *Mum*! When? Why didn't you tell me? Oh, I'm so sorry. Not Billy. I can't believe it.'

'Nor could I,' I said glumly. 'A PhD student? I mean, *really*. How can that possibly last?'

To give her credit, Rachel didn't even smile. 'Poor, poor you. What a nightmare. What are you going to do?'

'You're not mad at me for not telling you sooner?'

Rachel looked puzzled. 'Of course not. I'm sure you thought I had enough on my plate.'

I nodded. 'I was going to tell you in Italy . . .'

'Have you told Gordana?'

I shook my head. 'I wanted to talk to her. But not until I'd told you.'

In my mind, I saw the photograph of Billy and me at Clinton Lake, and pain zigzagged through me. It was funny how I rarely thought of him in the flesh now that I didn't see him that way any more. I only pictured him in the photos which had been on display on the sideboard: that Clinton Lake shot; a picture of us walking up a mountain, rucksacks on shoulders, grinning back at the camera; another, of us jumping hand-in-hand into a swimming pool. It was as if he'd been reduced from three dimensions to one.

'So what are you going to do?' she repeated.

'I don't know. I need to decide. I quit my job, though. And I'm not sure that I can stand living in Lawrence while he's there with . . . her. I just can't bear the thought that the second relationship I thought was permanent, isn't. Thank God I didn't marry him, eh? I couldn't stand being divorced twice.'

Rachel leaned across the table and squeezed my hand. 'I'd love it if you came back to live over here, Mum.'

I couldn't speak for a moment. 'Really?' I managed eventually. We stared at one another, and I felt so many things: sorrow, loss, love, relief that we were close again. It was terrible to admit, but for a long time it almost felt as if I didn't even have a daughter. It would be so lovely to have her back.

On the other hand, if I stayed in England, there would be no chance of a reunion with Billy. And, although it felt strange to acknowledge, England no longer felt like home, even though Rachel was here. I craved to be somewhere I belonged – but where was that place? I'd thought it was Kansas, but without Billy, I wasn't so sure. Maybe my best chance of finding a home was to stick near the only remaining family I had: Rach.

I missed my own parents then. But they were long dead, and my childhood home in Salisbury near the cattle market had been demolished to make way for a sports centre. They paved over what was our back garden to lay tennis courts . . . There was a certain irony to that.

'I don't think I'll know what to do until I know for sure it's over. I kept thinking it was a moment of madness, and he'd wake up one morning and want me back. But it's been over two months now, and he hasn't been in touch. He may not even be aware I'm over here.'

'Two months?' Rachel looked even more shocked. 'I wish you'd told me, Mum. I mean, I'm not cross or anything, but you could have let me know on the phone, even before Italy. I hate it that you thought you couldn't talk to me. And there was me, wibbling on to you about how Mark broke my heart . . .'

'It's not that I felt I couldn't talk to you, honey. It's just timing. That's why I wanted you to come skiing with me. I thought I'd tell you then, face to face.'

'Well, it doesn't matter,' she said briskly. 'We're a right sorry pair, aren't we?'

I smiled weakly. Now that the secret was out, I felt exhausted. And even more starving. 'Maybe we can tell each other what to do with our lives,' I said. I was glad now that I hadn't told her sooner. The couple of months' grace meant that at least I'd been able to hold it together. Even a month ago, I'd probably have sobbed my heart out in the telling, but in comparison to Gordana's cancer and Rachel's career-threatening injury, it no longer seemed such a tragedy. Hell, relationships broke up all the time. People got over it. It wasn't even as if we were married.

'Do you miss him?' she asked me, as the waitress brought our food over.

'Yeah,' I said. 'I do. A lot.'

Luckily, my seabass had arrived needing a great deal of attention. It was the whole fish, cooked intact and put on my plate, so what with all the decapitating, deskinning and deboning required, I was able to push Billy out of my mind, at least until I got some food inside me.

It turned into a bizarrely enjoyable evening, considering the circumstances. We talked and talked, through our main courses, through dessert (syrup pudding with custard for me – not a pudding you'd find in Lawrence, Kansas. It was delicious), coffee, and then more coffee. Rachel was telling me all about life on tour, and the friends with whom she had fleeting contact a few times a year in different places all round the world.

I was curious. 'Is it hard to be friends with girls you know you'll be playing against the next day? Do you ever hang out with the ones who've beaten you? Wouldn't it be better to be really aggressive towards them?'

283

Rachel shrugged. 'We're all in the same boat. We all want to win. We can't go round hating each other if we don't win. Usually people are cool. Sometimes they surprise you. My last match, actually, was a weird one – you rang me straight after it, and I had to go and throw up, remember? I was in such a state. Mark had just dumped me. I was in bits. But I got through to the semi-finals; and this girl I beat in the quarters, Natasha, just spooked me—'

I stiffened. 'Natasha?'

'Yeah. Hungarian. She looked familiar but she certainly wasn't a friend or anything – but she just seemed to detest me! It was the strangest thing. I mean, normally people are competitive, obviously, and often quite aggressive, but this was something else.'

'Hungarian . . . Natasha who?' My mind was racing. Could it be the same girl as the one in the photo, Tasha? Surely not; not after all these years. But Natasha was a Russian name. Were there many Natashas in Hungary?

'Natasha Horvath. I don't know what her ranking was. Or what her problem was, come to that.'

'Maybe she was just being immature; couldn't handle herself,' I said as casually as I could, although my heart was thudding. 'How old was she?'

Rachel shrugged. 'Dunno. About my age, I think. I don't think that was any excuse. It probably wasn't anything personal – I mean, I beat her, so she was never going to be over the moon about that. But the weirdest thing of all was that after my accident, I got a get-well card from her! I mean, I don't know her from Adam, and she seemed to hate me. Why would she send me a card?'

Oh, crikey. It had to be her. 'And how did she know your address?' I could have guessed the answer, and I wasn't wrong.

'She didn't post it. Apparently she bumped into Dad at the club and gave it to him to give to me. Dunno what she was doing down there . . . Oh, I think he said a friend of hers trains with him.'

So that was it. It was entirely possible that Ivan was still involved with her. Ten years later! And Ivan with a long-term, live-in girlfriend? That man was outrageous. I quickly did the maths in my head: surely Natasha couldn't be the same age as Rachel, because Rachel had only been thirteen in summer 1995, when that photograph was taken! Natasha looked young in it, but not that bloody young. If Rach thought they were the same age, though, it was unlikely that she was more than a few years older. Which still made her too young in 1995 . . .

Hang on a moment, though, I told myself. Perhaps it's innocent. It might not be the same Natasha; and even if it is, it could all have been over years ago. Maybe she resented Rachel for taking Ivan away from her, through her career?

Then why send her a card?

'Are you OK, Mum? You look very distracted. Is it Billy?'

No, I thought. It's your father: the other lying, cheating scumbag of a man in my life. The man who's just been accused of downloading child porn from the Internet.

'I'm fine,' I said, managing a smile. 'We'd better get the bill, don't you think? I don't want Ted to get back to an empty house.'

37

Rachel

It's a combination of the alcohol in my system, and Mum going all quiet when we leave the restaurant, but as I hop towards the car on my crutches I feel like a sink being unblocked. I can't stop talking. It's as if I've saved up all the things I needed to say to her since she moved to Kansas, and now the words are pouring out of me. I know that drinking does that to me, but I suppose I get drunk so infrequently that I don't usually allow myself to reach quite this stage of verbal diarrhoea. Even if I'm not in a tournament, I don't tend to drink more than one or two, because I know it will affect my training the next day. Mum had stopped after two glasses so she wouldn't be over the limit; so I ended up polishing off the bottle. And tomorrow there is no training.

So I talk and talk as Mum frowns over the steering wheel, her shoulders hunched forwards, glasses perched on the end of her nose. She has these big tortoiseshell-framed specs which I always think are at odds with the rest of her fashion-conscious image. Perhaps they're very stylish in Lawrence. Or maybe she's going for the Diane Keaton look.

I tell her about me and Mark, in far more detail than I did when we were in Italy. In Italy I hadn't been able to confess how much it upset me to think of him meeting somebody else – somebody he'd go to bed with.

'Why?' asks Mum. 'Was that a particular strength of your relationship with him or something? I'd say it's pretty natural to hate the idea of your ex with another woman. In fact, I know it is.'

She sighs, and I feel bad for making her think about Billy and his new girlfriend.

'No,' I say hesitantly. 'It wasn't a strength of ours . . . because we didn't. Sleep together, I mean.'

'Oh? Why not?'

I'm half relieved, half horrified that Mum is talking so naturally about it. It's the sort of full and frank discussion I'd never be able to have with her if I was sober. Talking about sex to your mother! Eurgh. Although it does kind of help that we're in the car, driving slowly through empty surburban towns and villages. At least I can look out of the window. It is only nine-thirty at night but there is hardly any traffic on the road.

'Because, well, actually, I've never done it before at all. I'm a virgin,' I blurt at the side window, blushing furiously, my admission steaming up the glass.

I glance across at her, to see that she is looking shocked. 'You're kidding.'

I shake my head, fiddling with my split ends to cover my confusion. Do I really need to tell her this stuff? Although, in a way, it feels good — as if my virginity is a deep dark secret I need to confess. I've never even told Kerry. She just assumed that Mark and I slept together, and I expertly fielded her none-too-subtle enquiries as to his prowess.

'But you must have had offers, surely! And what about Mark?'

'Well. Yes, I suppose so. But I'd never have a one-night stand, it just doesn't interest me. And I wouldn't do it unless I really liked the person; and I've never liked anybody enough, until Mark. I thought he was the one . . .'

'You'd have done it with him?'

I nod. 'I'm pretty sure I was ready to. I wanted to. I dunno . . . I suppose, well, I think, maybe I've got a bit of a problem with it. I've left it so long that I don't feel very confident – I mean, what if I get it all wrong? I was so scared of doing it with Mark, because he's so experienced. But in the end, that's what made him dump me. I'm sure it was. So now he's got Sally-Anne Horseface Salkeld to shag to his heart's content, and I'm still the oldest virgin in town.'

Mum smiles pityingly at me and squeezes my hand, before changing gear to go over a speed bump.

'Honey, first of all, you won't get it wrong. It just happens. Some sex is better than other sex, but really it's all about how you connect emotionally. I know I seemed shocked, but for what it's worth, I'm really, really proud of you for waiting. For not giving yourself away to the first man who comes along. You've obviously broken out of the mould your grandmother and I created, haven't you; and aren't you glad for that? Gordana, pregnant with Ivan at eighteen, and me not much older, having already chucked away my degree. At least you've got a chance to realize your full potential before you settle down.'

'If my knee heals, that is,' I say automatically.

'It will,' she replied, nodding to herself as if to re-inforce the power of positive thought. 'I'm sure it will.'

It's interesting, though. Why is it that my heart sinks when people say that? Surely I should be relieved beyond measure at the prospect of a full recovery? And of course I am – it would be terrible to be left with a limp, or worse. But when it comes to 'realizing my full potential', I find that I'm not thinking about tennis at all.

'Mum,' I say, my throat tight.

'Yes, angel?'

'Can I tell you something, in private?'

'Of course. What?'

But I can't say it. It's too blasphemous, too

frightening to contemplate, to even voice a doubt. I'm not *that* drunk.

'Oh. Nothing. Just – don't tell anyone what I told you about me and Mark, will you? It's so personal.'

'I won't,' she says, smiling at me.

We eventually pull into the long driveway leading to Gordana and Ted's house. I can see Adele, the cleaner, standing outside, a lit cigarette in one hand and Jackson's lead in the other, as he bounces around her feet, spotlit under the security lamp.

'Is that her idea of taking him for a walk?' I say indignantly, and the discussion is closed. Although when Mum runs round to hand me my crutches and help me out of the car, she gives me one of her giant, hard hugs, and I think she is never going to let me go.

'Thanks for talking, Rach,' she whispers in my ear so that the curious Adele can't overhear. 'It's so lovely to talk to you. Everything will be fine, for both of us. Talk to me again, whenever you want to. About anything, OK?'

With a bit of a shock at my selfishness, I realize that I'd almost forgotten what she told me, that Billy had left her. I hug her back. 'Yeah, Mum, I will. You too.'

She nods, and I feel her clench her jaw against my shoulder before she releases me.

38

Susie

It was the same Natasha. The writing on Rachel's get-well-soon card was unmistakably identical to the writing on the back of the photograph I had, now hidden in the inside zip pocket of my suitcase. But I still didn't know what, if anything, to do about it.

I had managed to avoid Ivan for the entire month I'd been in the UK with Rachel. I was sickened by him. I looked up Natasha Horvath on the Internet on Corinna's computer, and found her on various tennis sites: current ranking 491; trained 1995–7 in the UK – not with Ivan, although he had obviously succeeded in getting her over here – but now based in Hungary, on the WTA tour. There were pictures, too. She was tall, thin, blonde; beautiful, but tired-looking in all of them. And, more importantly, she was twenty-four years old – which would have made her fifteen when she gave Ivan that photograph. Fifteen years old . . . I felt afraid at what the further implications could mean for us all, in Ivan's current situation. The burden of such knowledge – or at least such strong supposition – was almost too great. I wish I'd never found the damn photograph.

I imagined Ivan running his dark hairy hands over her pale skin in bed, squeezing her muscles appreciatively like a trainer checking a racehorse's legs. Had he loved her? Did he still? Or had he seen it as protecting an investment . . . And if so, how many others had there been? I wanted to know – and yet didn't, at the same time.

Gordana had begun her chemo. She professed to be fine, but spent whole days in bed, looking out over her garden, listening to Radio Four. She wouldn't let Rachel do anything for her except read aloud to her (they were two-thirds of the way through *Rebecca*, although Gordana already knew it so well that her lips sometimes moved along in time with the reading). She permitted me to do a little shopping and cooking for us all – but only because I absolutely insisted, and said I would go and stay in a hotel unless she allowed me to.

Ted and Ivan put together a rota for driving her to her chemo appointments. I did volunteer too but was, politely and in the nicest possible way, refused by Ted.

'She's using it as an excuse to talk to Ivan,' he said, tapping his nose knowledgeably. 'It's the only way the bugger's actually ever going to tell her what's on his mind – and you know she's desperate to find out. Her theory is that if he's trapped in a car with her, he'll have to spill the beans eventually.'

I smiled sympathetically, thinking that I could fill Gordana in with a few salient facts about her precious boy . . . but of course I wouldn't do that. There was no way I was going to make Gordana's life any more difficult than it already was.

Gordana had another session today, and she and Ted had left a couple of hours earlier than usual, because she wanted to get her nails done first. Rachel had got a lift to Kingston with them – she was going to physio – and Jackson and I were alone in the house, which was quite a relief.

I'd been out with Corinna the night before, and felt hungover. Corinna could drink me under the table, and even a low-key dinner at a restaurant in Richmond had turned into a marathon drinkathon, ending up with me getting the last train and then a cab back to Ted and Gordana's, very much the worse for wear.

Jackson and I had been dozing on the sofa, his head on my shins, drooling and snoring softly into my knees – more male attention than I'd had for quite some time, I reflected, trying to shift his heavy head to avoid my leg cramping up. I heard a car coming up the drive, and tutted.

'Oh great,' I said to Jackson, who jumped up and barked frantically. 'Company. Just what we didn't need. Excuse me, buddy, I'd better see who it is.'

Staggering over to the window on wobbly legs, my heart plummeted when I saw Ivan parking his BMW at an untidy angle in the driveway. I caught him glancing over at the house as he climbed out of the car, and I ducked underneath the windowsill, my head pounding from the sudden movement. He looked a lot older than when I last saw him. He looked a lot older than me, come to think of it, although we were nearly the same age. I had to confess that I got a frisson of pleasure at the fact that he hadn't aged as well as I had – not that I thought that I had, particularly, either.

'Bother, damn, bother,' I muttered, crouching on the carpet. 'What am I going to do?'

I heard his footsteps snarling across the gravel, and the ensuing decisive stab at the doorbell. At least he didn't appear to have a front door key. I waited, holding my breath, wishing I had some Alka-Seltzer for my churning stomach. Jackson danced around my feet, still barking.

Ivan rang the doorbell again. I considered continuing to ignore it, but conscience got the better of me. I sighed. Typical of him to catch me unawares and hungover, without make-up. I hated the thought that he would look at me and decide that it was I who hadn't aged well. Still, I guessed he probably had more pressing things on his mind.

I straightened up, smoothed down my hair, and probed the corners of my eyes to remove any stray blobs of sleep. If my make-up bag had been within reach, I'd have been able to make an emergency application of lipstick, but unfortunately it was up in my bedroom. I'd just have to brazen it out.

I bit my lips and pinched my cheeks – which always made me feel like a Jane Austen heroine, but which did work, as a short-term beauty measure – and, shutting Jackson in the living room, went to open the front door.

'Oh . . . it's you. Hi,' said Ivan unenthusiastically.

'Hello, Ivan,' I replied frostily, standing aside to let him in. 'Long time no see.'

He nodded, not meeting my eyes. 'Is Mama ready?'

'Ready? No . . . Gordana left ages ago, with Ted.'

'What?' he exploded. 'We arranged that I'd drive her today – I've had to rearrange my whole schedule for this!'

I held up my hands in mock surrender and backed away a couple of steps. Ivan's tantrums no longer bugged me, I noticed with detachment. In fact, they were rather entertaining, now that they didn't impact on me. I felt sorry for Anthea.

'I think you might have the wrong week. Ted mentioned this morning that you were taking her next time – he sounded very certain. In fact – look, come and I'll show you. It's on the kitchen calendar. Why don't you come in and have a cup of tea, since you've come all this way?'

I fully expected him to say no and flounce off again, but instead he gazed at me appraisingly for a moment. 'No reason we can't be civil to each other,' he muttered eventually.

That's what you think, mate, I thought, smiling sweetly. I hadn't planned to say anything to him about the photograph, especially on top of all his other problems – but this just seemed too much like the perfect opportunity. Surely I had a right to know? Although I did run the risk of ending up with egg all over my face if there turned out to be an innocent explanation . . . and even if there weren't, he was bound to deny it. But what the hell. I'd know, straight away, from his expression.

He marched past me into the kitchen and examined the calendar on the wall, clearly expecting me, or Ted, or both of us, to have made a mistake. 'I wish people would be clearer about arrangements,' was all that he conceded, when he saw *Ted –R.M.* (for Royal Marsden) scrawled next to the day's date in black marker. I resisted the impulse to comment that it couldn't really have been much clearer than that.

I put the kettle on. 'Excuse me. I'm just going to the loo,' I said, escaping upstairs to retrieve my make-up bag. Answering the door to Ivan au naturel was one thing, but I couldn't countenance an entire conversation with him without the armour of Beauty Flash Balm and lipgloss. It wasn't that I was trying to impress him – far from it! – but I'd just feel far more confident once I'd powdered my nose.

When I returned, Ivan was looking at Jackson's bowls on the floor, puzzled. 'Ted and Mama have bought a *dog*?' he asked.

'Jackson? He's been here for weeks now. Surely you knew that? But they didn't buy him. He was originally a present for Rachel, from her ex-boyfriend – Mark? She said she couldn't keep him because Anthea would go ment— um . . . Anthea wouldn't like it. And she hasn't exactly been able to walk a lively puppy twice a day. So Ted offered to keep him instead. He's cute. He's shut in the living room at the moment.'

'Huh,' said Ivan, bemused. 'Maybe she did tell me.'

Rachel probably had, I reflected. Ivan had a very bad habit of not listening to things he was told.

He tutted. 'So Mark gave her a puppy. What a dickhead. Poor Rach.' He sounded affectionate, and I smiled at him for the first time, feeling almost fondness – until I remembered the mess he'd made of all our lives.

I made the tea, annoyed with myself for still knowing that he took his black with one sugar.

'How've you been, then?' he asked gruffly. 'How's the old man?'

I hesitated, then thought: Sod it. He had to find out some time. At least I could be the one to tell him. 'We broke up. He left me for another woman.'

Ivan looked sheepish. 'Oh. Sorry to hear that, Susie.'

I shrugged. 'It happens,' I said in loaded tones.

'S'pose it does,' he acknowledged. Natasha's card was still up on the kitchen windowsill, mixed in with both Gordana's and Rachel's other get-well cards. I actually saw his eyes flicker towards it, and away again.

Suddenly I felt angry. Perhaps it was the humiliation of having to tell Ivan about Billy, or perhaps it mattered more to me than I was allowing myself to admit that Ivan had also cheated on me, but I didn't want him to get away with it.

'How's Anthea?' I asked breezily.

'OK, under the circumstances, thanks. Working on a new collection.'

I suppressed a shudder at the thought of another of Anthea's 'collections'.

'And how's Natasha?' I added slyly, but in just as matter-of-fact a voice.

He was so startled that his hand twitched in the act of bringing his mug to his mouth, slopping tea on to the kitchen table.

'Natasha . . . Natasha who?' he said, panic flaring in his dark eyes.

'Natasha Horvath,' I said, taking a J-cloth from the sink and mopping up the spillage. 'Elbows, please,' I added bossily, making him lift his arms from the table so I could wipe underneath them.

'I recognize the name,' he stammered.

I stopped wiping the table and stood over him, my arms folded.

'Ivan. Of course you recognize the name. She's your bit on the side, isn't she? Or at least she was, when you were still married to me. And I'm guessing you're still in touch, otherwise I don't know how she'd have got that card to you for Rachel. I'm surprised you passed that on – bit careless of you, wasn't it?'

'It fell out of my pocket and Rachel found it,' he admitted, shoulders slumped.

'So you're still seeing her – nine years later? That's quite some fling. Or is it "true love"?' I made sarcastic quote marks with my fingers. 'In which case, what are you doing with Anthea? No – on second thoughts, don't tell me. It's too sordid. I don't have any interest in what you're up to now. It's what happened when we were still married that interests me.' I paused. 'Especially since, nine years ago, she was only fifteen, wasn't she?'

He buried his head in his arms. I noticed that he was almost completely bald on top.

'Perhaps she was only one of many,' I continued, a hard, ruthless streak of pent-up rage flaring within me. 'All those innocent little Eastern European girls who looked up to you? How many of them did you sleep with and promise to make into superstars?' I put my mouth close to his ear and hissed into it: 'How many of them while we were married, Ivan? How many times did you cheat on me, you worthless bastard? This is not a good time for all this to come out, is it? Arrested for downloading obscene photos of children, and then it turns out you've had underage sex? You'd lose your club, and your licence. You'd definitely go to jail.'

I had never seen Ivan looking so completely paralysed with fear. He reached out and gripped my forearm hard, his face completely white.

'Get your hands off me,' I said, wrenching him away. 'I asked you a question: how many were there?'

His leg jiggled convulsively under the table, making it jog and the tea spill again. This time I ignored it, and the puddle slid silently to the edge of the table and began to drip in a thin stream on to the floor.

Ivan continued to look at me in terrified appeal. 'Susie,' he said urgently, 'you have to believe me: this has *nothing* to do with the charges, nothing at all, I swear. I didn't even know she was that young; she told me she was seventeen.'

I snorted. 'Seventeen – oh well, in that case, that's fine . . . God, Ivan, what were you thinking?'

He didn't answer. 'How did you find out?' he said instead, through gritted teeth.

I put my hands on my hips. 'Let's just say I found some pretty compelling evidence,' I said. 'You ought to be ashamed of yourself; a man in your position. You give coaches a bad reputation.'

'What are you going to do?'

I considered, a finger on my chin. I wouldn't say I was enjoying this – in fact, I felt sick – but I knew Ivan well enough to know that I had to sound like I meant business, or he'd think he had got away with it.

'I want you to tell me if it's still going on.'

'How do I know you won't tell Anthea?'

'You don't. But if you don't talk to me now, I definitely will.'

He sighed. 'You probably won't believe this, Susie, but I love her – Tasha, I mean. We met when I went over to Hungary for three months to coach, do you remember? Ages ago.'

'You took Rachel with you,' I said, appalled. 'Rachel was only a couple of years younger than Natasha!'

'I had no idea,' he replied, rubbing his sleeve over the puddle of tea still dripping off the table. 'I believed Tasha when she told me she was seventeen. If you must know, it scared me just as much. But we kept in touch. You and I split up. I brought her over and had someone else coach her for a few years, but then her

297

visa ran out and she had to go back. She wrote and told me it was all off, and that's when I met Anthea. But then about two years ago I bumped into her at a tournament with Rach, and . . . well . . . it started up again. I'm crazy about her, Susie. I don't know what to do.'

I almost felt sorry for him. There was a pleading tone in his voice that I'd never heard before.

'Why don't you finish with Anthea if you're in love with someone else? It's hardly fair on her, is it?'

He spread his hands wide on the table and examined them, as if he was about to have a manicure. I remembered his hands. They were like unformed implements to him – he couldn't do anything which required delicacy or precision. He held tennis rackets and cutlery in the same way: fisting them with his grip. No wonder he was no good in the sack.

'I know. But Tasha, well, she won't make up her mind about what she wants. I only ever see her when she's playing in the same tournaments as Rachel. She's pissed off with me for even having another girlfriend.'

'Is that why Rachel got such bad vibes from her that time, when Rach beat her?'

He nodded miserably. 'She's completely threatened by Rachel. She thinks that I should coach her, Tasha, instead – she only wants me if I'll commit a hundred per cent to her – even though she won't commit to me either.'

So I was right. 'And Anthea's got no idea about all this?'

He looked up. 'No. Please don't tell her, Susie. She knows things haven't been great between us, but I can't tell her. I don't want to risk losing her too. I'm already in such shit with all this computer stuff. Although I didn't do it, you know – it'll come out that I'm innocent.'

'Ivan! That is so pathetic, hedging your bets like that! How do you think Anthea would feel, knowing that you're only staying with her until you find out whether someone else will have you or not? And what about Rachel? It would be terrible for her to find out that you cheated on me when we were married, and even worse for her to think that the only reason you insisted on coming to her tournaments with her was to see Tasha! It's bad enough for Rachel, knowing that you're on bail for—'

'It's not a barrel of laughs for me, either, you know!' Ivan interrupted querulously. 'Besides, it's not true about her tournaments. I come with her because I'm her business manager, not for any other reason. It just happens to be the way I get to see Natasha too.'

'Convenient,' I said, walking down the hall and back to release Jackson, who had started to paw and whine at the living room door. 'OK, buddy, keep your legs crossed. Tea makes me want to pee, too. I have to walk the dog,' I added coldly to Ivan, unclipping Jackson's lead from the coat hooks behind the back door. 'I think you'd better leave now. I need to think about all this stuff.'

'Right,' Ivan said, trying to regain his composure. I could see how much he was loathing all this. 'But please remember, Susie, that there are other people involved here, who stand to get a lot more hurt than you've been. Yes, I cheated on you, and I'm sorry. But I've got so much on my plate, and besides, it's ancient history now—'

'So that makes it OK, does it?' I flared back at him. It wasn't ancient history to me, not right at that moment. I remembered exactly what it felt like to be almost certain that Ivan was lying to me and seeing someone else, but being unable to prove it; the twisted worm of unease which made me hate myself for doubting him, but equally convinced that I had every right to. And now, it seemed, there were a whole lot more reasons to doubt Ivan.

'I'm not saying that. It was wrong of me. But don't

punish Anthea and Rachel for it. Not to mention Mama – just think what it would do to her . . .'

That was it. I saw red. I marched over to him and slapped the tabletop hard with my palm, wishing it could be his pouchy, hard-done-by face.

'How *dare* you bring Gordana into this! If you had any consideration at all for her feelings, you wouldn't be such a lying, cheating shit to begin with. After everything she's done for you – she loves you, unconditionally, and you can't even give her the courtesy of a chat when she needs one! You do nothing for her unless it suits you; nothing . . . And now you're trying to worm your way out of this situation by making out it's Gordana's feelings you're trying to spare? You make me sick, Ivan. I am so glad I'm not married to you any more. Apart from Rach, I consider the whole time we were together as a total waste. You're nothing. Billy was twenty times the man you'll ever be.'

Ivan shoved back his chair and stood up, towering over me. I wondered if he was going to hit me, and almost wanted him to. I wanted to wind him up, make him do something which would prove to everyone what a toad he really was.

'You think you're so perfect, don't you, Susie, lecturing everyone else about their faults, but you need to take a long hard look at yourself, wouldn't you say? I mean, even Saintly Billy couldn't stand you, could he? And I don't blame him. No wonder he cheated on you, you bitter old cow. So, you go right ahead and do your worst, then. Ruin Rachel's life as well as mine and Anthea's, if that'll make you happy. Do what the hell you want – I don't care any more. But just don't try and tell me that you know anything about my life, or what I'm going through, because you know jack shit, OK?'

He was breathing heavily into my face, challenging me with his dark eyes, and his breath was as sour as the insults issuing from his mouth. I marvelled at the number of mornings I'd spoiled, waking up with that breath wafting lies across my face as my welcome to the day.

He turned abruptly, yanked open the back door and stormed out. Jackson was so freaked out by the fury crackling in the room that his hair had flattened against his back, and he didn't even try to escape out into the garden when he had the chance. He backed up against the wall and shivered.

I heard Ivan's car start up and screech away down the drive, scattering gravel so far that a few stones rattled up against the glass of the conservatory on the side of the house, in a horrible parody of the lover who throws pebbles at his beloved's window.

39

Gordana

Now that these chips are down, I suppose I must start being a little more honest about some things. My feelings, I suppose. Honesty doesn't come that easily to me, although I never realized it before. It's like something unpleasant you find in your mouthful of food at a dinner party: gristle or a fishbone or something which must be dealt with, in the most discreet way possible, with nobody else noticing. Don't make big fuss about it, just spit it into your napkin and carry on as normal. I do dislike people who boast about how honest they are. It's so distasteful.

But even though I have said this, I am not going to be completely honest about my prognosis, apart from to Ted. I have decided that whatever happens, I will pretend everything is A-OK, for as long as I can. I mean, what is the point of letting them all worry so much? There is nothing they can do to change anything, if things are not good. Besides, I believe that if you run around weeping and wailing and gnashing the teeth it does not help. Much better to believe that all will be well. 'The power of positive thought': I read an article about this in my *Woman's Journal*. So I am always going to look forward, and make many plans.

We are going to go on a cruise every year. I am so much looking forward to it. I will wear those funny sweatbands on my wrists to stop me getting sea-sick.

We will of course be asked to dine on the captain's table. I specifically want to go on one of those cruises which goes to Korčula, to look at Marco Polo's house. How funny it will be! I will dress up in my best clothes to get off the ship that day. I've seen Marco Polo's house many times as a child, so I'm not interested in that. All which interests me is to swan ashore, the prodigal daughter returning. I used to dream I'd go back with Ivan a star; but it didn't happen. Then, in my head, the scenario was of me boasting about my champion granddaughter, but that hasn't really happened either. Although I will settle for just bringing a few snapshots of our house with me, to show all my old neighbours and cousins and so on. They will gawp in admiration for a while, running their eyes over my beautiful silk suit and my expensive handbag, and then I'll look at my watch (Tag Heuer, not that it will mean anything to them), and say, 'Sorry, our cruise ship leaves shortly. We're off to Greece next. So long!'

But this is all fantasy, and there are more important subjects I must consider too. For one, I think I must be honest with Ted about Ivan. There are a few things that I haven't ever told him, and he probably needs to know. I tell him everything else, so I must tell him this too.

40

Susie

After the scene in Gordana's kitchen, a lot of things were beginning to come back to me from my years with Ivan: doubts confirmed; small mysteries unravelled. There was one party, a smart LTA bash, black tie and five-course dinner. I couldn't remember what it was in aid of, but I'd been so looking forward to it. I remember it because it was the beginning of the end of our marriage.

Ivan had been coaching at this academy in Budapest, with Rachel training as an up-and-coming Junior, and I had missed both of them, a lot. Of course I was used to Ivan being away from home, but it was the first time Rachel had travelled with him for any length of time, and three months was a very long time for me not to see her.

At the time I'd had a nagging feeling that Ivan would find it a struggle to have sole charge of Rachel – thirteen, hormonal and stroppy – but I hadn't envisaged him meeting the love of his life out there, a girl not much older than Rachel herself . . . I mean, really – how had they begun their courtship? Out for pizza and coke as a threesome? It didn't bear thinking about.

Anyhow, the invitation to the party had arrived while they were away, for a date about a month after their return. I propped it against a vase on the mantelpiece in the front room, admiring daily its gilt wavy edges and embossed writing. Despite Ivan's stature in British tennis, I didn't actually get to go to many parties with him. He usually went on his own. But this invite was to both of us: Mr and Mrs I. Anderson, and I had already RSVP'd, going to the library especially to consult *Debrett's* on the correct way to reply to such a formal invitation. The week before Ivan's return, Gordana took me to a little boutique she knew, where the owner greeted her with a kiss on both cheeks, and where they both helped me buy a beautiful chiffon evening dress. The dress was purple and a dark, dark blue, with spaghetti straps on the shoulders. It fell around my shins in fronds which wafted when I moved, and made me look, I thought years later, rather like a sexy version of one of the Dementors in the Harry Potter film. I couldn't wait to show Ivan. One of his rare compliments to me had been regarding my shoulders. I never forgot the night he said I had beautiful shoulders, and after that I always used to wear strappy dresses. I bought sexy underwear too, thinking that perhaps if I made more of an effort, we might resurrect our woeful sex life. It could be a new start.

When the two of them got back from Hungary, things did initially seem to be looking up. Rachel was genuinely happy to see me again, and Ivan was making an effort to be nice. He even let me show him the dress, hanging in our wardrobe in clear plastic, waiting for the night of its debut.

But the week before the party, he came back from the club with a frown and a hangdog expression.

'Susie, listen,' he'd said. 'That LTA party.'

'Yes? Oh, that reminds me. I have to get my nails done for it. Maybe you could run me down to the hairdresser first, my appointment's at—'

'There's a problem,' he said, holding up an imperious hand.

'What? It hasn't been cancelled, has it, because—'

'It hasn't been cancelled. But the thing is, do you remember me telling you about Tracy?'

I shook my head, bemused. 'Who's Tracy?'

'My ex,' he said, rather impatiently. 'The psycho one I went out with for about six months, and then dumped when I got the scholarship to KU. She never forgave me. Well, you won't believe this, but she rang me today.'

'Oh? What's this got to do with the party?'

'Um. Well, the thing is, she's always had it into her head that I dumped her for you.'

I was still confused. 'But you didn't know me before you came to Kansas.'

'I know. But when I came back with you, and you were pregnant, she convinced herself that the whole scholarship thing was an elaborate set-up to enable you and me to start our new life together, away from her.'

'But that's crazy!'

'I know. I told you she was psycho. You must remember me telling you about her.'

I remembered no such thing, other than vague mentions of a girl called Tracy with whom Ivan had gone out for a while when he was at school.

'I still don't see what this has to do with the party.' I had a feeling of unease creeping up my chest and neck, like a blush.

'I haven't heard from her for years,' he said. 'But she rang me this morning on the mobile. I couldn't even work out who she was at first – I certainly didn't recognize her voice. Turns out that she got a job as a sports journalist – she was always pretty sporty. She'd found out that I'm invited to the party—'

'*We're* invited to the party,' I corrected frostily.

'Sorry, *we're*,' he conceded. 'And then she went all funny, and said, "Is *she* going?" I said who do you mean, and she goes, "Her. The bitch that stole you off me." I told her, Susie, that you had nothing to do with our break-up, and I said it was fifteen years ago anyway, so what was the big deal, etc. etc., but then she said, "We need to talk about this. I'm coming over to your club, now." '

'*What?* She didn't, surely. After fifteen years?' I was horrified.

'She did. She turned up when I was coaching two Juniors. Stood at the side of the court, crying, can you believe it.'

I couldn't – and didn't – believe it. 'Was she on drugs?'

'Possibly. I had to stop my lesson halfway through to go and talk to her, but then she started screaming at me. It was very embarrassing.'

Ivan looked really upset now, so I put a semi-sympathetic hand on his hard leg.

'What was she saying?'

He sighed theatrically. 'She said I'd ruined her life, that she thought we were going to get married, that she'd been waiting for me to break it off with you and come back to her . . . All that kind of stuff. I kept saying she couldn't possibly have waited fifteen years without contacting me until now, but she said she had been married herself for a bit, to someone who she thought would help her get over me – but it hadn't worked out. Then she started, um, being rather threatening about you.'

'Me?'

'Yeah. She said she was going to this party, and if she saw you there with me, I'd regret it.'

'What the hell is that supposed to mean?'

'I don't know. She's quite a well-known journalist, apparently. She could make things very awkward for me if she started printing lies. Or worse, she may have meant that she'd do something to hurt you . . .'

I couldn't believe what I was hearing. 'You're not

307

seriously suggesting that I can't go to the party because of her?'

'Well, I'd hate for you to be in any sort of danger. Or for her to cause trouble for me.'

I was outraged. 'Danger? That's a bit bloody melodramatic, isn't it? Who does she work for? I'll phone them up and get her fired. I'm your wife, for heaven's sake. She can't threaten us like that! It's totally unacceptable, and there's no way I'm not going to that party.'

Needless to say, Ivan got his way, and I didn't go to the party. I was so upset about it that I actually cried, burying my face in the soft fabric of the Dementor outfit after Rachel had gone to bed, picturing Ivan having a great time, flirting and drinking and appraising women with that particular hungry expression on his face which he never wore when looking at me.

When he slid into bed beside me in the small hours of that morning, I badgered him to tell me about the party, and if Tracy had given him any grief, but all he managed to mumble was, 'She didn't show up', before rolling over on to his back and snoring, loudly, for the rest of the night. I could tell that he was pretty drunk, though, because I punched him in the side three times to try to get him to turn over, and he didn't budge at all.

I lay awake all night, my teeth gritted, silent tears of rage falling sideways into the pillow. It wasn't just the party, of course, it was Ivan. If he'd cared at all about me, he could easily have called me a taxi and got me over there, better late than never. Hell, I'd have called the taxi myself, if he'd only rung me.

His argument later, of course, was that he was afraid she'd show up at any minute, or that perhaps she hadn't been invited after all but was hanging around outside.

'I wouldn't want her to do anything stupid,' he said. 'How terrible would we feel if she lost it completely and topped herself?'

Personally, I thought, I'm not sure that I would feel all that terrible. Sad for her, of course, but really, I did not see that I had anything at all to feel guilty about, and I resented the fact that Ivan was implying somehow that I did.

I attempted to find out about Tracy; who she was, whom she worked for, but it was 1995, before the Internet was in every household, and I only drew blanks when I rang up all the major daily newspapers' sporting desks to see if anyone knew or employed her. I asked Gordana if she remembered her, but all she said was, 'Oh yes, Tracy. Nice girl, I always thought. Very quiet, though. What is that expression: wouldn't say boo to a pigeon?'

'Goose,' I'd replied, thinking that that didn't sound a bit like the woman Ivan had described. Next time I'd taken Rachel to her tennis practice I'd asked some of the other Juniors' mothers if they'd witnessed the scene with a strange woman crying and screaming at Ivan, but nobody had.

In fact, the mysterious Tracy appeared to make a miraculous recovery from the terrible loss of a relationship which had apparently obsessed her for fifteen years, and promptly vanished out of Ivan's life again. But I couldn't forget her. Something inside me had buckled so far under the weight of my suspicions about Ivan's liberties with the truth, that I just couldn't stand it any more. I hated myself for it, but I became a checker for lipstick on collars, a pocket-rummager, a phone-bill analyser. Nothing concrete came out of it, except the gradual erosion of my self-respect, and trust for Ivan – for he did nothing to assuage my increasing fears.

'This is not me,' I thought one morning as I was feeling through the lining of his washbag in search of condoms that we had no need of, since I was on the Pill.

'I don't want to be like this,' I thought later, checking his diary for tiny inexplicable initials or restaurant bookings.

'I want a divorce,' I announced quietly a few weeks later, one evening after he'd just got in from squad training. 'I don't trust you any more, and I don't think I love you, either.'

He was sweaty and stubbly, in his oldest tracksuit and beat-up tennis shoes, but I still had to sit on my hands to stop myself opening his racket bag to see if he had a smart suit in there, the suit he must have worn on the date he had probably just been on. Perhaps he was sweaty from making love all evening to some girl in a hotel bedroom. Perhaps the stubble was a decoy to throw me off the trail.

He had leaned against the doorframe, exhausted, baggy-eyed, filling the doorway with his bulk, just looking at me, a wreck on the sofa. There was no fight left in me. And as I sat there, I remembered good things about him: his face when Rachel was born; the way he cried for joy when she slithered out of me and looked up at us with her own perfect little face. His dedication to so many things – although no longer to me – his enthusiasm and energy and drive. His gorgeous eyes.

I waited for the outraged refusal to accept what I had said. The impassioned pleas for another chance; the protestation of the love he really had for me, but which had become buried under the pressures of competition, travel, and perhaps just the inevitable familiarity of a marriage. The apologies, the tears, the wooing back again.

'It's probably for the best,' was what he said instead. Then, 'I'm going for a shower.'

Two days later he moved out. Two months later I moved back to Kansas.

We were divorced within a year, on the grounds of his unreasonable behaviour. He never admitted to his affairs, but I knew he'd had them – at least one. And now, all these years later, I knew that I'd been right.

41

Rachel

'Want a cup of tea, Gordana?' I ask.

From where she is propped up on pillows on the sofa, Gordana looks over at me standing in the doorway. She rarely goes to bed, unless she is feeling particularly sick, instead choosing to rest fully dressed on the sofa downstairs. She says it's so that she can see out into the garden, and also so Ted and I don't have to run up and down stairs after her all day – like I could run up and down stairs! – but we all know that really it's because she can't bear anyone to think of her as an invalid. She hates to be seen in her dressing gown and slippers.

Today she has a sketchpad and a charcoal pencil balanced on her lap, and she is making a few desultory black lines on an empty sheet, which I think are supposed to represent tree branches. She didn't want to be seen doing nothing – as if we'd judge her for that, I think, almost indignantly.

'Thank you, darling, if you're making one, that would be lovely. Be careful with the trolley, though, won't you? And perhaps you could help me with this drawing? I cannot make this tree look like that one out there. You are so good, please explain to me how you do it. And, Rachel—'

'Yes?'

'We do love having you here, you know. You will

stay as long as you like, won't you?'

I hop into the room, feeling the tickle of the thick carpet fibres beneath my bare foot, and sit down on the arm of the sofa. Unlike me, Gordana is wearing tights, as usual, underneath neatly pressed navy slacks, and even through the tea-brown stocking toes I can see that her toenails are beautifully pedicured. I give her toes an affectionate squeeze. In the background, the radio is playing old jazz songs.

I pick up her sketchbook and inspect the drawing, which is indeed pretty poor. With a few quick strokes, I transform the tree into a towering oak, and then sketch in a little Jackson, jumping around underneath it. It earns me a laugh from Gordana, and a feeling of pride in my chest, not unlike the pleasure of winning a match against a tricky opponent.

'I love being here. It's so different to living with Dad and Anthea. I always felt so in the way there, as if Anthea only ever relaxed when I went out. They just needed their own space, I guess . . .' I hesitate, concerned. 'But you and Pops do, too – need your own space, I mean,' I add awkwardly. 'You've got Mum coming and going too, and what with all the stress of Dad's court case coming up, and Jackson and everything – I do worry that you're just being polite, and really you both would love us to leave you to it. Isn't Pops sick of ferrying me to physio three times a week?'

She laughs faintly, and adjusts the neat bandanna covering her patchy hair.

'Come on, Rachel darling, you know us better than that. If we wanted to be alone, you'd be the first to hear about it. And Ted loves giving you lifts in and out of Kingston, you know he does. He says you are big breath of fresh air for him.'

I smile a watery smile. Gordana always knows the right thing to say to make me feel better – although at the moment I feel more like a hole in the ozone layer than a breath of fresh air.

'Thanks,' I say, hauling myself up again and out into the kitchen on my crutches, before she can see how much her words mean to me. I am relieved, because it's been playing on my mind considerably. I don't want to go back to the place I used to call home. I don't want to live with Dad and Anthea, either or both; and not just because of what Dad's going through. I'm not a rat abandoning a sinking ship. I'd stay there if I thought for a moment they needed me more than Gordana and Pops, but they definitely don't.

And I can't stay here for ever, either. It's fine now, while Gordana still needs company and a bit of help, but despite what she's just said, they won't want me or Mum here for too much longer. They are so independent.

I'm not doing too badly myself, either, in terms of independence. I'm getting pretty nimble, though I say so myself. I'm able to make the tea on one leg, put pot and cups on to a gilt hostess trolley and, leaning on the bar of the trolley instead of on my crutches, hop back into the living room, pushing it in front of me like a wheeled zimmer frame. Luckily it's a sturdy piece of equipment. It hasn't seen so much service since the 1970s, and it makes me feel like a one-legged dinner lady; but it gets the job done.

When I return with the tea for Gordana, she is singing along to 'Summertime' on the radio, in a low, wistful voice whose depths and clarity makes my stomach twist with fresh emotion. I pause just outside the door to listen. She has the most beautiful voice. I wonder if it is a source of real sorrow to her that she never became a singer; or whether it was just another lost dream: something she grumbled about not achieving but which wasn't ever a serious proposition. You could never be sure with Gordana. Sometimes the telling was what was important, rather than the content. I've heard the story of how Sandie Shaw took

314

the life Gordana wanted so many times that it is more like a myth.

Have I followed my dream, I wonder? Everyone always congratulates me, tells me that I have – but I'm starting to wonder what my *real* dream is?

I decide it might finally be time for me to rent somewhere; get a new life. Perhaps Kerry will know a place. She's the one with the wide social circle – she even has friends who don't play tennis! I certainly don't have any of those. I've been half thinking about asking Mum to go halves with me on the rent of a small house, if she's planning to stay, but she is beginning to make noises about going back to Kansas again.

Mum seems very down lately, and has been spending more and more time at her friend Corinna's. I worry that she's bored of being with me, or feels uncomfortable being around Gordana, but whenever we cross paths, she hugs me or touches my face, trying to smile, saying, 'Sorry, Rach, it's not you.'

I put it down to her sorrow about losing Billy, but she eventually confessed that she can't bear the thought of bumping into Dad. I don't really understand why. Neither of them will admit to a confrontation, although something must have happened. I mean, it was only a couple of years ago that we all had Christmas dinner together and that, whilst not exactly a bundle of laughs, hadn't been too bad.

'Oh, Rachel, I didn't see you there,' says Gordana, turning mid-song to look at me.

'Sorry. I didn't mean to eavesdrop. I just love listening to you singing.'

'I love singing,' she says softly.

I wheel in the trolley and park it in front of a nest of tables by her side, letting her sit up and do the honours. I wouldn't dare serve tea to Gordana without milk in a jug and sugar in a bowl. I watch her thin hands put the tea strainer over the cups and pour.

'So, what are you up to today?' she asks, handing me a cup and saucer.

It's been so long since I've 'done' anything that I'm kind of surprised she has even asked. We have all fallen into a quiet, safe routine, centred on Dad or Pops driving Gordana to and from her chemo treatments.

Between chauffeuring duties, Dad then vanishes again, coaching (privately, we assume, because he's not at the club) and placating Anthea, or whatever his life consists of. I fit in my physio sessions at Kingston Hospital and some basic non-weight-bearing training in the little gym in the village near Gordana and Pops's house, but nothing more exciting than that. I like it this way. Dad's next hearing and Gordana's recovery hang over us all, like two great boulders teetering on the edge of a high cliff, and so the quieter life is, the better, as we wait with bated breath to see if they are going to drop. And if they drop, how hard they shatter; how much damage they do.

Days are measured by Gordana's cycles of rest and activity; if she is feeling wiped out, we do jigsaws, reading out loud, sketching: invalid activities carefully disguised as hobbies, like a mother trying to get her child to eat vegetables by chopping them up into tiny pieces and smuggling them into the bolognese sauce. How much would she hate that I'm thinking of it like that! But on the days she feels more normal, we do other stuff: shopping trips and the cinema or theatre, with Pops a willing driver and bag-carrier.

The only thing neither of us wants to do is to go to the tennis club. Gordana's good friends come to visit her here, but she can't face the inevitable nudges and whispers about Dad's scandalous arrest that she knows would fly around her if she went down there. The same goes for me too, but in addition, I don't want to have to see Mark and Sally-Anne together. I can't bear the thought of him flashing her secretive little smiles from the next court, or seeing his arm resting casually around her shoulders.

I wonder if I'll ever have a serious boyfriend again. Maybe it's because twenty-three is, in tennis years, well into middle age, but I have a horrible nagging fear that maybe I'm destined to be an old spinster in all walks of life.

'Actually,' I say, remembering that Gordana has asked me a question, 'I was thinking of getting the bus back to Dad's this afternoon. I'm easily nifty enough on the crutches now, and I need to collect some gear from the house.'

'Are you sure you're up to the walk from the bus stop?' she asks carefully.

I shrug, but suddenly can't stop the frustration from bubbling up inside me.

'I don't see why not, if I take it easy . . . Oh, I *hate* this! I hate not being able to walk! What if I can never walk again? I know it's only been a month, but sometimes I just can't even remember what it's like! Let alone running around a tennis court . . . Now it's a big deal for me even to go to the sodding bus stop!'

'Oh darling,' she says, her big violet eyes full of concern. The dark grey shadows in the wrinkled skin beneath them make their colour stand out even more vividly. 'You're doing so well with your physio. I know there's not much I can say to make you feel better, but you just have to be patient.'

I stand up on my good foot and reach for my crutches again, a gesture which has become totally instinctive. 'I just want to know, one way or the other. I didn't before, but I do now. I've got to plan for the future.'

'I know what you mean,' says Gordana, so matter-of-factly that I feel humbled. I'm only worried about my career, while she is waiting to find out if she even has a future to plan for. For the first time, I feel something positive about my accident. If I hadn't injured myself,

I would have been able to spend hardly any time with Gordana while she was ill, and I certainly wouldn't have been living here. I'd have popped in for the odd visit, of course, telling myself that I was doing all I could to be supportive to her, but I bet she'd have had to be at death's door before I'd pull out of a tournament voluntarily to be at her side. To my complete shame, I'm not even sure I'd do that; not if I was doing well. What if I'd got through to the semi-finals? The final?

No, of course I would. Of *course*.

42

Susie

Gordana had called me at Corinna's to say that he'd rung and wanted to meet me. At first I couldn't even think who he was. My brain seemed a little scrambled from the stress of recent events, as well as the confusion of being based in two different places. I didn't like to spend more than a few days at a time at either Gordana's or Corinna's, not wanting to get under anybody's feet or outstay my welcome.

'Karl who?'

'He says he met you on the skiing holiday.'

I was astounded. 'Oh, that Karl! Good grief, I don't believe it.'

'Did you have time to have a holiday romance?' Gordana asked, a little frostily.

'No! Of course not! He was just really good to me – to both of us – when we were out there. He gave me lifts to the hospital and so on. He said he's often in London on business, and because I didn't know if I'd have a mobile phone over here, I gave him your number. I hope that's all right.'

'That is fine,' said Gordana. 'He says he's going to be here until Friday, and if you wished to give him a call, he'd love to hear from you. He asked about Rachel too.'

I copied down the number she read out, trying to remember what Karl looked like. I had a memory of blond eyebrows and thick stubby fingers, and bits of popcorn stuck in his stubble, but whenever I tried to picture him, I saw Paul Newman instead. Oh, and beetroot – that's right, he made me that supper when we got back from the hospital. That was all a bit blurry, after the brandies I'd consumed and the day I'd had. What had we talked about? I thought I must have done all the talking, because I couldn't for the life of me remember any information about him at all. I remembered the iron dragons in the fireplace, and the beige snow falling, and being out on the mountainside in zero visibility, but that was about it. What a truly awful vacation. Meeting Karl had been the only nice part of it, apart from the time spent with Rachel before the accident. But I couldn't say I'd given him more than a passing thought since our return.

He must fancy me, I thought uncertainly, to look me up. Usually when you met people on holiday and exchanged numbers, that was as good as saying, 'Have a nice life, it was good meeting you but I'll never see you again.'

'Ring him!' said Corinna when I told her. She was doing the Saturday *Times* music crossword at the time, frowning at the few remaining unsolved clues. Her bare feet were propped up on the coffee table and her purple sparkly toenail polish was chipped. We were having a lazy Saturday morning together. 'Go and have a date, it'll cheer you up. Wish some handsome Aryan knight in shining armour would ring *me* up.'

'He was quite handsome, actually,' I reflected. 'Quite a bit younger than me though, I'd say. Nice body. I can't remember what he looked like, other than he had a touch of the young Paul Newman about him.' I remembered that I'd thought of setting him and Rachel up, but that obviously hadn't happened. Suddenly I no longer wanted her to have him. That wasn't to say that *I* wanted him ... at least, not yet. But I decided I'd quite like the option, if there was one going.

Corinna cackled. 'Oh dear, it gets worse and worse . . . You sound like "younger" is a problem! A young, fit, decent, man who looks like Paul Newman is ringing you up? I'd be jumping for flaming joy if it was me. Eight letters, second letter L, Britpop band whose single was "Connection". Ooh, I'm sure I know that . . .'

'Don't ask me,' I said. 'There wasn't a lot of Britpop in Lawrence; not that I ever heard. It was more bluegrass or reggae instead. I'd like to see him again,' I added. 'If only to thank him for everything he did for us in Italy. I could take him out for a meal, couldn't I? But what if he—'

'*Elastica!* Of course.' She scribbled it in. 'What? What if he what?'

'Well. You know, does fancy me?'

Corinna shook her head pityingly. 'Oh come on, Susie, get a grip. I mean, literally. Get a grip. If he fancies you, go for it. Have some good old-fashioned uncomplicated sex! It'll do wonders for your ego if nothing else, and put a smile on your face. You lucky bitch.'

I laughed and slapped her shoulder affectionately. Perhaps she was right. I suppose it felt a bit funny, Gordana being the one who passed on the message. She made no bones about the fact that she'd love to see Ivan and me back together again, which of course was completely preposterous, but I had too much regard for Gordana to tell her that her son was an arrogant, devious cheat, and I didn't even want to be in the same room as him, let alone in another doomed marriage.

'I can't imagine having sex with anyone other than Billy,' I said dolefully. 'And I don't think I'm ever going to get married again. I'd have married Billy years ago if I'd wanted that.'

'Who's talking about marriage? You're going to meet up with a new friend, who may or may not fancy you . . . Oh, I can't do this one: the Rainmakers' only single, four words, last word ends in O. I've never even heard of the Rainmakers.'

I got up. 'It's "Let My People Go-Go".'

Corinna gaped at me in mock admiration.

'They're from Kansas, don't you remember?'

'No, I can't say I do. But thanks. Now go and ring your Karl bloke.'

Karl and I arranged to meet on Monday night for dinner, although I made him promise to allow me to pay, which he harrumphed about Germanically before conceding. Once I heard his voice on the phone, I remembered how relaxed I felt in his company. I still couldn't visualize his face, but I heard the smile in his voice and how he had that wonderful 'port in a storm' quality of making me feel safe. A bit like Billy had.

It was an odd feeling, getting ready for a date with a different man. I found myself dressing to impress Billy: a squirt of the perfume he liked, my hair up the way he approved of, the matching underwear he'd bought me (Lord knows how he managed that. I think he must have stood in the doorway of the lingerie shop in Lawrence looking lost until a sales lady took pity on him. For which I'm most thankful, otherwise I might have ended up with a purple polka-dot bra two sizes too large and some orange nylon briefs . . .).

Corinna lent me a funky pink charm bracelet, and her pink suede boots, which were a size and a half too large, but so lovely. I felt like I did as a five year old, dressing up and clunking around the house in my mother's clothes, and it gave me an unexpected pang of loss. As well as my parents being long dead, Billy never saw his folks: they were divorced, and one lived in Canada, one in Tallahassee. Gordana was my substitute mother, and I knew that whatever happened with Ivan and me, she would always be there for me. I couldn't stand the thought that she might not survive this illness. She was the hub of the closest thing I had to a family, however dysfunctional and fractured it was.

'What's up, Susie?' said Corinna, who was teasing my hair into big waves with her curling tongs.

'Just thinking about Gordana,' I replied, concentrating on applying shiny pink eyeshadow. 'I want to spend as much time as I can with her, but I don't want to have another run-in with you-know-who. He's like a bear with a sore head. I'm getting enough grief from one ex, I don't need it from the other as well.'

Corinna squeezed my shoulder. 'Think about your date instead. You can't change anything by worrying about Gordana.'

I sighed. 'I know, but . . .'

There wasn't much else I could say.

All the way into town on the train, I was still seeing Paul Newman's face on Karl's body. But when I met Karl at the bar of the tapas restaurant near Waterloo Station that Corinna had recommended, Paul Newman vanished with a pop, and I couldn't think how I'd ever made the association. They weren't a bit alike, apart from the hair. I also couldn't think how I hadn't been able to remember what Karl looked like – as soon as I saw him, he looked utterly familiar. Having felt nervous about meeting him, I instantly felt nothing but pleasure.

'Hi!' I said warmly, kissing him on both cheeks, enjoying the feel of faint stubble against my lips. I tried and failed to recall the last time I'd had sex. 'It's really nice to see you again.'

'You also,' he said, appraising me at arm's length. 'You look great.'

I laughed, remembering the Tweedledee salopettes that were my sartorial lot the last time he'd seen me. His trademark 'alt-zo' hit the spot, too.

'Well, rented ski gear from the Eighties doesn't do

much for a girl's appearance. Not to mention the trauma of that week.'

'No, I don't suppose they do.' I was half waiting for him to say that I'd looked great in Italy too, but he didn't.

'How is Rachel?' he asked.

'She's much better, thanks,' I said, accepting the seat he pulled back for me. 'She's still on crutches, but the physio's going well, and she'll find out if she can play competitively again in a couple of months' time.'

'I looked her up on the Internet,' said Karl with enthusiasm. 'She's done very well, hasn't she?'

'Yeah. Although she's convinced she could go a lot further. She wants to be at least the British number one – she's number eight at the moment. Well, at least she was, before the accident.'

'That sounds impressive to me,' Karl said. 'Please send her my best wishes.'

'Did you meet her?' I asked curiously. I couldn't remember that they'd even had a conversation, only that he'd brought her up with the rest of us in the van, and then seen her semi-conscious in hospital.

'Of course,' he said. 'We had a good chat the first morning over breakfast. I think you were not awake yet. We . . . how do you say it? Hit it off.'

'Oh right. Shall we order?'

In the end, the evening was somehow not quite how I'd imagined it would be. Whilst I'd been unable to get to grips with Corinna's idea of having a therapeutic, confidence-boosting one-night stand with Karl, I had thought that it would be . . . well, more of a date, I suppose. It was more like a comfortable, companiable dinner with an old friend I hadn't seen for a while.

Which was fine, of course, and infinitely preferable to a stilted meal full of pregnant pauses or, worse, unwanted advances. But on reflection, I think I was slightly hurt that there were no advances, unwanted or otherwise. Karl was utterly natural, and funny, and sweet. He told me all about his magnet-supplying business, which was a sideline to his 'real' work as a wine-importer, and how he loved the time he spent at the hotel in Italy.

He didn't volunteer any personal information at all, apart from saying he'd never been married. He didn't ask me anything personal either – although, recalling how I'd banged on relentlessly for several hours at the hotel that night, there probably wasn't anything left that he felt he didn't already know about me. Our chat was strictly present tense: I told him how I was dividing my time between Gordana and Corinna's places, and we talked a lot about how great London was after the small towns we were used to. It was all very . . . polite.

At the end of dinner, there was an unseemly tussle for the bill – he had reneged on his promise to let me pay – in which our hands accidentally brushed one another; but that was the only physical contact we had, apart from kisses hello and goodbye. We eventually agreed to split the bill, and after we'd got our coats and walked out into the still-noisy bustle of the Cut, to my surprise he asked me out again.

'Lunch, perhaps, on Wednesday? I could come out to where you are staying. I would like to say hello to Rachel also.'

I felt puzzled. He wasn't even looking in my eyes as he spoke. Instead, he was watching the progress of a homeless man weaving drunkenly along the pavement opposite, swamped by a huge macintosh which made him look like a Dalek. I might have been horribly out of practice, but Karl wasn't giving off signs that he liked me in any way other than as a friend. Perhaps he was gay? Lonely? No social skills? I discounted the last one – he was charm personified. The first two were far more likely.

Oh well, I thought. Go with the flow. You like him,

he obviously likes you enough to see you again, very soon. Perhaps it's a German thing: trying to look at all costs as though there was no question of fancying the person whom you were asking out . . .

'That would be lovely,' I said, trying to sound brisk and not coy. 'Give me a ring on the mobile, and we'll fix something up for Wednesday. I'm not sure whether I'll be in Surrey, though, or at Corinna's place. But I'll give Rach a ring to find out if she's free. I'm sure she'd love to see you too.'

Karl beamed at me, tearing his eyes away from the swaying drunk.

'Wednesday then,' he said.

43

Rachel

I managed to get the bus all the way to Dad and Anthea's, but it was more traumatic than I'd envisaged it would be. Partly because I timed it badly – I left it till mid-afternoon, and the schoolchildren had all just come out. The bus was a blur of off-white shirts, wonky ties and talk of bands I'd barely even heard of: McFly and Busted. A backpack in front of me was painted with the words '50 Cent' in big white letters. Was that a band or a solo artist? Kerry would know. I was worried that my crutches would slide to the floor and trip someone up, or that someone would accidentally kick my bad leg.

I listened to the teenagers' conversations with interest, as I always do when around non-tennis players. Until the accident, I found it hard to imagine how people not on the tour managed to occupy their time. What did they think about if they didn't have first-serve percentages to improve, or core stability to increase? What did they say to one another? What the hell did they *do* all day?

When I wasn't playing matches myself, but watching my friends or rivals from the stands, I used to love eavesdropping on crowd conversations, too. They gave me clues about what preoccupied people. Sure, a lot of those conversations pertained to the match, and were hilarious enough to listen to in their erroneous suppositions about the players or the technique, but what I really liked was the staggering inanity of many of the non-tennis related ones. After I got knocked out in the second round at my last British tournament, I sat in front of two middle-aged women who occupied an entire game of a thrilling quarter-final between Kerry and Tatiana Garbin in a discussion about jelly. Garbin was an Italian player ranked fifty-second in the world, and it was Kerry's biggest match to date. She'd done really well to get that far, and it went to three sets before she succumbed, so I felt quite outraged on her behalf that these two women weren't paying more attention.

'Do you like jelly?' one had asked the other. 'I make a lot of jelly at home, you know, with the cubes that you melt. Although I'm not so keen on the lemon sort.' She continued in this vein for some time, with her friend agreeing or disagreeing on the relative merits of different flavours, until the score in the game reached a fourth deuce, the crowd was biting its collective nails, hollering and gasping, and her friend said conclusively, 'We eat a huge amount of yogurt in our house.'

Perhaps it was because they didn't have anything more important than jelly to concern them. I fear that kind of existence; the thought of being unemployed, or trapped at home with babies or dependants, makes me feel ill with itchiness.

Although now I've had several weeks of it, I do feel a little differently. I can understand how days pass in cycles of small activities. Time just moves more slowly, that's all. The physio's going well, and I have filled two entire sketchpads with my drawings. I feel really good about that. So perhaps life doesn't have to be an endless round of extreme stimulation in order to be fulfilling. Perhaps I am beginning to understand how little things can matter too: a few hours chilling out in the company of a loved one; a good soap opera;

a nice cup of tea . . . Oh Rachel, listen to yourself! You sound about ninety-seven.

'Excuse me,' said an uncertain voice, accompanied by a tap on my shoulder.

I automatically shuffled across towards the window, thinking that the voice's owner, an acne-ridden skinny boy in his early teens, was asking me to move up so he could sit down in the other half of my seat. But he remained standing in the aisle, weighed down with sports kit and backpack and racket bag, blushing furiously.

'Are you Rachel Anderson?' he said, looking from side to side of him to make sure his mates weren't witnessing this exchange.

'Yes,' I replied equally cautiously, instinctively reaching my hand down to shield my knee. Tennis nerd, I thought.

He thrust a grubby scrap of paper at me. 'C'n I have your autograph? I saw you play at Surbiton last year. You beat that big French bird, didn't you, in the second round? Great match, that was. She was ranked much higher than you, too, wasn't she?'

I was impressed and flattered. It had, actually, been a great win for me. I'd got knocked out in the quarter-finals by a Japanese girl ranked thirty-eight in the world, but my win against the French player had upped my own ranking by quite a few places. And Mark had been watching the match, beaming all over his face when I hit a good passing shot or put away an overhead.

It all seemed like a lifetime ago.

I signed his paper for him, although the bus's movement made it come out rather wobbly. 'Sorry,' I said. 'There you go. Although it's probably not worth that much, not now my ranking will have dropped to the low hundreds.' I was trying to be funny, but realized that it just sounded self-pitying.

The boy looked as sympathetic as a teenager was

329

able – i.e. not very. 'So is that you out of tennis for good, then, or what?' he asked bluntly, apparently noticing my crutches for the first time. He was blushing again because his friends had stopped their conversations when they saw him chatting to an older woman, and were beginning to heckle and whistle.

'No,' I said. 'At least, I don't think so. But it'll be a while yet till I can play again.'

'Oh. Right.'

I could tell he was itching to get away now, so I decided against asking him about his own tennis prowess. Mercifully, the bus jolted to a halt and he gathered up his things to leave. 'Ta, then,' he said, turning and bumping his way back down the aisle to the door, banging into all the other passengers with his various bags. When he got off the bus, he shot me a sideways glance from under his fringe, and the faintest traces of a smile, while his mates shoved him scornfully and pointed through the window at me. He'll be quite good looking in about five years' time, I thought, smiling back at him.

By the time I have hopped on my crutches the short distance from the bus stop to Dad's house, my good leg is tired from the exertion, and my injured leg aches badly. I told myself that I could handle distances, but it is a bit of a shock that a short walk – hop – feels so debilitating.

The house looks empty and forelorn, the windows need cleaning, and the two wheely bins are abandoned haphazardly in the front garden rather than being stored neatly out of sight down the side of the house. I'm surprised: Anthea, whilst not being a great one for your actual cleaning, is a stickler for neatness and order. Dad's car isn't there, but Anthea's turquoise Fiat Punto is.

I realize with a slight shock that I haven't seen Anthea at all since before Mum and I went to Italy –

and I hadn't even noticed. She sent me a get-well card, but hasn't bothered even to ring me at Gordana and Pops's. It kind of confirms to me that she would much prefer that I wasn't such a fixture in her life. Well, I won't be for much longer, not if I can get a place of my own.

I let myself in with my key. 'Hello?'

There are three bulging suitcases standing in the hall, arranged like the Three Bears in order of size, all neatly trussed with Anthea's initialled luggage straps. Something looks different about the place, and I have to concentrate to think what it is, before working out that things are missing: the striped hall rug and the framed floral prints which had been on the walls.

'Anybody home?'

Mystified, I go through into the back room. The French windows opening out on to the garden have been flung wide, and an assortment of objects is piled in the middle of the lawn. At the edge of the pile I can see the bread machine, the Hoover, a large stack of glossy magazines, a bicycle, the clothes-drying rack and the Swiss ball she gave me.

Anthea appears through the back gate, which is also wide open, followed by a fat man in a stained T-shirt.

'Put that in next,' she commands over her shoulder, pointing at the bicycle. Behind her back, the fat man rolls his eyes and gurns at the back of her head. I can't help smiling.

'Hi,' I say, coming into the garden. 'Having a clear-out?'

Anthea jumps with fright, and her expression is one of utter shock. She looks like she's seen a ghost. 'Rachel!'

It's more than shock, though. Guilt and rage are clearly written on her face, too. What on earth is going on?

She comes towards me and embraces me, stiff-armed. When I look at her closely, I see that her face is

331

a mask; her make-up is applied in twice the usual quantities, and with the sort of precision which implies great attempts at disguising emotions. Her eyeballs are shot through with red spidery blood vessels, and face powder has settled in the deepening wrinkles on her cheeks.

'I wish you weren't here to witness this, Rachel, but I'm afraid I'm leaving your father.'

I gape at her. 'What? Why?'

She struggles to remain composed, and just about succeeds. The fat man comes back up the garden empty-handed, picks up the clothes rack and a bubble-wrapped mirror, and waddles towards the gate again, bumping the edge of the mirror against the side of the garage as he passes it. His bum crack clearly shows between the top of his saggy jeans and the bottom of his T-shirt.

'You'll have to ask Ivan that.'

'Where is he?'

She shrugs. 'He said he'd be out all day. Something about seeing his solicitor, I believe. Actually, no, I never know what to believe. He could be anywhere. Excuse me, Bob,' she calls. 'Please be more careful with that mirror. You'll have to pay for it if it's broken.' She turns back to me. 'Anyway, I intend to be gone by the time he gets home.'

'Does he know you're going?'

'No. And that's how I want it. I don't want any scenes.'

'Anthea, are you sure about this? You two have been together for ages. I know Dad's not easy, and he's got a lot on his mind at the moment, but—'

She holds up an imperious hand. 'Please, Rachel. Just don't. There are things that you aren't aware of, but it's not up to me to tell you what.'

'Can't we sit down and talk about it over a cup of tea?'

'No. I'm afraid I have to get on. I only have the van and that man booked for one afternoon, and all this stuff has to get to the storage facility by six o'clock.'

'But where are you going?'

'I'm afraid I can't tell you that either, except that I will be out of the country for a few weeks. Rest assured I will inform your father of anything he needs to know.'

She's changed, I think to myself. I recall the woman who stayed up all night frantically trying to pedal her tension away on the exercise bike when Dad had been arrested. This is different. She seems harder; stronger. I wonder how Dad will react, and my heart goes out to him: this, on top of everything else.

But then I remember the way he had split Mark and me up. The way he never invited Anthea to tennis club functions. The way he's so mean to Gordana, and so rude about Mum. He's brought it all on himself, the silly old sod.

I still feel sorry for him, though.

'How is Gordana?' Anthea asks abruptly. 'I'd like to have come to see her, but you know, I think it's better for ill people not to be pestered by visitors all the time when they're trying to focus on getting better.'

Isn't that up to the ill person to decide? I think to myself, knowing how much Gordana loves a good chat and some company. She would so loathe the thought that people were keeping away from her because she was unwell.

'She's doing well, thanks,' I say. 'I'll tell her you asked after her. The chemo's not affecting her too badly; not yet, anyhow. Her tennis-club friends pop in quite a lot, and that keeps her spirits up.' Oops, I think, that was a little bit too pointed. But Anthea doesn't seem to have noticed.

'Good,' she says. 'I was terribly upset to hear that she had . . . that she was . . . um, you know.'

'That she has cancer,' I say bluntly. I hate it when people pussyfoot around, not mentioning the 'C' word as if to speak it out loud is somehow inappropriate or embarrassing.

'Yes. Well, I must get on.' Anthea licks her middle finger absently and smooths down her thin eyebrows, as though eyebrow-grooming is an essential element of 'getting on'. Then she steps back inside the house and, uninvited, I follow her.

'I'll, er, leave you to it, then,' I say. 'I'm just going to get some clothes from my room . . .'

I don't know what else to do. I silently beg her not to make me promise not to tell Dad, and thankfully she doesn't. I suppose she thought he'd be home in a couple of hours anyway, and by the few objects remaining on the lawn, I assume she and Fat Boy are almost ready to go.

I can't say I feel sad about the prospect of Anthea no longer being in my life. But it's another change, in a year which has so far held so many scary changes for all of us, and I'm worried about how Dad will take it.

'Well . . .' I'm not quite sure what to say, and I feel almost shy. 'For what it's worth, Anthea, I'm really sorry. I hope you'll be OK. Keep in touch, won't you?'

For the first time, her eyes fill with tears, and she half stretches out a hand towards me, before dropping it back down by her side again. She has got so thin that her rings are twisting around on her fingers. But then the sorrow on her face swells into a rage so potent that it appears to stream through her body. It must be my imagination, but it seems even to fill out her fingers, momentarily fixing the rings. She is puffy with anger.

'I expect I will be OK, Rachel, eventually. But your father has really hurt me, and I'm afraid it is going to take me some time to get over that.'

'Sorry,' I repeat awkwardly. 'But he says he didn't do it . . . innocent until proven guilty, and all that. I thought you were standing by him?'

She takes the bunch of dusty blue fabric flowers out of the vase on the dining table, and begins to wrap them in a couple of sheets of newspaper that she picks off the floor. I'll be glad to see the back of those stupid flowers.

'I'm not referring to the charges against him, Rachel,' she says, and I can't suppress a wave of antipathy which sweeps over me at her frosty tone. 'I have discovered something else. Something more personal . . .' She hesitates. 'Well, I don't see why you shouldn't know. Your father was cheating on me. Probably the entire time we were together. As far as I'm concerned, he deserves everything he gets. He's a—' She checks herself. 'Did you not notice, Rachel? I mean, he was seeing her whenever you two went away for tournaments. I would hope you'd have had enough respect for me to have told me, if you had known.'

I am flabbergasted; angry and shocked, but somehow not surprised. I draw myself up to my full height – not easy, on crutches. I feel like putting my hands on my hips, but I can't. Bloody crutches.

'Anthea,' I say. 'Firstly, no, I had no idea. Secondly, if I had, I wouldn't have told you anyway. It's nothing to do with respect for you; it's none of my business! Dad's no saint, but of course I'd be loyal to him if it came down to a conflict of interests.'

'Of course you would,' she says stiffly. 'Silly me.'

I don't want to ask, but I just can't help myself. 'Who is she?'

Anthea looks as if she doesn't want to tell me, and then obviously realizes it will cause more trouble for Ivan if she does. 'Natasha Horvath.'

'Natasha,' I say flatly, remembering the hard-fought victory of our match in Zurich. It all clicked into place then: Natasha's aggression – perhaps it had all ended badly between her and Dad. The way Dad looked at her – he clearly still had feelings for her, even if the affair was over. The card she'd sent me, probably just to annoy Dad (I felt a moment's appreciation for her then, for knowing exactly how to wind him up. She obviously wasn't a pushover). I bet Dad would never have given me that card if it hadn't fallen out of his pocket.

'One of your little friends, is she?' Anthea asks sarcastically.

I tut with irritation. 'No, Anthea, I don't have any "little" friends, and if I did, she wouldn't be one of them. I only played her once. She looked vaguely familiar but I couldn't say I'd ever met her before.'

Anger is simmering between us now, building up and up like steam in a pressure cooker. I have a vision of it suddenly beginning to hiss out into the room, so loudly that neither of us can hear our 's's when we speak.

I look down at the bundle of newspaper-wrapped silk flowers, and a word jumps out at me: '*Porn*'. That horrible word again. Wait a second. I look more closely. '*Ivan Anderson*'. It's a report of Dad's arrest, from a different newspaper to the one Pops brought home; a tabloid, but the same story. Why has she kept it?

'Why have you still got this?' I ask, pointing at it. Without at all meaning it, I add sarcastically, 'Wasn't you who leaked the story to the press, was it?'

Her reaction gives her away immediately. She blushes puce and is visibly rattled. The rage drains out of her and shame flickers over her made-up features.

'You *did*!' I say incredulously. 'How could you do that? As if things weren't bad enough already, you compound his misery and ruin his reputation by letting everyone know about it? You Judas! How much did they pay you? You're despicable!'

'I don't have to listen to this,' she snaps, her composure back again. 'Like you said, Rachel, it's none of your business. It was wrong of me, I know, but like *I* said, I was very upset with your father. Now, if you'll excuse me, I don't think we have anything left to say to one another at all.'

'I'd like my Swiss ball back, if you don't mind,' I say, glaring at her.

'Your . . . ? Oh yes. I beg your pardon, Rachel, I forgot that it was yours. I wasn't trying to steal it.'

'No, no, of course you weren't,' I say, over-politely, wishing she'd tried to appropriate the hair-straightening device instead of the Swiss ball – I'd have let that go without comment. I don't think I've ever felt such dislike for someone. Why had she leaked the story ages ago, and then only left him now, if she'd known about Natasha Horvath for that length of time?

'I'm going to use the loo, if you don't mind, then I'll get some stuff out of my bedroom, and then I'll be off.' *And I hope I never see you again, you horrible woman.* 'I'll get the ball first,' I add, hobbling out into the garden, before Fat Bob packs it into the van.

I stoop slowly and pick up the Swiss ball off the grass, holding it awkwardly under my arm, before turning back into the house. It's difficult to manoeuvre with the crutches. Leaving the ball by the suitcases in the hall, I climb slowly up to the bathroom, lock the door and immediately text Dad: 'COME HOME NOW, ANTHEA LEAVING YOU!!' I resist the urge to add, 'SHE'S THE ONE WHO TOLD THE PRESS, THE EVIL COW.'

I sit on the closed toilet lid, idly taking in the brown sticky rings of different sizes left on the shelf by the bath where Anthea's numerous pots of unguents and jars of cosmetics had stood in regimented rows. Neat and tidy, but never cleaned underneath. This under-the-surface grubbiness was another reason I enjoy living with Gordana and Pops: their house is always spotless. This place seems doubly filthy now, the air tainted with what Dad might have been up to on his computer, or with Natasha Horvath. I was finding it very difficult to imagine the two of them together.

You just never know what's around the corner, do you? You think you've got it all mapped out – I mean, I knew I wouldn't be playing professionally for ever, but I really thought I had a few more years in me, and now . . . well, I just don't know. Mum thought she and Billy would grow old together. Gordana thought she had plenty of time yet – and hopefully she still does – and Dad thought he'd be building his little empire, not watching it crumble and vanish like a washed-away sandcastle. The best-laid plans, and all that. Presumably Anthea thought she and Dad had a future, too. It's distressing, to see how relationships unravel. And then there's Mark and I . . .

I get up and hop from the bathroom to my bedroom. My leg is really hurting now. I swear stress makes it worse.

I retrieve an assortment of creased clothes from my drawers, pack them into the empty backpack I brought with me for the purpose, and get out of there as quickly as I can. After all that, I leave the Swiss ball by the front door. I'd like to deflate it and take it with me, but I don't know where the pump is to reinflate it at the other end, and I don't want to stick around to search for it. I don't want to be here when Dad gets home – it's between him and Anthea. I can't help him with this, or with anything else.

As I close the front door behind me and hoist the backpack on to my shoulders, Anthea is nowhere to be seen. At least I've escaped without having to endure a final one of those horrendously awkward hugs, which are the only ones she knows how to do – all elbows and bony shoulderblades, and too much space between our heads. I wonder where she's going. I don't really care.

It doesn't really hit me, not until much later on. My dad is a cheating two-timer. But instead of thinking 'poor Anthea', I find myself thinking 'poor Dad'.

44

Gordana

I must confess I am in a poor state of mind today. I do not want to complain, or worry anybody, but it's so hard to be positive when I feel so sick. It is not a nice feeling. I'm not sure if it's the chemo, or the cancer, but I feel terrible. It is a little bit like the feeling I had when Ted and I went to Malaga last year, and we went out on a three-hour cruise to do the dolphin-watching. Five minutes after leaving the harbour I began to feel nauseous. Ten minutes later I was vomiting discreetly into sick bag. Fifteen minutes later I couldn't even be discreet about it any more; I was chucking up over the rail of the boat, while everyone was on the other side oohing and aahing at the grey shiny dolphins curving through the water.

I did not care at all about the dolphins; in fact when Ted took my arm and tried to get me to come and look, I shook it off and said something very rude indeed about the damn dolphins. I just wanted to get back on dry land, but I knew there was another two hours and forty-five minutes to roll around the deck before it ended.

It's so horrible, feeling like this and knowing that it won't stop. With the dolphins, it was only three hours, and they didn't make my hair get so thin. With this chemo, it's another five months and almost certain baldness. And then five weeks of radiotherapy every day. And then what? Still the cancer? I could go through all this and, at the end, nothing has changed. Mr Babish says he got it all out in the operation, but just one tiny speck, and it's back, spreading through me again like mould on cottage cheese. At least with the dolphins, I was not afraid, just sick. With this, I am scared stiff. I am terrified of dying. I look at Ted's face, and see this fear for me in him too. The only time he look relaxed is when he sleep. So, I'm enjoying watching him sleep, even with all the snoring and dribbling what is going on. I am taking pleasures where I can, and eating a lot of ginger root in syrup, to try and make the nausea go away. But I keep crying, in private, which is not at all like me.

I have been trying so hard to Think Positive. But sometimes this is not so easy. I will keep trying, though, and I will not tell anyone how afraid I am. I must think of poor Ivan and these terrible charges. It is vitally important that I get better to see him through it all. And I must also be there for Rachel, to encourage her through her recovery. I have things to do! I must pull myself together, like the curtains.

I went to a yoga class the other week. The teacher was a pregnant but very bendy young woman in a leotard which disappear right up her bottom, and she told us that we must imagine our bodies are full of golden sparkly light travelling around it, booting out all illness and so on. It is a nice idea, although I could see her bottom in the big mirror on the wall behind her, and her thong leotard bother me so much it made me itchy and then I couldn't think about the golden light, only about how she might get a yeast infection unless she start to wear less invasive clothing. It surely could not be good for the baby.

I wish Ted and I could have had a child together. Susie says the same thing about her and Billy. She and I have a lot in common. I feel so sorry for her. I still have my Ted, and I know she loved that strange Billy with his vests and his baseball caps round the wrong way. I only met him once and, I must say, I didn't really see what the appeal was. He was not nearly as handsome as my Ivan, and he had no social skills that I could see. Although perhaps she just wanted an easy life. I know how hard it is, trying to keep Ivan in line. Ivan should have realized how good Susie was for him. It would be so wonderful to see them back together again. Although not very likely, I think.

Speaking of Ivan, I must remind him that it's his turn to give me a lift to chemo tomorrow. The time since the last bout has gone so slowly, because of the feeling sick all the time. And now I must do it all over again and probably feel more sick . . . Oh well.

I ring him up, but there is no answer from his home; no point in calling him at the club, and his mobile phone is switched off. So I leave a message telling him to ring me back, but not between three and four-thirty, because the nice aromatherapist is coming then. Of course what does he do but ring me back at four. When I come downstairs after my massage, on woolly legs, smelling beautiful and miraculously not feeling sick, I press PLAY on the answerphone.

'Mama, it's me,' he says. His voice sounds tight, like he doesn't want to waste it. 'I hope you're OK. I can't give you a lift tomorrow, sorry, but something's come up. I need to see Susie, though, it's urgent. Please let me know when she will next be at your place.'

This is alarming, at the way he spits out the word 'urgent'. Uh-oh, I think. Here is trouble. For Susie, and probably for all of us. I must find out what's going on. I pay the nice aromatherapist, and she packs up her towels and oils and the big table she carries with her, telling me she'll be back in a fortnight. Then as soon as she's gone, I ring Ivan back on his mobile. It still goes straight to the voicemail.

'Darling, it's me. I'm afraid I really do need you to give me a lift tomorrow. Ted is out all day at a Rotary meeting. Susie is still at Corinna's, and Rachel's got physio at that time – not that she'd be able to take me anyway, of course. Otherwise I will have to take a taxi. You wouldn't make me take a cab to chemo, would you, darling . . . ? I thought not. It won't take long. So I'll see you at eight-thirty then? Thank you, Ivan, you are a sweetheart. Bye bye.'

Sometimes, I reflect, it is best to be firm, to treat him like a seven-year-old again. Seven-year-olds don't like to have too many choices; they need boundaries. Ivan, too, need boundaries in his life.

I am quite afraid that he won't turn up, and I really will have to get a taxi, but at eight-thirty-five the next morning I hear his car roaring up the drive. Even from the front door I can see that his face is like thunder-clouds. I brace myself as he gets out of the car to meet me, pressing myself slightly against the wet ivy which grows up the side of the porch wall. It leaves dark patches on the shoulder of my cream Burberry macintosh.

'Hello, my baby,' I say, kissing his stubbly cheek.

'Mama,' he replies curtly. 'Ready?'

He looks more tired than ever, with pouches under his eyes, but he holds the passenger door open for me, and waits to close it until I have arranged my skirt and handbag on my lap. For some reason I feel like the Queen. Perhaps it is the Burberry, and the headscarf I have started to wear outside the house now. I'm not bald yet, but I'm anticipating it. They said I wouldn't necessarily lose my hair, but I don't want any nasty surprises. I have already looked at wigs, and found a nice chestnut one not unlike my own hair at its best.

I am gearing up for our usual game of Twenty Questions, to try and discover what is going on his life from just yes and no answers, but to my surprise he begins talking first, as soon as the car has pulled away. It is like he is accelerating himself into conversation.

'OK, Mama, listen. I may as well tell you now because if I don't, Rachel or Susie will – in fact I'm surprised they haven't already. Anthea's left me. She's packed all her things and buggered off abroad somewhere, I don't even know where. But what I do know is that I think Susie's been stirring things. She couldn't bear to see me happy and settled, so she put the boot in to get her own back for ... well, things that happened between us in the past.

'I have to say, I feel very strongly that I don't want you and Ted to make her welcome her any longer. She's outstayed her welcome. She's broken up my relationship for her own selfish reasons, and I think it's completely intolerable. Just because she's been dumped by that hippie, she's—'

'Stop!' I put up my hand, trying to quell the flow of words. I am shocked at what he is saying, and struggle to take it in. 'Anthea's gone?'

I hadn't really ever warmed up to Anthea, but this is big change for Ivan. They seemed settled.

'That's what I said.'

'Oh darling, I'm so sorry. Perhaps if you talked to her . . .'

'I told you, Mama, she's left the country. I don't know where she is. Portugal, probably, at her mother's.' He shifts in the beige leather seat and scratches his head. I reach out and stroke his leg.

'But how do you know it was anything to do with Susie? She's not like that, Ivan, I'm sure she wouldn't have—'

'She did,' he says curtly. 'She must have done. Anthea left me a note, mentioning ... that she knows about ... Well, there's this other woman, you see, and ... Oh, it doesn't matter. The thing is that she found out.'

'Oh, Ivan.' You silly, silly boy, I think. Aren't you in enough trouble? I know that he used to sometimes not be so faithful to poor Susie, but I thought he had grown out of that by now.

343

'And frankly,' he adds, spitting out the words, 'what use am I to Anthea now? I can't afford to buy her anything any more. I'm stressed all the time, worried about my the court case, my debts . . .'

I glance at him sideways. I hope he is not blaming me for that.

We have slowed down to a crawl in the rush-hour traffic on the Kingston Bypass, and I look at my watch. I don't want to be late for chemo because it is done on a first-come first-served basis and there are only so many of the old *Hello!* magazines I can read without them getting blurry if I don't get there when they open at nine.

'Who is this other woman? Some little fling, or somebody you want to be with?'

Ivan sighs. 'Not a fling. Someone I've got a lot of history with, if you must know. Her name is Natasha, and I really like her . . . But she doesn't want me either, Mama. She's grown out of me. Who can blame her? Not exactly a catch any more, am I?'

'Calm down, Ivan darling,' I say soothingly. 'This will not do your blood pressure any good.'

'There's one more thing I wanted to tell you . . . I mean, well, confess, actually,' he mutters. I can tell it feels like having his teeth tugged out to admit it, and my heart sinks even lower down. It feel like a balloon with water inside. I close my eyes with terror that he will confess to computer stuff.

'What is it, Sonny Jim?'

'The money I owe you.'

'Yes? You have been paying it back; there is no problem.'

'Well, no, there is. A problem, I mean. The thing is—'

We have eventually got to the hospital, and I interrupt him to point out an empty parking space. He scowls at me.

'As I was saying, I was wondering if I could defer

the rest of the payments for a while? At least until after the hearing?'

'Of course, Ivan. I am sure things are difficult for you at the moment, with not being able to work and so on.'

'It's not just that,' he says, and he looks so ashamed that I am surprised. 'I haven't been able to afford to pay you back for some time now.'

'But you *have* been paying us back?'

'Yes. But I . . . Oh, this is hard to tell you . . . But I . . . had to get the money from elsewhere.'

'Elsewhere? Where else?'

An ambulance screeches up to the doors of the A. & E. department, and two men unload a body on a stretcher bed. It makes me shiver.

'I owe money to loads of people. The builders who renovated the club. The people who laid the new courts. Even the kitchen suppliers, and the brewery. I can't even pay the bar bill! I've been getting threatening letters – I'm sure it's one of these bastards who set me up with the porn. I told the police about it at my initial interview, so they're investigating all that now too. I'm going to be declared bankrupt, whatever else happens. So, I'm sorry. I'm sorry for being such a disappointment to you, and a failure. I didn't download that porn, but I did carry on paying you back when I ought to have been paying back other people. I just couldn't bear you to think of me as the loser that I am.'

What can a mother say to that? What sort of a bad mother was I, that Ivan worry more about paying me back than about getting so much into debts that he will be bankrupt?

'I go for my chemo now,' I say, in a big daze.

'I'll wait out here,' Ivan replies, not looking at me.

I get out of the car very slowly. It would be so nice for him to offer to come with me, just a little chit-chat while I lie there, to take my mind off it. But I guess it doesn't occur to him.

* * *

345

The needle into my vein hurts more and more with each visit, but this time I barely notice it for worrying about what will become of my boy. At least with Anthea he had a bit of stability in his life – although it did not stop him getting into big money troubles. Oh Lord, how could he let such a thing happen? Now it really will be the end of his dreams of the clubs.

I don't believe Susie would do anything to spoil things between Ivan and Anthea, though. Whatever Ivan says, it's just not like her.

Ivan has managed to spoil everything all by himself.

45

Rachel

It's very strange, being back here, and I am getting rather tired of telling people the same things, as I hop on my crutches to and from the club toilets:

'. . . Yes, I did it skiing.'

'. . . Significant fracture of the tibial plateau . . . The top of the tibia, just under my kneecap.'

'. . . On crutches for three months. A few more months after that till I can play again.' (I can't bear to admit that it might be longer; it might be never.)

'. . . No, it doesn't hurt much, not now.'

Then I take the leg brace off and pull up my tracky bottoms to show them my scar, the seven-inch line down the front of my knee, and that shuts them up.

The attention is nice in one way, but in another way it's a bit overwhelming. I haven't talked to so many people in one fell swoop for weeks; probably not since the Zurich tournament. Plus, I wonder if they are fussing over me so much because they feel more sorry for me about Dad. Nobody asks me about him, or how he is. It's a relief – I'm not sure what I'd have said, anyway:

'. . . On bail for child porn crimes, thanks for asking.'

'. . . Downloading images from illegal websites.'

'. . . I don't know, really – six months in jail? We don't even know when the trial is.'

I hate what he's supposed to have done; hate it. But

I'll stand by him, of course, at least publicly. He is my family. That's what families do, isn't it? In my Fantasy Family, we all stick up for each other. (But of course in my Fantasy Family, there are no allegations of child porn, or divorces, or cancer. Probably the biggest problem we all might have would be trying to decide where to cycle to on our picnic, and what sort of fillings to put in our sandwiches . . .)

I'd stand by Dad. What sort of daughter would I be, if I didn't? Not that I've seen much of him since Anthea left. I can't bear to ask him about Natasha Horvath, although I admit I'm curious. The only thing I can see them as having in common is their grumpiness, judging by that match she and I had.

All in all, I feel queasy with stress in case one of his Junior players' parents, or one of Gordana's friends, asks after him. They ask after Gordana, I notice, and that is easier to respond to: 'She's doing well, thanks.'

It was Kerry who persuaded me to come down to the club in the first place. I hadn't wanted to, but I couldn't really say no; not after I've been moaning so excessively to her about how bored I am. Besides, I'm meeting Mum for lunch in a restaurant down the road later, so it sort of makes sense to combine the two outings.

José is on holiday, Kerry said, and in his absence she needed some advice on her serve, which she claimed had 'completely gone'. She asked one of the first team ladies' players to give her a match, and she said she wanted me there to watch.

We haven't talked much about Dad, and the charges, although of course she knows. I guess the squads are talking of little else, although nobody mentions it in my presence. I asked Kerry if there have been journalists or photographers down here, and she said she hadn't seen any. The fact that I haven't noticed any further reports in the newspapers seems to back this up.

It occurs to me that this will probably all change around the time of the trial; assuming there is a trial. There's bound to be press interest then. The day is probably coming when people begin to look at me not as a tennis player, or an ex-tennis player, but as the daughter of a paedophile. It is more painful to me than my knee has ever been.

It is a cold December day. I can see my breath in the air, and frost is sparkling on the red fake-clay courts. I dressed with more care than usual this morning, in a proper matching tracksuit, and I even cleaned my trainers, washed my hair, and put on a bit of make-up. Just in case Mark is here. My leg-brace is on the out-side of my tracky bottoms, partly so that it doesn't press on the recently-healed wound, and partly out of vanity – it doesn't make my leg look huge that way. I'm self-conscious enough as it is, knowing that I've gained so much weight in the past weeks. I'm eating almost the same amounts that I used to, but without burning off any of the energy.

Today, however, adrenaline is probably burning off quite a few calories for me: a weird, jittery feeling of discomfort at everyone's knowledge of Dad's crime, and the necessity of pretending everything is OK. Then there is the possibility of Mark being there, whom I haven't heard from since the arrival of Jackson and my embarrassing sob-fest. I want him to see how much better I'm looking. Podgier, yes, but I know I have colour back in my cheeks, and I am practically leaping around on my crutches. I want him to see that he was wrong to write me off. I'll be playing again in no time; far sooner than everyone thinks, especially Mark.

'You look great!' exclaims Kerry, swallowing surprise when Pops drops me off at the club. Despite the well-wishers quizzing me about my knee, it is still quieter than usual. There are a couple of squads train-ing on the far courts; a quartet of elderly men playing

349

a sedate set on Court One; and a bored-looking coach I don't recognize giving a beginner a private lesson. I am simultaneously relieved and disappointed that Mark isn't there.

'Thanks, Kerry.' I'd like to have added, 'So do you', but as usual, Kerry's hair is unkempt and unwashed, and her mismatched sweatpants and WTA sweatshirt have weird reddish stains down the front, which she later confesses to be old Ribena. I give her a hug. I haven't seen much of her at all since I've been staying out at Gordana's; she's been on the tournament circuit as usual, and it has been hard to find time to meet up more than once or twice.

'Wish you were playing with me,' she says as her partner, Zoe, approaches, stubbing out a cigarette on the path and waving cheerily. Zoe is a huge orange-haired freckly girl who chain-smokes and looks like a turkey when she runs, but she is a very useful player, with a superb eye for the ball. Kerry of course will thrash her, but at least she'll get a decent game out of it.

'Me too,' I say, doing up my puffa jacket as I get settled with my leg stretched out on the bench nearest their court. I watch with envy as they warm up, smacking the ball up and down. It's so reassuring, to be able to control the ball the way we all could. In fact, there's nothing else in my life that I can control, I think to myself. I can't control Gordana's cancer, or the happiness of either of my parents. I certainly can't control Dad or Mark; and at the moment, I can't even control my own career. But once I'm playing again, I'll be able to control that little yellow ball. However many months I am away from this game, I know that, nine times out of ten, I will still be able to make it go where I want it to go, over that net, into one corner or another, high, low, fast, slow ... *If* I want it to, of course.

But perhaps controlling the damn ball doesn't even

matter any more. Just because I can doesn't mean that I have to. Perhaps I'd derive more satisfaction from training to be a . . . I can't think of anything. What would I train to be? Not a tennis coach. Not a TV commentator, like Dad wanted to be, until they told him that he mumbled too badly to be trusted with a commentary. I don't mumble, but I'm not exactly articulate in front of a microphone either. A physio? I've had so much physiotherapy since the accident that I could probably qualify automatically. But I don't really fancy the three- or four-year degree.

As usual, my thoughts on the subject go round in circles, until I realize that I'm not going to reach a conclusion, and knock them on the head. I'd like to talk to Mum or Gordana about it, just to broach the subject of me doing something else other than playing tennis – but every time I think about it, I chicken out.

When Kerry is at five games to three in the second set, a black cab chugs up to the gates of the club and a man gets out. I don't pay him any attention at first, until he comes and sits on the bench next to me. I glance across at him and he smiles. He looks vaguely familiar; cute, too – burly and blond. He doesn't say anything, though, until Kerry has polished off the final game with no difficulties. Zoe, disgruntled (although surely she couldn't have hoped to beat her), stomps off court and lights a cigarette, and Kerry bounds over to me.

'Rachel,' the man says then, holding out his hand and smiling.

'Um, hi?' I reply, reciprocating with a question in my voice. Kerry and I exchange wary looks. *Journalist*, I think.

'You don't remember me, do you? I am Karl, from the hotel in Italy. Last time I saw you, you were in the hospital.'

'Oh. Oh! Yes. Of course. How embarrassing . . . !'

'Why?' ask Kerry and Karl in unison.

351

'Well . . .' I remember my woolly concussed state after the accident, lying burbling in a bed, probably with my nightdress twisted up around my armpits. I could cope with my nearest and dearest seeing me in a state of disarray, but not really the van driver from the hotel. 'I must have been a right state.'

Karl shrugs. 'No. They gave you drugs; you looked peaceful. Your mother was more in a state than you were. I think she needed some of your medications.'

'I remember now. You brought me flowers. Mum did tell me that you were over, and that you two had dinner,' I say, feeling better. 'But what are you doing here?'

Karl looks around him, almost as if he is also surprised to find himself here. 'I am meeting Susie for lunch. She said she might invite you also, since she knew you would be here this morning. I found that I was too early, and I saw the signpost to the club. So I thought I would come and say hi. And to ask if you are going to join us for lunch?'

Kerry and I make eye contact again. This is a bit weird: why would he want me to come on their date with them? Mum had invited me for lunch, but she hadn't mentioned anything about Karl. Perhaps she thought I wouldn't want to come if he was going to be there. Perhaps she was right. But then I remember how she'd left me a message which had got cut off halfway through. I'd got the when and where bits, but evidently not the why. So she probably had told me.

'I thought it would be nice to see you again,' he repeats. 'To check that you are now OK. It is nice to see you up and about, even with these . . . what are they called in English?'

'Crutches. I've been using them since the accident. They wouldn't let me leave hospital until I could go up a flight of stairs on them,' I say, rather awkwardly, wondering what possible relevance that has to anything. I'm really not great at small talk. Flustered, I watch Kerry rub her sweaty face with a towel she takes out of her racket bag. It's probably been in there for months – I can smell it from where I'm sitting. Her face is going to smell like that now, I think idly.

My mobile phone rings in my bag. 'Excuse me.' I fish it out. It's Mum.

'Rachel, hi, are you still at the club?' she demands. She sounds stressed. 'I'm really sorry, but there's an accident on the A316 and I'm stuck in horrendous traffic. I don't know how long I'm going to be. I've lost Karl's number, so I can't get hold of him. He's probably on his way over.'

'He's here already,' I say brightly and loudly, thinking it was just as well he'd turned up and explained that we were all having lunch, otherwise I wouldn't have had a clue as to what she was talking about.

'What, at the club? What's he doing there? Anyway, could you take him off for a coffee? I'll meet you in that place on the High Street; you know, the one with the grapevine in the conservatory. I'll be about half an hour, probably.'

'Mum!'

I don't want to take a strange man out for coffee. I was looking forward to going for a drink with Kerry. But just then a blue Mazda pulls into the club car park, and a tall blonde jumps out. It's Mark's new girlfriend, Sally-Anne. I grit my teeth; but worse is to follow.

'Hiya, Kel!' she honks. 'Fancy a set or two? I absolutely have to work on my volleys. Oh . . . hello Rachel, long time no see. How's the leg?'

'I'm great, thanks, Sally-Anne,' I say sweetly, managing not to add: *No thanks to you for nicking my boyfriend.* But I suppose we had split up before they got together, so I can't really accuse her of stealing him, tempting though it is. 'You'll come for a coffee with us, won't you, Kerry?'

To my surprise, Kerry looks at me awkwardly, brushing her lank hair out of her eyes. She has the most amazing eyes: bright green and clear. But she never has much luck with men, either.

'I wouldn't mind another couple of sets here, actually,' she says. 'I don't have fitness training till two o'clock.'

I make pleading faces with her behind Karl's back, to no avail. Karl wanders over to the boards outside the clubhouse, where he skulks about, reading the names of all the members' tags, up there on Dymo embossed tape attached to metal tags and stuck on hooks.

One of my earliest memories is of Gordana letting me punch out labels for new members' names myself, clicking the dial to each letter on the handheld Dymo machine as she dictated the name. I must only have been four or five. Many of those same labels still hang up there on the board, nearly twenty years later, their hardy owners playing regularly, battling on in all weathers through arthritis or sprains, middle-aged spread and back problems. Or, in Gordana's case, cancer. I glance at the tag bearing her name, and my chest constricts.

'Just a quick one?' I ask Kerry again.

'Nah, thanks, Rach, but I think I'll stay here.'

Great, I think to myself. Sally-Anne's got her claws into Mark *and* Kerry. It's silly, but I am more hurt than I care to admit.

'No problem,' I say stiffly. 'See you around, then. Karl, would you like to go and grab a coffee down the road?'

He rushes back over with alacrity and hands me my crutches. I notice Sally-Anne's eyes widen to take in Karl's good looks, so I decide not to mention Mum's lateness until Sally-Anne is out of earshot. Excellent, I think, that'll get back to Mark.

A couple of minutes later, we are sitting in the warm cappuccino fug of the coffee shop. I send Kerry a discreet text under the table: 'PLS DON'T TELL S.A. THAT KARL'S NOT MY BOYF', hoping that she can do this much

354

for me. When I look up, Karl is watching me, and I feel uncomfortable. I'm never sure how to interpret that particular type of look, so loaded with unspoken words, as if it is trying to explain something I'd never in a million years understand. Why's he looking at me that way when he fancies my mother?

'Mum says sorry,' I say awkwardly, sliding my phone back into my tracksuit pocket. 'She's stuck in traffic, and she says she'll meet us here, and then we can walk along to the restaurant.'

'OK,' he says easily. He leans back in his chair as the waitress brings us our coffee. Everything he does seems easy for him. He is very different to Mark, I think, who was a bundle of nervous energy. Of late, I have been concentrating very hard on remembering all Mark's bad points, in an attempt to get over him once and for all, and slowly it seems to be working. It's strange how someone's 'bad points' don't even exist when you first fall in love. Then, gradually, you begin to identify them, and although they still don't bug you, you can see how they have the potential to.

'What are you thinking about?' asks Karl, amused. I blush, realizing that I must have been frowning.

'My ex-boyfriend's bad burping habit,' I reply, pouring milk into my coffee, and Karl snorts with laughter.

'I see. Well, thank you for the honest answer. Is this why he is your ex-boyfriend?'

'No,' I say moodily. 'He didn't want to be with me any more because he thought that my dad was too domineering.'

'Ah. The famous Ivan.' Karl blows on his black coffee and takes a sip. 'Susie has told me quite a lot about Ivan.'

'None of it good, I expect.' I suddenly feel grumpy and out of sorts, and wish Mum would hurry up. I wonder if she's told him about Dad's charges? I hope not. I decide to bow out of the lunch and leave her and Karl to it – I don't want to play gooseberry.

'He's actually not a bad person,' I say abruptly. 'He's just his own worst enemy. He pisses people off without really meaning to. He's so driven that he expects everyone around him to be the same, and sometimes it comes across as arrogance or bullying. But I feel sorry for him. He felt that his own career was a failure – at least, in his eyes – so he put everything into mine . . . but mine isn't working out how he planned either. Now his girlfriend has left him too. He can't keep a relationship . . .' I laugh cynically. 'But then again, neither can I. Like father, like daughter.'

The door of the café swings open and Mum bursts in, sooner than expected, waving hesitantly at us and simultaneously smiling and grimacing as she narrowly avoids tripping over a pushchair which has been carelessly parked by the counter. She's got such a beautiful smile, although it looks a little strained today, probably as a result of having to rush. She hates being late. But it usually lights up her entire face – when she smiles, she could pass for a woman my age. Her hair is bright blonde –not a bit brassy – and shiny in the way I'd love mine to be. I watch Karl watching her, and think: Yes, they'd make a nice couple.

'Sorry, sorry,' she says, rushing over and embracing us both over-enthusiastically. 'But luckily it all cleared just after I rang you. How are you, Rach? How's the physio going?'

'Really well, Mum. He says I'll be off the crutches in a few weeks. It's killing me today though.'

She kisses the top of my head as I pop a couple of ibuprofens, washing them down with still-hot coffee.

'Poor baby. You'll be back in the tournaments in no time,' she says, and I feel that old wash of emotions: fear, excitement, resignation . . . confusion. Do I want to?

I shake my head slightly as if to disperse the thought. 'I don't think I'll come for lunch after all, thanks, I'm just going to get a cab back to Gordana's and put my feet up.'

Mum pulls up a seat and shrugs off her coat. 'Oh Rachel, are you sure? We were looking forward to you joining us. I wanted to take you to that nice little bistro round the corner, and I thought we could— Oh!' She stops abruptly, staring at the door.

Dad is standing in the doorway, letting in all the cold air, glaring at us. He looks appalling: unshaven, his hair unkempt, eyes bloodshot, clothes rumpled as though he's slept in them. He moves almost stealthily towards us; it's more frightening somehow than a lunge, although he still manages to knock into the same pushchair Mum nearly tripped over. He doesn't seem drunk, just clumsy with rage. The pushchair's occupant, a lolling toddler, wakes up and starts to wail. The staff behind the café's counter exchange worried glances across the domes of choc-chip muffins as Ivan advances, pointing a shaking, accusatory finger at Mum. Even Karl loses his complacent laid-back expression and straightens up.

'Happy now?' Ivan snarls at Mum, whose face has turned the colour of the dirty magnolia wall behind her. She reaches out to try and put a restraining hand on his forearm, and then obviously thinks better of it and drops it back down again, knocking over the salt grinder on the table. It falls with a bang, and the top comes off, scattering salt crystals like rough diamonds.

'What are you talking about, Ivan?' she asks quietly.

'As if you don't know!'

'I don't know, Ivan. Sit down and say what you've got to say without embarrassing us all, or just leave now.'

She begins methodically to pick up each spilt salt crystal on the plastic tablecloth by pushing her index finger down on top of it, then flicking it off on to the floor, trying and failing to act unconcerned.

'Dad. Please, just sit down with us. Have my seat – I'll get another one.'

'No, don't get up, Rachel,' says Karl, quickly

dragging another seat over to our table. 'Here is a spare chair.'

'Who's he?' Dad demands like a madman, jerking his head towards Karl. It crosses my mind that maybe he really has had a breakdown.

'Dad – Karl; Karl – Ivan. Karl's a friend of ours from the skiing holiday.'

'I need to talk to you, alone,' Dad says, ignoring the introduction and glaring at Mum again.

Colour is rising back into Mum's neck and face, but apart from that, she remains cold and composed. People at the nearby tables are staring and whispering.

Dad crumples suddenly, sinking on to the chair and burying his face in his arms. Now he's closer, I can smell that he has been drinking after all. I've never seen him drunk before, except at parties or Christmas. I try to exchange glances with Mum, but she won't look at me. Karl scratches his head.

'Everything's ruined,' Dad says in a low, hopeless voice. Tears spring into my eyes at his tone. I've heard him angry, defensive, leery, accusatory; but this is new and, frankly, much more worrying.

Karl pushes back his chair and stands up. 'Right,' he says calmly, 'I think we should all leave. You three need to talk privately. I will wait somewhere else.' He takes in the agog faces of everyone else in the café. 'OK, everybody, the show is over.'

All the other customers suddenly become deeply interested in their bacon sandwiches or custard slices as Karl marches up to the counter and pays for our coffees. Numbly, Mum and I follow, and Dad reluctantly brings up the rear.

What a sorry excuse for a parent, I think as we trail outside again into the cold December air. This would never, ever, happen in my Fantasy Family.

'You go with Karl,' Mum says, clutching at my elbow. 'I need to talk to your father. I'll call you when we're finished and maybe we can meet up later.'

I am so worn down with emotion that I'm not even sure I can summon up the energy to find out what this is all about. I feel like lying down in a darkened room for the next six months with a cool damp facecloth over my eyes. In the end, though, I do ask.

'What's going on? Is this to do with you getting arrested, Dad? With Anthea? What?'

'Don't worry about it, Rach,' says Mum, still in that strained voice. 'Go and have some fun.'

Fun? I've just told her my knee's killing me and I want to go home and chill out. But it doesn't look like I have any choice.

'Karl, I'm ever so sorry about all this,' she continues. 'You don't really need to be plunged into the midst of our family dramas, do you?' She smiles, but it's not a real smile.

'It is no problem,' he replies. 'I certainly am not complaining.' He turns to me. 'Come on. I think a nice bottle of wine to start will be good.'

'I never drink during the day.'

I crane my neck to see where Mum and Dad are going. They appear to be heading back towards the club.

'You don't have to train, drive, or play later, do you?'

'No, but . . .'

'We have a nice time then,' he says firmly. 'Let them sort out what they need to sort out. Where shall we have lunch?'

I stop on the pavement. My knee is hurting, and I feel it is a little insensitive of him not to ask me if I'm up to it, since I've already complained that I'm in pain.

'Actually, Karl, I'm not really all that hungry. I'm happy to hang out with you for a while, but I'm just not sure that I want to sit in a restaurant. My leg gets really stiff when I can't stretch it out.'

'You want to go for a walk instead?' He looks doubtfully at my crutches, and then up at the cold grey sky.

'No . . . sorry, can't really do that either.' I am partly

doing this out of bloody-mindedness – I feel pushed into it and, while Karl seems perfectly nice, I'm not sure that I want to spend time with someone just because I'm told to go and 'have fun'. In truth, it probably wouldn't kill me to go for a hobble, since the painkillers will kick in soon, and I'm supposed to keep things moving . . .

'Well, what shall we do then?'

We stand in silence for a moment. I can't think of anything, except girly stuff like shopping, or a manicure. Wonder what he'd say if I suggested that?

'I am a tourist,' he announces after a while. 'This is a historic part of London, ja? Are we near the Hampton Court Palace?'

'Quite near,' I say doubtfully. 'We'd have to get a cab there. It's just along the river a way.'

'The river!' he says, brightly. 'I love to go on boats. Can we go on a boat trip?'

At first, I look at him as if he's crazy. It's December. It's cold. I'm not even sure if boats are running at this time of year. In the end, I shrug.

'I don't see why not. There's a boat which goes from here to Hampton Court, actually – or least in summer it does. The jetty's just around that corner. But I doubt that there'll be anything to eat on board, other than crisps and so on. And I thought you were after a nice bottle of wine?'

'Good thinking, Batman,' he says, and in his German accent it sounds funny enough to make me smile. 'But this is no problem. If the mountain will not go to Mohammed . . .' He drags me in through the automatic doors of a convenient branch of Marks & Spencer and sits me down in the café area while he rushes off with a wire basket draped over his forearm. 'Is there anything you don't like to eat?' he calls over from the fruit and vegetable section.

'Well,' I call back. 'I'm not keen on anchovies, All-Bran or Brussels sprouts, but since none of that is standard picnic food, I think I'll probably be OK.'

To my surprise, I feel an unaccustomed lightness of spirit, as if I know that I'm going to escape from all the doom and gloom for a few hours. Loath as I am to admit it, something tells me this afternoon might be fun.

46

Gordana

I'm so tired today. My insides hurt and my skin hurts. It is so dry that it feels like it's all going to flake right off and float away from me. And now I cannot stop worrying about Ivan.

Even Ted can't understand how Ivan turned out the way he did. Nor can Rachel, or Susie, or my friends at the tennis club – the ones who know me well enough to acknowledge Ivan's grumpiness and all the shortcomings.

'But he had everything!' they say. 'You've given him nothing but love and encouragement and support!'

The thing is that they don't know the truth. Not even Ted, to whom I tell everything eventually. And when you find yourself in a situation like this one; a situation where you must lay everything out for scrutiny like tidying an underwear drawer, not knowing if there's going to be time to reassemble it all in the correct way – I believe this is called 'putting your house in order' – well, then you suddenly realize that it's time to start getting a little more honest.

So this is what I ask myself now: is it my fault that Ivan is the way he is? Cross, over-competitive, even perhaps a liar. Nobody knows what a bad mother I was – still am. I cover it up with my 'Ivan darling's and my 'baby boy's, but they are just sweet words.

I wanted to be pregnant so that Paul Tyler would

marry me and I wouldn't have to work in the Ford factory any more, but I didn't think as far as being stuck with the baby those long five years before I managed to get Ted.

I went into some sort of big emotional freezer when Ivan was born and I realized I was going to be on my own; that I'd never be the next Sandie Shaw. It sounds silly now, but I remember how my chest ached with the importance of it to me then. I had nothing, and I could see nothing good to come. My parents didn't like me; they died believing me to be a disgrace and a burden.

And Ivan was so difficult, especially when he was a toddler, pooing on the floor and hitting me and shouting 'NO' whenever I ask him to do anything. He got a bit better once he went to school, and once Ted came into his life. I decided with a big relief that perhaps he'd just needed a father figure, and the absence of one during his early years caused the troubles I had with him.

Ted saved me from the worst of myself regarding Ivan. I remember the first time he took us both out, rather than just me. We had done many dates: drinks and dancing, movies and kissing; and I'd been putting it off for weeks, but eventually I gave in to Ted's constant suggestions that the three of us had a day out together.

'I'm going to be in your life,' he kept saying. 'So it'll be the three of us, not just you and me.' I knew he was right – but oh, how much I dreaded it.

Ivan was five. Ted took us to Bournemouth for the day in his white Hillman Imp – the only car I have ever seen with the boot in the front and the engine in the rear, like some sort of unfortunate deformity, although Ted was stupidly proud of it. We drove for what seemed like hours with Ivan whining down the back of my neck. In the end I had to let him sit in the passenger seat, and I was sent to the back seat, which made me feel so car sick that I couldn't speak. Ivan cheered up then, of course. He always does when he gets his own way.

It was not the sunny day that the weather forecaster had told us it would be, with his stick-on sunshine over the outline of the south coast. Instead there were dark purple clouds rolling across the sea, turning it choppy and cross-looking. I sat huddled in a mackintosh, shivering on a thin groundsheet while Ted and Ivan played cricket. They kept asking me to join in, but I didn't want to. I didn't want to take off my shoes – too cold, and so many shells with the razor edges – and I have never been able to catch a ball properly. We were the only ones brave enough to sit on the beach.

Ted had thought of everything: picnic hamper, two windbreaks, thermos flasks of tea, fish-paste sandwiches. It was a big surprise to me that a single man could be so organized without a woman to help him – in fact, I almost wondered if he had a wife back at home, cutting the sandwiches into their neat crustless triangles and wrapping them carefully in the grease-proof paper. None of the men at the Ford factory would ever have done that for a girlfriend and her son, I was sure of it.

I was also pleased to notice that he did not wear a knotted hankerchief on his head and a string vest, like men at the seaside often did. He looked quite handsome, I thought, in his crisp white shirt rolled up and open at the collar, and dark trousers held up with braces. I had picked a good one. A bit short, but no matter.

Ivan was loving it, at least, so for a while he was cheerful. It was such a big space for him to play in, not like my parents' tiny square back garden with the high fences all round, and the grey patches of grass. I even managed to read a whole chapter of my book without interruptions.

Ted said, 'What extraordinary ball skills he has, for a child of his age!' and for the first time, I noticed it myself. Ivan had never played cricket before, but he was taking great big whacks at the ball and nine times out of ten, hitting it. He could run fast, too, skidding for the stumps over the wet sand. He was winning, and drinking up Ted's admiration – until Ted decided to put some pressure on.

I watched anxiously as Ivan's mood changed. I could see he needed a poo, but when I called him over and asked him, in a whisper, he declared that it had 'gone back in again'. But this also made his temper worse.

'Not fair!' he yelled as Ted hit a mighty six. Ivan didn't even try to run after the ball, which the wind was carrying away along the edge of the waves.

'Run, Ivan,' I called from the groundsheet, and he just scowled at me, folded his arms and stamped his foot, leaving little hoof-shaped hole in the sand.

'Run, Ivan,' said Ted, pointing towards the escaping ball. 'Otherwise you won't get a chance to keep winning, will you?'

This was incentive enough, and Ivan trotted off after it, as Ted winked at me, and I rolled my eyes at him. Ivan threw back the ball with one powerful heave for a five-year old, and it landed at my feet.

'Mama, you be bowler now!' he ordered, and I reluctantly stood up.

'All right, but I cannot run,' I said, wishing I had brought some deck shoes instead of my sandals with heels.

I cannot really remember how the big row started – I suppose that I did not throw the ball to Ivan's satisfaction, but soon he was having a monstrous tantrum. I think I also by accident kicked over one of his sand-castles, such a puny effort that I didn't even realize it was meant to be a fortified building; I just assumed it was a small hump on the beach. Anyway, he began to shout and scream and lash out with his bare feet at me.

I was embarrassed, and ashamed, at his behaviour in front of Ted, whom I was still wishing to impress. There was a scuffle as I tried to restrain his windmills of arms. I accidentally trod on his toe, and he yelped with pain.

The worst thing of all: I felt moment of gladness when I first realized I'd stepped on his foot, and then what did I do? For one second, I stepped harder. I let the hard heel of my sandal grind into his bare foot. I wanted to hurt him. I wanted to cause him a tiny portion of the pain he'd caused me, compensation for the life he had snatched away from me with his own many demands.

Then I came to my senses, the guilt shooting through me like a red firework, so strong that I was nearly sick. A bruise the colour of the dark clouds was already coming up on Ivan's skin, and I thought I must surely have broken his toe. I wanted to die from the guilt. His tantrum became huge sobs as I tried to rock him better.

That was the first time I wanted to hurt him. The first of many, many times; and I worry now that this is what has made Ivan the way he is. I never beat him out of rage – although I did smack him when he was naughty, same as my parents smacked me; and like he used to smack Rachel to make her learn things on court.

Instead, when I hated Ivan, I used to ignore him. I withheld the hugs, the kind words, even the eye-contact. I put him into the same freezer I was in; lifted the lid from inside and let him climb in to shiver next to me. Not touching me. I punished him that way. And I never told Ted I did it.

I saw a mother at the Marsden do the same thing to her two-year-old when I went for my most recent chemo session. The little girl was whining and pulling her mother's skirt, jumping up and down and begging, just begging to be picked up and loved. But the mother wouldn't even look at her. I saw the desperation in her blank eyes as the child's cries got louder and more insistent and I thought: *You must just pick her up!* It look so cruel when you see someone else do it. But when I did it, it was because I just couldn't face it. I couldn't face that big amount of neediness. I wanted to say something to the mother. I wanted to shout loud at her: For goodness' sake, look at what you are doing to that child. She's two years old, she doesn't understand what you're going through! Another part of me wanted to put my arms around that mother and say: But I do understand. It's wrong, and if you keep doing it, it will damage you and your relationship with this child – but I understand, because this has happened to me too.

'What's the matter?' Ted asks me as he watches me thinking about all this. There am I, believing I am doing a convincing impression of somebody trying to make a banana cake in the bread machine – but it won't cook, so I am wondering whether to put whole tin in the oven instead – but he knows that I am not worrying about banana dough.

'Nothing,' I say, but the timing of his question is, as always, on the spot, and I have to turn my head away from him and switch on the oven. Sometimes I wish I hadn't married such an honest man.

He puts down the financial section of the Sunday newspaper he has been reading – or I thought he had been reading. Jackson is sitting adoringly at his feet, good as gold, dribbling on a chew, and I can't remember what it was like before he lived with us. He is good companion for Ted, and he will take Ted's mind off things when I go.

No, don't think that. I will not allow it to happen.

'Come on. What's on your mind?'

'It was very bad idea to try and make a cake in this machine. It is going to be heavy as a brick. I don't think it is ever going to cook! The instructions say cook for forty minutes. It's already been an hour and a half, I don't know . . .'

Ted comes to me and puts his arms around my middle from behind, pressing his cheek in between my shoulders. Because I am taller than him, he fits there very nicely. He's always done this. It makes me feel safe, like a boat tied to a big ring on a harbour wall.

'Dana,' he says, using the pet name that only he calls me. 'Are you afraid? Because you know Mr Babish says you're doing well, fighting really hard. I know it's awful for you but—'

'It's not that.'

'What, then? Surely not the banana cake.'

I feel his mouth form a smile into my spine, and I manage a little fake laugh. But I am a fake, so that is no surprise. The surprise is how he could have lived with me for all these years and not known the sort of woman I am. The sort of woman who maybe does not even really love her only child.

I shove the bread tin into the oven and turn to face my husband.

'It's Ivan.'

Ted sighs. 'What's he done now? Good grief, it's like when he was at school, always getting into trouble. Has the headmaster called?'

I burst into tears, and Ted is shocked. I cry so rarely. 'No, then, it's not Ivan. It's me. There is something I must tell you about me and Ivan.'

Ted steers me over to a chair and sits me down at the kitchen table. He hands me a piece of kitchen towel. Jackson regards me mournfully and then flops his head back on to his paws, and Ted crouches down next to me. 'Tell me.' They both have the big anxious eyes.

I jiggle my leg up and down. 'That money Ivan borrowed . . .'

'What about it?'

'We ask him to pay it back every month.'

368

'Yes? He has been, hasn't he?'

'Yes. But I thought he couldn't really afford it.'

Ted looks puzzled. 'Then why did you ask him to pay it back? And how is he paying it back? I let you take care of all that because you insisted you wanted to. If there were problems, you should have let me know!'

I feel the shame of it, perhaps for the first time. Ted is like a mirror to my conscience. A speckly old mirror that you can't see clearly into, but still a mirror. I reach out and grasp his hand.

'He is paying it back because he knows I don't love him. He doesn't want to let me down.'

Ted shakes his head. He looks very tired. 'What do you mean, Dana? You aren't making sense.'

I breathe in, feel my fake reconstructed breast rise with my real one, pulling at the scar. 'He owes money to many other people, builders and what-not. But he pays me back instead of them. He hasn't paid anybody else, and now he will be bankrupt.'

'What in God's name did you let him do that for?' Ted drops my hand and stares at me incredulously. 'He's in enough trouble already!'

'I didn't know. He just told me. And then I check with Esther —you know her husband took job as accountant for Ivan – and she told me in secret that it's true; many red bills and demands come in, and Ivan gets grumpy and takes them away quickly. I was cross with her for not telling me this before.'

'But . . . But . . . you've let him get into such debt, just to pay you?'

I lift my chin and look him in the eye. 'I told you, I didn't know. He would have lost the club by now anyway if he had to pay it back to a mortgage company.'

'Ivan is a fool,' says Ted, who never say bad things about anybody.

'But it is my fault,' I say. 'Imagine! He is so afraid of letting his mother down that he goes bankrupt first. What kind of mother am I?'

This is the trouble with too many changes in life. They make you look hard at everything which went before, and you will see what mistakes you have made.

Ted stands up and hugs me – how high his waistbands have got! He cannot change the white hair and the saggy skin, but we can stop him dressing like an old man too. I must buy him some new trousers.

'Dana, you aren't a bad mother. You weren't, I mean; and you aren't now. Ivan's an adult. He's responsible for his own mistakes; accountable for his own behaviour. He was a difficult child! Nothing you did; it's just the way he was. I think him paying you back before his creditors is more because he's too proud to admit that the business was failing, not because he was afraid of your criticism. I know you're feeling under the weather, but try not to make yourself feel worse by blaming yourself. It's not your fault.'

Ted releases me from the hug, picks the dog lead off the peg, and clips it on to Jackson's collar.

'Let's take him for a walk,' he says. 'We can go slowly. Fresh air will do you good.'

I have heavy heart as I put on my coat and follow him outside. I believed that I would feel liberated by telling Ted the truth, but now I have just worried him more. I should have kept quiet. But I have been feeling so bad for Ivan, sorry for him, now that Anthea has gone and Rachel's not speaking to him and Susie's found out about Natasha. Even Natasha doesn't want him now. He's broke and alone. And Ted is disgusted with him. I do not feel liberated. I feel rather depressed, actually. And no matter what Ted says, I am still a bad mother.

47

Susie

'We'll go and sit in the car,' I said to Ivan, more firmly than I felt. He was being so aggressive, yet I could sense the inherent weakness and despair fuelling it. I also sensed that perhaps it wasn't just me he was angry with. But my knees were shaking so much that I was worried I wouldn't even make it back to the car, which was parked on a meter in the High Street.

I unlocked the passenger door and held it open for him. As soon as he got in, he leaned forwards in the seat, rocking to and fro, his shoulders hunched in defeat. A broken man. He wrapped his arms over his head in a curiously childlike posture and moaned.

'How can you be so vindictive, Susie? I mean, talk about kicking a man when he's down.'

'I haven't been vindictive!' I said hotly. 'I don't even know what you're so upset about. If anything, it's *me* who has a right to be upset.'

He snorted. 'You? Oh, do me a favour.'

'Yes, me. You haven't even bothered to apologize for cheating on me – and I don't care that you think it's ancient history, because it matters to me.'

'And so you thought you'd make me suffer for it, all these years later, and in the process break Anthea's heart? You say that's not vindictive . . . ? Huh.'

He made an 'I rest my case' gesture, palms open,

371

which so infuriated me that I felt like punching him in the ear.

'I haven't said a word to Anthea. If she knows, she's found out some other way.'

'I don't believe you.'

I shrugged. 'Fine. Then don't believe me. But it's true, and I'd appreciate it if you stopped accusing me of things I haven't done.'

He sighed. The windscreen was beginning to steam up, so I turned on the engine and put my window down by a few inches, letting in some welcome cold air.

'How did you find out about Natasha, anyway?' he asked sulkily.

'I found a photo of you two in a box of stuff I'd left at Corinna's. It wasn't positive proof, but there was something about the way you were looking at her, and the message she wrote on the back. It was clear that she was more than just one of your players.'

'You *must* have told Anthea . . .'

He was so infuriating. 'Ivan, is that really how little you think of me? Why would I want to do something like that?'

'Any number of reasons,' he said, the old defensiveness creeping back into his voice. 'Because you hate me. Because you wanted revenge on Rachel's behalf, because she thinks I split her and Mark up . . .' That one was a bit far-fetched, I thought. 'Because you decided it was only fair to warn Anthea I was a two-timing "creep", as you would doubtless put it.'

'Well, there is that,' I said. 'But I didn't tell her. Maybe somebody else did. Maybe, like me, she found something: a photo or a letter or something. People who cheat on their partners usually get found out. I'm amazed it's taken me this long to find out about you and her.'

'I didn't two-time Anthea,' he said wearily. 'Not really. Tasha just keeps me on a string. Tells me she loves me and wants to be with me for ever, and then dumps me. It's been going on for years. Then I met Anthea, and started to get over Tasha. But she came back, a little while ago. I met her for a drink in Zurich, and again in London – she came over for a time. But I had too much going on, what with being on bail and all – it was right after I got arrested – and she was still really holding back. I just couldn't be sure she really wanted me the way I want her. Hell, for all I know, she was only after free coaching. Maybe she never really loved me at all . . . Anyway, I told her that it was too late. I just couldn't face going through all that again, however much I love her.'

I waited to feel the swelling of outrage and disbelief in my chest, but none came. Deep down, I knew he was still telling the truth. He was a self-pitying bugger, though.

A woman tapped on Ivan's window and we both jumped. For a moment I thought it was someone else from his murky past, but when he put down the window, we saw she was pointing at the parking ticket balanced on the dashboard.

'Terribly sorry,' she was saying, 'I was just wondering if you were going, and if so, could I have that? I've got no change and there's a traffic warden on the prowl.'

She was in her fifties, jolly and posh. She probably knew Gordana, I thought. Probably pitied her for the deliciously juicy scandal of a son being accused of paedophilia. Prior to now, everyone thought of Gordana as a pillar of the community; a brave soul who'd overcome hardship and poverty. We'd all heard the stories: how she got pregnant and all her hopes and dreams were crushed, then Ted came along. What did they all think now?

Ivan handed my ticket to the woman, who beamed and nodded and backed off. Typical.

'Ivan! I haven't finished with that – I'm supposed to be meeting Karl for lunch.'

'I'll buy you another one. I just wanted to get rid of her.'

When the woman had gone, we sat in silence again as I digested what he'd told me.

'So, do the police know about your debts?'

He nodded wearily. 'It's all come out because they've been investigating my finances, so now I'm going to be declared bankrupt too. I know I've been an idiot. It's just that the club means so much to me. And being a success means so much to Mama, I just couldn't admit that I was struggling with it; that I couldn't pay her back.'

'She'd have let you off. She'd never have insisted you paid her back.'

'I know. But I so wanted to prove myself to her.'

I shook my head. Poor, sad Ivan. I felt so sorry for him; and with my pity came a kind of release; an end to bitterness and resentment I'd harboured towards him for so many years.

'Let me help you,' I said impulsively. 'Gordana and Rachel have got too much on their plates at the moment. Ted needs to be there for Gordana. Anthea's gone. I'm not as involved. I want to help. You need a friend.'

He sniffed and looked out of the window. But he didn't instantly refuse.

'Just tell me one thing, Ivan. I swear that what you say will stay inside this car; I won't tell a soul. But I have to know: *did* you download and pay for any of that porn?'

He shook his head instantly, turning to face me with burning eyes. 'I really didn't, Susie, I promise you, on Mama's life. I'd swear on fifty bibles. Someone else must have done it.'

'On your computer?'

'I think so. I don't know much about these things but I don't think it could've been done from any other computer.' He leaned his head against the side

374

window. 'I'm not remotely interested in children in that way. In fact, I hate the way they get exploited like that . . .'

'*Natasha* was only fifteen when you met her. A child.'

'I know. But she looked twenty-one. Not that it's any excuse, but she didn't look or act like a child; and I certainly didn't coerce her into anything. I wasn't actually even coaching her in Hungary, not at first, until after we'd met up. Then she got herself transferred to my Junior squad, and that's how I found out how young she was. I was horrified, but I was involved by then. I know I'm a bit of a Lothario, Suze, but since then I swear I've never looked twice at a girl without checking her age first, and if she's under eighteen, I've run a mile.'

Tears ran down his cheeks again, and he swatted them away with the backs of his hands, sniffing like a child. 'If I get convicted, I'll definitely lose the club. But if I'm declared bankrupt, I'll lose it anyway. Mama will never get her money back. Rachel will suffer . . . Oh God, I can't bear it. I know some of it's my own fault, but not all of it. And all I've been trying to do is avoid Rachel getting hurt. Give her the best chance she can have of success. Now I've ruined everything.'

He scratched the stubble beneath his chin. I noticed that the car was filling up with a strange kind of sweaty fug: the scent of Ivan's despair. I wound down the window even further, almost gasping in the fresh, damp air. Imminent rain hung in the atmosphere; the thick dark grey clouds were so low they seemed to press down on the buildings and pavements.

The first drops of rain began to fall on the car roof, gathering speed and momentum. Within a minute, it was hammering all around us, sending people scurrying to their cars or into shop doorways. Funny how Ivan and I were back in a rainstorm, I thought, although the last thing he was likely to do was to bend

me over a balcony and impregnate me. Thank goodness. I wound the window back up as rain was
splashing into the car and on to the side of my face and
my shoulder.

'While you're being honest with me, for once, I want
to ask you something. About that LTA party back in
'ninety-five?'

Ivan looked at me as if I'd lost my mind. 'What
party?'

'The one I was invited to as well. That you ended up
going to on your own, because you claimed that you
were being stalked by a psycho ex-girlfriend called
Tracy, who then mysteriously vanished out of your life
as fast as she'd appeared?'

He looked shame-faced. 'Oh. Yeah. Her.'

'There was no Tracy, was there? That was a cover, so
you could meet up with Natasha, wasn't it?'

'Sorry,' he said lamely, fiddling with a packet of
chewing gum I'd left in the pouchy leather surround
of the clutch.

I tutted with irritation. 'Ivan, you are the worst liar
in the world. I knew you were lying, even back then! I
knew there was no Tracy. You just wouldn't admit it.
Have a piece of gum — your breath smells like a
brewery.'

'Actually, there was a Tracy, an ex of mine. She
wrote to me around that time and asked to see me
again. I just, um, exaggerated it.' He put a lozenge of
chewing gum in his mouth and a fresher, mintier scent
replaced the stale alcohol halitosis.

'The only good thing about you being a dishonest
cheating pig of a man is that at least you're bad at it.
That's how I know you're telling the truth about the
downloads. I can see right through you, you know.'

'You never used to be able to.'

'Well, call it perspective, or experience, but I can
now. You're a total bloody idiot, Ivan.'

'I know,' he said humbly, and for the first time in

almost ten years, I thought I might be starting to be fond of him again.

Two young girls in tennis whites ran past, obviously heading back to the shelter of the club. Ivan shrank down in his seat, but even through the rain, one of them spotted him and nudged the other, who stared unsubtly back at him over her shoulder. He pretended he hadn't seen them. Rachel said there'd been rumours of reporters and detectives down at the club in the first weeks after his arrest, so the whole place was probably agog with speculation and censure.

'I'll take you home. You can sleep it off,' I said. 'Let me think about all this, see if there's anything we can do.'

'What about your date?' said Ivan gruffly as I got my phone out of my handbag.

'I'll stop by the restaurant after I drop you off and see if they're still there. But it doesn't matter. I'm not really in the mood anyway.'

I started up the engine and pulled out into the slow traffic. The storm had already blown over, as suddenly as it started, but rain still flooded the streets, and queues had built up both ways.

'Susie,' Ivan said, chewing his gum with his mouth open in the way which had always irritated the hell out of me, but which he did when he felt awkward about something.

'Yes?'

'Thanks. I mean, thanks for believing me. I know I can be a shit, and I've done some wrong things in my time – some of them to you – but I'm not that much of a shit.'

I didn't look at him as we stopped at some red traffic lights near his house.

'Listen, Ivan, we've had our differences. But I don't like seeing you in this state. Are you getting any help? Counselling, I mean?'

I waited for him to snort derisively, but instead he

gave a meek nod. 'Yeah. Been going since I was arrested.'

'Oh, right . . . well, that's good.' I was astonished. Ivan had always been the type who'd rather pluck out his own eyes with toothpicks than voluntarily seek help from a professional. 'If there's anything I can do, just let me know, OK? '

'OK.'

Good grief, I thought, after I'd dropped him off. How the mighty – or not so mighty – fall. I watched him shambling up his unkempt front garden path, a crushed, drooping figure, such a contrast to the once proud, fit athlete who could hit a ball as if each smash were a personal triumph. I felt so sad for him.

But at least I now knew for sure that he wasn't connected with the child porn. There had to be some other explanation. And, really, it didn't matter about Natasha, not any more. I would never admit it to Ivan, but he was right; it was in the past. It was Anthea's problem now, not mine.

48

Rachel

We get to the jetty, and I'm quite surprised to see a big launch bobbing up and down in the murky water, and a coachload of Japanese tourists embarking along a precarious-looking gangplank. But when I limp over to inspect the timetable, I discover that the scheduled boat services only run between April and September.

'We can't get on this one,' I call to Karl. 'It must be a private party.' I look around to see if there are any nearby benches where we can sit and eat our lunch; but Karl is not so easily deterred. He marches up to the Japanese tour guide – identifiable by the large, furled umbrella he points straight up towards the sky – and I watch with amusement as he bows politely. I don't hear what he says, but the next minute, he turns to me and gives a big thumbs-up.

'Have you just scrounged us a lift on someone else's boat?' I ask, laughing in disbelief, hopping towards the gangplank.

'You don't ask; you don't get,' he says philosophically, steering me carefully up. I nod thanks to the tour guide, and he nods back again.

'Are you sure this boat is going to Hampton Court? I don't want to end up at Westminster Pier. It'll cost a fortune in a cab to get home again.'

'I checked,' he confirms, settling me on a wooden bench which runs around the open back of the boat.

'Now, madam, please relax and enjoy the scenery. It seems there is a bar inside so perhaps it will be best if we drink our wine – what's the word in English? – discreetly.'

Karl has thought of everything. He's bought red wine in a screwtop bottle, serviettes, plastic cups, little trays of salad with plastic forks attached to the lid, fresh bread, crisps ('I love your English crisps!' he says, with such enthusiasm), fruit, chocolate . . . I didn't realize I was so hungry until he starts getting it all out of the M&S bags.

He unscrews the wine and pours me some, handing it over with a flourish. I rest my crutches on the floor of the boat and touch cups with him. It's cold out here, but not unpleasant with my big jacket done up and my fingerless gloves on.

'Cheers!' he beams. 'This is very exciting for me, I must say.'

I toast him back, smiling at him in admiration. I'd never in a million years have the nerve to barge (no pun intended) on to someone else's boat trip, but Karl makes it appear perfectly natural. He strikes me as someone who probably gets his own way most of the time, just through charm and chutzpah. And it really doesn't seem to be a problem – the Japanese tour group are inside the main area of the boat, listening to a commentary. Nobody is paying us any attention.

The boat revs up its engines and begins to chug away downstream as Karl and I make inroads into our impromptu picnic.

'This is delicious,' I remark, tucking into my pasta salad.

The riverside developments slide past, block after block of architecturally complicated apartment complexes in shades of sand and rust, terracotta and cream. They have wavy balconies, big windows, private jetties.

'I'd love to live in one of those flats,' I say, pointing

at one with the end of my fork. 'They look so nice, don't they?'

Karl inclines his head slowly, in contemplation. 'Ja-a,' he says doubtfully. 'It is nice, but I think for me I prefer countryside. A house with fields around, and not too many other houses. Perhaps a horse to ride also.'

I think of my Fantasy Family. We'd live in a house like that. I always wanted a pony. Karl is so approachable that I almost tell him about this invented family of mine. Thankfully, I manage not to; partly because it might make him think it's an inherent criticism of Mum, and partly because it makes me sound like a right sad sack.

'Yes, wouldn't that be great? I'm thinking about moving soon myself, actually. Can't afford a flat like these, but hopefully I'll be able to get a little one-bedroom place somewhere nearby. Even a studio. I don't want to live with Dad any more.'

I swallow a mouthful of wine, alongside a big gob of guilt that I'll be leaving Dad too, so soon after Anthea, and when he's at his lowest.

'He seems . . . I don't wish to sound rude . . . a little intense,' Karl ventures, popping open a big bag of sea salt and vinegar crisps and extracting a large handful, which he holds out to me on his palm, as if offering sugar lumps to the pony we both wanted. 'Is he always like that?'

I accept some crisps, transferring them from his palm to mine. Crumbs of salt and crisp stick to my woolly gloves, and their sharpness hits the back of my tongue. They taste so good with the wine. I can feel my shoulders beginning to relax, and my knee has stopped aching, even after the walk down to the jetty.

'No. I've never seen him this bad.' I hesitate, wondering if Mum's told him about Dad's charges. 'He's under a lot of stress at the moment. His girl-friend's just left him – I think that's why he was so mad at Mum. He thought she had something to do with it, but of course she didn't. She's so over Dad, by the way,' I add hastily, not wanting Karl to think that Mum is still hung up on Dad in case it puts Karl off her.

I look at Karl again, through fresh eyes, as a potential stepfather, but I can't quite see it somehow. He's got to be a lot younger than Mum. And besides, the way he is gazing at me is far from fatherly . . . For a brief moment I realize with embarrassment that we are looking into each other's eyes, and I snap my head away, concentrating on the riverbanks slipping by.

Something occurs to me, and I gasp with horror at my thoughtlessness. 'Oh no – wasn't Mum meant to come and join us? She thinks we're in that restaurant near the tennis club . . . She can't join us on a boat!' I feel mean and selfish, rail-roading her date like this. How awful. I've practically kidnapped her potential boyfriend.

Or rather, he's practically kidnapped me . . . but Mum might not see it that way.

Karl is, as ever, unfazed. 'Don't worry. She said she will ring you when she is ready. This will not be a long boat ride, the guide told me. Susie has a car, doesn't she? She could meet us at Hampton Court.'

I feel better again. He's right: it's hardly as if we've set off down the Limpopo on a six-month expedition.

Karl fills up my glass again, and I'm surprised that I got through the first one so quickly. The wine is warming me, mellowing my insides and making my fingers tingle. I don't usually drink red wine, but this is delicious.

'I never understood before what it means when people talk about the "notes" in the taste of a wine,' I say. 'But I can taste all sorts of things in this one. Blackberry, for example.'

Karl exaggeratedly swooshes wine around inside his

mouth and pretends to think. 'Let's see now . . . a hint of peppercorn.'

I laugh. 'No way!'

'Yes way. It doesn't matter that you can't taste pepper, because I am only describing what *I* can taste. It is funny that people often think wine tasting is so difficult and mysterious, when it is really just describing what you personally taste. Nobody would laugh if you said "that motorbike sounds like a chainsaw", would they? It's just your comparison of the sound to something else.'

I am impressed. There is something about Karl which is refreshingly sophisticated, at least to my impressionable eyes. For the first time, I am making a mental comparison between Mark and somebody else which reflects *un*favourably on Mark. Mark knew sod all about wine. He'd never have the brass neck to hitch a lift on someone else's boat. He only ever ordered chicken in restaurants (and then only if they didn't serve burgers). I get the feeling that Karl's tastes are a lot more mature.

Suddenly, two things occur to me: the first, that perhaps at last I'm getting over Mark, and the second, that I would really like to go out to dinner with Karl some time. I wonder how serious Mum is about him . . .

'Liquorice,' says Karl thoughtfully.

My turn. Another big mouthful. 'Um . . . Tobacco!'

'Interesting one. Plums.'

I can't think of anything else, but my cup is empty again, and once more Karl fills it.

A young Japanese boy comes out on the rear deck of the boat. He is trendy, with thick-rimmed black oblong glasses, floppy black hair and baggy Evisu jeans. He has a Polaroid camera around his neck and another digital camera in his hands. He nods and smiles, and points towards the sky behind us. We look around to see a huge black cloud lowering over the horizon, but it's lit up by the weak winter sun, and it makes the sky seem alive, almost fizzing with dark energy. A full rainbow is curving over the river, its colours clear and sharp against the darkness.

'That's a big storm,' I say in awe. 'Hope it doesn't come this way.'

The boy leans on the rail next to us and raises his digital camera to his eye. There is a sudden flurry of movement from the trees on the riverbank to our left and a large flock of bright green birds flies across the river, their feathers almost fluorescent in the sun against the black cloud. They shriek joyously as they cross exactly beneath the rainbow.

'It's the green parrots!' I exclaim with delight.

'But I didn't think England had wild parrots?' Karl looks mystified. 'Germany does not.'

'No, we don't, generally. But for some reason, there are loads of them in this area. Nobody knows where they came from originally; there are all sorts of theories, like they escaped off a film set in the seventies, and bred in the wild. They're a bit of a nuisance in people's gardens, but they look nice.'

The Japanese boy is overjoyed. He shows us the photo he's just taken, on the screen of his camera. It's beautiful: parrots, sunlight, cloud, rainbow.

'That's perfect,' I say, smiling back at him. 'What a lovely souvenir.'

On impulse, the boy lifts his Polaroid and gestures for Karl and me to move closer together. Karl puts his arm around me and for a moment my breath stops. We lift our cups and beam at the camera. A square of plastic shoots out of the boxy contraption, and the boy hands it to Karl.

'Thank you very much,' Karl says in that formal way of his. 'Would you like to join us for a drink? You could perhaps get another glass from the bar.' He gestures to the wine bottle. The boy clearly doesn't speak any English, but he smiles and shakes his head and nods, all at the same time, before retreating back inside to join the rest of the group.

After that, we are undisturbed. People pop in and out to take photos, but they don't approach us. We peel the plastic covering off the Polaroid and laugh at our grinning heads framed in the photograph. The first bottle of wine is finished, so Karl braves the bar inside to buy another. I surreptitiously examine the photograph while he's queuing, and it makes me smile. I tuck it safely in my jacket pocket, feeling happier than I have for ages. I was a little concerned that the large amounts of lunchtime alcohol might render me over-emotional, possibly even tearful – which would be mortifying – but instead I feel a weird euphoric freedom, as if being on the river with Karl grants me a sort of diplomatic immunity to all the year's worries. The parrots are still swooping back and forth across the water, wheeling and banking in perfect synchronicity. It's magical to watch.

'I don't think this wine will be quite so nice,' Karl says, coming back with an open bottle and two proper wine glasses, 'but never mind.'

It doesn't taste much different to the first one, to my untrained palate. We finish our picnic, and Karl packs away the empty salad containers and crisp packets. He looks up and smiles at me, and my belly does something strange. I am tempted to ask how long he's over here for, but am worried that he might think I'm being too forward. I am also tempted to text my mother and tell her that I really like Karl . . . I mean, she's talking about going back to Lawrence soon, so surely she and Karl would be a non-starter? Mind you, he doesn't even live in England, so the same might go for us . . . and maybe he doesn't even remotely fancy me. I'm not very good at picking up signals. Perhaps that's because he hasn't given me any? Aargh. I don't know. I feel totally at sea.

'So where do you stay when you're in London?' I ask him as the reddish brown chimney stacks of Hampton Court Palace appear in the distance, to the right-hand-side of the boat. The starboard side? I'm never sure.

'I have good friends who live in Hammersmith. They are from my home town of Stuttgart – I went to school with Pieter. He married an English girl and moved over here ten years ago. They have a spare room which they call "Karl's room". I stay there often.'

'That's nice,' I say drowsily. The wine has really gone to my head now. I am fighting an urge to sink down against Karl's broad shoulder and have a snooze. I wonder what on earth we're going to do once we get to our destination. Get a cab back, I suppose. I realize that I'm really disappointed that the boat trip is about to end.

'Thank you for this, Karl, I've really enjoyed it.' I force myself to wake up a bit, and smile at him. 'Everything's been so grim lately, with . . .' Again, I wonder how much he knows about our family, '. . . all the various traumas which've been going on. It's so nice to get away from it all and not think about anything.'

'I have enjoyed it too, very much. It's a pity your knee is injured, otherwise perhaps we could go for a walk along the river now.'

'Nice idea, but if my knee weren't injured, I wouldn't have time to walk anywhere. I'd be on court, or in the gym, training.'

'How do you feel, since you cannot train or play for these past months?'

I consider the question for a minute. 'Well. It's awful being this immobile, obviously, and it's a drag having to be doing physio all the time. But . . .' I hesitate. This is something I haven't been able to admit to anyone else, and I say it in a rush. 'Actually, I'm not missing the tournaments. I'm not missing the airports, or the waiting around, or the being knocked out, and all the endless drills and matches and fitness regimes, Dad shouting at me, being knackered all the time . . . I feel like I'm really having a rest. And I've done a lot of stuff I wouldn't normally have done.'

'Such as?'

'Well . . . er . . . sketching, I suppose. And some watercolour things, nothing special, just little crappy pictures. But I really enjoy it.' Why do I feel so defensive admitting it, as if it's a vice?

'Don't put yourself down. I am sure they are very good. I would like to see them.'

I laugh. 'Come up and see my sketches some time . . .' Good grief, am I flirting?

I think I must be. Karl leans towards me and looks in my face. He has the most amazing hazel eyes. 'I would love to,' he says slowly, and his hand comes up to cup the side of my face. My skin is cold, but his hand is warm. Just as the boat chugs alongside a little wooden jetty by the magnificent palace, he leans further in and kisses me, so gently that at first his lips and mine just brush together. It's so sensual that the shock reverberates through my body, making my bad knee jump.

I wince with pain and put my hand protectively on my knee. He puts his on top of mine. And kisses me again, this time more firmly, pressing me back against the boat rail. My head is spinning from the wine and the pleasure of it. As far as things that hurt my knee go, this is a whole lot more fun than physio . . . I close my eyes and sink into the kiss.

When I open them again, the Japanese tour party is filing past us off the back of the boat, politely averting their eyes. Karl laughs and hugs me.

'I have wanted to do that ever since I met you in Italy,' he says.

I am astonished. 'Italy? Really? But . . . I thought . . . Mum . . .'

Karl looks a little embarrassed. 'I think Susie is a wonderful woman also,' he says. 'I like her very much. But not in the way I like you. I did want to see her

again, and I would like to have her as a friend. I hope
she won't be offended, but, most of all, I wanted to see
her so that I could meet you again. I really like you,
Rachel.'

'How old are you?' I blurt drunkenly, too non-
plussed properly to acknowledge what he's just said.
My cheeks have gone from freezing to flaming in the
cold river air.

'I am thirty-two,' he says solemnly. 'Single, mature,
loving, sensible, solvent. All my own hair and teeth.'

'But you live in Germany. Or Italy. Or both.'

'*Ja*. But I am still single, mature, and so on. And in
fact I am thinking of settling down in one place soon.
I am tired of not having a real home.'

'And which place might that be?'

We are alone on the boat now, apart from the bar
staff and boat crew. Karl stands up and hands me my
crutches, then he picks up the bag of our lunch
remains. He puts a proprietorial hand gently on my
back as I hop towards the gangplank.

'I think English crisps are so good,' he says, giving
me a sideways glance. 'I would like to live somewhere
which had good crisps.'

'Yes,' I reply, limping slowly back on to dry land,
feeling the earth rock slightly beneath my feet in an
echo of the boat's motion. The palace looms next to us,
huge and imposing under suddenly blue skies.
'English crisps are excellent.'

49

Susie

After I dropped Ivan home, I went back to the restaurant where Karl and I had initially planned to meet. It was only an hour later, but to my surprise he and Rachel weren't there, and the waitress insisted that nobody on crutches had been in. There didn't seem to be any other restaurants nearby, and when I tried Rach's phone, it went straight to voicemail.

I felt a little hurt, in one respect, but relieved in another. I wasn't really in any fit state for a date, and it would do Rachel good to get out and have some fun. Karl was a gentleman; he'd look after her. Who knows, I thought idly as I got back in Gordana's car, perhaps he'll be her stepfather some day – but the thought seemed so preposterous that I stamped on it immediately. I didn't want to marry anybody else. I just wanted Billy.

Oh, snap out of it, Susie, I told myself. It wouldn't do me any harm to play a little hard-to-get. Let Karl ring me if he wanted to reschedule our date. I don't have to marry the man. It was just nice to have the attention.

Gordana had her car radio tuned to a talk radio station and, as I was driving in the direction of Corinna's house, an item caught my attention. A man was discussing how he and his family were trying to rebuild their lives after he'd spent three months in jail for viewing images of child pornography, and explaining why he thought the Internet industry should take more responsibility for this crime.

I sat up straighter at the wheel and listened carefully. From the UK alone, he said, there had been seven thousand customers downloading stuff from just one illegal site in Texas, all traced by their credit cards. More than three thousand people arrested, seventeen hundred charged, and thirteen hundred investigations still ongoing . . . Wow. I wasn't sure if it made it better or worse to think that Ivan was not alone in his charges.

But I was sure by now that Ivan hadn't done this. I believed him when he'd said he was innocent – although I wondered if all three thousand people arrested were saying the same: 'It wasn't me, I didn't do it'.

I was distracted by a grey squirrel running into the road right under the wheels of the car in front. I saw the car jog slightly as it extinguished the animal's life in an explosion of guts, and I felt sick at the sudden, unintentional brutality of the death. The injustice of life sometimes felt almost unbearable.

Then the interviewer asked something interesting, and I forced myself to concentrate on the radio again:

'How can the police prove that someone else didn't download the material with your credit card?'

I'd been wondering about that, too.

'Well, of course it does happen. People are often reluctant to use their own cards, in case it gets traced back to them. Most people are aware that it can be . . .' Not Ivan, I thought. Ivan couldn't even do his grocery shopping online, from what Rachel said. *' . . . so they use a stolen card or, more commonly, a borrowed one.'*

'But surely the police can tell which computer the material has been downloaded on to?'

'Yes, of course, and when the same person owns the computer and the credit card, it's pretty conclusive,

but it takes the police months to sift through all the files on all the computers they've impounded, which is why the cases often take so long to come to trial.'

Huh, I thought. That explained a lot. I had a mental image of a huge warehouse piled to the rafters with a jumble of impounded computer equipment and a team of weary-looking investigators standing in the doorway looking at it all in despair. Two words caught my attention: 'time stamp'. I listened more closely.

'Anything you do on a computer creates a "time stamp" which can be easily checked – it's one of the first things the analysis team would look for. If the suspect is denying it, it's his chance to come up with an alibi.'

Prickles ran down my back and in my excitement I mounted a pavement when turning the corner into Corinna's road. If someone really had set Ivan up, they'd have to have broken into the house to do it, when neither he nor Anthea were there. He and Rachel travelled so frequently, and from what I understood, Anthea didn't like being in the house on her own when he was away, so once the investigators got the time stamp sorted out, surely there was a good chance Ivan could prove his innocence, since he could well have been away when the crime was committed?

Parking badly over Corinna's neighbour's driveway, I was rushing inside to call Ivan – but I hadn't even reached the front door before doubts began to assail me again. Surely this was the first thing Ivan's solicitor would have suggested? Ivan hadn't mentioned it as a possible get-out clause, though. Was it possible the solicitor wouldn't know about time stamps? Also, there had been no evidence of a break-in at the house. Unless – and this was more likely – someone could have done it from the office at the tennis club? Perhaps the police had just seized the wrong computer? After all, all they had to go on was the evidence of payment on Ivan's credit card . . . oh. That hadn't been reported as stolen either. And presumably there'd be a date and time recorded on the credit card transaction too.

My head was still whirling when I let myself into Corinna's house with the spare key she'd lent me. As I stood in her small, silent front room, surrounded by her tasteful vases and arty prints, with the smell of her perfume faintly hanging in the air, I wondered how long I'd be staying in other people's houses, feeling like an intruder amongst their possessions and taste in decor. Maybe not for much longer – Corinna had been hospitable, but I knew she wouldn't want me there long-term, and I didn't feel comfortable at Gordana's, not with everything that was happening.

As I reached for the phone, I felt a sudden pang of yearning for Lawrence, and for my own things in my own house.

My house – our house, as it was – wasn't immaculate and shiny and minimalist like Corinna's. Our house had cat hair in the sugar bowl, a blow-up armchair mended with Band-Aids (I was amazed Billy hadn't popped it altogether by dropping lit joints on it), and an unfortunately swirly bedroom carpet we'd never got around to changing. There was no art on the walls, just a few dream-catchers and some old film posters in clip-frames, which I'd never stand for if I lived in England, but which in Lawrence was perfectly fine.

In just a few months, it would be spring again; in Lawrence, the stabbing cold and bleakness of winter would be melting into something green and fresh, skies swept clean and blue by warmer winds, trees budding and people shedding their overcoats and mufflers like a rebirth. Newport and Pavonia would stop pretending they didn't know how to operate the cat-flap and would be frisking in the garden again, chasing birds and beetles. It was too early for mosquitoes and chiggers, so I could be outside in the grass all day and evening without first having to poison myself with insect repellent, and I could be in the sun without getting burned to a crisp. It was my favourite time of year.

I want to go home, I thought. Surely I'd be back in time for spring.

But how could I leave Rachel with all this going on around her? I still felt responsible for her knee injury. Besides, I still wasn't sure if I could face going back to my house without Billy in it. At least, not before Christmas. Christmas without Billy was far too depressing to contemplate.

I didn't call Ivan. Not straight away. On impulse, I dialled Billy's number at the garage instead. He always started work early, so I thought he ought to be there. I hadn't spoken to him since he'd come round to take more of his stuff to Eva's, about a week after I discovered them holding hands in the deli.

'Billy Estes Mechanics, Billy speaking.' His familiar voice wavered a little over the distance, and I imagined with wonder the speed of it, travelling through sea-bed cables.

'Hi, Billy, it's me.'

There was a pause, infinitesimally longer than the transatlantic delay. 'Hey, Susie, how are you, honey?' He sounded formal but friendly.

Not your honey any more, I thought. 'I'm OK. I'm in England, staying at Corinna's.'

'Yeah. I ran into Audrey at the drug store and she mentioned you were taking some time out after your ski trip, and that she was feeding the cats. How was it, by the way, your trip?'

'Terrible. Rachel broke her leg really badly. She still can't walk on it. She might not be able to play again for a year.'

I heard him exhale. 'Wow, that's awful. Tell her I'm sorry, would you?'

'Sure.'

Another pause, more awkward this time. Annoyingly, my eyes filled with tears.

393

'So how have you been?'

Now he sounded tender, and I bit my lip so hard I tasted blood.

'Well. You know. Not great, really. I want to come home, but I don't want to . . . I can't face . . .' Come on, Susie, I told myself. Hold it together. I took a deep breath. 'There's been all kinds of awful stuff happening here. Gordana's got cancer—'

'Oh, man, that's terrible.'

'That's not the half of it. Ivan got arrested for downloading child porn. He's waiting to go on trial, in a total state. Swears he didn't do it. And Anthea's dumped him – it turns out he's been sleeping with some young player behind her back; well, behind mine, too, it started when we were married . . .'

As usual, once I began, it all came falling out. I could imagine the surprise on Billy's face; the way he'd be looking into the middle distance, frowning with concentration as he tried to keep up with my torrent of words. It was such a relief to talk to him. I'd missed having him to confide in, so much.

'Jeez, Susie, sounds like you landed right in it there. But what about you? Are you OK?'

He keeps asking me that, I thought irritably. 'No, like I said, Billy, not really. I'm coping fine. I think I'm even maybe starting to get over you. But I'm worried about Rachel and shocked about Gordana and feeling sorry for Ivan, believe it or not. I want to come home to Lawrence, but I feel trapped here by everything that's going on, and it'll be a long time before I'm really going to be *OK* again.'

'Sorry.' Another pause. 'Susie. Look, I really am sorry about what happened . . .'

'I don't want to hear it, Billy. Don't tell me. I'm sorry I called – I just missed you. I wanted to hear your voice.' The tears came back, although I was fighting them as valiantly as I could. I had to go before he heard them creep into my voice.

'I miss you too, Suze,' he said quietly.

I leaned back in Corinna's huge beige leather sofa ('Taupe, sweetie,' she called it). It made a loud farting noise for which I hoped Billy wouldn't think I was responsible.

'I've got to go now,' I said, feeling worse than before.

'When are you coming back?' he asked, a plaintive note in his voice.

'I don't know,' I said. 'I need to make sure Rachel's all right first. And Gordana. Even Ivan, in a weird sort of way. I just heard something on the radio which might possibly help him out. I was about to call him when for some reason I found myself calling you instead . . .'

'Well, give me a holler when you're back. It would be . . . I mean . . . Can I ask you one thing? Have you, you know, met anybody else? You and Ivan seem to be more close than you used to be . . .'

I rolled my eyes and tried to sniff discreetly. 'Would you care if I had met someone else? Or got back together with Ivan?'

'I know I've got no right to . . . but yeah, I guess I would care. Sorry. I know it's out of order of me.'

Sorry for what? I thought. Sorry for caring that I'd met someone else, or sorry for blowing my life apart? All these sorries, none of them making a blind bit of difference to the way things were, and would be for ever.

'Yes, Billy, it's way out of order.'

I considered telling him about Karl, but decided against it, mostly because nothing looked like it would ever actually happen between us, and I wasn't even sure if I wanted it to now.

'But for what it's worth, no, I haven't met anybody new. Or re-met anybody old, either. And I don't even want to . . . I really am going now. Take care, OK?'

'You too, Susie.'

There was a pause into which I was sure, absolutely

certain, that we were both silently whispering 'B.I.L.Y.' to one another. I put down the phone, made a note of the length of the call so I could reimburse Corinna for it, and then howled into one of her expensive embroidered silk cushions. I had to replace it upside down on the sofa, in the hope that she wouldn't notice the large teary mark all down the middle of it.

What the hell did I go and call him for? I thought. As if I wasn't missing him enough already.

Later, when I'd calmed down again, I reflected on how odd it had been to hear Billy hesitant like that. One of his most endearing qualities was his utter naturalness. You could put him into any situation and he would be completely at ease. Even when I plunged him into an Anderson family Christmas that time, with Ivan glowering and Gordana fussing and Anthea uptight enough to cause stress to a coma victim, even then he took it all in his stride. He just sat back, beamed at everyone, offered to help as if he'd known them all for years, and generally exuded calm.

Or perhaps he'd been high . . . Oh well, whatever the cause, it was his default characteristic, and he sounded different without it. I remembered when we first got together, that too had seemed so natural that I felt none of the pressure of a first date or a new relationship. Billy had just said to me one day at the Crossing, after Ivan and I had split up and I'd moved back to Lawrence: 'Hey, I'm going to the grocery store. Wanna come with me?'

I'd shrugged; my heart simultaneously leaping. As it happened, I was out of Cheetos and bin-liners. 'Sure,' I said, even though I'd never before exchanged more than a little chit-chat and a few meaningful smiles with him, and in fact hadn't even seen him for nearly fifteen years. He hadn't aged much, just got a little softer around the edges. As soon as I clapped eyes on him again, the latent attraction I'd always felt for him came roaring back in a tidal wave.

The visit to the grocery store turned into a round trip to unload both our loads of shopping, then dinner at Billy's place, blissful sex on the rag-rug in his living room, and a year later we were engaged. You'd think I'd have been wary of committing again so soon, but this was Billy; my Billy. I just knew I'd finally met the right man.

50

Gordana

So it is Christmas already. It does not seem a moment since I was last arranging the wooden Nativity characters on top of the Pembroke table by the fireplace: Joseph with his nose chipped off; the cow with three legs from when Ivan threw it against the wall once, when he was little. And yet here we are again, with so much in between . . . It has not been an easy year – at least – not the last couple of months.

It's very nice, though, to be sitting in my warm flickering church at a quarter to midnight; it is like a cocoon, with the wind howling outside, and inside golden and sacred. The smell of incense is so comforting, like the feel of Ted's hand in mine, and the deep colours of the priest's Christmas robes. I am alive, and I am not in pain. My family is here, now. Not one of us will be here for ever, this is true, and I must accept that it is not up to me when I go.

I look along the pew: my Ted next to me, his wrinkled eyelids closed in prayer. I bet he prays for me, and I love him for it. I hold his hand very tight. We are in this together. I am glad I told him all my secrets, even the bad ones. He says he is glad to know them, even though they are hard to hear.

Then there is Ivan; and it must be a Christmas miracle but even though this awful thing is still hanging over his head, he look more peaceful. Good grief, I think he is almost smiling . . . Next to him is Susie, who has trouble of her own, but who always thinks first of everyone else. I know she is still here because she feels so guilty for Rachel's accident, but I also think perhaps it is good that she's stayed. We are all healing slowly, in our own ways, and the best way she can heal is by believing she's helping us all.

Then Karl. I have decided I like Karl very much. Somehow he seems like part of this family already. I like that he is sitting between Rachel and Susie, even though Susie told me in private that she thought Karl wanted her at first, and that she was hurt when he turned out to love Rachel . . . But there is no awkwardness between them, not like there was for years between Elsie and the garden gnome man, Humphrey, at the tennis club. Elsie thought he liked her – ha! As if! – when all along he like Valerie. She never spoke to him again, but that is Elsie for you. And I think he was very relieved by this. I must have some Christmas spirit when I think of Elsie, but even the Blessed Virgin herself would find that hard, I bet. Anyway, Susie is nothing like Elsie.

At the end of the row is Rachel, so she can stick her leg out the side into the aisle. She is still with the crutches, but her leg brace is hiding beneath a long black velvet skirt, and there is a big red flowery clip in her hair. I approve very much of this skirt, although she grumbled when I bought it for her. She is a good girl. She is wearing it for me. Although now she's with Karl, I have noticed that she does not wear the terrible tracksuit bottoms so often any more. And she wear lipstick now too. She is lovely looking, especially now that she isn't frowning so much. She has – what's that word – flowered? No. Blossomed.

Susie looks sad. She always tries to hide it, but when she think nobody is watching her, it leaks out of her. Now we are singing 'In the Bleak Mid-Winter', and I see how her lip wobbles. How was it that the

Queen described her very bad year? Her *annus horribilis*. We have all had an *annus horribilis*, that is for sure.

The bells strike midnight, and we hug and kiss and shake hands with everyone in the nearby pews, smiling and chatting like nothing is wrong. One more carol; the collection – even though Ted and I give weekly to the church on a standing order from the bank, I still always put money in the collection bowl. I know that God is aware of our standing order, but my fellow parishioners are not, and I do not want them to think I am mean. A little chat with the priest on the way back out into the frosty car park in front of the church – he looks tired, his eyes are bloodshot and his handshake limp. I want to make him a hot toddy and send him to bed, because the poor man doesn't have a woman to look after him.

I clutch Ted's hand even harder, and he makes a face as my rings dig into him.

'Sorry, darling.'

I put both my arms around him, right there in the car park, and kiss him full on the mouth like we are two young lovers. He kiss me back, and the others laugh as we stand there. But nobody except Ted knows that I'm crying and kissing at the same time, because my back is turned to them.

'Merry Christmas, Dana,' he whispers, and holds me tight.

51

Susie

I was on a mission to help Gordana prepare the best Christmas they'd ever had in that house. I was determined it would be a good day. We would be a family, however fractured; we would be together and we would have fun. Even Ivan, who had recently done a good impression of someone who doesn't know the meaning of the word.

By mid-morning it was all going to plan, although in a more subdued atmosphere than I'd have liked. There was a large turkey crammed into the Aga – we'd had to stuff it in, apparently resisting all the way – and, in the hall, a fir tree of a size which wouldn't have looked out of place in a shopping mall. Ivan was out somewhere. Being Ivan, nobody knew exactly where, and it could hardly be a business meeting on Christmas morning, but we all knew there was little point in asking. Rachel and Karl had gone for a quick pre-lunch visit to Karl's friends in Hammersmith, and Doris Day's voice was warbling festive songs from a boombox on the kitchen counter.

So it was just Ted, Gordana and I at home, in the kitchen preparing vegetables for dinner. Sprout leaves were mounting up in a pile beside the chopping board as I scored crosses in the bottoms of the undressed buds. Ted stood next to me, and I watched his knobbly old hands paring the parsnips; long dull gold strips fell next to the cut green curls of the sprouts, reminding me of the floor of a hairdresser's. Ted wasn't looking particularly well either these days – he was much more subdued than he used to be. But I supposed we were all getting older, and he'd had so much stress lately, it was bound to take its toll. Because it all concerned other people, I thought he was probably quietly absorbing it into his once-broad shoulders, trying to soak up the problems of others like a big sponge. Sometimes it was painful to see him and Gordana. But I was determined not to let today be painful.

'Funny, isn't it, how regional some vegetables are, but not others . . .' I said, trying to inject more levity into the not-quite festive enough atmosphere, despite Doris's best efforts. '. . . I remember you telling me ages ago, Gordana, that you never had sprouts in Croatia; and Billy had never heard of parsnips when I first met him. I brought some over to him from England once, after a trip home, and when I cooked them for him, he treated them with such suspicion anybody would think I'd sprinkled them with arsenic . . .'

I remembered Billy's face, the hesitant tasting of the unfamiliar vegetable through pursed lips, like a child being forced to eat his greens; and it gave me another big pang of missing him.

A traditional British Christmas Day was in itself fairly alien to me – in fact, something of a novelty, which was another reason I wanted to make the most of it. I missed the family Christmases of my childhood – and the festivities in Lawrence had always been unconventional, with assorted hippie guests for lunch, and the cashew and cheese roast I used to make, because the hippies were always vegetarian. There was no wishbone or church service or post-prandial country walk, just a sort of stoned fuddlement which settled on the house after lunch. Billy and I used to sneak off upstairs to make love, because all our guests had fallen asleep and there was nothing else to do except the washing up. After a couple of years, this became one of our traditions: the Christmas cuddle, as we called it.

No Christmas cuddle for me this year. I wondered jealously if he and Eva would continue the tradition themselves, and momentarily lost concentration on the job in hand, nearly cutting off the end of my thumb with the vegetable knife. Blood oozed out of a half-inch cut and splashed neatly into an upturned boat of sprout shell.

'Oh darling, I will get you a plaster,' said Gordana, who was sitting at the kitchen table peeling potatoes into a washing-up bowl. She made to get up when she saw my injury, putting her palms flat on the tabletop to help press herself into a standing position, and she looked so exhausted it was almost unbearable.

The knowledge that she'd finished the first round of chemo, and that the doctors seemed pleased with her progress, was a relief to everyone. But I supposed that she and Ted were just too worn out really to celebrate. For a moment I felt guilty about trying to chivvy them into a big festive day when probably all they wanted to do was go away to a country hotel somewhere and let other people do all the work. Although they had vehemently insisted they wanted to host lunch.

'No, don't,' I said hurriedly. 'You stay there, just tell me where they are.'

'Cabinet in Rachel's bathroom,' she said gratefully. 'Thank you.'

'No problem.'

With Jackson trotting beside me, claws clicking on the tiles, I walked down the hall and round the corner towards Rachel's room. She was living here more or less permanently, with Karl already a regular visitor. Apparently he was looking for a flat nearby.

They had been inseparable ever since the day Ivan had confronted us in the coffee shop. I did, undoubtedly, feel a sting of rejection – had he only ever been interested in Rachel, and not at all in me? I suspected as much, but I didn't want to know for sure. The fact that it mattered to me, even slightly, was just a shallow, egotistical reaction; and whenever I saw the bloom in Rachel's cheeks, or the smile back on her face, I couldn't possibly begrudge her her happiness. There was no way I'd have been ready for a new relationship anyway. And besides, Karl was far too young for me . . .

I was about to push open the door of Rachel's room when I heard a noise from inside, and hesitated. I pressed my ear up against the wooden panel and listened, genuinely wondering what it was. At first I thought it was Jackson yelping, until I remembered that he was sitting at my feet. He was looking up at me with an expression which seemed as puzzled as my own. As soon as I realized what was going on in there – Rachel and Karl had evidently sneaked in for a quickie, not saying hello first in case they got roped into spud-bashing – colour flooded up over my face, and I leaped away from the door as if it had scalded me.

I cantered back down the hall, mortified, my bleeding thumb still rammed in my mouth, and my blush still warming my cheeks. Thank goddess I hadn't burst in . . .

Still, at least Rachel appeared to have overcome her fear of intimacy, and for that I felt relieved. The accident had changed her in a lot of ways: her priorities, her dependence on Ivan, her lack of confidence. Her new relationship seemed a further indication of this new-found maturity. I had a sudden flash of intuition for her, that she should embrace this new life, not go back to the old. Things were different now. Perhaps there was no going back.

'Come on, Jackson, let's keep it under our hats, OK?' I whispered to him outside the kitchen door, stooping to pat his bristly neck. He panted obligingly and licked my hand. I was just wondering how to prevent Gordana marching into Rachel's room to find the plasters I'd been unable to locate, when I remembered that I probably had a couple in the side pocket of my handbag, which was in the coat cupboard. As I went to investigate, the front door opened and Ivan came in.

'Hi,' I called, my head buried in the coat cupboard. I backed out, with the scent of lavender and mothballs in my nostrils, and turned to face him. I was expecting the hangdog, bitter expression which – despite his slight increase in optimism of late – still dragged down his jowels and furrowed his brow, but instead I barely recognized him. Dour, grumpy Ivan Anderson was smiling; in fact, beaming broadly. I marvelled at how much younger he looked – like the Ivan I'd fallen in love with, all those years ago, over a Velvet Underground LP and some strong Kansas pot.

'You look cheerful,' I said, tearing the plaster wrapper open with my teeth and winding it around my bleeding thumb. 'Christmas spirit finally got through to you?'

'*You*,' he said, pointing a finger at me, and even though he was still smiling, my instinct was to think: Oh no, now what have I done?

'What?' I said, slightly nervously. But his smile was so infectious that I couldn't help joining in.

'You have no idea what a huge favour you've done me.'

'Really? How come?' I closed the coat cupboard door so that Jackson didn't go in and eat all the shoes.

'Well, you know you told me to mention that time stamp thing to my solicitor? I did, as soon as you heard about it. I thought for sure he'd already be aware of it, but he wasn't! He got on to it straight away, badgering the police to let him know what the time stamp said. In conjunction with the date of the credit card transaction, that'll be much greater proof that I couldn't have done it – the credit card alone isn't enough, in case I did it from another computer – and they've already established that the transaction was done when I was out of the country. I was away at a tournament in Russia, with about a thousand alibis . . . So, assuming the time stamp is the same as the transaction – which it's bound to be – then I'll be in the clear! They still haven't finished sorting through the evidence, and they said that a specific analysis of the time clock can't be done at the same time as the file interrogation. That's why the hearing's been adjourned again. But I had a meeting with the solicitor yesterday, and he's convinced it's going to make all the difference to my case.'

On impulse, he picked me up around the waist and swung me around the hallway. It was the first real physical contact I'd had with him since we were married. I laughed with him, flinging my arms round his neck and letting him spin me as Jackson barked at our feet, confused and delighted at the commotion.

'Ivan, is that you? What is going on out here, for goodness' sake?' Gordana came out into the hall in her Marigolds, potato peeler in hand, with a headscarf covering her remaining patchy strands of hair. She looked bemused – as well she might – at the unfamiliar sight of her son showing any spontaneous affection, particularly towards his once-reviled ex. 'Please mind that vase with your feet, Susie!'

Ivan hastily put me down and hugged her instead. 'Hello, Mama, how are you today?'

'Have you been drinking?' she asked suspiciously, patting her scarf to check that it was in place.

'No, I haven't. Aren't I allowed to be cheerful for once?' he said, a hint of the old defensiveness in his voice.

'Of course you are allowed, my darling, we are just

not used to it, that is all,' she said, kissing his cheek. 'What has made you so jolly?'

He opened his mouth to tell her, when Rachel and Karl appeared in the hall behind her, dressed, but dishevelled and pink-cheeked. If I'd been in any doubt as to what they were up to in there, I wasn't any more. Good for you, Rach, I thought.

'Hi, Dad, happy Christmas,' said Rachel guardedly. 'Have you won the lottery or something?'

Gordana looked hard at her and Karl. 'I thought you two kids were out visiting somebody,' she said suspiciously.

'Oh, we were, Gordana, we just got back a while ago,' Rachel replied disingenuously.

Karl rubbed his big hands together. 'Shall I make a cup of tea for us all?' he asked, as at home in Gordana's house as he was everywhere else. 'Then we can hear what Ivan's exciting news is.'

I stood back to let them all troop back into the kitchen, Rachel swinging on her crutches with the ease of a chimp swinging through trees. I was about to follow, when a pang of loneliness overtook me, and I slunk upstairs into my room instead.

Downstairs I could hear the excited chatter of voices, but the air in my big, grand guest room was as still and empty as the atmosphere I'd been trying to escape at Corinna's. Perhaps it wasn't the house at all; perhaps it was me? Maybe I was constantly trying to escape something which was inherently impossible to run away from, because it was in me. Was this why I went back to Kansas in the first place, after the divorce; and then why I left again when I found out about Billy and Eva . . . ?

But how could I ever escape it, if I didn't even know what it was?

It looked as if Ivan was going to be all right, despite all the chaos around him. Maybe it was because *he* never ran away, he just squared his shoulders and let

407

it all rain down on him. But then again, although he made out that he was so independent, underneath it, he was as needy as an infant. It was true that he didn't run when the going got tough, but what he needed to learn was not to push away the people who, in spite of it all, loved him. Gordana was on the mend, which was clearly a load off his mind too, although he never spoke about it.

I went and stood by the window, looking out over the frozen, bleak garden, wanting to feel as happy for Rachel and Karl, and Ivan, as I kept telling myself I was. Instead, a sense of isolation clutched at my chest, twisting at me like the bare barbed-wire branches of the rose bushes outside. In spite of my resolution to enjoy this Christmas, I couldn't help thinking that there was something deeply sad about the deadness of a much-loved garden in the middle of winter, too far from spring even for snowdrops or crocuses – and at that, it all started to crash down on me.

Apart from Rachel, this wasn't even my family any more. Gordana had Ted, Ivan had Gordana, and Rachel had the lovely Karl. I didn't even have a *job*, let alone a partner. I'd been too preoccupied with worrying about Rachel's injury to bother pursuing the life-coaching qualifications about which I'd felt so enthusiastic a mere two months ago. I had given up the real-estate job. There was nothing I even wanted to do – but I had to do something. I had to support myself from now on. I couldn't continue sponging off Gordana or Corinna, eking out my meagre savings, which had already dwindled to almost nothing. Panic, and something strangely like rage, began to swell inside me, mingling with the self-pity.

Nobody needed me here. For a brief time, I'd been a mother to Rach, when she needed me; I'd been a friend to Ivan, when he had none; and I'd – hopefully – been a support to Gordana. But now everybody seemed to be sorting out their lives. I felt like a dandelion clock, blowing aimlessly about, shedding filaments in different places but not knowing where I'd end up, nor where I wanted to be.

A flash of red caught my eye, on the driveway, by the big wrought-iron gates. Someone wearing a Santa Claus hat was walking hesitantly up the drive: a small figure with a large rucksack on his back, which looked from this distance like a hump. It was too far away to hear the gravel crunch, or to make out any of the person's features, but he looked familiar and absolutely out of place at the same time. It was like seeing a fur-clad Eskimo sunbathing on a tropical beach. I pressed my face against the window to try and see more clearly. The figure came closer. I stared incredulously, snapping out of my self-pity. Jackson was barking downstairs, trying to alert the others to the intruder, but presumably they were still celebrating Ivan's news.

I ran down the stairs, flung open the front door, and ran down the drive in my socks. Gravel pricked the soles of my feet, but amongst all the other, more powerful emotions, I felt no pain from it. The figure stopped, hefted the big rucksack off his back and dumped it on the drive, opening his arms to me. The stones didn't hurt, but what was physically painful was seeing those familiar, stubbly, red-eyed features, with the dimples punctuating that tentative, sheepish smile.

'Merry Christmas, Suze,' he said. 'Jeez, it's hard to get around in this country on a public holiday. I thought I'd never get here. I haven't missed dinner, have I?'

I put my hands on my hips. The self-pity had dissipated, but the anger most certainly had not. 'If you think I'm going to rush right into your arms and forgive you just because you managed by some miracle to get yourself organized enough to get a passport and plane ticket – without even checking first that I'd be here, or that you can foist yourself on Gordana and Ted at a time like this – well, then you are very much mistaken, you cheating, lying, useless HIPPIE!' I shouted, in my best impression of a fishwife.

'A passport, a plane ticket *and* a cab all the way from the airport,' he added, sounding offended. 'It cost me a fortune!'

I punched him in the stomach, almost knocking him off his feet. He gasped for air and bent double.

Then I hugged him tightly. The sheer relief of his familiar contours and his engine-oil plane-scented Billy smell made me feel as if I'd been winded too.

'B.I.L.Y., Billy,' I whispered into his ear.

'B.I.L.Y., Susie, baby,' he whispered back, when he'd recovered his breath enough to speak.

'This doesn't mean I'm taking you back,' I said firmly.

'No. Sure. I understand,' he wheezed, coughing weakly over my shoulder. 'Any chance of a beer and a bed for the night though? Even us useless hippies need to sleep . . .'

52

Gordana

It's a good thing we have enough chairs for everyone to sit at the dining table. I do wish that Billy could have telephoned to let us know he was coming, but Susie says that it's a miracle he even manage to find his way here on his own, all the way from the Yellow Brick Road, the little Munchkin. She is being quite rude about him when he's not listening. But then she keeps staring at him, like she cannot believe it. So I don't know if she is pleased to see him or not. Fortunately Ted bought a turkey that was bigger than Jackson, so we had enough food. I notice that Billy did not eat his parsnips.

Jackson of course thought the turkey was just for him, and was most upset when we all had some. Even now all that is left of it is just bones and bits and pieces of unpleasantness on the spiky silver platter, and Jackson has had a big bowlful of turkey meat, he still wants more. Ted shut the carcass in the larder, and Jackson went to sit patiently outside the door. Every now and again he whined and scraped. Finally he put his head down on crossed paws, and now he is having a little sleep while he waits for the turkey to come outside again.

The rest of us are leaning backwards in our chairs, full up to the top, drinking coffee and cracking nuts. When Rachel was little we used to have to cut this part short because she was so desperate to open her presents. Now we have some more time to digest our dinner, and do what Ted calls the Christmas Wishes bit. He started this tradition a long time ago, where we all say what we want most to have happened by next Christmas. They must be personal wishes, for our-selves. For years, all Ivan ever said was 'to win Wimbledon'. Then, for years, all *Rachel* said was 'to win Wimbledon'.

I wonder what they will say this year? I am a little worried that Jackson will get his wish before any of us get ours. It is more likely that the remains of the turkey will open the larder door, walk across the kitchen floor and climb into Jackson's bowl than that any of our wishes will come true. But I must not be so negative. I will not be able to do what I have to do if I am negative like this.

'Christmas Wishes time!' I chink my teaspoon against my port glass. 'Who will go first?'

There is a pause. Karl and Billy look around with confusion, everyone else with hesitation.

Susie stands up. She is fiddling with a tiny pack of cards which came out of her cracker; turning it round and round in her hands. Nobody except the fairies could play a game of cards with those tiddly things.

'OK, I'll go first,' she says. 'My wish . . . and I've been thinking about this all through dinner . . . is to stop running away from myself. To be settled. To have decided who I am, what I want to do, and where I am going to live.' She glances at Billy. 'And who I am going to live with.'

We clap, and she sits down. Billy pats her on the knee and she glares at him. Then smiles at him. 'Your turn, Billy,' she says.

Billy clears his throat and scratches his head. He has a big mop of curly hair, which I feel tempted to ask Manuel to mow, next time he comes to do the grass.

Everyone else is dressed up for Christmas, but Billy is wearing sandy-coloured canvas trousers with many pockets, big boots, a once-navy sweatshirt with a rip at the neck, and a bracelet with brown beads on a leather lace.

'I guess it's pretty obvious what I want,' he says, not taking his eyes off Susie, who looks cross again. 'I want my Susie back. I was a fool, and I don't blame her for being mad at me, but . . . Suze . . . I dumped Eva. I realized right after you left for Italy that I didn't really love her; I was just fooled into thinking I did; it dragged on way too long and I—'

Susie held up a hand, like traffic cop, although her voice was soft. 'Later, Billy. Not now, OK?'

He bites his lip and nods. I feel sorry for him. I hope those two kids work it out. He obviously really does love her. I suppose it depends whether or not she will forgive him, and if they can fix whatever the problem was what make him run off with this Eva person in the first place.

I pass round the bowl of nuts. Susie takes out two big whole walnuts, which she holds in the palm of her hand for a moment like she's weighing them up, and then she cracks them, viciously, with the nutcrackers. Billy looks *very* nervous.

'Ivan, darling, you next,' I say quickly, giving him a nudge to stand up. I never know what to expect with Ivan. It would not be a surprise to me if he refuse altogether to join in.

But he takes a deep big breath, and then a big swallow of port. 'I want Mama to have got the final all-clear,' he says.

'No, that is not allowed as your wish,' I cry indignantly. 'It must be something for you!'

'That is for me. It's for all of us.'

'You know what I mean. Something about your life.'

He sighs. 'OK. Well, you know the obvious wish – and, thanks to Susie, it looks like I might have got it:

413

for this whole nightmare to be over, soon.' We all think this is it, but he opens his mouth and speaks again, with a curious shyness. 'There's another one, though . . . a wish, I mean.'

Something strange is happening to his face. For a second I am worried; it is going a funny dark red colour, and his cheeks are blotchy, but then I realize: Good grief, my boy is blushing! This is not a thing which happens very often. He does not look comfortable; as if the blush hurt his skin.

'What else, Ivan?' I ask, with much interest.

He clears his throat, and by now we are all sitting up and leaning forwards to hear, even Billy.

'Um, well, I think probably most of you know that I was seeing someone, before and . . . well, anyway: there's been someone in my life on and off for quite a few years now. Natasha.'

Susie and Rachel give one another meaningful looks across the table. Billy examines his fingernails, and Ted pretends that this is the first time he has heard of this, although of course I tell him all about it ages ago, when Ivan first mention it.

'I may at times have been less than complimentary about her, and not very positive about our relationship, for fairly obvious reasons, but what I wanted to tell you is that I saw her this morning. She came back to England a few days ago; and she wants to give things a real go with me, at last.'

He is trying to look serious but a little smile wobbles at the corners of his mouth. Rachel looks shocked, and raises her eyebrows at Susie.

'Ivan, that's great,' said Susie, 'but I thought you said she was only after free coaching?'

My goodness, she is brave to just come out with it. I would not want to – what is the expression? – 'wreck his buzzing' like that. But I am desperate to hear what he says. I don't want any silly little tennis player breaking his heart; not now, not ever.

Ivan does not even look cross; instead, a little embarrassed.

'Yes, well, I may have mentioned to you that at one point I worried that was the case. I was angry, because she'd rejected me. But she says she was just scared of all the changes she'd have to make to be with me – and that she wants to make them. She wants to move over here and be with me, properly. She even knows about the charges, and she's going to support me – she's offered to make a statement giving me another alibi! So, my wish is that this time next year, we're still together, and settled. I can't wait for you all to meet her. You'll love her.'

We all look at each other again. Rachel in particular looks very doubtful. But anyway we clap and raise our glasses, and Ivan sits down again, with the biggest smile I have seen on his face since Ted gave him BMX bicycle for his twelfth birthday.

'Karl's turn,' Rachel says, leaning into him and stroking the side of his head. 'Go for it, gorgeous.'

Karl stands up and gives a little cough-cough-cough. He looks as if he is about to make a speech to five hundred people from a big stage, perhaps like he has just won the Oscar statue.

'First, I would like to thank Gordana and Ted for inviting me into their home like this. It is most kind, and I have very much enjoyed staying here.'

Then I think he will thank his agent, the public, his mother . . . He is not shy, this Karl. But also not arrogant the way that Mark was. I nod graciously, like the Queen. We have missed her speech this year, again. But then we always do. After we open the second bottle of wine, everyone always forget.

'Get on with it!' Rachel heckles, poking him in the side.

'OK, my wish then? My wish is that by next Christmas, I will have a nice flat in this nice part of

415

England. And many boxes full of your good English crisps.'

Rachel laughs, but nobody else does.

'Do you want some crisps now, Karl?' Ted asks seriously. 'We have some in the kitchen. Aren't you full yet?'

'No, thank you, Ted, that is very kind but it is a private joke with me and Rachel. There is one last part of my wish, that with the crisps in my flat there will be Rachel living also. Even though it has only been a very short time since we are together, I am sure of this.'

He sits down again, and they smile fondly at each other. Rachel does not look surprised, so they must have discussed this already. Everyone says 'Aaah', even Ivan, which is a miracle.

'Ted?'

But I know Ted's wish already. Ted's face is purple, same as his party hat from the cracker. He need to watch that blood pressure.

'Mine . . .' he says slowly, 'is to be able to dance with my beautiful wife, on our fortieth wedding anniversary, which, for those of you who aren't aware of it, is next June, June the twenty-fifth . . .' He stops speaking and his lip is wobbling a great deal. I need to help him out here.

'Yes!' I stand up and clap my hands together. 'There will be big party! I am thinking about it already. We will do it at the tennis club, with purple and green balloons for Wimbledon fortnight, and a barbeque, and maybe even a Midweek tournament first. Lots of dancing, and whirly disco lights for my special dance with my darling but soppy husband. That is my wish, but also, there is another part of mine too: I want there to be a band, and I want to sing for everyone, on the stage. My career of singing may be a little bit late starting, but who cares? Better late than never, that's what I say!'

Everyone claps and cheers, and I smile at the dream of it. I know what I will wear; my long royal blue dress what is all sequins. I will have to get matching shoes. Perhaps an evening bag with many beads to sparkle on it.

Ted gets up. 'I'll just get some more coffee on,' he says in a funny voice, and leaves the room. I think I must give him a moment. Poor Ted. I can hear him blowing his nose in the kitchen.

'My turn now,' says Rachel as Ted comes back in, looking less purple. 'Forgive me if I don't stand up. But I've got a big wish. It's an announcement, really, too. I have something to go with it. Karl, could you . . .?'

Karl right away jumps up and leaves the room. We all look at each other. What is going on? This year it can't be a Wimbledon wish. And surely they are not getting married so soon, they only just met.

He comes back in with an armful of square, flattish parcels in Christmas paper, about the size of a record sleeve but thicker. He gives one to me, one to Susie, and one to Ivan. Then he checks the label on the last one and puts it on his own place mat.

'I have to give you all your Christmas presents now, as part of this,' Rachel says. She sounds embarrassed and her cheeks are pink. 'Pops and Gordana, that one's for both of you. Go on, everyone, open them. Sorry, Billy, I didn't know you were going to be here. I haven't got you anything.'

'No problem,' says Billy, raising his glass to her. His midwest accent sounds funny. What a mixture of accents, I think: my Croatian; Karl's German; Billy's Yankee Doodle Dandy.

'Open them, everyone,' repeats Rachel in her very English one, even more English in her awkwardness.

She takes a mouthful of the coffee at the bottom of her cup, but it must be cold, because it's been there for ages. I think she just wants something to do with her hands, which are trembling. I have no idea what is in the packages. Ted rips the paper off ours first and holds it up: it's a picture, a big rosebud with dew drops, crimson against a plain pink background. It's lovely. I haven't got my reading glasses on but it looks like a fuzzy photograph.

'Thank you, Rachel, it's very nice, darling,' I say, leaning over and kissing her.

Ivan's is a dark, heavy purple and black tulip head. 'Thanks, Rachel,' he says, a bit puzzled. I can see that he wonders why she give him a picture. Art and decorations and so on was Anthea's business. He only bothered with electrical appliances and gadgets, or sporting equipment.

'What's this got to do with your Christmas wish? Not thinking of becoming an art dealer, are you?'

She smiles mysteriously, but says nothing.

Susie opens hers last. It's a beautiful dandelion clock, up close, each individual fluffy stem glowing silver against the black background. I cannot tell if it's a photograph or a painting. I look more closely at my rosebud, and realize it is a painting.

'Oh!' says Susie, and for some reason she starts crying. She gets up and hugs Rachel. 'Oh Rach,' she says. 'It's gorgeous.'

Suddenly I get it. Rachel did not buy these pictures. 'My darling, you surely didn't paint these yourself?'

She nods, half proud, half embarrassed. 'I did. Do you like them?'

There is a big noise as everyone talks at once, a big noise of praise and delight and surprise and admiration. The paintings are so much life-like.

'But what's this got to do with your Christmas wish?' says Ivan. In a *very* worried sort of a voice.

I do not think any of us are too surprised when she tell us.

'I wanted to let you all know at the same time.' She is holding Karl's hand very tight. 'I've decided . . .'

418

She looks at Ivan and gulps. Then she speaks in a big rush. 'I've decided that I'm not going to play professionally any more. My wish is that . . . by next Christmas I'll have finished my first term at college. Art college. I want to do a degree in art.'

There is total silence, except for the distant sound of Jackson serenading the dead turkey outside the larder door. Susie's eyes are sparkling and she is smiling a big smile, even with her face still wet from tears. Everyone else is staring anxiously at Ivan, who has gone the colour of the Stilton. He look for a moment like he is going to cry too, but not in a good way.

Then slowly, slowly, he push away his chair and stands up. Oh no, darling, don't walk out, I beg him in my head. Don't do this to her, it's not fair. I can see the big muscle tick-ticking away at the corner of his jaw, and it seems like it's going in time with the tick-ticking of the grandfather clock in the corner of the room.

He walks over to Rachel. Karl squeezes Rachel's hand more tighter. Rachel is shaking so much now that she knocks over her port, and it makes a stain on my beautiful lace tablecloth. The stain is the same colour as the rose she painted me. Karl picks up the glass and mops at the spillage with his napkin, not letting go of Rachel's hand even though it means he has to cross his other arm awkwardly over his body to reach it.

It's like the whole room is holding its breath. Ivan leans down – and then he hugs her. She puts her arms around him and hugs him back. He doesn't say a word. I know my boy – sometimes he doesn't speak because he doesn't want to. Other times he doesn't speak because he can't. Now is one of those times. He can't.

He kisses the top of her head. Then he walks back and sits down. Nods once at her. Smiles. And that's the end of it. It's over. Rachel's new life begin here.

53

Susie

Long walks were one of the things Billy and I always did well together — surprisingly, considering his general inactivity for much of the rest of the time. Some of our best chats had been tramped out in time with our marching feet and the backdrop of a spot of impressive scenery. Perhaps it was because our legs were the same length; we could keep pace perfectly. Something about the rhythm of it always used to turn us on, too. Some of our best sex was had after, or during, a long walk — all that fresh air and blood rushing around the body . . . And it always helped us figure out problems too, away from the stale familiarity of our home, puffing out the cobwebs of our discontent and our dreams.

Up in the thin air of the Adirondacks we set up Billy's new mechanics' business. In the Ozarks, I told him the sorry story of my marriage to Ivan in more detail than I'd ever told anyone else; and then Billy leaned me backwards over a hollow fallen tree-trunk and made it all better. Across the smaller peaks and glassy waters of the Lake District, scuffing through an autumn carpet of orange and red on a holiday soon after we got engaged, we discussed having kids. That conversation lasted for miles, I recalled, and never was really concluded.

Billy reminded me of it as we did circuits of Bushy

Park, near Hampton Court, on a damp foggy Boxing Day. There were no mountains for us to walk up in south-west London, but there was an austere beauty to the bare ancient chestnut trees, and the deer skittering across the grass lent an otherworldly quality to the setting, despite the fact that we usually preferred to be alone in our landscapes – and we were far from alone. Families were out in force: little girls in bright-coloured wellies and ladybird or frog mackintoshes, new and shiny like the carefully pedalled trikes and brand new Christmas scooters bumping over the ruts as parents strolled behind issuing warnings and injunctions.

Billy gazed at them. He'd always taken it harder than I had, us not having children of our own.

'Was that anything to do with it?' I asked abruptly. 'Kids, I mean.'

We still hadn't talked properly yet. He had slept on a camp bed in Ted's office last night (Ivan, Karl, Rachel and I taking up all the other available spare beds in the house), and I hadn't suggested he shared my bed. I let him be in the dog-house, and he had humbly acquiesced. I'd half expected, half hoped that he might creep into my room in the dark of night, but he hadn't, so I had lain awake, itchy with frustration and long-suppressed lust, dying for my Christmas cuddle but not quite ready to forgive him yet. Not sure that I would be able to forgive him.

Billy reached out and took my hand. I was wearing woollen gloves but I could still feel the warmth of his touch. Ever since I was a little girl I'd always loved the feeling of wearing gloves and holding hands with someone.

'It's hard to explain,' he said cautiously.

'Try.'

A squirrel shot out of a patch of long grass nearby and hurled itself up the closest tree, hotly pursued by a yapping cocker spaniel. The dog's owner, a rotund

421

woman in a red jacket that made her look like a lagged hot water tank, called out to it: 'Trevor, stop it! Naughty boy!' Then she turned to us. 'Sorry! isn't he dreadful? Did you have a nice Christmas?' – as if we were old friends.

'Yes, thank you,' I replied politely. The woman opened her mouth to say something else, but I allowed Billy to drag me away before we got engaged in any more of a conversation. We had rather more important things to discuss.

'I thought you said Brits weren't as friendly as Americans?'

I grimaced. 'Only when you don't want them to be . . . So. Kids. Was that it? Or did you tell Eva that I didn't understand you? Come on, Billy, we've never even talked about all this, and it's time we did.'

'I know,' he said. 'But to be fair, it's not like you gave me a chance. You kicked me out and then you went to Europe.'

I stopped walking, outraged. 'Oh right, so if I'd said we needed to talk, and I hadn't gone to Italy, you'd have dumped Eva then and there and everything would've been fine? I don't think so!'

Spaniel Woman was catching us up, with a determined look in her eye and another conversational gambit hovering on her lips. We ducked off the main path, through the long, wet grass, to avoid her.

'No, I'm not saying that at all. But we should've talked earlier. We talk when we go on walks, but, Suze, how many years has it been since we went on a walking vacation, or even for a hike? We stopped walking, and we stopped talking. I was so busy at the garage, you were always at work, or with Audrey, or planning your next trip to see Rachel; or emailing Rachel; or talking to Rachel on the phone – I just felt shut out of your life! You never included me in anything, I felt like a spare part. And yeah, maybe if we'd had kids of our own, we'd have been more of a family.'

We stopped to let a herd of deer stroll past, which at least made the spaniel and her owner run in the opposite direction. Not so brave now, are you, Trevor? I thought, watching the dog yelp and scarper. I was furious with Billy.

'*You* felt shut out? We hardly ever had the bloody house to ourselves, with all your buddies round the whole time buying pot and then staying half the night to smoke it. What was I supposed to do, since I don't smoke? Sit on the sofa in silence with you all, or talk about Spinal Tap for seven hours on the trot?'

'Suze, that's not fair. I was always asking you if we could do more stuff together. I got all those brochures for photography classes, and we were going to take up t'ai chi, remember? I wanted us to have folk round for dinner once a month, a proper dinner party, but you just made a joke about us not having enough trays, and that was that. It never happened. I wanted us to put some weekends aside to redecorate the house, remember, but you were always too busy, and I so wanted it to be a joint project.'

I supposed he was right. Billy had at various times tried to get us to do more stuff. I hadn't thought he was all that serious about it; I'd assumed they were just more of his stoner ideas that would never happen. It never before occurred to me that the reason they didn't happen was due less to his lethargy and more to the fact that I'd ignored them or poured cold water on the suggestions. Guilt began to prickle at me.

He stopped walking. A heavy drizzle was beginning to surround us, coating our faces and settling on his hair like dew. He had tears in his eyes.

'It wasn't just that, Suze. I've been feeling for ages that . . . well, that you weren't really mine any more – maybe that you never felt you were; that you'd been running away from Ivan and you rushed into getting engaged to kind of make up for the crap marriage you had with him, without ever intending to *commit*. You just talked about him and Rachel and Gordana all the time, and your life in England, and the fact that you wanted to come back here one day, and that you didn't like Kansas—'

'I do like Kansas! I loved our house, and living in Lawrence, and being engaged to you. I thought we were happy; I thought that was committed!'

'But I didn't know that. You always seemed like you wanted something different to what you had. You never said you were happy. And if you liked being engaged to me, why the hell wouldn't you marry me?'

A flock of crows all suddenly rose as one from a big bare oak tree, cawing so loudly that I had to speak up to be heard. They flew over our heads to settle on the branches of a different tree, all flying as if they knew exactly where they were going. Why couldn't we have been more like that? Why was it so difficult to communicate, even with the ones closest to us? There'd only been me and Billy – how could it have been so easy for us to misread each other's needs?

'I didn't know it meant so much to you. I thought you understood how scared I was of getting married again, after the first one went wrong. I thought we were OK as we were. I'm sorry, Billy. I just didn't know it was upsetting you so much.'

'You hardly ever even said you loved me; not with passion, anyhow. Only B.I.L.Y.'

'I liked B.I.L.Y.,' I said miserably. 'I thought that was our thing; our way of saying it. I'm sorry if you needed me to spell it out.'

He sighed. 'Yeah. No, you're right. It was. But it's not just that. I mean, we used to have a great sex life – but we haven't for years, have we? No wonder I thought you didn't want to marry me.'

'You were always up half the night after I'd gone to bed. I was tired from working. You often worked weekends.' I felt angry again, and defensive, like he was trying to blame me for the fact he'd cheated on me.

'You shut yourself off from me, Susie. I tried to talk to you, but you stonewalled me. I thought you didn't love me any more. Then I met Eva—'

'Where did you meet her?' I hadn't wanted to ask, but curiosity got the better of me.

'At a show, at Liberty Hall. Leon Russell – remember? I asked you if you wanted to come with me, but you said no, so I went on my own. She was at the bar at the same time as me, and we got talking, 'cos she was on her own too. She listened to me, Suze. I just felt, for the first time in years, like I was really connecting with someone, the way I wanted so bad to connect with you, but couldn't . . . I know it was wrong, and I feel truly awful about it, please believe me. Now I've hurt Eva as well as you, and I can't forgive myself. But I couldn't pretend to her any longer. When you went away, I just couldn't bear it. I used to go and sit in our yard at night, looking at the empty dark house and petting the cats. They were always real happy to see me. But I'd sit there and cry, because I'd lost the one person I love more than anything, and I didn't know what to do to make it right again. I'd destroyed everything we had together, just because we couldn't talk properly.'

He was really crying now, in that hopeless way that men did; dragging his sleeve across his eyes, all wet-mouthed and red-faced, his shoulders shaking silently. I hugged him, loving the way that we were the same size. With Ivan, I'd always had to crane my neck to reach up to kiss him. Since both our legs and trunks were the same length, it meant that Billy's mouth and mine were exactly opposite each other's too, and all we had to do was to lean forward and . . .

I leaned forward. He tasted of salty tears, garlic and, faintly, old pot. It was the best taste in the world. He kissed me back, hiccuping slightly. He smelled wonderful too.

'It's not all destroyed,' I whispered, the rim of his ear

soft and velvety against my lips. 'I still love you, really, Billy, I always did. I was devastated when I found out about you and Eva. I've never, ever not wanted to be with you.'

'But how can you ever forgive me for cheating?'

I shrugged. 'It might take a while. But I will, because I want to. I want you. I want our lives back; just you, me and the cats. I didn't see it before, but I'm to blame as well, by not talking to you. But things can change. We can do all that stuff together: courses and holidays and stuff. Perhaps you might stop selling pot for a while, so we don't have so many people in the house . . . ?'

Billy nodded into my neck. 'Definitely. I'm sick of it anyhow, and they're really coming down harsh on the dealers these days. It's not worth the risk. And to tell you the truth, I don't really care much for Flamingo Dan and his buddies either . . . I just couldn't piss 'em off or they'd buy their pot elsewhere.'

'Shame about the weather!' trilled Spaniel Woman, popping up again from nowhere. 'It's lovely when Boxing Day is crisp and clear, but this—'

Billy looked up, wet-faced and irritated. 'Madam, I don't mean to be rude, but we're having a—'

I clamped my hand over his mouth. 'Yes, *such* a shame about the weather, isn't it? Oh well.' I slid my hand around the back of Billy's head. 'Some things are more important than a bit of fog, aren't they?' And I kissed him, long and hard, right in front of her. She looked on, horrified, as Billy walked me over to the nearest tree, still kissing me back, and pressed me hard up against it, ramming his knee between my legs and sliding his hands inside my coat to feel my breasts. I reciprocated, running my own hands over his backside and down the sides of his legs, both of us giggling helplessly within the kiss.

'Well!' said Spaniel Woman in tones of horror and disgust. 'I never saw such an appalling . . . I can't

426

believe people can be so . . . I don't think I'll . . .' She tailed off and, peering over Billy's shoulder, I saw her clip the lead on to the dog's collar and drag him off back towards the car park.

'That's sorted her,' I said briskly, going to push Billy away from me again. But he wouldn't move; he just rubbed himself harder against me and kissed me again. The relief of it almost made me cry – except I was too turned on. I'd go off like a rocket, I thought, if we made love now; a whirling Catherine wheel of desire. It had been so long.

'Come on.' I grabbed his hand impulsively and led him towards a dense copse. 'No one will see us in here.'

Billy said nothing, but smiled his wicked, dimpled smile and followed me until we were surrounded by dark, tight-packed tree trunks. He laid his coat down on the damp ground and pushed me on to it – but my knees were so weak by then, I probably couldn't have stood up for much longer anyway.

Some time later, we stood up and brushed bits of bark and soggy leaf off ourselves, our bodies two patch-works of hot and cold, wet and dry. I had indeed gone off like a rocket, my strangled cries issuing up into the treetops and scaring away the birds. Billy shook out his coat and put it back on, a look of sudden anguish on his face as he began to delve in the big pockets of it.

'What have you lost?' I asked.

'Oh man, don't tell me, oh man – wait – oh. Phew. Here it is,' he said, visibly relieved, pulling what looked like a piece of crumpled kitchen towel out of one of the pockets. It wasn't like Billy to be so con-cerned about being out without a tissue, I thought, unless he'd changed a great deal since we were together . . .

'Kitchen towel?'

427

He grabbed my hand, looking over his shoulder to check we were still alone – or perhaps to check that Spaniel Lady wasn't about to pop up and start commenting on his technique.

'Close your eyes,' he commanded, and I obliged, smiling a languorous, post-coital smile, half expecting him to wipe my nose with the scrunched-up tissue. It was the best feeling in the world: to have Billy's familiar warm voice in my ear and the imprint of his skin against mine, after thinking he was lost to me for ever. But things were about to feel even better: he was still holding my left hand, and I felt the small cold slide of metal on my third finger. My eyes immediately popped open to the flash and gleam of my engagement ring, the opal greedily catching what meagre winter light was filtering through the trees on to it.

'My ring,' I said fondly, examining it like the face of an old friend, tilting my hand up and down to watch the colours change.

'You want to wear it again?' asked Billy anxiously. 'I had to break into the house to get it. But I mended the window afterwards, don't worry.'

'Yes,' I said. 'I want to wear it again. And I want us to go shopping for the wedding ring that'll sit next to it, right there.' I took his finger in my right hand and rubbed it gently on my own ring finger, just below the knuckle and just above the opal. 'Tomorrow. I want to go shopping tomorrow, so we can take the ring back to Lawrence with us when we go.'

Billy nodded, speechless, leaning his forehead against mine.

'Then we'll book the register office. OK?'

He just nodded again, and I hugged him. Over my shoulder, I saw the opal flash pink and red and green and turquoise.

EPILOGUE
Six Months Later
Rachel

I haven't been to the tennis club for months, not since the day that Karl turned up and we gatecrashed the Japanese party's boat. The day our relationship began.

It's nice to be back, in a bittersweet kind of way. There is cheerful bunting draped in loops along the gutters around the pavilion, tubs of salmony-pink begonias and lurid fuchsia are in full bloom, and there is white surfinia in hanging baskets outside the club-house. It all looks somehow more technicolor and super-real than I remember. The Midweek ladies have been here all afternoon getting the place ready for the party. I should probably have offered to help, but I couldn't quite face the prospect of several hours of being bossed around by Elsie and Gordana's friends – and I didn't think it fair to inflict that on Karl either.

Elsie herself seems to have mellowed quite a bit, though. Dad sees her going in and out of her house sometimes, and reported recently that she's actually got a boyfriend. Turns out it's one of the garden gnomes, a sweet white-haired old boy; the same one Gordana reported gleefully that Elsie wouldn't speak to for years because she thought he fancied Valerie. His name is Humphrey. I didn't know there were any

Humphreys still alive; I thought they'd all died out with Colonialism.

When Karl and I arrived, the Midweek tournament was just finishing, and Elsie and Humphrey were coming off court after the Senior Mixed Doubles. They were wearing matching blue elastic knee supports – sweet! (I shouldn't mock. I have to wear one myself, at least for the next few months.)

Elsie spotted us and made a beeline for me, actually hugging me. The sun visor perched on top of her perm knocked into my forehead as we embraced awkwardly. I've known her since I was four, but that's the first time I've ever had the dubious pleasure of physical contact.

'Rachel dear,' she said in a tone that, if I didn't know her better, could only be described as nervous. I notice that her lipstick matches the begonias, and wonder if this is intentional. She looks round at Humphrey for support, who gives her an encouraging nod and a thumbs-up – she's obviously been preparing this speech. 'You look beautiful . . . I just wanted to let you know that it's very nice to see you up and about again, without the crutches. We miss you down here; the place isn't the same without you all. And I'm really sorry for . . . well, you know, the trouble I caused before over your father's . . . ahem . . . problems. I ought to have kept my speculation to myself – even if it did turn out to be correct. I've made my peace with your grandmother already, but if Ivan's going to be here later, I'd like to apologize to him too. He's been through a terrible time. You all have.'

I'm touched, even though the entire speech appears to have been delivered at the top of one of the floodlight poles and not at me at all.

'Thanks, Elsie, that's really nice of you. No hard feelings.'

She hesitated, and looked at me for the first time. 'I never did care for that Anthea, you know. She used to ignore me when she saw me in the street!'

As someone who has studiously ignored Elsie in all sorts of places on many occasions over the years, I blush slightly. 'To be honest, we didn't much like her either,' I say.

'Have you heard from her?'

I shake my head. 'Oh no. We won't do, either, I'm sure, not directly. The police are going to have her extradited to face charges, even though Dad said he would let it go. But they told him that the offences are too serious: downloading child porn *and* attempting to subvert the course of justice. They tracked her down at her mother's retirement home in Portugal, although it took them a while. She confessed straight away.'

I have an interesting mental picture of Anthea in her Chanel velour tracksuit, pedalling her way around continental Europe on an exercise bike, a international fugitive from justice, stopping only for cans of Slim-Fast and manicures, until the constabulary caught up with her and she crumbled under the pressure of interrogation . . . Poor old Anthea.

Elsie's eyes get bigger and rounder at the scandal, and she purses her lips. I decide not to add fuel to her fire of gossip by telling her that, despite Anthea's act of treachery, Dad does feel bad towards his former girlfriend. She had only done what she had when she found out about Dad and Tasha's on-off relationship. Apparently, Anthea had discovered a letter from Tasha to Dad, and she'd downloaded the porn then, on the spur of the moment, to get her own back. She had to wait months for the police to discover the offence, but even after that, she wasn't satisfied. That was when she tipped off the press.

None of us could really understand why she'd bothered to stay with Dad throughout all this if she hated him so much, but it seemed she couldn't bear to let him go, either. It's so sad. She was waiting for him to wake up and realize that he wanted her, not Tasha. I don't know how she could have kept silent for so long, knowing Dad had been in love with someone else, not knowing whether it was still going on . . . And not knowing which day would be the one the police came after him. Or, as it turned out, her. She hadn't been aware of what Mum subsequently found out, and got Dad to tell his solicitor: that every command you perform on a computer, every file you download, has a time stamp to it.

After Anthea's confession, the police took statements from José, Kerry and myself, all testifying that Dad was with us at a tournament on the dates in question. It took them a while to sift through the files on the computer and check the credit card statements, but eventually it all came together.

On a frosty February day, Dad, his solicitor, Gordana, Ted and Tasha had put on their smartest suits and attended Kingston Magistrates Court for the official announcement, surrounded by a phalanx of journalists and photographers, and even a crew from the local TV station. Despite Anthea's best efforts, it was the first time that his case had attracted TV coverage – so it was an unbelievable relief for us all that Dad could emerge from the court and stand on the steps with an ear-to-ear beam, as his solicitor announced that he was fully exonerated of all charges, and that the CPS had dropped the case against him.

I smile at the memory of the celebrations we had on that day. It was the first time I'd met Natasha, properly, and I'd bitten my nails to the quick with nerves beforehand. I had this horrible image that she'd be glaring at me across the table like she had across the net on court that time. But when I met her, she had the sort of mega-watt smile which lit up the whole room, and her hand rested on Dad's arm almost the whole evening. She even apologized for her behaviour in our match. I don't think she'll ever be my closest friend or anything (heaven forbid: she might tell me about her sex life, eurgh), but I think we like each other.

And here we are now, at a different sort of party, just four months later . . . Suddenly I feel a frown of emotion squeezing my forehead, and I have to take a deep breath. Time has gone so fast . . .

Karl sees, and reaches for my hand. Elsie of course doesn't notice.

'Well, it should be a jolly good bash tonight. Everyone's coming, you know.'

'Great,' I said, managing to smile at her. 'And yes, Dad said he was coming too.'

I hadn't been at all sure that Dad would agree to attend the party. Of course he ought to be here, but Dad being something of a law unto himself, it wouldn't have surprised me if he'd said no. It's going to take a lot of courage for him to show up here tonight, after he was declared bankrupt in April. The club was on the market for a little while, until a collective of the old guard of members, mostly the wealthy Midweek ladies, decided to pool their resources and buy it out. They've asked Ted to be club secretary, and he's delighted.

He and Jackson spend most of their time down here now, much to the disgust of Timothy the club cat. Jackson's even taken over Timmy's favourite sleeping place, in the large cardboard box of lost property. I don't think anyone ever reclaims anything which goes into that box: all the mislaid T-shirts and sweatshirts are covered with cat and dog hair now, and unappealing bits of dirt dropped from muddy paws. Timmy has been relegated to the club car park, where he sits on car bonnets hissing and hurling kitty insults at Jackson whenever he and Pops trot past.

Anyway, Dad is different now that all the charges have been dropped against him, and Tasha's moved in with him. He seems to be able to handle things much better than he ever used to. The house is no cleaner

433

than when Anthea lived with him, and neither of them can cook to save their lives, but he's so much happier. He's no longer anyone's business manager – who'd have him, with his track record? – and most of his squads train elsewhere now, except for Kerry's and Mark's, who stayed based here, because José still coaches them.

'You haven't been in here before, have you?' I ask Karl as we push open the door and go inside. It's just as it was before, dusty-floored village hall adjoining the newer, smarter carpet-tiled bar area representing Dad's failed investment. As per Gordana's strict instructions, purple and green balloons are dangling all over the ceiling like small bunches of outsized grapes on a vine. They clash horribly with the yellow and red patterned curtains, but nobody seems bothered about that. A little stage has been set up in the corner and an elderly man in a shiny waist-coat is hunched over, tuning a guitar and testing microphones.

'No. It's very sweet,' says Karl in an entirely un-patronizing voice, looking around him at the championship boards on the walls, dating back to the 1940s. The women's board for the seventies features Gordana's name as Singles champion on several occasions, and mine crops up over and over again in the nineties (every year, in fact, except '97 when I was out with a hamstring injury). Dad's name of course dominates the men's board for the seventies and eighties. It's a family thing, I think proudly. Funny how I can have won tournaments all round the world (albeit not many of them, and not big tournaments, but still . . .) and yet our names in gold letters on the little local club championship board inspires in me the most pride of all. My Fantasy Family may have good picnics and a harmonious home life, but even in my imagination I can't picture any of them having half as much success as my real family has had. It's the first time this thought has occurred to me, and suddenly the Fantasy Family seems a little . . .well . . . goody-goody and *wet*.

I lean back against the wall and survey the activity around me. Lots of ladies, many familiar, some not, are flapping around engaged in various activities: salad-mixing, window-cleaning, flower-arranging. Someone even appears to be checking that the name-tags on hooks on the membership board outside are all in the correct alphabetical order.

The folded and propped-up table-tennis table against the wall next to me has an A4 sheet sellotaped to it reading: 'DANGER! DO *NOT* USE TABLE!'

'I wonder what sort of danger we would be in if we used the table?' Karl asks reflectively, following my gaze.

'Could ruin your forehand swing for ever, perhaps?' I suggest. 'Table tennis is almost as bad as squash for that.'

'Mine is already ruined,' Karl says, and I laugh. It's true, he's a terrible tennis player. I've only just started playing again myself – the leg brace came off at the end of January, but it was a good few more months before I could actually run – and Karl and I recently had a very gentle hit on the courts at my gym. I tried to give him a bit of coaching, but we gave up after an hour. I could tell right away he was an ex-squash player; he just wouldn't stop whacking the ball straight out of the back of the court, and he had no service action whatsoever. It got a bit boring after a while, although at least he remained good-natured about it.

I'm still doing regular physio on my knee, and am back at the gym three times a week. Obviously I don't need to be as fit as I used to be, but I don't feel right when I'm not exercising. I don't sleep so well, and my digestion doesn't function as efficiently. It also passes the time for me when Karl has to be away, working. He goes between here and France, Germany and Italy on a regular basis for his wine-importing business. Needless to say, I'm not in any hurry to go skiing again, but we did go back and spend a wonderful weekend at his sister's hotel. It was a bit weird, being back there, but lovely to get to know Karl's family a bit better.

But mostly I've been trying to build up my portfolio. I've been accepted as a mature student on to the BA (Hons) Fine Art course at Kingston University, and I can't wait. The walls of the flat Karl and I moved into last month are already covered with my flower paintings, and every time I look at them, I feel another thrill of satisfaction; much more tangible and lasting than the brief warm glow from applause, or a few points hike in ranking. And so much less hard work too! I've been going to art galleries, and reading tons of art history; I love the feeling of mental instead of physical stimulation (I have Karl to give me physical stimulation now – every night!). It's such a new experience: facts and images jostling for position inside my head; the sensory blossoming which comes when I see colours combined in a certain way, or touch the smoothness of a cold marble sculpture. Karl's body and mine together is like a work of art too, something which mingles and curves into a new sort of beauty, astonishing to me in its depth.

Mum and Billy went back to Kansas just after Christmas. They've finally set their wedding date, for this coming New Year. They're getting married in Barbados, on the beach, and Karl and I are going to fly over as witnesses. I can't wait. The only sad thing about it is that it means they couldn't afford to come over again this year. I wish Mum could be here tonight, but it's enough knowing that they're happy. Apparently Billy has stopped both smoking and selling pot; and Mum's training to be a life coach. Billy's keeping his mechanics business but cutting down on his hours, and they're planning to set up a gallery together in Lawrence as well. I told her she could sell my paintings, and she didn't even laugh.

'Definitely,' she said with total conviction. It was lovely.

Guests arrive: most of the members of the tennis club, past and present. It's hard to recognize women with their hair loose around their shoulders, in party dresses and make-up rather than tennis gear and blotchy, sweaty skin. Everyone looks so much more attractive, and younger. The barbeque smell intensifies: a heavy, smoky scent of summer and of party; and people sit down outside on benches and grassy banks, attacking burgers and potato salad with insufficiently sturdy plastic cutlery. All Gordana's Midweek friends are here now, and Ted's golfing buddies and their wives, whom Ted is greeting with backslaps and kissed cheeks. A few fellow cancer-sufferers turn up: people Gordana met during her treatments at the Marsden; and her Cancerkin Volunteer Visitor, a lovely red-haired lady called Christine who supported Gordana and Ted through Gordana's illness with great practical efficiency and compassion. We are all really fond of her (especially Jackson, because she always brought him doggy treats).

Dad and Tasha turn up just as the band – four-piece, jazz, average age sixty – clamber with difficulty on to the small stage for their first set. It is still light outside, and children are playing Giant Jenga and Connect 4 on the red shale tennis courts, but inside people are already dancing as if it's midnight in a jazz club, rather than nine-thirty on a balmy summer's evening. Gordana instructed everyone to dance, and dance they do.

I rush over and kiss them both as Karl goes off to buy more drinks. 'Hi! It's lovely to see you.' And it is. It's lovely to see Dad looking so smart in the clothes which Tasha has – very evidently – bought for him: trendy

437

chinos and a Paul Smith shirt. It's lovely too, to see the pride with which he gazes at Natasha. He's only coaching her now, and they are inseparable. I haven't seen him on court with her, though. I wonder if he slaps her legs when she misses a shot? Bet he doesn't. She'd deck him. She's almost as tall as him, and looks as if she could swing a hefty punch.

'I can't believe you've got Dad into those great clothes,' I say admiringly, and she laughs.

'Oh, it was easy. He does whatever I say, don't you, Ivan?'

Dad, the erstwhile belligerent, sullen, self-contained power freak, does something which approximates a simper.

'We can all change,' says Tasha in her precise English. 'Even men, but it takes them longer. We women are much better at adapting to circumstance, though, don't you think?'

I think of Mum, and Gordana, and me, and of all the circumstances of the past year. 'Yes. We are,' I say, and my throat tightens again.

The door opens and a new group of people arrives: the younger, team players – fashionably late, of course. José is in the midst of them, talking to Kerry, who sees me and waves wildly in my direction. Miracle of miracles, it even looks as if she's brushed her hair and put on some mascara. Behind her are my other old squad members, including Sally-Anne – and Mark, holding her hand. Sally-Anne's long blonde hair has been sprayed so much that it looks as if it's been moulded out of plastic. When she moves, to kiss Mark's cheek, the hair stays still.

I notice that Mark doesn't turn into her kiss; his eyes continue to rove around the room, sizing up any woman under the age of fifty. Funny how, when we were together, I never noticed how predatory he was. But then again, it doesn't really surprise me. I feel like I was an innocent back then, in all ways.

I turn to watch Karl fighting his way to the bar, his broad shoulders dominating the crush. I seem to have a thing for large men. Perhaps it's true what they say about women always going for partners who look like their fathers. Karl isn't nearly as conventionally gorgeous as Mark, but seeing Mark now, his arrogant eyes and his artfully tousled hair, probably as carefully styled as Sally-Anne's, I am left cold. Karl turns and waves a cheery beer bottle at me from across the room and, conversely, something melts in me. The best thing to come out of my relationship with Mark is currently tied up on the porch outside, whining disconsolately.

Kerry is just rushing over to talk to me and Karl when Ted steps hesitantly up to an unused microphone, centre stage. The band have stopped for a little sit-down in between numbers, and they lean aside to let him in. He taps the microphone and clears his throat, and suddenly the silence is louder than the music.

Someone notices through the window that a speech is in the offing, and sends the word around amongst all the people still outside. They hastily put their paper plates down on to the long trestle table next to the barbeque and start making their way into the pavilion, much to the delight of Timmy the cat, who jumps up and curls around the leftovers, in heaven, licking at bits of kebab and pulling at chicken wings. I can see his dusky shape weaving unchecked through the debris. It's driving poor Jackson mad, from his helpless bondage by the wooden steps, watching Timmy tucking in.

It's finally getting dark now, and one set of floodlights wavers into life, illuminating the partygoers as more and more squeeze into the clubhouse.

Inside, the whirling disco lights are stilled, leaving Ted standing uncertainly in a lone spotlight on the stage. His face, lit from above, is a series of the crags and soft hollows of age, until he shades his eyes with a hand to peer out at us all. Light bounces off his bald head.

I am unbearably fond of him.

His eyes are watery, but his gaze is firm as he looks around the room as if looking for Gordana; waiting for her to emerge in her long gloves and her sparkly blue dress, still with the shape of a thirty-year-old, smiling and taking the stage for her big number. She'd rehearsed for it for weeks, in the bath, in the kitchen, in the garden, secateurs in hand, wrestling with roses as prickly as her son, and with bindweed as tough as her beloved husband and as tenacious as their love for one another. She rehearsed until she had no energy left to breathe in enough air to sing out again, and until she was too ill even to lift her head off the pillow.

'I won't talk for long,' he says. 'I just wanted to thank you all for coming tonight. We all know why we're here. Forty years ago today, I married the most beautiful woman I'd ever seen. I have loved every minute of being married to Gordana, all the ups and downs – of which there have been many, this past year . . .'

He looks in our direction, and Dad scratches his chin and looks at the floor. Karl hugs me on one side; Kerry on the other.

'This party was her idea, right down to the last detail. We've been planning it for months. It kept Dana occupied through all those last awful treatments she had to endure. She never complained. She just kept planning . . .'

His voice breaks, and everyone's eyes fill, instantly. He takes out an enormous handkerchief, and wipes his own eyes.

'But we've all done enough crying in the last three months. Tonight is for celebrating, not crying; Dana made it quite clear that it should be this way. So, before the band comes back, I want to propose a toast: to my family, who mean the world to me. To Rachel, in her new life at art college . . .' There is loud clapping and cheering, led by Kerry, Mark, Dad and Karl, and I bury my burning face in Karl's chest.

'To Ivan, who has gone through hell, but who came out the other side, and we're all so pleased that you were cleared, old chap. We all knew you were innocent.'

Even louder cheering, especially from the men's teams.

'To the members of this club, for keeping a very old tradition going. Everything changes, including us. It is encumbent upon us to realize this, and to move with the times; to evolve into something better, and stronger, and not to cling to old habits and ways of thinking.'

'Hear, hear,' calls Elsie, the biggest opponent of change in history. She still moans about decimalization, for heaven's sake.

'But most of all,' Ted says finally, into total silence – even Jackson has shut up outside, 'most of all, I want to propose a toast to my beloved wife, Gordana. More than anything, I wanted to dance with her tonight, on our fortieth wedding anniversary. I wanted to hold her in my arms, and gaze at her face the way I did when I first danced with her more than forty years ago. I wanted to show everyone how beautiful she is; boast about her to my friends the way I did then. She wanted to sing tonight, as you know. She held on as long as she could, but really, what she'd been holding on for most was to see her son cleared of his charges. Once that happened, it . . . it wasn't so easy . . .'

Hang in there, Pops, I silently beg him, tears pouring down my cheeks. He takes a deep breath.

'Anyway, Gordana being Gordana and never one to miss out on an opportunity to show off' – subdued laughter – 'here, by the miracle of technology, is Gordana. If not in the flesh, then at least by courtesy of a digital tape. It's her goodbye to us all . . . so let's drink to that. Cheers, everyone.'

He raises his glass with a shaking hand, and everyone toasts. Amid the chinking glasses and murmur of voices, a brisk but muted trumpet introduction fills the room, followed by some shuffly drums, and then there it is: Gordana's voice, as strong and constant as she herself was.

She is singing the old Sandie Shaw classic 'Always Something There to Remind Me', and as soon as I realize it's Sandie Shaw, I can't help smiling. I knew she'd recorded a few numbers before she got too sick – Ted had hired, at great expense, a local recording studio and a sound engineer – but she had kept what she was actually going to sing a big secret. I never asked, because to ask was an admission that I knew she wouldn't be there to perform in person. We had hoped and prayed she would be, right up to the last day.

But the cancer hit her again, with a vengeance, after Christmas. Perhaps it had always been that bad, and she just hadn't wanted us to know. She had been waiting for Ivan to be cleared, that much was obvious. I wanted her to fight it, so badly, but it was as if she knew that it was too big for her slender frame to cope with. Once she decided she was going, typically for her, she hadn't hung around. She wanted to spare us all those torturous long-drawn out months of watching her suffer.

She died a month after Ivan was cleared, back in March, and I still feel as if I could never cry enough tears for her.

Everyone is crying now, despite Gordana's edict. Everyone except Ted, it seems. He has stepped down from the stage, and walks over to me, smiling. He pulls out his large hanky again, and tenderly wipes beneath my eyes, as if I am five years old again.

'She wanted us all to dance tonight,' he says. 'And since I can't dance with her, I'm afraid you're the next best thing.'

He holds out his hand to me, and together we move into the centre of the pavilion. My grandfather puts one arm around my waist, stretches out the other for me to hold, and we dance. It's not an easy song to dance to, and I can't dance nearly as well as Gordana could, but we do our best. Tasha peels Dad away from the wall, where he's been standing next to the fire extinguisher, scrubbing at his eyes, and they begin to dance next to us. I smile gratefully at her. Then others follow: Elsie and Humphrey; Mark and Sally-Anne; all the old married couples who have been coming here to parties for years. Karl goes over and makes a small, gallant bow to Christine, the Cancerkin lady, and they take the floor together. Everyone is dancing.

Gordana sings four more songs, and after each one, we all clap and stamp and cheer as loudly as possible, in the hope that she might somehow be able to hear, and savour it.

I picture her up on stage, the sequins of her dress jumping and moving in the spotlight, pink spots of life and excitement on her cheeks. She loved sequins – she even had a tracksuit with a row of sequins down the arm and leg seams. She used to wear it with a perfectly crisp white T-shirt, showing off her figure as she moved as gracefully on a tennis court as she would have done on this stage.

'Can we go outside for a minute?' I ask Karl. 'This is all getting a bit much for me.'

'Of course,' he replies, taking my hand and leading me off the dance floor. I untie Jackson on my way down the steps, and he grins and pants at me gratefully, clearly thinking he's finally going to get a shot at the leftovers, but the barbeque has been dampened to embers, and the indefatigable Midweek ladies have cleared up all the paper plates and food remains.

We sit down on the brand-new bench which takes pride of position in the front of the clubhouse. Jackson slumps against my feet and Karl puts his arm around me. We look out across the courts, and I think of the weeks and months I've spent on them, in the low blinding sunshine of winter, in lashing rain and freezing fog. Combine that with the time that Gordana and Dad have spent out here too, and it probably runs into years.

But nothing lasts for ever. Nothing ever stays the same. Inside, Gordana's voice has been replaced by the gruff bass of the band's lead singer as they start another set, and her moment is over. It feels like the end of an era.

'I miss her so much,' I say to Karl.

He hugs me tighter. 'I know,' he says. There isn't really anything else he could say.

The door opens with a blast of heat and noise. Ted comes slowly outside and sits down next to me. Jackson puts his head in his lap and gazes adoringly at him, and Ted pats him. 'Good boy,' he says absently.

'Great turn-out,' he adds to us. 'Well, I think that went all right, didn't it?'

Again, I marvel at his courage.

'It went really well, Pops. Gordana would have been proud of you.' Pops nods, once, his arms hanging down between his knees. Jackson licks his fingers.

I twist around and look through the pavilion windows to see Dad and Tasha still dancing, holding each other close, whispering and kissing.

As I turn to hug my grandfather, something shiny at the back of the bench catches my eye.

'Have you seen this?' I ask, pulling at his sleeve, as I notice the plaque: '*In memory of our friend and fellow Midweek stalwart, Gordana Anderson. 1942-2005. She loved this place, and we loved her.*'

'Ah, there you are, Ted,' says a cheery voice, and Gordana's friend Esther sticks her head around the door. 'I see you've found our bench, then.'

'It's lovely,' says Pops in a choked voice, tracing the words with his forefinger as if he is tracing the lines on Gordana's face. 'Thank you all so much.'

'No need to thank us!' she said brusquely. 'No need at all. Now come on, this is a party, and she wanted us to dance: so let's dance!'

She pulls Ted up by the hand and leads him back inside.

'Life goes on,' says Karl, squeezing my shoulders. 'For us also, I think.'

'Alt-zo'. Mum told me once how she loved the way Karl said that.

'Yeah,' I said. 'For us alt-zo.'

We sit together in silence for a while longer, and then, hand in hand, we go back to the party.

THE END

Acknowledgements

Thanks are due to lots of people for this one, for generous help with research, or just vital moral support:

For tennis-related information and fact-checking, big thanks to Danny Sitton, Tony Marshall, Anne Keothavong, and Heather Purchase from Ace Magazine.

For enormous amounts of help on internet-related crime, thanks very much to Dr Neil Barrett and Rob Welling.

For all the gory details about 'significant fractures of the tibial plateau' (first-hand!) thanks to Alison Meredith.

Thanks to the usual suspects, my friends and fellow writers, who've really supported me over this past year: Jacqui Lofthouse, Linda Buckley-Archer, Jacqui Hazell, Kate Harrison, Stephanie Chilman, Marian Keyes, Sharon Mulrooney, Claire Harcup and Mark Edwards.

Thanks to all at Transworld: Selina Walker (with love and gratitude for being such a brilliant editor), Diana Beaumont, Judith Welsh, Cora Kipling, all the sales team.

I also wanted to thank the following: Jean Lancaster, Jon Woolcott, Jane Landymore, Patti Norman, Rolli Rigiani, Richenda Todd (for her usual indefatigable copy-editing), and Carol Jackson at Curtis Brown.

Finally, biggest thanks of all this time go to my agent, Vivienne Schuster. Can't imagine this would have got written without her encouragement, enthusiasm and suggestions.

A SELECTED LIST OF FINE WRITING
AVAILABLE FROM BLACK SWAN

77084 1	COOL FOR CATS	Jessica Adams	£6.99
77115 5	BRICK LANE	Monica Ali	£7.99
99934 2	EVERY GOOD WOMAN DESERVES A LOVER	Diana Appleyard	£6.99
77186 4	ALL INCLUSIVE	Judy Astley	£6.99
77105 8	NOT THE END OF THE WORLD	Kate Atkinson	£6.99
99947 4	CROSS MY HEART AND HOPE TO DIE	Claire Calman	£6.99
99990 3	A CRYING SHAME	Renate Dorrestein	£6.99
99954 7	SWIFT AS DESIRE	Laura Esquivel	£6.99
99898 2	ALL BONES AND LIES	Anne Fine	£6.99
99656 4	THE TEN O'CLOCK HORSES	Laurie Graham	£5.99
99890 7	DISOBEDIENCE	Jane Hamilton	£6.99
77179 1	JIGS & REELS	Joanne Harris	£6.99
77111 2	SHOPAHOLIC & SISTER	Sophie Kinsella	£6.99
77104 X	BY BREAD ALONE	Sarah-Kate Lynch	£6.99
77200 3	NO WONDER I TAKE A DRINK	Laura Marney	£6.99
77190 2	A GIRL COULD STAND UP	Leslie Marshall	£6.99
99991 1	THE MEN IN HER LIFE	Imogen Parker	£6.99
99909 1	LA CUCINA	Lily Prior	£6.99
77145 7	GHOST HEART	Cecilia Samartin	£6.99
77173 2	BROTHER & SISTER	Joanna Trollope	£6.99
99902 4	TO BE SOMEONE	Louise Voss	£6.99
99903 2	ARE YOU MY MOTHER?	Louise Voss	£6.99
77155 4	LIFESAVER	Louise Voss	£6.99
99864 8	A DESERT IN BOHEMIA	Jill Paton Walsh	£6.99
77221 6	LONG GONE ANYBODY	Susannah Waters	£6.99
99723 4	PART OF THE FURNITURE	Mary Wesley	£6.99
77228 3	COCKTAILS FOR THREE	Madeleine Wickham	£6.99
77101 5	PAINTING RUBY TUESDAY	Jane Yardley	£6.99